George Gilbert Ramsay

Latin Prose Composition

Vol. 2

George Gilbert Ramsay

Latin Prose Composition
Vol. 2

ISBN/EAN: 9783337370985

Printed in Europe, USA, Canada, Australia, Japan

Cover: Foto ©Andreas Hilbeck / pixelio.de

More available books at **www.hansebooks.com**

Clarendon Press Series

LATIN PROSE COMPOSITION

ADAPTED FOR THE LEAVING CERTIFICATE AND
UNIVERSITY PRELIMINARY EXAMINATIONS

BY

GEORGE G. RAMSAY, M.A., Oxon.

HON. LL.D. (EDIN.), LITT.D. (DUBLIN)

PROFESSOR OF HUMANITY IN THE UNIVERSITY OF GLASGOW
EDITOR OF 'SELECTIONS FROM TIBULLUS AND PROPERTIUS,' ETC.

FOURTH EDITION

VOLUME II

*CONTAINING PASSAGES OF GRADUATED DIFFICULTY
FOR TRANSLATION INTO LATIN*

TOGETHER WITH

AN INTRODUCTION ON CONTINUOUS PROSE

Oxford

AT THE CLARENDON PRESS

1897

PREFACE TO THE FOURTH EDITION.

——++——

THE present Volume consists of a collection of passages of various difficulty, and in various styles, for translation into Latin Prose, together with a general Introduction upon the art of writing Continuous Prose. Every passage has been subjected to a careful scrutiny, to make sure that no passage should be admitted which was not specially suitable for translation into Latin, both in style and matter, and such as to bring out, fairly and squarely, the essential points of difference between the two languages: and to secure this end, every piece of English in this volume has been either actually translated into Latin, or specially studied with that view.

In addition, pains have been taken to select passages that should be both interesting in themselves, and excellent as specimens of English style. If a student is to acquire a good style in Latin, he must have placed before him a sample of good style in English ; both thought and language should be such˙ as to be worth the labour to be expended on them in translation. The passages chosen may serve to show how rich our literature is in forcible and beautiful prose : how different is the English written by our best writers from what often passes for English nowadays. The titles prefixed to each passage will, it is hoped, prove both helpful and interesting to the student.

The aim of the *Introduction* is to put before the student a general idea of the essential differences between English and Latin modes of expression, between English and Latin composition ; and to indicate the main principles on which he must proceed in translating from the one language into the other, if he would arrive at a satisfactory result. No attempt is made to supply a series of 'tips'; or to suggest how a set of stock phrases may be skilfully introduced so to give a veneer of Latin to what is essentially a passage of English expressed in Latin words. There are two main things which a student has to be taught if he is to write good Latin : the first is to appreciate the fundamental differences between the two languages ; the second is to gain an understanding of the sort of process which he must apply to the English if it is to be moulded in a Latin form.

I have now for thirty years been engaged in teaching Latin Prose, not only for the purposes of higher scholarship, and with a view to classical examinations, but also to provide for the wants of those students whose main requirement is to gain a command over their own language for the practical work of life ; to acquire clearness of thought, power of logical comprehension, correctness and purity in the use of language, and, if possible, simplicity and force of style. For this purpose, the study of Latin Prose forms an unrivalled discipline : and the *Introduction* contains a short summary of the method which I have found most useful in so teaching it, encumbered with as little detail and technicality as possible.

In the preparation of this Volume I have received help from many friends, and from various books, amongst which I must specially mention Dr. Potts' *Hints*, Dr. Postgate's *Sermo Latinus*, and M. Berger's *Stylistique Latine*, to which I am indebted for some excellent illustrations.

In connection with the present Volume there has been published a Volume of *Latin Prose Versions* contributed by many of the best Latin scholars of the day. That Volume contains translations into Latin of 158 English passages, of which 112 form part of the present collection. As this collection contains 492 passages, teachers have an ample choice, in selecting passages for translation, between those included, and those not included, in the *Versions.*

With the exception of some necessary corrections, the present Edition is an exact reprint of the Third.

G. G. RAMSAY.

University of Glasgow.
October 1, 1897.

TABLE OF CONTENTS

—◆—

INTRODUCTION TO
CONTINUOUS LATIN PROSE.

—•◦•—

On Continuous Prose.

§ **1.** In Vol. I. we dealt with Simple Sentences, and with Compound Sentences of a simple kind, explaining and illustrating the various kinds of Subordinate Clauses one by one. We have now to consider the more difficult art of writing Continuous Prose; that is, the art of Composition, properly so called. To write a single sentence correctly is one thing: it is quite another thing to put together a number of sentences, whether in a single period, or in a passage containing several periods, so as to form a well-composed and harmonious whole. For the genius of the Latin language requires that a passage should be considered as a whole, and that the whole should be something more than a collection of parts.

§ **2.** The treatment which is satisfactory for a sentence standing by itself, may be unsuitable for the same sentence when taken in combination with others. It must then be considered with reference to what goes before, and to what comes after; the construction, the order of the words, the very words and expressions used, may have to undergo change, in order to fit the sentence into its place, as sense or sound may direct. Emphasis will demand some changes; variety will suggest others; and the order in which the sentences follow one another will demand as much consideration as the order of the words in any single sentence.

§ **3.** We have seen (Vol. I., App., p. 237) that for the writing of correct Latin Prose, three things are needed:

(1) Each word must be put into its proper Construction;

(2) Appropriate words and expressions must be used, so as to convey adequately the sense of the English: that is, we must choose such terms and modes of expression as a Roman might have used to convey a similar meaning to Romans;

(3) Each word must be placed in its proper Latin Order.

No. (1) has been fully treated in Vol. I.; some hints as to the differences between Latin and English modes of expression (no. 2) will be found in the Notes to the Exercises in that volume; and the primary rules for Latin Order (no. 3) are given in the Appendix, §§ **29** to **32.** But both (2) and (3) require to be considered more fully in relation to Continuous Prose.

§ **4.** We will suppose that the student has before

him a piece of good literary English to translate into Latin; not of the simplest narrative kind, but containing some thought in it, and with some pretensions to style. What are the special difficulties which he has to face in the task of clothing the English ideas in a Latin dress? What are the special qualities which his Latin should exhibit if it is to be considered good Latin, or indeed Latin at all? It is not enough to be correct only, or to avoid what is absurd in expression, or what is confused and unnatural in order. *He must express himself in the sort of way in which a Roman would have expressed himself if he had had to say the same thing;* he must have a conception not only of the characteristics of the two languages, but also of the fundamental differences between Roman and modern modes of thought.

§ **5.** What then are the salient features of Latin? It has not the flexibility of English; it has not its variety and exuberance; its vocabulary is limited, and wholly inadequate to the needs of modern life. Its great feature is that it is essentially *a law-abiding language*: Law and Order are the pillars on which it rests. Intolerant of inexactness, confusion, and redundancy, it compels the writer to think out exactly what he has to say, to state it in clear and simple terms, and in the order prescribed by the natural sequence or prominence of the ideas. Its inflections reveal every inaccuracy of thought; and the positive Roman mind permitted no writer to wrap up his meaning in obscure generalities. Clearness, directness, simplicity, order, symmetry: these are the qualities in which Latin stands pre-eminent, and on these all sound thinking and all clear writing must be based.

§ **6.** The first thing, then, that a student has to do in writing Latin is to know exactly what he means to say. This hint is by no means unnecessary. Modern English writing is often so slip-shod that it may mean several different things, or nothing at all : modern readers read so quickly and so carelessly that they seldom carry away more than general impressions of what they read. The newspaper, the lecture, and the sermon, all foster the growth of this 'impressionist' school, which shirks the labour of continuous thought both in reading and in writing ; and many a scholar has felt that he had never in his life thought out connectedly the meaning of a difficult piece of English, until taught to do so by the exigencies of Latin Prose.

§ **7.** So long as we confine ourselves to Simple Sentences, and to ideas of the simplest and most universal kind—the external objects, the common incidents and actions, of every-day life—the differences between Latin and English thought do not appear. A mere knowledge of Latin syntax will carry the student pretty safely through Parts I. and II. of this book. But the moment we step out of this simple order of ideas, and have to do with man's inner thoughts and feelings ; when we deal with such complex and variable topics as society, literature, history, morals, politics, religion, philosophy, etc., we cannot translate well unless we realise what the life of the ancient Romans was, and under what aspects these various departments of thought presented themselves to the Roman mind.

§ **8.** The process of translating English into Latin is thus wholly different from that of translating into a modern language. When we translate into French or German, we have only to change the language : we are addressing people who, with minor differences, lead the same lives, have the same thoughts and general aims as ourselves. But in translating into Latin, we have to pass from one era of civilisation into another. We have to take the ideas of a highly complex age, and represent them as they might have appeared to a simple age ; we have to pass in imagination from an age rich in knowledge, but comparatively indifferent to form, to an age whose circle of ideas was narrow, but whose sense of form, and power of logical analysis, were very highly developed.

§ **9.** These differences are stamped upon the face of the two languages. English is a very rich language, carrying along, as part of itself, the results of all the past thought and action of the world ; Latin is, in many respects, a very poor language. English has many ways of expressing one idea ; as a rule, Latin has but one. English is a loose and flexible language ; Latin is a rigid, precise, and logical language.

English revels in the use of abstract terms where concrete things are meant; Latin is severely concrete, and seldom uses abstract terms except to denote abstract things. English is a complex language, enriched by the experience of many civilised nations; Latin is a simple language, expressing in a plain direct fashion the thoughts of a practical unimaginative people, whose life was for centuries confined to a single province of Italy. English abounds in metaphor of the most varied kind, much of it now unconscious; in Latin the metaphors are few, simple and direct, and drawn from a very narrow circle of ideas.

§ **10.** To translate well, therefore, from English into Latin, the student must perform an act of imagination. He must think little of the words; he must go straight for the thought of the original. He must strip the expression of all that is non-essential, redundant, or allusive, and put the actual thing intended into its most simple and direct form. He must eschew all so-called embellishments, using nothing but plain natural metaphors, and regarding purity and straightforwardness as the first great ornaments of speech. These once secured, a little practice, and a careful study of good model passages, will train his ear to appreciate good rhythm, and feel the beauty of that balance and harmony of sound which marks the distinguished Latin style.

§ **11.** It follows, from what has been said, that the main object for a student to set before him is not to look out for special phrases or idioms, to borrow or to imitate particular tricks of speech : he should seek to reproduce the general character of the language as a whole. As Dr. Potts well says[1], ' *The* idiom of the Latin language is to be logical, clear, distinct ; to be intolerant of haze in thought or expression ; to be rhythmical and sonorous in sound.'

Let the writer of Latin therefore before all things bear in mind that he must aim at *clearness.* Baldness, roughness, dulness, are pardonable faults : ambiguity, obscurity, complexity, are unpardonable. Variety, point, rhythm, are qualities to be aimed at ultimately : but the first indispensable quality of good Latin is to be clear.

On the Choice of Words.

§ 12. As soon as the general sense and connection of the passage have been mastered, the next thing to do is to find the nearest Latin equivalents for the separate ideas which it contains. Except in the case of very simple objects and ideas, it is seldom that the first Dictionary substitute, still more seldom that the corresponding English term, will answer the purpose. Do not be satisfied with finding a word in the English-Latin Dictionary; look it up in the Latin-English Dictionary, consult the passages there quoted, and satisfy yourself that the word or the phrase is used just in the sense wanted.

[1] *Hints towards Latin Prose Composition*, cap. v. p. 23.

§ **13.** Cases in which the English word is the same as the Latin word are very apt to mislead: a word adopted from Latin into English has usually either worn off some of its meaning, or added something to it, so that it has come to represent something quite different, or carries with it quite different associations, from the original Latin word. The following is a short list of simple words which differ widely in meaning, or in use, from the same or corresponding words as used in English :—

abhorrere, 'to shrink from,' 'to be widely different from': not 'to abhor' (*detestari*).

adhuc, 'hitherto,' should only be used of present time, 'up to this moment': not as we use 'hitherto,' of past events (for which *tum, ad id tempus*, etc. should be used).

adquirere, 'to gain in addition': not simply 'to acquire' (*parare, consequi*, etc.).

aestimare, 'to value,' 'to appraise': not 'to esteem' (*magni, parvi*, etc., *aestimare*).

affectio, 'a state,' 'a condition': not 'affection,' 'love' (*amor, benevolentia*, etc.).

alludere, 'to play,' 'to joke' or 'do sportingly': not 'to allude to' (*significare, designare, spectare ad*, etc.).

annuus means 'that lasts a year,' as well as 'recurring yearly.'

antiquitas, 'age,' 'antiquity': not = 'the ancients' (*antiqui, veteres*, etc.).

argumentum, 'the subject' of a writing, 'the plot' of a play, etc. ; not 'an argument' (*ratio, causa, res, disputatio*, etc.).

auctor, an 'originator,' 'guarantor,' 'adviser,' 'authority for,' etc.: not properly 'an author' (*scriptor*).

casus, 'a chance,' 'an accident': not 'a case,' 'an instance' (*genus, causa, res, exemplum*, etc.).

celeber, 'crowded' of places: not 'celebrated' of persons (*vir illustrissimus, amplissimus*, etc.).

conscientia, 'privity to,' 'knowledge in one's own mind of': not 'conscience' (*religio, religiosum*, etc.).

crimen, 'an accusation': not 'a crime' (*scelus, culpa*, etc.).

disputare, 'to discuss': not 'to dispute.'

diversus, 'in a different direction,' 'different': not 'divers' (*complures*).

doctrina, 'teaching,' 'science' in general: not 'a doctrine' (*praeceptum, ratio, disciplina*, etc.).

elevare, 'to depreciate': not 'to elevate,' 'to raise up' (*tollere*).

exsistere, 'to stand out,' 'to shew oneself': not 'to exist' (*esse*).

experientia, 'a trial,' 'proof': but not (in the best period) 'the knowledge gained thereby,' 'experience' (*usus*, or *rerum usus*, etc.; *re doctus*, 'taught by experience').

familia, properly 'an establishment of slaves'; also technically, a subdivision of the *gens*: not 'a family,' 'a household' (*domus, sui, mei*, etc.).

gratia, 'favour,' 'thanks': not 'grace' (*decor*); notice esp. that the usual phrase is *gratiam* (Sing.) *habere, debere, referre*; but *gratias* (Plur.) *agere*.

habere, 'to have' or 'hold'; not so usual in the sense 'to possess,' as the phrase *est mihi*, etc.: with Abstract Subs. it constantly means 'occasions,' 'gives rise to,' 'involves': e. g. *habet admirationem, terrorem,* etc.

historia, 'a narrative,' 'a story' : not 'History' as = 'recorded events' (*res gestae, res ipsae*, etc.).

honor, 'a public office,' 'a public distinction,' 'repute': not usually for 'honour' (*fama*), or 'honour' as a personal quality (*fides*).

instructio, 'a constructing,' 'an arranging': not 'instruction' (*doctrina*).

libellus, 'a written document,' 'a petition': not 'a libel'.

meritum, 'a kindness done to a person': not 'a merit' (*laus, virtus*, etc.).

momentum, 'a movement,' 'a turning point,' and so 'a cause' or 'influence': not 'a moment of time' (*punctum temporis*).

mundus, 'the world,' 'the universe,' 'the heavens': but not 'the earth' specially (*orbis terrae* or *terrarum*); nor yet in the sense of 'mankind,' 'society,' 'life,' etc.

obnoxius, 'liable to,' 'subject to': not 'objectionable (*molestus*).

obtinere, 'to hold fast,' 'to retain': not 'to obtain' (*acquirere, parare*) ; nor yet intrans. of a custom, opinion, etc. (*consuetudo est, valet opinio*, etc.).

occasio, 'favourable occasion,' 'opportunity' (=καιρός): not merely 'occasion.'

perdere, 'to destroy,' 'to squander': not merely 'to lose' (*amittere, omittere*).

persona, 'a part,' 'a character': not 'a person.'

regnare, 'to be king,' or 'to play the tyrant': but not metaphorically in the sense of 'to prevail' (*esse* or *valere*; e. g. 'silence reigned,' *silentium fuit*).

reparare, 'to procure over again,' 'to recover,' or 'to restore ': but not properly ' to repair.'

scientia, ' knowledge ': not absolutely, for ' a science ' ; nor yet ' science in general ' (*ars, doctrina*).

sententiam dicere, ' to state formally one's opinion ' in a court or assembly : not merely ' to express an opinion ' (*dic mihi quid sentias,* etc.).

stilus, ' a (Roman) pen ' or ' pencil ': not our ' style ' (*oratio, dicendi,* or *scribendi genus,* etc.).

studere, ' to be keen about,' ' fond of' (with Dat.) : not ' to study ' (*operam dare, laborare in,* etc.).

traditio, ' a handing over ': not in the sense of oral or written ' tradition ' (*memoria, fama, ferunt,* etc.).

usurpare, ' to make use of' : not ' to usurp.'

vivere, ' to be in life,' or ' to feed upon ' : but ' to live at such a time ' is *esse eo tempore,* etc.

vultus, ' the expression ' (from *volo*) : not ' the face ' (*facies,* ' the make,' ' the features '; *os, lineamenta oris,* etc.).

On Latin Modes of Expression.

§ **14.** Having got hold of the right word or words, the next thing is to use them in the right way : to combine them in the sort of expression which a Roman writer might have used to express the sense intended. To do this with nicety, is to have command of the Latin language[1]; but every student

---

[1] See the excellent comparison of English and Latin modes of expression in the matter of social and political ideas in Prof. Nettleship's Introduction to *Passages for Translation into Latin Prose,* G. Bell & Sons, 1887, p. 10.

should at least have an idea of the general objects to aim at in the conversion of literary English into literary Latin.

§ 15. Dr. Potts tells us that the main features of Latin expression, all more or less connected together, are (1) **Concreteness**; (2) **Directness**; (3) **Lucidity**; (4) **Realism**; and (5) **Precision** (in tenses, etc.). To these we must add (6) **Conciseness**, a most marked characteristic, which, however, occasionally interferes with no. (3) (*Lucidity*), and is itself sometimes incompatible with no. (2) (*Directness*). Quality no. (4) (*Realism*) is scarcely to be separated from no. (1) (*Concreteness*): it means a putting of ideas simply, as they actually are, or as they appear primarily to the mind or senses, rather than a describing of them through the medium of other ideas, representations, or associations imported by the mind itself.

§ 16. As said above, these qualities are not always compatible; one or another may have to be sacrificed. *Clearness* demands that an idea or a thing must be fully indicated; but there are many modern ideas which were unknown to the ancients, and which cannot be expressed fully by one word: a periphrasis must be used. No one word could express a complex idea like 'civilisation'; and a single English adjective may have to be expanded, for the sake of clearness, into a whole relative clause. *Directness* is analogous both to *concreteness* and to *realism*: it means that a thing must be expressed at first hand, as an object is reflected by a mirror, not indirectly by an allusion to something else.   An English author writes : ' How noble is Xenophon's description of the death of Socrates !   He tells us how *the philosopher* sat calmly amongst his friends,' etc.   Here the words *the philosopher* give an allusive description of Socrates : if we were to translate by *philosophus*, some new person, different from Socrates, would be indicated [1].

§ **17.** *Clearness*, we have seen, is the most important end to aim at : yet it is often interfered with by *conciseness*, and still more often by the fact that on many subjects the Romans had not thought out differences of meaning which are familiar to us, and so allowed one word to stand for very different things.   Thus words are sometimes used both in an Active and a Passive sense : *exspectatio* may mean ' a waiting for others,' or ' the being waited for by others'; *caecus* may mean ' blind ' or 'unseen'; *gnarus* is both ' knowing' and 'known'; *illacrimabilis*, ' incapable of weeping,' or ' of being wept for.' In other cases no distinction is made between a thing itself, and the consciousness of that thing by the mind; *libertas* may mean 'liberty,' or ' the love or sentiment of liberty'; *officium* may mean 'external acts of duty,' or 'the sense of duty in the mind.'   The word *memoria* may mean three things : (1) 'The faculty or act of memory'; (2) 'The time to which the recollection extends'; (3) 'An account of past events,' 'a narrative.'   And a whole host of ideas may be repre-

---

[1] But we might add, for emphasis, *philosophus ille illustrissimus*, etc.

sented by such vague words as *res*[1], *ratio, esse, habere, agere*, etc. For, as said above, Latin is a poor language; and it may often be better to use vague words like the above, somewhat empty of meaning, rather than run the risk of conveying a wrong meaning.

§ **18.** *Preciseness* and *conciseness* again are some-times opposing qualities. Latin is very precise in its use of tenses; preciseness often requires a clause where we use a single word (*id de quo agitur*, 'the subject'; *is cuius causa agitur*, 'the defendant'; *id quod animo proposuit consecutus*, 'having gained his end'); rejoices in expanded phrases like *ex quo efficitur ut, quae cum ita sint*, etc.; or adds unneces-sarily a defining word, as in *causae rerum*, 'causes'; *natura rerum*, 'nature'; *angor animi*, 'distress.' On the other hand, for the sake of shortness, pronouns, personal or possessive, are constantly omitted; verbs are frequently omitted, as in *quid plura?* (sc. *dicam*); *ne multis* (sc. *utar*); *quid, quod?*; *Sus Minervam* (sc. *docet*), = 'Teach your grandmother'; or substan-tives, as *illud egregium* (sc. *dictum*) *Catonis*; *Hectoris Andromache* (sc. *uxor*).

§ **19.** We thus see that the qualities of *lucidity, concreteness, directness, realism, conciseness*, though sometimes incompatible, yet as a whole run into one

---

[1] On the wide use of *res* see Dr. Postgate's *Sermo Latinus*, p. 34; for both *res* and *esse* see Dr. Potts' *Hints*, pp. 32, 33. Dr. Potts happily calls the word *res* 'a blank cheque, to be filled up from the context.'

another, and are all the results of one tendency. They may be summed up in the saying that *Latin always speaks the truth*; and loves to speak it in a plain simple way. It may not be possible always to write so as to exhibit all these qualities; but, if possible, let clearness never be sacrificed. Intelligibility is the first requisite of all language; it is better to be clear than to be short, and better to be inadequate than to be misleading.

§ **20.** Let us next consider some of the main peculiarities of English which would appear, to a Roman mind, inconsistent with the above qualities: what are the kinds of expression which, however good in English, cannot be translated literally into Latin without a sacrifice of them. We may then consider what means Latin employs in such cases to express the required meaning in its own way.

Use of Abstract Terms.

§ **21.** A marked peculiarity of English, as of all modern languages, is the constant use of abstract terms where concrete things are meant. It is impossible to turn over a page of English without finding such expressions as 'Society is censorious'; 'Literature is an exacting mistress'; 'Genius is always sensitive'; 'Public life had no attractions for him'; 'Humanity demands it'; 'Old age is penurious'; etc. In each of the above sentences an abstract term is used, not in its proper sense to denote the abstract idea involved in each, but to denote things or persons. As a rule, such expressions are to be carefully avoided in Latin[1]. Say exactly and directly what you mean ; do not express it indirectly through an abstraction. All the above expressions refer to *men* of some sort, and you must say so, with such qualification as may be necessary. If 'Society' means 'mankind at large,' say *homines* or *plerique hominum*. If it means 'Society' in the technical social sense, *qui urbani et venusti sunt*; and so on. Think out in each case what the thing actually meant is, and express that. 'Honesty is the best policy' is an abstract way of saying that 'Men succeed best by honesty,' or that 'Honest men are prosperous.' 'Temperance is the best guarantee for health,' may be expressed directly by saying 'Men preserve their health by temperance'; or 'Temperate men are healthy.'

§ 22. We may take a few examples at random from the English passages in this volume :—

(*a*) 'The excellence of his administration': Latin would say *quod rem bene gesserat*, 'the fact that he had governed well.'

(*b*) 'To give stability to his throne': *ut imperium firmaret*.

(*c*) 'To prevent its abstraction': *quod ne auferretur*.

---

[1] There are exceptions, as *inventus*, *mancipium*, etc., but they are not numerous. Cicero uses Plural Abstract Nouns with great boldness and beauty, as *omnes honestates civitatis*, Pro Sest. 51, § 109 ; *fontium gelidas perennitates*, De Nat. ii. 39, § 98 ; *fugae, timiditates*, Pro Mil. 26, § 69. The force of the Plural is to suggest the idea of various persons, places, or occasions.

(*d*) 'His exultation at the successful completion of an important enterprise': *gaudebat quod rem tantam tam bene perfecerat.*

(*e*) 'Government during this period was Asiatic, but it was commonly able': Latin would say, 'The governors (kings or emperors, etc.) ruled in Asiatic fashion, but ruled well.'

(*f*) 'He met with a kind reception': say 'He was kindly received.'

(*g*) 'The division of the gold took place in the presence of the chief': *Aurum praesente principe divisum est.*

To quote further examples were endless. Modern thought loves to express itself by such abstract vague generalities; but Latin, where a definite precise thing is meant, prefers to state it in a definite precise way.

Latin Equivalents to English Abstract Terms.

§ 23. Let us examine more closely the concrete Latin forms of speech which correspond to such abstractions as those quoted above.

(1) In many cases a concrete noun, denoting things or persons, may be at once substituted for the abstraction. Thus, 'the majority of mankind' will become 'most men,' *plerique*; 'old age is talkative' will be rendered by *senes loquaces sunt*; 'philosophy is ever prone to doubt' will become *amant semper philosophi dubitare.*

(2) An abstract term may be represented by an Adjective, or a Participle, agreeing with a Noun ; as

'The rising and setting of the sun make day and night,' *Sol oriens et occidens diem noctemque conficit*;

'It was not liberality but levity which led Atticus to suppose,' etc., *Atticus non liberalis sed levis arbitrabatur*, etc.;

'After the foundation of the city,' *Post urbem conditam*;

'His presence was an inspiration,' *Praesens animos erigebat*;

'The assassination of Caesar seemed to some a fine deed,' *Occisus Caesar aliis pulcherrimum facinus videbatur.*

(3) By an Adjective in the Genitive :

'It would be madness to imitate such an example,' *Dementis esset talem hominem imitari.*

(4) By a Finite Verb, as in the example above, *Praesens animos erigebat*;

'Knowledge is power,' *Quo plura scies, eo plus valebis*;

'After the disastrous engagement of Cannae,' *Cum apud Cannas adverso Marte pugnatum esset.*

(5) By a Verb in the Infinitive :

'Self-command is nobler than empire,' *Imperare sibi quam aliis praestantius est*;

'Drinking is more injurious than eating,' *Plus nocet bibere quam edere.*

(6) By an Ablative Absolute :

'The assassination of Caesar left Antony master of the State,' *Occiso Caesare Antonius quasi dominus reipublicae imponebatur*;

'Under the leadership of Caesar,' *Duce Caesare.*

(7) By a Gerund or Gerundive :

'He cleared for himself a road by the assassination of his enemies,' *Viam sibi ad regnum inimicis interficiendis patefecit.*

(8) Sometimes by a whole Clause :

'His popularity with the masses secured his unanimous and enthusiastic election to the consulship,' *Quod apud plebem gratiosus fuit, ideo summo omnium studio consul creatus est* ;

'Having accomplished his design,' *Quod animo pro-posuerat consecutus* ;

'Nothing but vain repentance remained,' *Nihil ultra quam ut frustra paeniteret restabat.*

§ **24.** Note especially that Latin keeps the form in *io* and *tas* to denote the abstract idea, while English uses them indifferently both as abstract and concrete. In the sentence

'The institution of a new system requires care,'

the word *institution* would properly be rendered by *institutio*, which means 'the process of setting up.' But to translate

'At such times *society* rallies round any *institution* which bears the marks of sovereignty,'

neither *societas* nor *institutio* can be used. 'Society' here means the individuals of whom the state is composed ; whereas *societas* means the state of being in association. *Institution* means, not 'a setting up,' or 'instituting,' but 'a something set up.' Here we must

use *homines* for ' society,' *institutum*, not *institutio*, for
' institution.' Compare in the same way the difference
between *inventio*, 'the discovery of a thing,' and *inventum*, 'a thing discovered,' 'a discovery'; *cogitatio*
and *cogitatum*, *promissio* and *promissum* [1], etc.

§ 25. On the same principle, Latin objects, as a rule,
to the abstract use of the Singular to represent a
plurality of things, or a whole class of things. We
say 'the eye' gets accustomed to this, 'the ear'
appreciates that, and speak of 'day and night'; in
such cases Latin says *oculi, aures, dies atque noctes,*
etc., because the Plural is at once more true, and less
abstract, than the Singular. So where we say 'the
philosopher,' 'the poor man,' 'the melancholy man,'
using one person to represent a class of persons,
Latin says *philosophi, pauperes*, etc. There are a few
special exceptions to this rule, consecrated by philo-
sophic usage, such as *avarus, sapiens*, etc.; similarly,
eques and *pedes* are used for 'cavalry' and 'infantry';
and occasionally, in war operations, *Romanus, Poenus,*
etc., may stand collectively for the Roman or Carthaginian army. But the rule of Latin is to prefer
the Concrete Plural to the Abstract Singular :—

' The poor man's cottage,' *Pauperum tabernae* ;

'Some devoted themselves to music, some to poetry,'
Totos se alii ad poetas, alii ad musicos se dedere ;

'He was popular with the aristocracy,' *Apud principes*
(or *optimates*) *gratiosus fuit.*

---

[1] See Berger, *Stylistique Latine*, p. 74.

§ **26.** In matters of age, date, office, etc., Latin states concretely what English states abstractly :—

'I have been devoted to books from my boyhood,' *Litteris a puero deditus sum* ;

'In the consulship of Plancus,' *Planco consule*;

'He did this in his private capacity,' *Privatus fecit.*

§ **27.** Even when both forms of speech are equally accurate and available, Latin tends always to the more concrete when it seeks precision : *sententiam dicere* is the regular phrase for 'pronouncing an opinion,' but *dicere quae sentio* states more clearly that I state what I really think ; similarly the expressions *ii qui accusant, qui audiunt*, etc., are preferred to *accusatores, auditores*, etc., when particular persons are referred to.

On Personification and other Non-realities of English Expression.

§ **28.** Again, English likes to use, for picturesque and quasi-poetical effect, all sorts of expressions which in their literal meaning have the stamp of unreality, and therefore of ambiguity, about them. As we use them, such expressions are not ambiguous, because they are understood ; they are not unnatural, because they have generally a known history ; they appeal to familiar associations, they suit the genius of the language : but.to the matter-of-fact Roman mind, with its limited associations, they would appear

grotesque, untrue, and therefore unmeaning, if reproduced literally in Latin. Many of such expressions
are founded on metaphors, to which modern life only
can supply the key ; but apart from metaphor, many of
our commonest modes of expression involve artificial
and indirect modes of regarding things which a
Roman would neither have appreciated nor understood. One of the commonest examples of this is
the tendency to give life to inanimate things by
personification; that is, by attributing to lifeless
things actions and qualities which are peculiar to
living agents. We see nothing odd in such expressions as the following[1]:

(*a*) 'Indolence kept him for six whole months at home';

(*b*) 'Neither fear nor favour could move him ';

(*c*) 'The perfidy of Napoleon made peace impossible';

(*d*) 'If anything of disappointment depressed his spirits';

(*e*) 'Our colder temperaments scarce enable us to conceive';

(*f*) 'His presence might have averted this calamity';

(*g*) 'Caesar's rule promised order and security';

(*h*) 'His success in this scheme encouraged him to
attempt another';

(*i*) 'An enquiry into these encroachments would have
stripped every Spanish nobleman of his estates';

(*k*) 'No pen can record the sufferings of a whole
people';

(*l*) 'The prison-house at last brought him to his senses.'

---

[1] These examples are almost all taken from passages in this
volume.

§ 29. To a Roman every one of the above expressions would have appeared to involve an outrage upon common sense. In each of them an external object, or an abstract idea, is invested with personality. In Latin this must be done but sparingly; only in simple instances, and on suitable occasions. A highly-coloured rhetorical passage may admit of some bold personification; and simple ideas, especially those representing human feelings[1], such as *ira, pavor, cupido, metus,* etc., are frequently used with verbs implying personal action. But in other cases, such expressions should be avoided. One simple mode of avoiding them is to turn the Active Verb into a Passive : it is more natural in Latin to describe a man as being *non gratia, non pecunia motus;* than to say, *eum nec gratia nec pecunia movere potuit.* The abstract idea, or the inanimate thing, which appears out of place as the Subject to a verb of action, will excite no surprise as an Ablative of the Instrument, or turned in some other way. The above sentences might all be Latinised as follows :

(*a*) ' He was so indolent that,' etc. ;

(*b*) ' Moved neither by fear nor favour' ;

(*c*) ' By reason of Napoleon's perfidy peace could not be made' ;

or ' Napoleon was so perfidious that,' etc. ;

(*d*) ' If, baffled in hope, he had let down his courage ' ;

(*e*) ' We indeed, as our minds are cold (*ut sunt*), cannot conceive ' ;

---

[1] See Potts, *Hints,* p. 35.

(*f*) 'Had he been present, he could have averted';

(*g*) 'Men expected that under Caesar (as) ruler they would enjoy law and order';

(*h*) 'Which since (it) had turned out well for him, he determined to dare something further';

(*i*) 'Concerning all which things had it been enquired (impers.), all the Spanish nobles would have been deprived of their estates';

(*k*) 'By no letters can be described what a whole people is able to endure';

(*l*) 'Thrown into prison, he at length learnt how things really held themselves.'

§ **30.** In translating such figurative phrases into Latin, we must in each case eliminate the unreal, imaginative element, and ask ourselves how the thing actually meant would be expressed by an unimaginative person of common sense, who knew perfectly well what he had to say, but had not at hand, ready to draw from (as we have), a fund of pictorial expressions, in forms consecrated by time. The Roman used language which he understood; if he said a thing, it was because he himself had thought it. But the modern is perpetually using figures of speech thought out by past generations, or suggested by past modes of life, without any sense of their proper original meaning. He uses representative words and expressions as if they had never denoted anything but the things for which they now stand. Hence the incongruities and redundancies of so much of our modern writing: in Cumberland, *Winder-mere lake*, even *Derwent-water lake*, are common expressions, people forgetting what *mere* or *water* mean. To such faults the writing of Latin applies the best of correctives ; for to write it well we must think out, at first hand, the exact meaning of everything we have to say.

General Precision and Truthfulness of Latin.

§ 31. The general precision of Latin, which requires that things should be stated truthfully and literally as they are, is further illustrated in the following points :

(1) It is strictly correct in the use of Tenses. Thus it will not permit the looseness of the English 'I shall see you when *I am* in Rome,' 'I shall call on you *when I arrive* in Rome.' Latin and logic alike require *cum Romae ero, cum Romam pervenero.* See Vol. I, Pref. note to Ex. IV. ; Ex. VI. n. 9 ; Ex. VII. n. 14, etc. ; and so with other tenses.

(2) Similarly, Latin Participles must be used in their strict and proper meaning. The Present must not be used for the Past Participle, as in the English 'Taking my passage by the quick steamer, I arrived in ten days at Alexandria' ; nor to denote a reason, as in 'Seeing all hope was gone, I came away.' Nor can the Present Part. be used (except in a strictly limited number of cases) in lieu of an Adjective, as in

c

the English 'a lying scoundrel,' 'a convincing speaker,' 'an irritating answer,' 'a domineering woman.' The Present Part. denotes that the act is actually going on at the moment; hence, to translate such phrases as the above, we must use an adjective in *ax* (denoting 'with a tendency to') if there is one, as *mendax*, *audax*, *pervicax*, etc., or else an Adjectival Clause. (See Vol. I. § 32.) Sometimes by a bold personification, such epithets may be rendered by nouns : *exercitus victor*, 'a conquering army'; *animus Catilinae cuiuslibet rei simulator ac dissimulator*, Sall. Cat. 5. 4. Sometimes, by a concreteness of expression peculiarly Latin, the Genitive Plural of a Present Part. may be used: 'encouraging opinion,' *comprobantium sententiae*; 'disapproving murmurs' (or 'murmurs of disapproval'), *frementium voces*.

(3) We say 'War was declared with France'; 'Our relations with Russia are on the most friendly footing.' Latin would say 'with the French,' 'with the Russians,' which is what is meant.

(4) Truthfulness, again, as well as force, suggest the frequent use of the figure *Hendiadys* (ἓν διὰ δυοῖν), that is, of two Substantives to take the place of what we less correctly express by a Substantive and an Adjective. Thus *ratio et doctrina* is equivalent to 'methodical instruction'; *antiquissimae litterae et monumenta* (In Verr. II. 4. 48) to 'ancient written records'; *vim et manus alicui adferre*, 'to lay violent hands on a person'; *natura pudorque meus*, 'my natural modesty.' The same effect may be produced

by joining two Adverbs together, in the place of an Abstract Noun with an Adjective : *modice ac sapienter rem agebat,* 'with a wise moderation.'

(5) For the same reason, a Noun in the Genitive will often take the place of an English Adjective : 'bodily pleasures' are *corporis voluptates*; 'literary pursuits,' *studium litterarum*; 'universal joy,' *omnium gaudium*; and so on. It is obvious, speaking with literal exactness, that joy cannot be 'universal,' nor a pursuit be 'literary,' nor a pleasure 'bodily.' Nor would truth permit us to say 'a learned book,' 'a strong argument,' 'a witty saying'; Latin says what is meant : *liber doctissime scriptus* or *a docto scriptus ; facete dictum*; and so on.

§ **32.** The following passage (No. CXC. in this volume) affords a good example of the changes which a simple piece of English may have to undergo in being translated into Latin :—

When the masses at Athens[1] had become more and more preponderant[2], the Areopagus was attacked[3] in the following manner by Ephialtes, a man reputed incorruptible[5] in his loyalty to democracy[6], and[4] who had become leader of the Commons. He first put to death many of its members by impeaching them[7] of offences committed[8] in their administration[9]. He then despoiled the Council of all its recently-acquired attributes[10]; and distributed these amongst the Senate, the Assembly, and the Courts of Law. In this work he had the co-operation of[11] Themistocles, who, though himself an Areopagite, was expecting to be accused of treasonable correspondence[12] with Persia[13]. Desiring the ruin of the Council, Themistocles warned

Ephialtes that it was going to imprison him; and at the same time told the Council that he would shew them a band of traitors in the act of conspiring [14] against the State. Then, conducting [15] a committee of their number to the residence of Ephialtes, he shewed them the gang assembling, and held them in conversation [16] on the spot; Ephialtes fled panic-struck to the altar, clad in nothing but his tunic, and sat there to the amazement of [17] all beholders.

Aristotle.

(1) 'The masses at Athens.' Instance of 'loose connection.' Vol. i. App. § 29 (o). If *Athenis* were used, the meaning would be 'When the masses had become preponderant at Athens.' Say 'The Athenian populace' (*plebs*).

(2) 'Had become more and more predominant.' Say 'were by this time very powerful' (*iam plurimum pollebant*).

(3) 'Was attacked.' No single word for 'attack' will here convey the exact meaning. What is meant is that Ephialtes sought 'to diminish the power' of the Areopagus.

(4) 'A man reputed incorruptible . . . *and* who had become . . .' To translate the '*and*' in this sentence as it stands would be incorrect in Latin. Say either 'reputed incorruptible . . . who had etc.'; or else 'who was reputed . . . and who had . . .'

(5) 'Incorruptible in his loyalty to democracy.' Loose connection. Say 'of uncorrupted loyalty towards the plebs,' placing *in plebem* between *incorruptae* and *fidei*, to show the connection.

(6) 'Democracy' must of course be translated by 'people' (*plebs*).

(7) 'He put to death many of its members by impeaching them.' It would be absurd to say this in Latin. He did not put them to death '*by impeaching them.*' They were impeached first, and put to death afterwards.

(8) 'Offences committed etc.' Clearness requires us to say 'offences which they had committed.'

(9) 'In their administration.' Too abstract for Latin. Say 'when they were magistrates,' or *in magistratu*.

(10) 'Attributes.' Say more definitely 'powers.'

(11) 'Had the co-operation of Themistocles.' Too abstract. Say 'had Themistocles (as) an associate.'

(12) 'Accused of treasonable correspondence.' Again too abstract. Say 'that he had treacherously sent letters to.'

(13) 'Correspondence with Persia.' The correspondence was not with Persia. It was with the Persians, or the Persian monarch.

(14) 'In the act of conspiring.' The Pres. Part. scarcely strong enough. Say 'who at that very time were conspiring' (*coniurare*).

(15) 'Conducting.' The sense requires 'having conducted.'

(16) 'Held them in conversation on the spot.' Loose connection. 'Conversation' must be expressed by a Verb or Pres. Part. in order that 'on the spot' may be taken with it.

(17) 'To the amazement of.' Say concretely 'all wondering.'

Use of Metaphor.

§ **33**. Great care should be exercised in dealing with Metaphors. A Metaphor is 'a condensed simile[1].' A simile states that one thing is *like* another thing : a metaphor states that it *is* that other thing, leaving the mind to draw for itself the conclusion that the writer or the speaker is not identifying the two things, but only indicating forcibly some point of similarity between them. If I say 'I see the deep's untrampled floor' I use Metaphor; if I say 'The sea is like a floor that has not been trampled upon' I use Simile : the difference being that in the one case the reader is informed, by express words, that a comparison is being made ; in the other case he is left to find out for himself that the words are

[1] See Nägelsbach, and Potts' *Hints*, Part V.

only figuratively used.   If he does not find it out he is misled, and the figure fails in its purpose.

§ **34.** The primary object of using either Simile or Metaphor is to help a hearer or a reader to form a clearer, more graphic conception of an idea by comparing it to something better known, and more familiar to him, than the thing compared. Hence most metaphors are drawn from natural external objects.   The internal operations of the mind are made clear and intelligible when compared to some simple external act, as in the words 'to comprehend,' 'to grasp,' 'to understand,' 'to reflect,' 'to suppose.'   The first object of all such comparisons is to render a less familiar idea intelligible by presenting it in the form of a known and familiar idea ; and the comparison must be of the unfamiliar to the familiar, of the unknown to the known.   This is what Quintilian means by saying that Necessity is the first reason for employing Metaphor : language would have been a mere catalogue of existing objects, progress in thought would have been impossible, if man had not possessed the power of representing and vivifying new or unformed ideas as they arose— especially all abstract and non-sensible ideas—by expressing them in terms of acts or objects that were already familiar to him.

§ **35.** Thus the first object of all Metaphor is to make the meaning clear; the second object, according to Quintilian, is to make it forcible[1]; in other

---

[1] On this point, see Dr. Potts, *Hints*, p. 115.

words, to make it doubly clear, and drive it home to the mind of the hearer with a force which he cannot resist. The third use of Metaphor (and it is emphatically the mark of bad writing to make this the most important) is for purposes of ornament. If we gain the first two ends, we may leave the third to take care of itself.

§ **36.** The first condition, then, of the right use of Metaphor being that it should make the meaning more clear, more vivid, more intelligible, it is essential that it should be drawn from something within the experience of those to whom it is addressed. An illustration can only make a thing clearer to me if it be drawn from something which I know better than the thing illustrated ; and if we use Metaphor in writing Latin, it must be drawn from materials which were familiar to the Roman mind, or could be made intelligible to it. There are multitudes of modern metaphors which cannot be translated into Latin at all, because they are based on facts and ideas essentially modern in their character. Such phrases may have a whole history behind them ; many have passed current so long in their figurative sense that we forget in using them that they are figurative at all. We are scarcely conscious that we are using metaphor when we speak of 'the foot,' 'the side,' 'the brow,' 'the shoulder,' 'the face,' 'the breast,' 'the spurs' of a mountain : yet Latin only knows the first three of these, while it speaks of the *gremium*, and *radices* of a mountain, figures unknown to English.   Again, Latin sometimes uses the same figures that we do, but uses them in a different way, as required by their original meaning : thus 'to propose,' 'to intend,' 'to conceive,' 'to object,' are all phrases used in Latin, but are not used absolutely as by us.   We must say *hoc mihi proposui,* not simply *proposui*; *intendo animum,* 'I stretch' or 'strain the mind,' not *intendo* alone ; *concipere animo,* not *concipere*; *haec mihi obiecit,* 'he cast up these things against me,' not *obiecit* absolutely.,   Latin preserves the proper meanings of such phrases ; we have forgotten them.

§ **37.**   But there are many English metaphors which are quite untranslateable.   'To beat time,' 'to kill time,' 'to take time by the forelock,' 'to steal a person's heart away,' 'to steal a march upon,' 'to be the victim of circumstances,' 'to nurse one's wrath,' 'famine now stared them in the face'—are a few out of hundreds of common English metaphors which Latin would decline to recognise in any form.   In other cases, even where the ideas drawn upon are comparatively simple, the modern mode of working out the metaphor may be too complicated to adapt itself to the simple realism of the Roman mind.   The following are chance instances of common English metaphors taken from passages in this volume :—

(*a*) 'France knew how to make atonement for the past';

(*b*) 'The reign of political superstition had set in ' ;

(*c*) 'Revolutions send capacity to the front with volcanic force' ;

(*d*) 'His wit needed an atmosphere of license in which to move freely';

(*e*) 'The quiet peacefulness of a face . . . which stirred not even the veil behind which it worked';

(*f*) 'A drama is itself the only adequate commentary on its persons';

(*g*) 'The promise thus held out is certainly not kept to the letter';

(*h*) 'The generality of writers render this tribute to the good fortune of conquerors';

(*i*) 'Man's will is mysteriously linked to the long chain of natural causes';

(*k*) 'Plato's writings are the touchstone of a hasty and shallow mind.'

Latin would eschew every one of the above metaphors. Some of the ideas are outside the pale of Roman thought: almost all are too drastic and violent in their substitutions, and involve acts of mental gymnastic which a Roman would not have performed. They are also too elaborate. A Roman metaphor must be simple, and must not be overdone. It should consist of one central idea clearly put, and not be expanded into detailed developments. A Roman might have compared increasing happiness to the increasing light of day: but he would not have endured to hear that 'The dawn of our happiness has not yet burst into the splendour of open day': he would have thought the metaphor was flogged to death.

§ 38. What then is to be done with metaphors like

the above, in which modern language abounds?
There are several resources open to us. We should
first scan the whole phrase carefully, and realise
exactly in what point or points its appropriateness as
an illustration consists. If it be a perfectly simple
and natural metaphor, and appeal to common familiar
experience, it may possibly be reproduced as it is in
Latin ; if it be complicated, or violent, or far-fetched,
or essentially modern in its character, we may be sure
that it can not. Before using a metaphor, let a
student consult his Dictionary, and see whether the
particular metaphor was actually used, and in what
form, by Latin writers. If no authority can be
found for the particular metaphor, let him seek
for some analogous figure actually used, of a more
simple universal kind, which will express the central idea of the comparison, though perhaps by
different means. Thus in example (*a*) given above,
the idea of 'pardon' for past offences might be
substituted for 'atonement'; in (*b*), though 'superstition' could not be said 'to reign,' it might be said
'to seize' or even 'to invade' the minds of men ; in
(*h*), though writers could not 'render this tribute,'
they might simply 'give this,' or 'concede this,' to
the fortune of conquerors.

§ **39.** If a simplification of this kind is not to be
found, the student has two resources. If the metaphor
be altogether too strange to introduce satisfactorily
into Latin, he may drop the metaphor altogether, and
express in a plain straightforward way, without

figure, the actual thing which the writer meant to say. This would probably be the best mode of treating the metaphorical expressions quoted above, in § 37, (*c*), (*f*), (*g*), and (*h*) :—

(*c*) 'In troubled times the most able men come forth as leaders'; or 'as each man is most able, so he,' etc. ;

(*f*) 'The characters of the persons in a play (*quales quisque sint*) can only be learned from the play itself';

(*g*) 'What was promised, that same thing was certainly not done';

(*h*) 'Each man in reading Plato is proved, whether he be of a shallow or a profound mind.'

§ **40.** But there are other cases in which a metaphor may be too strong to be taken as it stands, and yet the idea may be such as would be natural and intelligible from a Roman point of view, if the mind were prepared for it by some explanation or apology. In such cases, the metaphor can be changed into a simile, by prefacing it with some word of comparison, such as *ut, ceu, haud secus ac*, etc., or it may be apologised for by introducing *quasi, quidam, tanquam, velut, ut ita dicam*, or some equivalent expression, to shew that the phrase is not to be taken in its strict literal sense. We think it quite natural to talk of 'incendiary language'; but Cicero, though the metaphor from a torch was a common one in Latin, thinks it necessary to tone it down by prefixing *quasi*:

Hic cum Philippo quasi quasdam verborum faces admovisset, de Or. III. i. § 4.

By similar means the metaphors in examples (*d*),

(*e*), and (*i*) as given above, might well be preserved. Instead of

(*d*) ' His wit needed an atmosphere of license in which to move,'

the Latin might say

' He was of that kind of wit (*eo erat ingenio*) that he desired all things to be free, as it were in the open air ';

(*e*) ' The quiet peacefulness of a face which stirred not even the veil behind which it worked,'

might be rendered by

' His face was so tranquil that it did not move even that which like a veil was placed before it.'

(*i*) ' Man's will is mysteriously linked to the long chain of natural causes,'   .

might be rendered

' Man's will is in some strange way bound by that chain, if I may so speak, by which the causes of things are bound together.'

§ 41. Thus in Metaphor, as in all else, Latin aims at the simple, the natural, the intelligible. Latin metaphors are all of a simple kind ; they are usually conveyed by a single word, not developed through several points of likeness, as modern metaphors so often are ; and that one word is more often a Verb than a Noun. Dr. Potts supplies a list (*Hints*, pp. 116–124) of the sources from which the greater number of Latin metaphors are derived. As might be expected, they are largely drawn from the ordinary sights and processes of nature: from rivers and fountains; from the flowering, seeding, and fruiting of plants; from seas and storms and ships; from floods and fires; from the members and actions of the human body; from animals; from the simple arts and processes of human life; and especially from the various institutions of Rome, whether social, legal, military, political, or religious.

On Latin Order.

§ 42. One of the main difficulties in writing Latin consists in placing the words of a sentence, whether simple or compound, in their proper order. In the matter of Order, Latin differs essentially from English. In English, as in all uninflected languages, words follow one another in the order of the syntax; if we change that order, we change the sense also. If we wish to change the order without changing the sense, we must vary the construction, so as to bring out the same sense in another way. In Latin, the syntax, being determined by the inflection, is independent of the order; hence the order may be varied to almost any extent, according as emphasis, or variety, or harmony may suggest, without making any fundamental change in the meaning. In the English sentence 'Brutus stabbed Cæsar,' no change of order is possible without a change of sense; but in Latin we may say *Brutus interfecit Caesarem, Caesarem interfecit Brutus, interfecit Brutus Caesarem, Caesarem Brutus interfecit*, and so on, without any change of sense : each sentence stating the same fact, only with a slight change of emphasis. To produce any special emphasis in English we must vary the construction : ' It was Cæsar that Brutus killed '; 'It was Brutus that killed Cæsar,' or else reproduce in writing, by means of the clumsy device of underlining or of Italics, that emphasis which is given naturally by the voice in speaking, and which the Romans were able to indicate equally well in writing by the mere order of the words [1].

§ **43.** As then, in Latin, the general sense is determined by the construction, independently of the order, a Latin writer is free to use the element of order for three main purposes :

(1) To arrange his ideas in their natural logical order, so as to add lucidity and intelligibility to his statement of them ;

---

[1] The Dean of Norwich used to quote the following sentence as an example of how the meaning of an English sentence may be changed according as we lay the emphasis on one word or another : 'The Novum Organon of Bacon was not intended to supersede the Organon of Aristotle.' It is apparent that various different meanings can be extracted from the above sentence, according as we lay the emphasis on the words *Novum Organon, Bacon, intended, supersede, Organon,* or *Aristotle* respectively.   If we say ' The .*Novum Organon* of Bacon,' etc., we imply that it was some other work of Bacon's that was intended, etc. ; if we say ' The Novum Organon of *Bacon*,' etc. we imply that it was the Novum Organon of some other author than Bacon that was intended, etc. ; if we lay the stress on *intended*, we mean that it was not Bacon's *intention* to supersede, etc. ; if on *supersede*, that he meant to supplement it, not to supersede it; and so on.   Latin would never leave the main sense of a passage in such ambiguity.

(2) To mark any particular emphasis which he wishes to add, as an indication of his own mind and opinion upon the subject matter of his statement ; and

(3) To please the ear by giving a sense of variety, of balance, and of harmony to the whole.

For sound has to be considered, as well as sense, in the structure of a Latin sentence. We must endeavour not only to express our meaning correctly, clearly, and forcibly, but also in such words and sentences as shall fall smoothly and melodiously on the ear. Nor is this melodiousness or rhythm in the sound a mere matter of ornament and pleasure : it has an important bearing on the sense. The rhythm should be so arranged that the emphasis in sound should fall on the same words and syllables which are important in the sense, so that the correct reading of the passage should of itself give a key to the general meaning of the whole. This subject will be treated more fully below, in the sections on Rhythm.

§ **44**. The main Rules for the order of words in simple sentences have been laid down in Vol. I. App. §§ 29-31. Let the student always bear in mind the following points :

(1) As a rule, the Subject stands first in a sentence, and the Principal Verb last. A Latin writer tells us at once what he is going to talk about ; but he reserves the most important idea, the idea which clinches the sense for the whole, for the end.

(2) After the Subject, as a rule, come Adverbial

phrases of all kinds, oblique cases with or without Prepositions, Ablatives Absolute, etc.

(3) Between these and the Verb come the Indirect Object and the Direct Object, the former usually preceding.

(4) All words, phrases, or clauses, explanatory of, or specially connected with, the Subject, Object, or other Noun, will be placed in close connection with such Noun.

(5) Adverbs go with the word which they qualify, usually the Verb ; and closely before the Verb will go any Prolate Infinitive which depends on it.

(6) As a rule, Adjectives (as also the Genitives of Quality and Definition) stand after the Noun ; but if the Adjective or Genitive contain the more important or emphatic idea, it will stand first. And. so with Apposition. If I say *Fabius consul fecit,* I mean that Fabius did it in his consulship, and *Fabius* is the leading idea ; if I say *Consul Fabius fecit,* I mean that the thing was done by the consul, the fact that Fabius was that consul being of secondary importance. Similarly, in the Ablative Absolute, the Participle or Adjective usually stands first, because it contains the operative part of the idea : *amissis armis periit,* ' Having lost his arms he fled ' ; *invalido corpore resistere diutius non potuit,* ' His weakness made it impossible for him to resist any longer.'

(7) Negatives, Interrogatives, Demonstrative words, and Adverbs of Time, stand at the very

beginning of a Sentence, before the Subject. In all Relative clauses the Relative must stand first.

(8) The natural order is often changed merely with a view to variety. A good instance of variety for variety's sake is supplied by the figure called *Chiasmus*: if two (or more) pairs of ideas are compared or contrasted, it is usual to change the order in which the ideas are given, so that one pair may be placed close to one another, the other pair apart. Thus in translating

· 'This would merely expose our troops to be butchered without inflicting a decisive defeat upon the enemy,'

we should arrange the ideas thus :

Hoc est trucidare nostros, non hostes debellare;

Or again,

' A course of conduct which brought reputation to himself but disaster to his friends,'

In quo famam sibi, suis exitium praeparavit.

See further instances in the passage quoted below under § 70 (5).

(9) If there are two Pronouns in one sentence, whether Personal or Possessive, they will usually be found in immediate juxtaposition : *ille mihi eadem abstulit; suum cuique ; hic mihi tuum reditum nuntiavit.*

(10) Subordinate Clauses in a Period usually follow one another in the natural order of the ideas which they contain. Thus clauses denoting the Time, the Cause, the Condition, usually come in before the Principal Clause, because they necessarily

precede in thought. In Comparative Clauses, for the same reason, the *ut* Clause comes first, the *sic* Clause afterwards. Final Clauses may come either before or after the Principal Clause : as the motive is prior to the act, they would naturally come first ; but if the end of the action be regarded, they would not less naturally come last.

(11) On the other hand, Consecutive Clauses and Indirect Questions come naturally after, not before, the Verbs on which they depend.

(12) When a Noun is Subject, or Object, both to, a Subordinate and Principal Clause, it should be placed, if possible, in the Principal Clause : *Rex Prusias, cum venenum bibisset, mortuus est.*

§ 45. But though the above is the usual and natural order, it is constantly departed from for special reasons of emphasis, variety, or contrast. The Verb frequently stands at the beginning ; and Substantive, Adjective, or Adverb may stand at the end, if emphasis or sound require it. Where there is a usual order, emphasis will be marked by any departure from that order. The two most important places in a sentence are the beginning and the end ; hence any word, however insignificant, can be brought into prominence by being placed in either of those places. The reason why Subject and Verb are usually placed at the beginning and the end respec-tively, is that they usually contain the most important ideas ; but if it happens that the construction or the connection of a sentence is such that the really new

and important idea is not contained in the Subject or
the Verb, then the emphatic idea must be put in the
emphatic place, whatever may be the part of speech
by which it is conveyed.

§ **46**. Again, even where there is no question of
emphasis, mere variety demands that sentences shall
not all be constructed on the same model. One of
the chief merits of an inflected language is its plia-
bility : the writer can marshal each sentence as he
pleases, with reference to the preceding and the
succeeding sentences, so as to give freshness and
point and harmony to the whole. In continuous
writing, the monotony would be intolerable if the
same order were followed in every sentence ; and
every Latin sentence must be constructed with a view
not to itself only, but in relation to the whole passage
of which it forms a part. Hence, while every really
important period, where there is a distinct pause in
the sense, should almost invariably be closed by the
Verb, the Verb may take almost any place in the
sentences which form the less important stages in the
passage, and whose sense is less conclusive. Such
sentences are made purposely to end with weaker
words ; the very fact of a weak ending to a sentence
shews that a true pause in the sense has not been
reached, and leads the mind on to expect the more
decisive character of the true pause when it comes.
In this way the order of the words in each separate
sentence serves as an index to the general progress
of the sense.

§ **47**. It thus appears that the order which is most suitable for a sentence taken by itself, may not be suitable, or even possible, when the same sentence is combined with others so as to form a *Period*. This leads us to consider one of the most marked characteristics of Latin style, viz. its partiality for the periodic structure.

The Period.

§ **48**. The Latin Period is but an expansion upon a large scale of the compactness and logical perfection of structure which are characteristic of the language even in its simplest sentences. If a Roman had several ideas to express, he preferred to state them in their logical connection with one another. Instead of expressing each idea in a sentence by itself, with a principal Verb of its own, he preferred to place several ideas in a single sentence, under one principal Verb; or to group together a number of sentences into those continuous, and sometimes complicated, passages which are known as *Periods*. Latin is singularly rich in devices for furthering in either of these ways the condensation of thought.

§ **49**. Thus a single Latin sentence may contain a meaning which has to be expressed by two or more sentences in English. The Past or Present Participle, the Ablative Absolute, the emphatic position of a single word, may express a meaning which would require in English a whole sentence with a Finite Verb of its own. Compare carefully the

following Latin and English sentences, and note
how Latin economises its Finite Verbs, and avoids
the stringing together of several Co-ordinate Verbs
by means of the copula 'and.'

Fugatus in castra se recepit hostis,
'The enemy was routed, and took refuge in his camp';

Oriente sole desertus a suis imperator interfectus est,
'As the day dawned, the general was deserted by his
men and slain';

Fugatos Publius hostes usque ad urbem persecutus est,
'Publius routed the enemy and pursued them up to
the city gates';

Comitiis habitis consul ad urbem rediit,
'As soon as the elections were over, the consul returned
to the city';

Privato mihi populus hunc honorem detulit,
'The people conferred upon me this honour before I
had held any public office';

Invalidus pede consul pugnam declinabat,
'The consul was averse to engage as he was wounded
in the foot.'

§ 50. Passing on from the consideration of single
sentences, we find that Latin differs essentially from
English in two respects;

(1) In its fondness for the Period;

(2) In its desire to exhibit by express words the
logical connection between successive sentences, even
though they may have grammatically no connection
with each other.

These two features are closely connected. The

Roman desired to find unity, continuity, logical connection, in what he heard or read; he desired to
have one train of ideas carried on as long as possible
in a single line of thought, interrupted as little as
possible by sudden jerks and contrasts. Hence Latin
prefers to put a number of ideas into a single sentence, keeping throughout a single Subject; to reserve the principal Verb or Verbs for the expression
of the main or central idea of the passage; and to
group round that idea, expressing these in the form
of subordinate clauses, the various accessory and less
important ideas, each having its logical place in reference to the whole, and arranged in the order most
favourable to apprehension and continuous thought.
A passage thus constructed is called a Period.

§ **51.** A glance at any two pages of English and
Latin side by side will shew how many more Principal
Verbs, how many more full stops, there are in the
former than in the latter. ´The two passages quoted
below give a good example of the contrast between
the periodic style of Latin, and that more detached
abrupt style which is preferred by English writers.
Modern French authors often carry this detached
mode of writing to excess. Instead of using continuous sonorous periods, they will tell a story in a
series of short unconnected sentences, which suggest
the idea of a succession of explosions. To us the
Latin Period may sometimes appear cumbrous, involved, and tedious; not so to the Roman. He
preferred to have the connection between his ideas

carefully elaborated, and to see them marshalled like an army in review before him, because this was to him the simplest, most intelligible, mode of presenting them ; we prefer to have ideas thrown rapidly before us, one after the other, and to trace the connection for ourselves. But if we would write Latin, we must adopt the Latin point of view ; and it is precisely because we cannot write Latin well without logically thinking out the connection of a whole passage—analysing rigorously each thought, and assigning to it its due weight and place in relation to the whole—that the practice of Latin Prose Composition forms so admirable a mental discipline.

§ **52.** The following Period is from Tacitus, Ann. I. 2 :

How Augustus gradually assumed imperial power.

Postquam Bruto et Cassio caesis nulla iam publica arma, Pompeius apud Siciliam oppressus, exutoque Lepido, interfecto Antonio, ne Iulianis quidem partibus nisi Caesar dux reliquus, posito triumviri nomine consulem se ferens et ad tuendam plebem tribunicio iure contentum, ubi militem donis, populum annona, cunctos dulcedine otii pellexit, insurgere paulatim, munia senatus magistratuum legum in se trahere, nullo adversante, cum ferocissimi per acies aut proscriptione cecidissent, ceteri nobilium, quanto quis servitio promptior, opibus et honoribus extollerentur, ac novis ex rebus aucti tuta et praesentia quam vetera et periculosa mallent.

Three main points strike us in the above passage.

(1) There are at least seventeen distinct proposi-

tions contained in it, each of which, if stated separately, would need a Verb of its own : and yet there are but two Principal Verbs in the whole passage, viz. the Historical Infinitives *insurgere* and *trahere*. Five of the propositions are expressed by Ablatives Absolute ; one by a Participle Present, agreeing with the Subject; the remainder are Subordinate Clauses, three introduced by *postquam*, three by *cum*, one by *ubi*, and one by the Relative word *quanto*.

(2) Complicated as the construction is, every single idea is placed in its natural order : if an event, in the chronological order of its occurrence ; if an idea, at the point where the idea would be naturally raised in the reader's mind. First comes the battle of Philippi, and the Republic thereby left without an army—Pompey's defeat, B.C. 36—the deposition of Lepidus soon afterwards—Augustus left sole head of the party. He gives up the title of triumvir—assumes the consulship combined with the tribunitian power—plays on army and populace alike—and gathers gradually all power into his own hands. This is the central fact of the picture: the idea naturally occurs, How was he permitted to do all this ? The closing clauses describe the torpor or the connivance of all that was best in Rome, and formulate in stinging sentences Tacitus' indictment against the Empire. The power and compactness of the historical summary, the logical completeness by which the establishment of monarchy is shewn to follow as a necessity from the preceding chain of events, and the art by

which the reader is led on to adopt as his own Tacitus' view of the situation, are unapproachable.

(3) Observe the careful balance of the sentences. The narrative clauses lead gradually up, by well-marked stages, to the central idea, expressed by the Principal Verb; but instead of abruptly closing at that point, the passage is prolonged through what musicians would call a 'Coda,' which at once balances the opening clauses, and though subordinate in form, reserves the writer's most earnest reflections to the end.

§ **53.** The structure of this passage would be intolerable in English. In translating it, we must break it up into its constituent parts, somewhat as follows :

'With the death of Brutus and Cassius, the Republic had lost her last army. The defeat of Pompey in Sicily, the deprivation of Lepidus, and the death of Antony, left Cæsar undisputed leader of the Julian party. Thereupon he laid aside the title of Triumvir, proclaimed himself Consul, and professed that he would be satisfied with the tribunitian power, for the protection of the people. But when he had won over the soldiery by donatives, the populace by cheap corn, and the whole world by the sweets of peace, his pretensions gradually rose : one by one he gathered into his own hands the functions of the Senate, the magistrates, and the legislature. Opposition there was none : for the most independent spirits had fallen in battle or in the proscriptions, and the rest of the nobles, advanced to wealth and office in proportion to their servility, found profit in the change, preferring the safety of the present to the dangers of the past.'

In performing the reverse process of translating from English into Latin it will often, conversely, be advisable to combine several sentences into a single period, in which the various parts shall stand in their due logical relation to each other.

§ 54. Another example, of a strictly narrative character, may be taken from Livy V. 47:

Dum haec Veiis agebantur, interim arx Romae Capitoliumque in ingenti periculo fuit. Namque Galli, seu vestigio notato humano, qua nuntius a Veiis pervenerat, seu sua sponte animadverso ad Carmentis saxorum adscensu aequo, nocte sublustri, quum primo inermem, qui tentaret viam, praemisissent, tradentes inde arma, ubi quid iniqui esset, alterni innixi sublevantesque in vicem et trahentes alii alios, prout postularet locus, tanto silentio in summum evasere, ut non custodes solum fallerent, sed ne canes quidem, sollicitum animal ad nocturnos strepitus, excitarent. Anseres non fefellere, quibus sacris Iunonis in summa inopia cibi tamen abstinebatur. Quae res saluti fuit; namque clangore eorum alarumque crepitu excitus M. Manlius, qui triennio ante consul fuerat, vir bello egregius, armis arreptis, simul ad arma ceteros ciens vadit et, dum ceteri trepidant, Gallum, qui iam in summo constiterat, umbone ictum deturbat.

Here note:

(1) The narrative begins with a short decisive sentence to preface the whole; then falls into two Periods.

(2) In both Periods, the exact order of the incidents described is followed.

(3) In the first Period, we have some eleven distinct circumstances, or steps in the narrative, expressed in various ways, before we come to the main idea in *evasere*; the subject *Galli* having been placed at the very beginning.

(4) The Period ends, not with the Verb of the Principal Sentence, but with the Subordinate Consecutive Clause, *ut . . . . excitarent.* A Consecutive Clause frequently occupies this position (see above, § 44. (11)), not only because it refers to a time subsequent to that of the Principal Verb, but also because it may contain the most important idea of the passage.

(5) The second Period begins with *Anseres*, partly for emphasis, partly to carry on the sense : the same Subject however (*Galli*) is continued in *fefellere*, and until we reach *M. Manlius*, the hero of the whole story.

(6) The character and first acts of Manlius are rapidly described ; but not till we come to the very last word (*deturbat*) do we learn of the decisive act of Manlius, the words immediately preceding (*umbone ictum*) telling us the means by which he performed it.

§ **55.** Another good example of the periodic structure is furnished by Livy V. 41,42, where he describes the scene in Rome after the massacre of the Senators in the forum by the Gauls.   He begins with three rapid Historical Infinitives :

'Post Principum caedem nulli deinde mortalium parci, diripi tecta, exhaustis iniici ignes.'

He then launches into two long periods, the first, with *ignis* for its Subject, descriptive of the conflagration ; the second, with *Romani* for its Subject, describes the horror of the scene as beheld from the Capitol :

Ceterum, seu non omnibus delendi urbem libido erat, seu ita placuerat principibus Gallorum, et ostentari quaedam incendia terroris causa, si compelli ad deditionem caritate sedum suarum obsessi possent, et non omnia concremari tecta, ut, quodcunque superesset urbis, id pignus ad flectendos hostium animos haberent, nequaquam perinde atque in capta urbe prima die aut passim aut late vagatus est ignis.   Romani ex arce plenam hostium urbem cernentes vagosque per vias omnes cursus, quum alia atque alia parte nova aliqua clades oreretur, non mentibus solum concipere, sed ne auribus quidem atque oculis satis constare poterant.   Quocunque clamor hostium, mulierum puerorumque ploratus, sonitus flammae et fragor ruentium tectorum avertisset, paventes ad omnia animos oraque et oculos flectebant, velut ad spectaculum a fortuna positi occidentis patriae nec ullius rerum suarum relicti praeterquam corporum vindices, tanto ante alios miserandi magis, qui umquam obsessi sunt, quod interclusi a patria obsidebantur, omnia sua cernentes in hostium potestate.

§ **56.** With passages such as these let us contrast a narrative from Macaulay, in his sharp staccato style :

William approaches the shore of England.

'When Sunday, the Fourth of November, dawned, the cliffs of the Isle of Wight were full in view of the Dutch armament. That day was the anniversary both of William's birth and of his marriage. Sail was slackened during part of the morning : and divine service was performed on board of the ships. In the afternoon and through the night the fleet held on its course. Torbay was the place where the Prince intended to land. But the morning of Monday, the fifth of November, was hazy. The pilot of the Brill could not discern the sea marks, and carried the fleet too far to the west. The danger was great. To return in the face of the wind was impossible. Plymouth was the next port. But at Plymouth a garrison had been posted under the command of Lord Bath. The landing might be opposed ; and a check might produce serious consequences. There could be little doubt, moreover, that by this time the royal fleet had got out of the Thames and was hastening full sail down the Channel. Russell saw the whole extent of the peril, and exclaimed to Burnet, " You may go to prayers, Doctor. All is over." At that moment the wind changed : a soft wind sprang up from the south : the mist dispersed ; the sun shone forth ; and, under the mild light of an autumnal noon, the fleet turned back, passed through the lofty cape of Berry Head, and rode safe in the Harbour of Torbay.'

Macaulay.

In the whole of the above passage there are only two Clauses that can be called Subordinate : there are no less than twenty-seven Principal Verbs, in independent or co-ordinate Clauses.

§ 57. If we take another passage, of a more reflective character, we shall find the same sort of structure.

William and the Coalition.

'No coalition of which history has preserved the memory has had an abler chief than William. But even William often contended in vain against those vices which are inherent in the nature of all coalitions. No undertaking which requires the hearty and long-continued co-operation of many independent states is likely to prosper. Jealousies inevitably spring up. Disputes engender disputes. Every confederate is tempted to throw on others some part of the burden which he ought himself to bear. Scarcely one honestly furnishes the promised contingent. Scarcely one exactly observes the appointed day. But perhaps no coalition that ever existed was in such constant danger of dissolution as the coalition which William had with infinite difficulty formed. The long list of potentates, who met in person or by their representatives at the Hague, looked well in the Gazettes. The crowd of princely equipages, attended by many coloured guards and lacqueys, looked very well among the lime trees of the Voorhout. But the very circumstances which made the Congress more splendid than other congresses made the league weaker than other leagues. The more numerous the allies, the more numerous were the dangers which threatened the alliance. It was impossible that twenty governments, divided by quarrels about precedence, quarrels about territory, quarrels about trade, quarrels about religion, could act long together in perfect harmony. That they acted together during several years in perfect harmony is to be ascribed to the wisdom, patience, and firmness of William.' *'Macaulay.*

In the above passage, there are sixteen Principal Clauses to ten Subordinate Clauses; and almost all of these are of the simplest Adjectival kind.

§ **58.** It must not be supposed, however, that all Latin writing is periodic. The Period, however varied it may be, would give a sense of long-windedness and pedantry if continually repeated; nor is it suitable for every kind of subject. The Period implies thought; a looking forward from the beginning of a passage to the end; time both for writer and for reader to consider and take in the connection and proportion of the whole. It is dignified, grave, and impressive; but for that very reason it is not suitable for the expression of sudden and sharp emotion. High feeling, quick action, familiar common-place incidents, must be expressed more rapidly and simply, and by a machinery less elaborate. Some of Cicero's most effective passages, delivered at excited or passionate moments, are composed of short isolated sentences. Such is the famous outburst against Antony (Phil. II. 22, § 55):

Ut igitur in seminibus est causa arborum et stirpium, sic huius luctuosissimi belli semen tu fuisti. Doletis tres exercitus populi Romani interfectos : interfecit Antonius. Desideratis clarissimos cives : eos quoque nobis eripuit Antonius. Auctoritas huius ordinis afflicta est : afflixit Antonius. Omnia denique, quae postea vidimus—quid autem mali non vidimus?—si recte ratiocinabimur, uni accepta referemus Antonio. Ut Helena Troianis, sic iste huic rei publicae belli causa, causa pestis atque

exitii fuit.   Reliquae partes tribunatus principii similes.
Omnia perfecit, quae senatus salva re publica ne fieri
possent perfecerat.   Cuius tamen scelus in scelere cog-
noscite.

And again his triumphant denunciation of Catiline
(Cat. II. 1, § 1) :

Tandem aliquando, Quirites, L. Catilinam, furentem
audacia, scelus anhelantem, pestem patriae nefarie mo-
lientem, vobis atque huic urbi ferro flammaque minitan-
tem ex urbe vel eiecimus vel emisimus vel ipsum egre-
dientem verbis prosecuti sumus.   Abiit, excessit, evasit,
erupit.   Nulla iam pernicies a monstro illo atque prodigio
moenibus ipsis intra moenia comparabitur.   Atque hunc
quidem unum huius belli domestici ducem sine contro-
versia vicimus : non enim iam inter latera nostra sica illa
versabitur ; non in campo, non in foro, non in curia, non
denique intra domesticos parietes pertimescemus ; loco
ille motus est, cum est ex urbe depulsus.   Palam iam cum
hoste nullo impediente bellum iustum geremus.   Sine
dubio perdidimus hominem magnificeque vicimus, cum
illum ex occultis insidiis in apertum latrocinium conie-
cimus.   .

In the former of the above passages there are thirteen Principal Verbs : in the latter there are fourteen.
Yet even with sentences short and independent as
these, the student will note how carefully the connection is maintained throughout, how often it is actually
expressed.   (See below, §§ 61–64.)

§ **59.**   So Livy, when he desires to paint some vivid
scene, and give the idea of rapid action, can write
almost in the style of a Macaulay.   Take IV. 37:

Ergo fortuna, ut saepe alias, virtutem est secuta. Primo proelio, quod ab Sempronio incaute inconsulteque commissum est, non subsidiis firmata acie, non equite apte locato concursum est. Clamor indicium primum fuit, quo res inclinatura esset; excitatior crebriorque ab hoste sublatus; ab Romanis dissonus, impar, segnius saepe iteratus incerto tenore prodidit pavorem animo- rum. Eo ferocior illatus hostis urgere scutis, micare gladiis. Altera ex parte nutant circumspectantibus galeae, et incerti trepidant applicantque se turbae; signa nunc resistentia deseruntur ab antesignanis, nunc inter suos manipulos recipiuntur. Nondum fuga certa, non- dum victoria erat; tegi magis Romanus quam pugnare; Volscus inferre signa, urgere aciem, plus caedis hostium videre quam fugae.

In this passage there are at least sixteen Principal Verbs. It will be noticed what force is added by the use of the vivid Historical Infinitive; and by that of the figure *Asyndeton.*

§ **60.** But whilst the special character of some passages, and the principle of variety in all, must put some limit to the use of the Period, nevertheless the proposition holds good as a whole, that English tends to prefer short and decisive sentences, each complete in meaning; to change frequently the Subject of its sentences; and to look for its effects to variety and sudden contrasts. Latin, on the contrary, tends always to revert to the periodic style; to change the Subject as seldom as possible; to use Subordinate

Clauses to express all ideas which are in sense subordinate to other ideas; and to make unity, order, and continuity its first essentials.

On the Connection between Successive Sentences.

§ **61.** But it is not in the Period only that Latin shews its preference for connected rather than detached writing. The same principle is shewn in the care which Latin writers take to link together the successive sentences or periods of which a passage is composed, and to make each successive sentence exhibit on its face the nature of its connection with that which has preceded.

Every logical sequence must be indicated, not left to be supplied by the imagination. If there is a relation of **cause**, it will be expressed by some causal word, such as *nam, namque, quia, quippe, enim, scilicet, enimvero, etenim,* etc. ; if of **effect**, by *ergo, itaque, ita, quapropter, propterea,* etc. ; if of **contrast**, by *sed, at, autem, verum, vero,* etc. If there is a relation of **time**, it will be indicated by some temporal word, as *tum, iam, mox, postea, deinde,* etc. If there be no logical relation at all, then a mere Demonstrative word— *hic, is, ille,* etc.—may suffice to carry on the train of ideas· from the last sentence. Most commonly of all, the Relative Pronoun is used in some of its various forms and meanings—*qui, quare, quapropter, quod, quod si, quae cum ita sint,* etc.—with no other purpose than to prevent a break in the sense, and to satisfy that desire for continuity which possessed the Roman mind. Latin is extraordinarily rich in such particles and phrases of connection ; even where no such word is used, a connection may be indicated by the repetition of some word from the previous sentence, usually in a different construction, or by use of some word in sharp contrast to one which has preceded.

§ **62.** Let the student carefully examine any continuous passage in Cicero or Livy, and mark how artistically the transition from sentence to sentence is effected. Let him take Cic. de Or. III, caps. 1 and 2, and note how every new sentence begins with some word or words which connect it with the last :—

Death of L. Crassus.

Instituenti mihi, Quinte frater, eum sermonem referre et mandare huic tertio libro, quem post Antonii disputationem Crassus habuisset, acerba sane recordatio veterem animi curam molestiamque renovavit. Nam illud immortalitate dignum ingenium, illa humanitas, illa virtus L. Crassi morte exstincta subita est vix diebus decem post eum diem, qui hoc et superiore libro continetur. Ut enim Romam rediit extremo scenicorum ludorum die, vehementer commotus ea oratione, quae ferebatur habita esse in concione a Philippo, quem dixisse constabat videndum sibi aliud esse consilium : illo senatu se rempublicam gerere non posse : mane Idibus Septembribus et ille et senatus frequens vocatu Drusi in curiam venit. Ibi cum Drusus multa de Philippo questus esset, retulit ad senatum de illo ipso, quod consul in eum ordinem tam graviter in concione esset invectus. Hic, ut saepe inter homines sapientissimos constare vidi, quamquam hoc Crasso, cum aliquid accuratius dixisset, semper fere contigisset, ut numquam dixisse melius putaretur, tamen omnium consensu sic esse tum iudicatum, ceteros a Crasso semper omnes, illo autem die etiam ipsum a se superatum. Deploravit enim casum atque orbitatem senatus, cuius ordinis a consule, qui quasi parens bonus aut tutor fidelis esse deberet, tamquam ab aliquo nefario praedone diriperetur patrimonium dignitatis ; neque vero esse mirandum, si, cum suis consiliis rempublicam profligasset, consilium senatus a republica repudiaret. Hic cum homini et vehementi et diserto et in primis forti ad resistendum, Philippo, quasi quasdam verborum faces admovisset, non tulit ille et graviter exarsit pignoribusque ablatis Crassum instituit coercere. Quo quidem ipso in loco multa a Crasso divinitus dicta efferebantur, cum sibi illum consulem esse negaret, cui senator ipse non esset. . . . Permulta tum vehementissima contentione animi, ingenii, virium ab eo dicta esse constabat, sententiamque eam, quam senatus frequens secutus est ornatissimis et gravissimis verbis, *Ut populo Romano satisfieret, numquam senatus neque consilium reipublicae neque fidem defuisse*, ab eo dictam, et eumdem, id quod in auctoritatibus praescriptis exstat, scribendo adfuisse. Illa tamquam cycnea fuit divini hominis vox et oratio, quam quasi exspectantes post eius interitum veniebamus in curiam, ut vestigium illud ipsum, in quo ille postremum institisset, contueremur. Namque tum latus ei dicenti condoluisse sudoremque multum consecutum esse audiebamus ; ex quo cum cohorruisset, cum febri domum rediit dieque septimo lateris dolore consumptus est. O fallacem hominum spem fragilemque fortunam et inanes nostras contentiones ! quae in medio spatio saepe franguntur et corruunt aut ante in ipso cursu obruuntur, quam portum conspicere potuerunt. Nam, quamdiu Crassi fuit ambitionis labore vita districta, tamdiu privatis magis officiis et ingenii laude floruit, quam fructu amplitudinis aut reipublicae dignitate. Qui autem ei annus primus ab honorum perfunctione aditum omnium concessu ad summam auctoritatem dabat, is eius omnem spem atque omnia vitae consilia morte pervertit. Fuit hoc luctuosum suis, acerbum patriae, grave bonis omnibus ; sed ii tamen reipublicae casus secuti sunt, ut mihi non erepta L. Crasso a diis immortalibus vita, sed donata mors videatur. Non vidit flagrantem bello Italiam, non ardentem invidia senatum, non sceleris nefarii principes civitatis reos, non luctum filiae, non exsilium generi, non acerbissimam C. Marii fugam, non illam post reditum eius caedem omnium crudelissimam, non denique in omni genere deformatam eam civitatem, in qua ipse florentissima multum omnibus gloria praestitisset.

§ **63.** In the two chapters given above, there are seventeen sentences or periods which end with a full stop. Exclusive of the first sentence, they begin respectively as follows: (1) *Nam*; (2) *Ut enim* ; (3) *Ibi cum* ; (4) *Hic ... quamquam* ; (5) *Deploravit enim*; (6) *Hic cum* ; (7) *Quo quidem ipso in loco* ; (8) *Permulta tum* ; (9) *Illa* ; (10) *Namque tum* ; (11) *O fallacem hominum spem ...* ! (12) *Quae* ; (13) *Nam quamdiu* ; (14) *Qui autem* ; (15) *Fuit hoc* ; (16) *Non vidit flagrantem bello Italiam*, etc.

In only two cases (11 and 16) is there no distinct word of connection ; and in both of these a sharp contrast is intentionally made.

§ **64.** Analysing chapters 3 and 4 in the same way, we find the following beginnings : *Et quoniam* ; *Quis enim* ; *Tenemus enim* ; *Iam M. Antoni* ; *Neque vero* ; *Neque enim* ; *Non vidit* (a rhetorical repetition); *Ex quibus* ; *Sulpicius autem* ; *Ego vero* ; *Nam tibi.*

In every single instance the sentences begin with an indication of their connection with what precedes. Let the student study in the same way the composition of the other Latin passages quoted in this Introduction.

On the Rhythm of Latin Prose.

§ **65.** It remains to deal with the important but difficult subject of rhythm. It is essential that we should express our meaning fully, correctly, and forcibly; but we should endeavour to do so in sentences which shall fall pleasantly and gratefully on the ear. There should be a proportion, and if possible a sonorous ring, about our sentences. Each word should have an importance of sound (or the reverse) adequate to the idea which it represents, and should come in where it will please the ear most from the appropriateness or novelty of its position ; each sentence should have a form and cadence fitted to the place which it occupies in the sense. The less important sentences should not attract attention; the principal clauses should shew their importance in sound as well as sense. For though it should be the first maxim in writing 'to take care of the sense, and the sounds will take care of themselves'; yet the second tells us that in Latin the sound may help the sense, and prepare the mind for its reception. In Latin, there is a rhythm of prose as well as of poetry; it is part of the spirit and genius of the language; and though it is difficult to catch, and cannot be caught at all by those who have no ear, it is essential to acquire some sense for it if we would write Latin well. Much may be done to develop this sense. The ear may be cultivated by the constant reading, and reciting aloud, of good selected passages, and thus gradually learn to recognise how the peculiar qualities of Latin — its strength, its lucidity, its logical grasp and stateliness — are enhanced by a certain kind of harmonious and musical expression. If we are to undertake the serious labour of learning to write Latin at all, we should aim at writing in good literary style; and if we would write as the best Roman authors wrote, *we must learn to hear, as well as to think, in Latin.*

§ **66.** It is not possible to reduce the laws of rhythmical prose to rule. Some writers on 'Stylistik' have indeed attempted to analyse minutely the structure and the cadences of various kinds of sentences, with a view to demonstrating how certain fine effects may be produced : but with small success. It is not so that our own good writers learn to write English. The Grammar and the Syntax once mastered, the true way for a student to learn to write good Latin is to read, read, read, from the best Latin writers, and to drink in the spirit of the language. Let him study good passages closely, read them aloud, and learn them off by heart ; but not seek to imitate them consciously, to borrow particular phrases, or to reproduce particular endings. Let the form and the sound of good Latin gradually sink into him, and he will get a better result than by combining all the *purpurei panni* in creation.

§ **67.** A few general principles, however, may be stated, some of which have been to some extent anticipated in the sections on *Order*.

(1) As the end of a period or a passage is the most important place in sense, it should be important in sound also. A passage should not end in an insignificant way. It should end with some decisive full-bodied word or words, on which the voice may rest, as it were, in safe anchorage, after the ups and downs of the passage. Hence no short, trivial word can stand last ; a sonorous combination of two or three important words, connected in meaning, will give weight and dignity to the close. Thus the verb *esse* scarcely ever ends a sentence, unless used emphatically, or as part of the Perfect Passive. Towards the end of a passage, long words and long syllables tend to prevail over short ones, with enough short ones between them to prevent a sense of heaviness. Cicero's favourite ending is a double trochee (*ārbĭtrā-tŭr*), or a trochee and molossus (*vĕrbă nōlĭmŭs*), while his fondness for the termination with a tribrach and

spondee in the phrase *essè vĭdĕātŭr* exposed him to the ridicule of his critics.

(2) The beginning of a passage is, so to speak, its business part : it has simply to introduce the subject, and set out rapidly the main features of the situation. For this, short decisive words, simply and tellingly arranged, are the most suitable : seldom does a sentence begin with a long-rolling word, unless in special relation to one that has gone before.

(3) All tags of verses, whether beginnings or endings of lines, are to be avoided, as giving a sense of jingle : it is strange what pains are taken to avoid the ending with a dactyl and spondee, which would otherwise appear a natural and euphonious ending, for no other reason than that they would suggest the ending of a dactylic hexameter.

(4) As parts of verses must be avoided, so also must care be taken to avoid anything like rhyme or jingle, such as would be caused by a recurrence of the same termination.   Inflection gives great importance and emphasis to the terminations : hence a repetition of the same ending is more offensive than in English.

(5) In this, as in everything else, variety must be studied : in a Latin inscription, half the point and elegance may depend upon a happy contrast of the final syllables.   Variety again forbids our placing together a string of words of the same length, or similarly accentuated, and especially of mono-

syllables: the marvellous force and beauty which may be given in English to lines, and even stanzas, composed wholly of monosyllables[1], were utterly unknown to Latin.

§ **68.** Variety and proportion are indeed the two main elements to consider with a view to a good Prose Rhythm, just as order and emphasis are the main factors in determining or aiding the sense. Just as in the pronunciation of a polysyllabic word the ear likes to hear one syllable accentuated, and the other syllables but lightly indicated; so the essence of a good Prose Rhythm consists in a happy succession of emphatic and non-emphatic words. The important places in the sense should be filled by important full-sounding words; the less important ideas, the less important parts of speech, should fill the interspaces. Thus the whole will move on with equal force and ease, emphatic but not ponderous, bright but not trivial, the light and the shade mutually relieving and setting off each other.

§ **69.** Let us see what Cicero himself has to say on the importance of writing *numerose*; that is, with a good rhythm, with a view to melodious and rhythmical cadence. The passage itself (De Or. III. 45 and 46) affords an admirable example of that grace and beauty of style on which it is a commentary :—

---

[1] As in Tennyson: see especially *In Memoriam.*

Everything that has a use has beauty.

Quonam igitur modo tantum munus insistemus, ut arbitremur nos hanc vim numerose dicendi consequi posse ? Non est res tam difficilis, quam necessaria ; nihil est enim tam tenerum, neque tam flexibile, neque quod tam facile sequatur, quocumque ducas, quam oratio : ex hac versus, ex hac eadem dispares numeri conficiuntur ; ex hac haec etiam soluta variis modis multorumque generum oratio. Non enim sunt alia sermonis, alia contentionis verba ; neque ex alio genere ad usum cotidianum, alio ad scenam pompamque sumuntur ; sed ea nos cum iacentia sustulimus e medio, sicut mollissimam ceram ad nostrum arbitrium formamus et fingimus. Itaque tum graves sumus, tum subtiles, tum medium quiddam tenemus ; sic institutam nostram sententiam sequitur orationis genus, idque ad omnem aurium voluptatem et animorum motum mutatur et vertitur. Sed ut in plerisque rebus incredibiliter hoc natura est ipsa fabricata ; sic in oratione, ut ea, quae maximam utilitatem in se continerent, plurimum eadem haberent vel dignitatis vel saepe etiam venustatis. Incolumitatis ac salutis omnium caussa videmus hunc statum esse huius totius mundi atque naturae, rotundum ut caelum, terraque ut media sit, eaque sua vi nutuque teneatur ; sol ut circumferatur, ut accedat ad brumale signum et inde sensim ascendat in diversam partem ; ut luna accessu et recessu suo solis lumen accipiat ; ut eadem spatia quinque stellae dispari motu cursuque conficiant. Haec tantam habent vim, paullum ut immutata cohaerere non possint, tantam pulcritudinem, ut nulla species ne cogitari quidem possit ornatior. Referte nunc animum ad hominum vel etiam ceterarum animantium formam et figuram : nullam partem corporis

sine aliqua necessitate affictam, totamque formam quasi
perfectam reperietis arte, non casu. Quid in arboribus,
in quibus non truncus, non rami, non folia sunt denique
nisi ad suam retinendam conservandamque naturam?
nusquam tamen est ulla pars nisi venusta. Linquamus
naturam artesque videamus : quid tam in navigio neces-
sarium quam latera, quam cavernae, quam prora, quam
puppis, quam antennae, quam vela, quam mali ? quae
tamen hanc habent in specie venustatem, ut non solum
salutis, sed etiam voluptatis caussa inventa esse videantur.
Columnae templa et porticus sustinent ; tamen habent
non plus utilitatis quam dignitatis. Capitolii fastigium
illud et ceterarum aedium non venustas, sed necessitas
ipsa fabricata est ; tamen, cum esset habita ratio, quem ad
modum ex utraque tecti parte aqua delaberetur, utilitatem templi fastigii dignitas consecuta est ; ut, etiamsi
in caelo Capitolium statueretur, ubi imber esse non posset,
nullam sine fastigio dignitatem habiturum fuisse videatur. Hoc in omnibus item partibus orationis evenit, ut
utilitatem · ac prope necessitatem suavitas quaedam et
lepos consequatur. Clausulas enim atque interpuncta verborum animae interclusio atque angustiae spiritus attu-
lerunt ; id inventum ita est suave, ut, si cui sit infinitus
spiritus datus, tamen eum perpetuare verba nolimus.
Id enim auribus nostris gratum est inventum, quod
hominum lateribus non tolerabile solum, sed etiam facile
esse posset.

Study carefully the rhythm of the above passage,
and note especially:

(1) All the endings are emphatic and sonorous.
If we examine the important pauses, we shall find
that seven sentences end with a Double Trochee (*ĕt*

fĭgūram—dīgnĭtātĭs—fābrĭcāta est—cōnsĕcūta est—cōn-sĕquātur—āttŭlērunt—ĕssĕ pōssĕt); five with a Trochee followed by a Molossus (*cōnsĕqŭī pōsse—pŏmpamque sumuntur—etiām vĕnūstātĭs—ārtĕ nōn cāsū—vĕlă quām mālī—vērbă nōlĭmus* , while we have *ĕssĕ vĭdĕātŭr, ĕssĕ vĭdĕantur*, and the same rhythm in *tuttūquĕ tĕnĕātur, pārs nĭsĭ vĕnūsta, ārtĕsquĕ vĭdĕāmus*[1].

(2) In three cases an idea is expanded without any addition to the sense, merely to prevent a clause ending too weakly with a single word standing alone : *formamus et fingimus—mutatur et vertitur—formam et figuram.* This desire to secure a good balance of sound is especially noticeable in Cicero, and frequently leads him into redundancy.

(3) Observe the ease and smoothness with which the whole passage runs. Every idea glides naturally into its place, suggested by the one which has preceded : so skilful is the *iunctura* that, to borrow the well-known Latin figure, the nail can scarce detect the several pieces out of which the beautiful mosaic is made up.

§ **70.** Another passage, exquisite in rhythm and beauty of expression, is to be found in the De Natura Deorum II. 39 :—

---

[1] Observe that this ending differs only from that of the dactylic Hexameter ($- \cup \cup | - -$) by the insertion of one short syllable ($- \cup \cup | \cup | - -$). It has exactly the same kind of stately ring : the extra syllable redeemed it from being a verse-ending. See above, § 67 (3).

Ac principio terra universa cernatur, locata in media sede mundi, solida et globosa et undique ipsa in sese nutibus suis conglobata, vestita floribus, herbis, arboribus, frugibus, quorum omnium incredibilis multitudo insatiabili varietate distinguitur. Adde huc fontium gelidas perennitates, liquores perlucidos amnium, riparum vestitus viridissimos, speluncarum concavas amplitudines, saxorum asperitates, impendentium montium altitudines immensitatesque camporum ; adde etiam reconditas auri argentique venas infinitamque vim marmoris. Quae vero et quam varia genera bestiarum vel cicurum vel ferarum! qui volucrum lapsus atque cantus! qui pecudum pastus! quae vita silvestrium! Quid iam de hominum genere dicam? qui quasi cultores terrae constituti non patiuntur eam nec immanitate belluarum efferari nec stirpium asperitate vastari : quorumque operibus agri, insulae litoraque conlucent distincta tectis et urbibus. Quae si, ut animis, sic oculis videre possemus, nemo cunctam intuens terram de divina ratione dubitaret.

At vero quanta maris est pulchritudo! Quae species universi! Quae multitudo et varietas insularum! Quae amoenitates orarum ac litorum! Quot genera quamque disparia partim submersarum, partim fluitantium et innantium belluarum, partim ad saxa nativis testis inhaerentium! Ipsum autem mare sic terram appetens litoribus alludit, ut una ex duabus naturis conflata videatur. Exim mari finitimus aer die et nocte distinguitur, isque tum fusus et extenuatus sublime fertur, tum autem concretus in nubes cogitur umoremque colligens terram auget imbribus, tum effluens huc et illuc ventos efficit. Idem annuas frigorum et calorum facit varietates, idemque et volatus alitum sustinet et spiritu doctus alit et sustentat animantes.

Various points call for notice in the above passage.

(1) *In media mundi parte reconditas auri argentique venas.* Note the position of *mundi* and of *auri argentique* : boxed up respectively between *media* and *parte*, and between *reconditas* and *venas*, they make the connection unmistakeable. See what is said on ' Loose Connection,' Vol. I. App. § 31 (o).

(2) *Vestita floribus, herbis, arboribus.* Mark the force of the *Asyndeton.* When several nouns are coupled together, the rule is to use the copula with each noun, or with none.

(3) *Quorum omnium.* This is the usual order. The relative almost invariably comes first.

(4) *Fontium gelidas perennitates. . . . speluncarum concavas altitudines*, etc. Note the especial force and beauty of these Abstract Plurals. The use of the Plural is to suggest the various particular instances of the thing mentioned ; hence it is more concrete than the Singular, and used for that reason. Yet we also have below *immanitate 'belluarum, stirpium vastitate,* etc., where the qualities are, as it were, poetically personified.

(5) Note especially the use of the figure *Chiasmus.* Where two nouns are strung together, or contrasted, each with an Adjective or other word qualifying it, it is usual to put the corresponding words either next to each other, or removed from each other, so as to emphasise the antithesis. Thus *montium altitudines*

*immensitatesque camporum; fontium gelidas perenni-
tales, liquores perlucidos amnium; nec immanitate
belluarum nec stirpium asperitate,* etc.

(6) *Quae si, ut animis, sic oculis,* etc. : this is the
almost invariable order of *ut* . . . . *sic* in comparisons.
The *sic* Clause comes last, because most important :
in English we usually prefer the reverse order.

§ **71.** Another passage remarkable for its ease of
style, and perfection of rhythm, is to be found in Cic.
de Orat. I, caps. 35 and 36 :—

Haec cum Crassus dixisset, silentium est consecutum ;
sed quamquam satis iis, qui aderant, ad id, quod erat
propositum, dictum videbatur, tamen sentiebant celerius
esse multo, quam ipsi vellent, ab eo peroratum. Tum
Scaevola, 'quid est, Cotta?' inquit, 'quid tacetis? Nihilne
vobis in mentem venit, quod praeterea ab Crasso re-
quiratis?' 'Immo id mehercule,' inquit, 'ipsum attendo:
tantus enim cursus verborum fuit, et sic evolavit oratio, ut
eius vim et incitationem aspexerim, vestigia ingressumque
vix viderim, et tamquam in aliquam locupletem ac refer-
tam domum venerim, non explicata veste neque propo-
sito argento neque tabulis et signis propalam conlocatis,
sed his omnibus multis magnificisque rebus constructis
ac reconditis : sic modo in oratione Crassi divitias atque
ornamenta eius ingenii per quaedam involucra atque
integumenta perspexi ; sed ea contemplari cum cuperem,
vix aspiciendi potestas fuit. Itaque neque hoc possum dicere, me omnino ignorare, quid possideat, neque plane
nosse atque vidisse.' 'Quin tu igitur facis idem,' inquit
Scaevola, 'quod faceres, si in aliquam domum plenam
ornamentorum villamve venisses : si ea seposita, ut dicis,
essent, tu, qui valde spectandi cupidus esses, non dubi-

tares rogare dominum, ut proferri iuberet, praesertim si
esses familiaris. Similiter nunc petes a Crasso, ut illam
copiam ornamentorum suorum, quam constructam uno in
loco quasi per transennam praetereuntes strictim aspexi-
mus, in lucem proferat et suo quidque in loco conlocet.'
' Ego vero,' inquit Cotta, ' a te peto, Scaevola :—me enim
et hunc Sulpicium impedit pudor ab homine omnium
gravissimo, qui genus huius modi disputationis semper
contempserit, haec, quae isti forsitan puerorum elementa
videantur, exquirere :—sed tu hanc nobis veniam, Scaevola, da: perfice, ut Crassus haec, quae coarctavit et
peranguste refersit in oratione sua, dilatet nobis atque
explicet.' ' Ego mehercule ' inquit Mucius ' antea vestra
magis hoc caussa volebam, quam mea. Neque enim tanto
opere hanc a Crasso disputationem desiderabam, quanto
opere eius in caussis oratione delector ; nunc vero, Crasse,
mea quoque iam caussa rogo, ut, quoniam tantum habe-
mus otii, quantum iam diu nobis non contigit, ne graveris
exaedificare id opus, quod instituisti : formam enim totius
negotii opinione meliorem maioremque video, quam vehementer probo.' ' Enimvero ' inquit Crassus ' mirari satis
non queo etiam te haec, Scaevola, desiderare, quae neque
ego ita teneo, uti ii, qui docent ; neque sunt eius generis,
ut, si optime tenerem, digna essent ista sapientia ac tuis
auribus.' ' Ain tu ? ' inquit ille : ' si de istis communibus
et pervagatis vix huic aetati audiendum putas, etiamne
illa negligere possumus, quae tu oratori cognoscenda
esse dixisti, de naturis hominum, de moribus, de rationi-
bus eis, quibus hominum mentes et incitarentur et repri-
merentur, de historia, de antiquitate, de administratione
rei publicae, denique de nostro ipso iure civili ? Hanc
enim ego omnem scientiam et copiam rerum in tua pru-
dentia sciebam inesse ; in oratoris vero instrumento tam
lautam supellectilem numquam videram.'

f

§ **72.** The examples hitherto given have been taken from Cicero or Livy; but Cæsar must not be overlooked. For ease and grace, for fulness and versatility of style, Cicero stands unrivalled. It was Cicero who first brought out all the power, all the resources, of the language. It was Cicero who first shewed that the Latin tongue could grapple with the whole field of human knowledge : could find expression for every problem, however profound, for every distinction, however subtle, which was to be found in the whole range of Greek thought and literature. And what he did for the vocabulary of Latin, he did for its form also : gifted with a fine ear for style, trained in all the delicacies of Greek rhetoric, and yet constrained by the necessities of the advocate and the statesman to make these subservient to the purposes of practical life, it was he who first took all baldness, all stiffness and roughness, out of the language, and proved that in every variety of style Latin could exhibit a strength and a dignity all her own, and at the same time a finish, a beauty, and an ease, not inferior to those of the purest Greek models. It was this mixture of theoretical and practical training, of literary and practical power, which raised Cicero to his unique position as the fashioner of the Latin language. His gifts, his training, and his experience were precisely of the kind fitted to make him a consummate master of speech ; and he lived at the very moment when Roman thought was maturing for its highest efforts, and finding its need of an implement more pliant, more rich, more susceptible of artistic moulding, than Latin had hitherto shewn itself to be. Thus everything conspired to give him an influence over his native tongue more great and lasting than was ever exercised over any language by any single writer before or since.

§ **73.** The style of Cæsar has merits of a very different order. It represents the perfection of the purely Roman style, and exhibits the great elemental features of the Roman character. The product of a great and busy mind engaged in great things, using words for the immediate practical purpose in view, and concerning itself not at all with literary or rhetorical effect, Cæsar's style is simple, direct, logical, severe, unconscious : he describes things exactly as they occurred ; he speaks by facts, not by imagination ; he lets each story tell its own tale, writing with clear and rapid vision of the men whom he has known, of the events which he has seen and felt. Livy has much more art ; he is frequently elaborate, frequently poetic, both in his choice of language and in his method of description : if he describes such an event as the disaster of the Caudine Forks, he throws himself into the spirit of the scene, imagines himself a soldier looking round powerless and speechless in dismay at the impending catastrophe, and summons up every element of horror and despair that can add colour to the situation. He has always the effect in view ; and though he writes as a student in his closet, often

careless as to facts which he might easily have verified for himself, his whole work is warmed with the
glow of patriotic feeling.   For specimens of this
feeling see the whole account of the fall of Rome
before the Gauls in Book V, cap. 32 sqq. ; the great
speech of Camillus in opposition to the proposal
to migrate from Rome to Veii, V. 51-54 ; or the
fine digression in Book IX, caps. 17-20, in which he
compares Alexander and Papirius, discusses the
probable event if Alexander had turned his arms
against Italy, and concludes that in commanders, in
soldiers, and in fortune, Rome would have risen
superior from the conflict. Such passages abound
in Livy, and give charm and warmth and colour to
his style.

§ **74.** As a sample of the more sober and realistic
style of Cæsar, as described above, we may take
the passage in the 5th book of the Gallic War,
in which he describes the only signal disaster
which befell his arms in Gaul, ending in the loss of
an entire legion.   The disaster was similar in many
respects to that of the Caudine Forks : a comparison
of Livy's account of that event (IX. 2, 3) with the
following description of Cæsar will give a good example of the points of difference between the styles
of the two authors.   The most striking part of
Cæsar's narrative is contained in B. G. V., caps. 33
to 37 :—

Tum demum Titurius, qui nihil ante providisset, trepi-
dare et concursare cohortesque disponere, haec tamen

ipsa timide atque ut eum omnia deficere viderentur; quod plerumque iis accidere consuevit, qui in ipso negotio consilium capere coguntur. At Cotta, qui cogitasset haec posse in itinere accidere atque ob eam causam profectionis auctor non fuisset, nulla in re communi saluti deerat, et in appellandis cohortandisque militibus imperatoris et in pugna militis officia praestabat. Cum propter longitudinem agminis minus facile omnia per se obire et, quid quoque loco faciendum esset, providere possent, iusserunt pronuntiare, ut impedimenta relinquerent atque in orbem consisterent. Quod consilium etsi in eiusmodi casu reprehendendum non est, tamen incommode accidit : nam et nostris militibus spem minuit et hostes ad pugnam alacriores effecit, quod non sine summo timore et desperatione id factum videbatur. Praeterea accidit, quod fieri necesse erat, ut volgo milites ab signis discederent, quae quisque eorum carissima haberet, ab impedimentis petere atque arripere properaret, clamore et fletu omnia complerentur. At barbaris consilium non defuit. Nam duces eorum tota acie pronuntiare iusserunt, ne quis ab loco discederet : illorum esse praedam atque illis reservari, quaecumque Romani reliquissent : proinde omnia in victoria posita existimarent. Erant et virtute et numero pugnando pares nostri; tametsi ab duce et a fortuna deserebantur, tamen omnem spem salutis in virtute ponebant et quotiens quaeque cohors procurrerat, ab ea parte magnus numerus hostium cadebat. Qua re animadversa Ambiorix pronuntiari iubet, ut procul tela coniciant neu propius accedant et, quam in partem Romani impetum fecerint, cedant (levitate armorum et cotidiana exercitatione nihil iis noceri posse), rursus se ad signa recipientes insequantur. Quo praecepto ab iis diligentissime observato, cum quaepiam cohors ex orbe excesserat atque impetum fecerat, hostes velocissime refugiebant. Interim eam partem nudari necesse erat et ab latere aperto tela recipi. Rursus, cum in eum locum, unde erant egressi, reverti coeperant, et ab iis, qui cesserant, et ab iis, qui proximi steterant, circumveniebantur ; sin autem locum tenere vellent, nec virtuti locus relinquebatur, neque ab tanta multitudine coniecta tela conferti vitare poterant. Tamen tot incommodis conflictati, multis vulneribus acceptis resistebant, et magna parte diei consumpta, cum a prima luce ad horam octavam pugnaretur, nihil, quod ipsis esset indignum, committebant. Tum Tito Balventio, qui superiore anno primum pilum duxerat, viro forti et magnae auctoritatis, utrumque femur tragula traicitur ; Quintus Lucanius, eiusdem ordinis, fortissime pugnans, dum circumvento filio subvenit, interficitur ; Lucius Cotta legatus omnes cohortes ordinesque adhortans in adversum os funda vulneratur. His rebus permotus Quintus Titurius, cum procul Ambiorigem suos cohortantem conspexisset, interpretem suum Gneum Pompeium ad eum mittit rogatum, ut sibi militibusque parcat. Ille appellatus respondit : Si velit secum colloqui, licere ; sperare a multitudine impetrari posse, quod ad militum salutem pertineat ; ipsi vero nihil nocitum iri, inque eam rem se suam fidem interponere. Ille cum Cotta saucio communicat, si videatur, pugna ut excedant et cum Ambiorige una colloquantur : sperare ab eo de sua ac militum salute impetrari posse. Cotta se ad armatum hostem iturum negat atque in eo perseverat. Sabinus quos in praesentia tribunos militum circum se habebat et primorum ordinum centuriones se sequi iubet et, cum propius Ambiorigem accessisset, iussus arma abicere imperatum facit suisque, ut idem faciant, imperat. Interim, dum de condicionibus inter se agunt longiorque consulto ab Ambiorige instituitur sermo, paulatim circumventus interficitur. Tum vero suo more victoriam conclamant atque ululatum tollunt impe-

tuque in nostros facto ordines perturbant. Ibi Lucius
Cotta pugnans interficitur cum maxima parte militum.
Reliqui se in castra recipiunt, unde erant egressi. Ex
quibus Lucius Petrosidius aquilifer, cum magna multitudine hostium premeretur, aquilam intra vallum proiecit,
ipse pro castris fortissime pugnans occiditur. Illi aegre
ad noctem oppugnationem sustinent; noctu ad unum
omnes desperata salute se ipsi interficiunt. Pauci ex
proelio elapsi incertis itineribus per silvas ad Titum
Labienum legatum in hiberna perveniunt atque eum de
rebus gestis certiorem faciunt.

§ **75.** One hint and one caution in conclusion.
We have seen that the first fundamental quality of
good Latin is that it should be intelligible and per-
spicuous. Whatever other qualities a student may
fail in exhibiting, let him make sure of these. With
this end, if he have a passage to translate into Latin,
let him first read and re-read the English until he is
sure that he has grasped the essential meaning of the
whole, as well as the logical connection between its
parts. Having translated it into Latin as well as he
can, let him put by his version for a few days, then
take it up again and read it through, without refer-
ring to the English. If the meaning of the whole
appear clear and connected at the first reading, he
may be content: but if it appear difficult or obscure,
or if he have to refer back to the English to make out
the exact meaning, he may be sure that there is
something wrong, and that he must re-cast the Latin
either in whole or part. Much has been said in this
Introduction about the higher qualities of style: but

let not the student aim at these until he has acquired its fundamental elements. In writing Latin, as in other things, it is well to aim high : but we must not attempt to fly until we have learnt to crawl. Grace, point, ease, beauty of expression, good rhythm, are admirable and delightful : but correctness and clearness are indispensable. Pure style, we have been told, is colourless like water ; and no criticism is more just than that contained in the well-known saying of Quintilian, that one of the greatest arts in writing is to know how to be simple.

PART III.

Easy Passages for Translation into Latin Prose.

—+—

I.

Lycurgus.

THERE once[1] lived in the city of[2] Sparta a man whose[3] name was Lycurgus. He belonged to[4] a noble family, and was the son of Eunomus, the brother of Polydectes the Spartan king. Upon the death[5] of the latter, his wife promised[6] Lycurgus to kill her own son and obtain[7] for him the kingdom. To this proposal Lycurgus seemed at first to consent : but fearing[8] treachery, he caused[9] the child's life to be saved, and, slaying[10] the mother, handed the kingdom over to her son.

[1] Note the two meanings of the English 'once:' *semel* means 'on a single occasion.'   [2] Use Apposition in all such cases.
[3] Use the Dative.   [4] 'belonged to': say 'was of.'   [5] Use the Abl. Abs.   [6] Remember Verbs of *promising,* &c. take the Fut. Infin.   [7] *Obtinere* means 'to hold fast.' not 'to obtain.'
[8] What does 'fearing' really mean ? See **Vol. I. Pref. Note** to **Ex. XXV.**   [9] 'To cause to': *efficere ut.*   [10] What does 'slaying' really mean ? See **Vol. I. § 32, n.** *

B

II.

The Laws of Lycurgus.

Lycurgus was the wisest of all men at that time. In order to make the Spartans more powerful than their neighbours, he instituted laws by which the citizens were prohibited from[1] possessing gold and silver. All the men were engaged either in cultivating the fields or in military exercises; the women were not allowed[2] to appear in public, and were enjoined to remain at home, attending to their children and their households. On leaving[3] the city for a time, that the people might not change his laws, he bound[4] them by an oath that they would not alter them during his absence[5].

[1] Use *quominus*: see **Vol. I, § 156.**   [2] Use *licet.*   [3] Say 'When he was leaving.'   [4] Use *devincio.*   [5] Say 'while he was away.'

III.

Demetrius and Stilpo.

Demetrius had taken the city of Megara[1]. Upon his asking Stilpo[2], the philosopher, if[3] he had lost anything, the other answered, 'I have lost nothing; for all my property is still mine.' At this the monarch marvelled much; for his patrimony had been plundered, his sons carried off, and his country conquered. No doubt the philosopher meant Demetrius to understand[4] that he cared nothing for[5] material possessions, and that no enemy could deprive him of the possessions which alone he valued, namely, those of[6] the mind.

[1] Use Apposition.   [2] Say 'when he had asked Stilpo.' [3] Use *numquid* : remember this is an Indirect Question.   [4] Say 'wished to signify to Demetrius.'   [5] Say 'valued at nothing.' [6] 'those' not to be expressed: see **Vol. I. Ex. XXXIV,** n. 3, and **App. § 12** (d).

IV.

The Gauls besiege Clusium.

The Gauls were now besieging Clusium, a city of Etruria [1]. The Clusians applied to the Romans, entreating them to send ambassadors and letters to the barbarians. Accordingly they sent three illustrious persons of the Fabian family, who had borne the highest offices of the State. The Gauls received them [2] courteously, on account of the name of Rome, and, putting a stop to their operations against the town, came to a conference. But when the ambassadors told them that the Romans ordered them to leave Italy and return to their own country, they replied haughtily 'that they knew of no master but their own will, and that they deemed all countries their own which they had conquered [3] with the sword.'

[1] Use the Adj.   [2] Say ' whom when the Gauls had received.'
[3] Use the Subj. (Orat. Obl.).

V.

Hannibal Conquered.

After having ravaged Italy for many years and won many victories over the Romans, Hannibal was at last beaten by Scipio in the great battle of Zama, which was fought in the year B. C. 201 [1]. After many wanderings, he at last found refuge with [2] Antiochus, King of Syria. Some years afterwards, ambassadors were sent from Rome to Antiochus to demand that Hannibal should be given up. Amongst the number [3] was Scipio, who in conversation asked Hannibal whom he thought to be the greatest general. Hannibal replied that Alexander, King of

Macedon, seemed to him to have been the greatest, because with small forces he had routed[4] innumerable armies.

[1] Say 'in the year before Christ born two-hundredth and first.'   [2] *apud.*   [3] Say 'in the number of whom.'   [4] Use the Subj., as 'routed' refers to the opinion expressed by Hannibal.

VI.

Appius wins a Sea-fight.

At six o'clock the enemy's fleet appeared in view. Appius at once made up his mind to engage the enemy, and gave the order to advance. No regular order was observed. Each ship moved on as best it could, singled out its own antagonist, and grappling at close quarters engaged in a kind of land-fight. The battle was fought[1] with the utmost obstinacy, and no quarter was given[2] on either side. The engagement lasted for four hours, and ended in a complete victory for the Romans. A great number of the enemy's ships were sunk or disabled.

[1] Use *pugnare* impersonally in the Pass.   [2] Say 'and it was spared to none.'

VII.

Regulus keeps his Oath.

Regulus was conquered by the Carthaginians under the leadership of Xanthippus[1]. Only two thousand men remained out of the whole Roman army. Regulus himself was captured and thrown[2] into prison. He was afterwards sent to Rome to consult about an exchange of prisoners[3], after giving an oath that he would return to Carthage if he did not[4] accomplish what he wished.

When the Senate assembled, he advised them to reject the terms of peace which had been offered, and bravely set out from Rome, accompanied by a great crowd, knowing well⁵ that death and torture awaited him on his return to Carthage.

¹ Use Abl. Abs.   ² Use one Finite Verb and one Past Part.
³ Say 'about exchanging prisoners.'   ⁴ Use the Pluperf. : see
Vol. **I. Ex. CIV, n. 2.**   ⁵ Say 'although he knew well.'

VIII.

A Panic in Rome.

Panic reigned throughout the city. No one knew whom to believe. Some said a battle had been lost ; others that the consuls were killed ; the rest that the army was in revolt, and on the march for Rome. Guards were posted at the gates ; a new levy was ordered and equipped ; an embassy was despatched, prepared for either peace or war, and amid universal gloom¹ the day came to a close.

¹ Say either 'all grieving,' or 'amid the greatest grief of all.'

IX.

Before Thrasimene.

Then Hannibal crossed the Alps, and after laying waste the plains of Etruria far and wide, encamped upon some rising ground above the lake of Thrasimene. Seeing Flaminius in hot pursuit, and knowing that if he entered the defile between the mountain and the lake he could surround him on every side, he halted his infantry on the hill beyond the pass, led his cavalry and light armed troops round the heights at the back, and having addressed a few

words of exhortation to[1] the soldiers, awaited with confidence the advance of[2] the enemy.

[1] Say 'when he had exhorted his (men) with few words.'
[2] Say 'the enemy advancing.'

X.

After Thrasimene.

The news reached Rome at about six o'clock. It caused
immense excitement ; and furious multitudes thronged
the streets. Some denounced the Senate. Others blamed
the consuls. Others believed that the anger of the Gods
had been aroused by the violation of the auspices. One
mother died of excitement on meeting her son unexpectedly at the gate, safe and sound ; another of sheer joy
at the appearance of her husband falsely reported as dead.
The Senate deliberated all through the night. Every
senator was asked individually to give his opinion. After
considering every plan, within hearing of the mob outside,
the Senate resolved to resist to the last, and ordered the
consuls to see that the republic took no harm.

XI.

To be turned into Oratio Recta.

Samnites, concilio Etruscorum coacto, dicunt se multos
per annos cum Romanis dimicasse : petisse pacem, cum
bellum tolerare non possent : rebellasse, quod pax ser-.
vientibus gravior, quam liberis bellum esset : unam sibi
spem reliquam in Etruscis restare. Samnitem illis exer-
citum paratum, instructum armis et stipendio, venisse :
statim secuturos, vel si ad ipsam Romam oppugnandam
ducant.

XII.

To be turned into Oratio Recta.

Tum Tribuni; 'quidnam id esset? num veterum contumeliarum memoriam deponere posse? an quicquam esse turpius? reminisceretur plebs pristinae virtutis; sed nolle se vana loqui.'

To be turned into Oratio Obliqua, after a Past Tense.

Unus ego sum ex omni civitate qui adduci non potui ut jurem, vel liberos tibi meos dedam. Ob hanc rem ex civitate profugi, quod solus neque jurejurando neque obsidibus teneri volui. Si mihi veniam dederis, numquam, mehercule, aut te aut senatum paenitebit.

XIII.

After Cannœ.

Of those that fought against Hannibal at Cannæ, some escaped by flight, others were taken prisoners. The latter were very numerous; but though Hannibal offered to release them for a small sum, the Senate refused it by a decree, and left them to be sold or put to death. Those that had fled were sent to Sicily, with orders not to return to Italy until Hannibal should leave it. These came to Marcellus, and begged to be admitted into the army; but though Marcellus was inclined to grant their request, the Senate decreed 'that the Commonwealth had no need of cowards.'

XIV.

Vespasian's Dying Jest.

It is said that [1] the Emperor Vespasian on his death-bed wished to comfort the friends who were weeping around him, and exclaimed with a smile, 'Methinks I am becoming a god!' Although [2] this jest now appears strange and almost incredible, it was very appropriate then. For the Romans were wont to render divine honours to the emperor while he lived, and believed that when he died he straightway was numbered among the gods. Nor was the emperor himself ever displeased with [3] such honours. Tiberius indeed once forbade a temple to be erected to himself; not however, if Tacitus is to be trusted, because [4] he hated flattery, but because he despised fame.

[1] In such phrases use the Verb personally, 'Vespasian is said,' &c. [2] Remember the distinction between *etsi. quamquam* (Indic.) and *licet, ut, quamvis* (Subj.). [3] 'displeased with': turn the sentence Act. [4] *Non quod,* or *non quo,* with Indic.

XV.

The Poet Æschylus.

The poet Æschylus was born at Athens four hundred and twenty-five years before the birth of Christ [1]. He composed many tragedies, but unfortunately very few have reached our age. Those, however, which are extant to-day shew how worthy he is [2] to be [3] reckoned among the greatest poets. Besides, so far was he from being a coward that [4] he was present at the battles of Marathon and Salamis [5], and displayed the utmost valour. In his old age he went to Sicily, and while staying there perished by

a strange chance. An eagle, having seized a tortoise, cast
it to the ground to break its shell, and struck the head of
the poet while he was walking by the sea. Thus he died,
and was buried at Gela.

[1] See Passage V, n. 1.   [2] Indirect Question.   [3] Use *qui*
with Subj.   [4] 'So far . . . that': see **Vol. I. § 115, Note.**
[5] Use Adjectives.

XVI.

Tiberius and Tacitus.

It is related in [1] Tacitus that the Emperor Tiberius was
gloomy, proud, and cruel, and that he loved no one and
was himself loved by none [2]. There are, however, persons
who say that these things are not true, and warn us not [3]
to believe false charges ; for, they say [4], Tacitus hated the
emperor because he was [5] the overthrower of the old republic, and accepted idle rumours without [6] inquiring if
they were true. Perhaps however such persons err ; for
though Tacitus hated Tiberius, still he was not the man
to [7] state what he knew to be false.

[1] *Apud* or *a*.   [2] Use *neque ullus*.   [3] 'To warn not': *moneo*
or *suadeo ne*.   [4] 'they say' to be omitted—use Or. Obl.   [5] Virtual
Or. Obl.   [6] Say 'nor enquired.'   [7] Use *is erat qui* with
the Subj.

XVII.

Socrates.

Wise men often appear foolish to the unlearned ; and
the wiser they are, the more foolish [1] they appear. Who
has not heard of the philosopher Socrates, who when condemned to death [2] by the Athenians refused [3] to escape
from the prison, although earnestly entreated by his

friend Crito ? For he compared himself to a soldier on
guard (*excubare*), and would not quit his post (*statio*)
until God commanded him. Therefore he remained in
the prison ; and during the whole of that day discoursed
beautifully about the immortality of the soul, and toward [4]
evening was put to death without fear or complaint.

[1] 'the wiser . . . the more' : *quo . . . eo.*   [2] *capite* (or *capitis*)
damnatus.   [3] Use *nolo.*   [4] *Sub.*

XVIII.

Archimedes.

I shall give you another example of the folly of wise
men. While the city of Syracuse[1] was being besieged[2]
by the Romans, the philosopher Archimedes taught the
citizens many devices[3] by which to drive back the enemy
from the walls. At last the city was taken, and the citizens
plundered or butchered by the fierce Romans.   But
meanwhile Archimedes was sitting at home intent on his
studies, and not knowing what was being[4] done. He was
drawing lines on the sand, and when a soldier burst in,
he forgot his danger and[5] cried out, ' Don't [6] confuse (*tur-
bare*) my circles.'

[1] Use Apposition.   [2] '*dum*' takes Present Indic. : see Vol. I,
§ 143, and **Ex. CVI**, n. 3.   [3] *artes.*   [4] Ind. Quest.   [5] 'forgot
. . . and'; use Past Part.   [6] Use *noli.*

XIX.

'I have found it! I have found it!'

But wise men appear not only foolish, but also sometimes ridiculous. The same Archimedes long pondered
on a very difficult and obscure question[1], and could not

understand it. But one day it happened that while he
was bathing in the public bath he discovered by chance
what he had long been searching for. Straightway, forgetting both where he was and what he was doing[2], he
rushed headlong out of doors and ran home through the
city naked, crying : 'I have found it! I have found it!'
Doubtless before[3] he reached home he moved many to
laughter[4].

[1] *res.*   [2] Ind. Quest.   [3] 'before' is a Conjunction = 'before that.' *Priusquam* takes the Perfect; **Vol. I, § 143.**   [4] Say
'moved laughter to many.'

XX.

National Characteristics

Charles V. used to say, that the Portuguese[1] appeared to
be fools, and were so ; that the Spaniards appeared wise,
and were not so ; that the Italians seemed to be wise, and
were so ; and that the French seemed fools, and were
not so : that the Germans spoke like[2] carters[3], the
English like blockheads[4], the French like masters, and
the Spaniards like kings.

[1] *Lusitani.*   [2] Say 'in speaking seemed to be.'   [3] Use
cerdo, -onis.   [4] *Stulti.*

XXI.

We must all die once.

A poor Irishman, who was on his death-bed[1], and who
did not seem quite reconciled[2] to the long journey he
was going to take, was kindly consoled by a good-natured
friend with the commonplace reflection, that we must all
die once. 'Why, my dear, now,' answered the sick man,

: that is the very thing that vexes me; if I could die half-a-dozen times, I should not mind it at all.'

¹ Say ' was just about to die.'   ² Use the Adj. *invitus.*

XXII.

Scepticism.

The sceptics, who doubt of everything, and whom Tertullian calls professors of ignorance, do¹ affirm something when they say we can affirm nothing, and admit that something is certain when they maintain that nothing can certainly be known.

¹ ' do ' is emphatic : use *re vera.*

XXIII.

The Big and the Little.

Alexander demanded of a pirate, whom he had taken, by what right he infested¹ the seas ? ' By the same right,' replied he boldly, ' that you enslave the world.   But I am called a robber, because I have only one small vessel ; and you are styled a conqueror, because you command great fleets and armies.'

¹ Say *infestum reddere* or *habere.*

XXIV.

A Happy Solution.

At a banquet, when solving enigmas was one of the diversions¹, Alexander the Great said to his courtiers², ' What is that which did not come last year, has not come this year, and will not come next year?' A distressed officer starting up, said, 'It must certainly be our arrears[3] of pay!'[1] The king was so diverted that he commanded him to be paid up, and also increased his salary.

[1] Use the phrase '*aenigmata animi causa proponere*.'   [2] *comites*.   [3] *reliqua*.

XXV.

Land and Sea.

A countryman once asked a sailor where his father had died. The sailor replied that his father, his grandfather, and his great-grandfather had all perished at sea. 'Well,' said the other, 'are you not afraid to go to sea, lest you should be drowned too?' 'Not at all,' answered the sailor; 'but tell me, I pray you, how your father, your grandfather, and your great-grandfather died?' 'In their beds,' rejoined the rustic. 'Well, then,' said the sailor, 'are you not afraid to go to bed every night?'

XXVI.

Conjugal Affection.

Vossius tells the following story of that great scholar, Frederick Morel. Whilst he was employed in his edition of Libanus one day, he was told that his wife was suddenly taken ill. 'I have only two or three sentences to translate,' he said, 'and then I will come and look at her.' A second message informed him that she was dying[1]. 'I have only three words to write, and I will be there as soon as you,' replied the philosopher. At length, he was told that his wife was dead. His only reply was: 'I am very sorry for it indeed: she was a *very honest woman*.'

[1] What does 'she was dying' exactly mean?

XXVII.

Home Once a Year.

Only once in the year is this visit to the home of our fathers permitted; we require[1] two of the longest days[2] for our flight, and can remain here only eleven days, during which time we fly over the large forest whence we can see the palace in which we were born, where our father dwells, and the tower of the church in which our mother was buried. Here even the trees and bushes seem of kin to us; here the wild horses still race over the plains, as in the days of our childhood; here the charcoal-burner[3] still sings the same old tunes to which we used to dance in our youth; hither we are still attracted, and here we have found thee.

[1] Use *opus est.*   [2] Say 'two days when days are longest.'
[3] *Carbonarius.*

XXVIII.

Troy Besieged.

For nine years and more the Greeks had besieged the city of Troy, and being[1] more numerous [and better ordered] and having very strong and valiant chiefs, they had pressed the men of the city very hard, so that these dared not go outside the walls. This being so[2], it was the custom of the Greeks[3] to leave a part of their army to watch the besieged city, and to send a part on expeditions against such towns[4] in the country round about as they knew to be friendly to the men of Troy, or as they thought to contain good store of provision and treasure. For having been away[5] from home now many years, they were in great want of things needful, nor did they care much how they got them.

[1] 'being': say 'since they were.'   [2] 'This being so': '*quae cum ita essent.*'   [3] Put 'the Greeks' in the Dat.   [4] 'such towns as': use *is* with the Subj.   [5] 'having been away': say 'since they had been away.'

XXIX.

The Trojan Horse.

At last the Greeks made as if they had given up the siege, and sailed away. Then the Trojans issued from the city and beheld with wonder a wooden horse which their enemies had left behind. They long doubted what should be done with it. Many of them were anxious to dedicate it to the gods as a token of gratitude for their deliverance; but all the more prudent spirits advised them to distrust an enemy's gift. Laocoön struck the side of the horse with his spear; but though the sound revealed that the horse was hollow, the Trojans heeded not the warning. Then two serpents came up out of the sea, and slew the unfortunate Laocoön with one of his sons in the sight of all the people; and this terrific spectacle, together with the perfidious counsels of the traitor Sinon, induced the Trojans to make a breach in their own walls, and to drag the fatal horse with triumph and exultation into their city.

XXX.

The Inquisitor's Ears.

An Englishman who stopped at [1] Ferney, on his way to Italy, offered to Voltaire to bring him from Rome whatever he desired. 'Good,' said the philosopher, 'bring me

the ears of the grand inquisitor.' The Englishman, in the
course of a familiar conversation with Clement XIV., related to him this piece of pleasantry. 'Tell Voltaire from
me,' answered the Pope, laughing, 'that our inquisitor is
no longer possessed of ears.'

¹ 'stopped at': use the phrase *deverti ad* or *apud.*

XXXI.

To be turned into Oratio Obliqua.

Imperator, milites hortatus, 'Instate' inquit. 'Cur nunc
hic moramur? Num hostis morabitur? Ne dubitate de
vestra virtute aut de mea vigilantia. Si ignavus fuissem,
vos descruissem; urbs enim, ut opinor, non facile capi-
etur, neque frigoris vis mitescet. Sed nolo ignavia vitam
emere. Quod imperatorem decuit id perfeci; quod si
pro patria moriar, mortem non invitus oppetam.'

XXXII.

A Detective Dog.

A Roman slave was murdered during the civil wars,
but no one knew by whom the crime was perpetrated.
His dog guarded the body, so that no one dared to touch
it.   King Pyrrhus, travelling that way, observed the
animal watching over the corpse, and learning that he
had been there three days without meat or drink, ordered
the body to be buried and the dog to be brought to him.
A few days afterwards every soldier had to march in
review past the king.   The dog lay quietly for some time,
but on seeing the murderers of his late master pass by,

he flew upon[1] them with great violence. This excited the king's suspicion, and the men were seized. They confessed the crime, and were immediately ordered for execution.

[1] Use *invehor in.*

XXXIII.

The Ides of March.

The meeting of Senate took place in the Curia of Pompey. Cæsar had been advised to be on his guard against the 15th of March[1]; on that morning his wife had a dream which terrified her, and she begged him to stay at home. But he went all the same: the conspirators awaited him; and when he came into the Senate house, Tillius Cimber approached, and laying hold of his robe, pretended that he had a favour to ask. Casca gave the first blow; the rest then fell on him; and the great Cæsar fell, pierced by three and twenty wounds.

[1] 'The 15th of March': for the Roman method of dating see **Vol. I, Pref. Note to Ex. LXXXVI.**

XXXIV.

A Letter.

Old age, which renders others talkative, imposes silence upon me. In my youth I wrote many and long letters, at present I write very short ones, and those only to particular friends[1]. With respect to you, whom I have never seen, whom I know little but love much, I shall write only this :—That your book pleases me, and that I am very thankful for your good opinion. I know that I am un-

worthy of your praises ; but you must indeed love virtue
much, if you value its shadow so highly. If you treat me
so generously, what kindness would you not show a man
who had in very truth proved himself to be virtuous?

    [1] 'particular friends' : use the Superl. of *amicus*.

XXXV.

Where is Aristotle?

A Gascon officer, in the regiment of the Duke de
Roquelaure, dining one day with the Duke, the conversation turned on Aristotle. Some one maintained, that there
were a great many admirable things in Aristotle, which
were to be found nowhere else. 'Well,' said the Duke,
turning to the Gascon, who was the butt [1] of the company,
'what do you think of the matter?' 'My opinion is,' replied the Gascon, 'that a great many people talk of having
been at Aristotle, who never were there in their lives.'

    [1] 'to be the butt of': *ludibrio esse, inter ludibria haberi.*

XXXVI.

Rape of Proserpine.

It chanced that Persephone was playing with the daughters of Oceanus in a flowery meadow, where they were
picking flowers and making garlands. She happened
to quit her companions for a moment to pluck a narcissus
which had caught her fancy : when [1] suddenly the ground
opened at her feet, and Pluto, the god of the infernal
regions, appeared in a chariot drawn by snorting horses.
Swift as the wind he seized the terrified maiden, and in

spite of all her struggles bore her off into the regions of darkness before her companions were aware of what had happened to her. When Demeter missed her darling child, and none could tell where she had gone, she kindled torches, and during many days and nights wandered in anguish through all the countries of the earth, not even resting for food or sleep.

[1] Note here that 'when,' as frequently in English, introduces the real apodosis of the sentence. In such cases, the 'when,' if expressed, should be attached to what is, in sense, the subordinate clause.

XXXVII.

Avarice.

When Dr. Franklin was asked why those who had acquired more wealth than was sufficient for all the purposes of comfort, should still desire to increase it, he answered 'that avarice was the most natural and common of all the human passions,' and illustrated his assertion by giving to a child, then in the room, a large apple. The moment [1] it had taken it he offered it another, which it also took; and before it could dispose of either, he presented a third; it vainly tried to hold it in its little hands, and at last, in a passion of tears, threw itself and the fruit on the floor.

[1] Say 'as soon as.'

XXXVIII.

Political Geese.

At the time of the revolution [1] in England, several persons of rank, who had been zealously serviceable in bringing about that event, but who, at the same time, possessed no great abilities, applied for some of the most considerable employments under the new government. The Earl of Halifax was consulted on the propriety of admitting these claims. 'I remember,' said his lordship, 'to have read in history, that Rome was saved by geese; but I do not recollect ever to have read that those geese were made consuls.'

[1] *Res novae* would not be suitable here to express ' revolution,' the term used to denote the constitutional changes made at the accession of William and Mary. You might say *post exactum Iacobum,* or *cum forma reipublicae commutata est,* etc.

XXXIX.

Athenian Courtesy.

The story runs[1] that once upon a time at Athens, during the celebration of the games, an old gentleman, much advanced in years, entered the theatre. Among his countrymen who were present in that large assembly no one offered him a place. So he turned to the Lacedæmonians, who as ambassadors had a certain place allotted to them. They rose in a body, and begged him to sit amongst them. Loud shouts of applause arose from the whole theatre; whereupon it was remarked that the Athenians knew their duty, but were slow to exemplify it in their conduct.

In translating stories like the above, consisting of many detached sentences, the student should use the *periodic* structure, putting the less important statements into subordinate clauses, and reserving the principal clause or clauses for the leading ideas.

XL.

A Conservative Voter.

A Liberal candidate applied to a yeoman of a certain county for his vote, promising, if elected, to do all he could to turn out the ministry [1] and procure a fresh set [2]. 'Then I won't vote for you,' cried the farmer. 'Why not?' said the patriot, 'I thought you were a friend to the people.' 'So I am,' replied the yeoman; 'and for that reason I am not for a change in the ministry. I know well enough how it is with my hogs; when I buy them in lean, they eat voraciously; but when they have once got a little fat, the keeping of them is not near so expensive. I am for keeping the present set of ministers, as they will devour much less than a new set.'

[1] *magistratus.*   [2] Use the phrase *novos creare (magistratus).*

XLI.

Alexander invades Egypt.

Alexander, in the three hundred-and-thirty-second year [1] before the birth of Christ [2], invaded Egypt, which had long been subject to the Persians. While [3] he was staying there, he founded the city of Alexandria, which at one time he wished to be considered the metropolis of his empire, and which to this day bears his name. Elated with success, he now laid claim to divine honours, and among the very priests there were found persons so base as to flatter him in this, and make him believe he was the son of Jupiter Ammon. Many of his soldiers died of fatigue and thirst while marching to the temple of this imaginary god, which was distant a journey of seven days from Alexandria.

[1] For Roman counting, see **Vol. I, Pref. Note to Ex. LXXXV.**
[2] Say 'before Christ born.'   [3] For the Constr. of *dum*, see **Vol. I, § 143,** and Note.

XLII.

Diverging Paths.

It is related of Justice Holt, who had been very wild in his youth, that one day when he was on the bench, a fellow was tried for a robbery, and very narrowly acquitted, whom his lordship recollected to be one of his early dissipated companions. After the trial was over, curiosity induced him [1] to send for the man in private, in order to inquire the fortune of the cotemporaries with whom he was once associated : he therefore asked the fellow what was become of [2] this one and that one, and the rest of the party to which they belonged ? 'Ah, my lord,' said the fellow, 'they are all hanged except your lordship and myself.'

[1] Carefully avoid in Latin such phrases as 'curiosity induced him,' &c., which are so common in English. Latin avoids them because too far removed from literal truth. They may usually be turned Passively : e. g. it is better to say *motus ira* than *ira movit.* Here say 'since he wished to know, &c., he sent for the man.'
[2] 'what was become of': *quid factum esset,* with the Abl.

XLIII.

King Log.

The Frogs, living [1] an easy free life everywhere among the lakes and ponds, assembled together one day in a very tumultuous manner, and petitioned Jupiter to let them have a king, who might inspect their morals and punish all wrong doers. Jupiter, being at that time in a good humour, was pleased[2] to laugh heartily at their ridiculous request, and throwing a little log down into the pool, cried, 'There is a king for you.' The sudden splash which this made by its fall into the water, at first terrified[3] them so exceedingly that they were afraid to come near it; but in a little time, seeing[1] it lay still without moving, they ventured by degrees to approach it; and at last, finding[1] there was no danger, they leaped upon it, and, in short, treated it as familiarly as they pleased.

[1] Do not use the Pres. Part. in any of these instances.   [2] Note that the phrase 'was *pleased* to laugh,' does not imply pleasure; it only implies condescension.   [3] Do not say 'the splash terrified them,' but rather that 'they were terrified by the splash.'

XLIV.

King Stork.

But they were not contented with so insipid a king as this[1], so they sent deputies to[2] petition again for another sort of one, for this they neither did nor could like. Upon that he sent them a stork, who, without any ceremony, fell a-devouring and eating them up, one after another, as fast as he could. Then they applied themselves privately to Mercury, and begged him to speak to Jupiter in their behalf, that he would be so good as to bless them again with another king, or to restore them to their former state. 'No, no,' says he, 'since it was their own choice, let the obstinate wretches suffer the punishment due to their folly.'

[1] 'so insipid as this': use *tam*, omitting 'as this.'   [2] For 'to' denoting purpose, see **Vol. I, App. § G d** .

XLV.

Perugian Eloquence.

The town of Perugia having sent deputies to Urban V., who was then at Avignon, they found this pontiff sick in bed. The orator of the embassy made him a long speech, without [1] paying any regard to his indisposition, and without [2] ever coming to the point. When he had done, the Pope asked the deputation [3] whether they had anything else to state. Seeing that he was heartily tired, they said: 'Our instructions are, to declare to your Holiness, that if you do not grant us what we ask, our orator will make his speech again before we go.' The Pope granted the demand instantly.

[1] The English 'without' before a Participial Noun may be rendered in various ways in Latin, but *sine* must never be used except with a Substantive. Use here the Abl. Abs., 'no regard having been paid to': 'to pay regard to anything' is *alicuius rei rationem habere.* [2] Here use *neque* with a finite Verb. [3] In such cases, as a rule, use the Concrete form, not the Abstract: 'deputation' means 'deputies.'

XLVI.

Sophia's Pet.

Of this bird Sophia, then about thirteen years old, was so extremely fond that her chief business was to feed and tend it, and her chief pleasure to play with it. By these means little Tommy, for so the bird was called, was become so tame that it would [1] feed out of the hand of its mistress, would [1] perch upon her finger, and lie contented in her bosom, where it seemed almost sensible of its own happiness; though she always kept a small string about its leg, nor would ever trust it with the liberty of flying away.

[1] 'would' here only denotes habit.

XLVII.

Congreve.

Congreve, the English dramatist[1], spoke of his works as trifles, upon which he placed no great account; which was beneath him. Voltaire, when he was in England, paid him a visit[2]. Congreve, during the first conversation, made him understand that he wished himself to be looked upon in no other light than as a *gentleman*[3] who led an easy and simple life. To this announcement Voltaire answered drily: 'Had you been so unfortunate as to be nothing more than a gentleman, I should not have given myself the trouble to wait upon you.'

[1] *Poeta scenicus*, or *fabularum scriptor.*   [2] to visit: *salutandi causa adire* or *visere.*   [3] Use *urbanus.*

XLVIII.

A Sly Dog.

A dog, that was kept constantly on the chain, found that he could withdraw his head from it when he pleased. Thinking, however, that if he did this when his master saw him, his chain would be made tighter, he never drew his head through it during the day, but waited till night. He would[1] then run off and roam through the fields, which were stocked with sheep and lambs, many

of which he either wounded or killed. To wash off the
marks of blood, he would go to a neighbouring stream,
and then return home before daybreak. He then slipped
into his chain again, and lay down as if he had been at
home all night.

[1] 'would' denotes habit.

XLIX.

Janus.

Among the most important gods of the Romans was
the celebrated Janus, a deity quite unknown to the
Greeks. He was god of the light and of the sun, like·
the Greek Apollo, and thus became the god of all beginnings ; New Year's Day [1] was his most important festival.
Now the Romans had a superstitious belief[2] in the importance[3] of a good beginning for everything, concluding
that this had a great influence on the good or evil result
of every undertaking. So neither in public nor in private
life did they ever undertake anything of importance without first confiding[4] the beginning to the protection of
Janus. When the youth of the city marched out to war,
an offering was made to the god by the departing general,
and the temple, or rather gateway, sacred to the god, was
left open during the continuance of the war, as a sign
that the god had departed with the troops and had them
under his protection.

[1] Say 'the Kalends of January.' See Vol. I, Pref. Note to Ex.
LXXXVI.   [2] 'A superstitious belief' or 'custom' is *religio*.
[3] 'in the importance of': use the phrase *plurimum interesse.*
[4] 'without confiding': say 'unless they had previously con-
fided.'

L.

An Honest Philosopher.

A follower of Pythagoras had bought a pair[1] of shoes from a cobbler, for which he promised[2] to pay him on a future day. He went with his money on the day appointed, but found that the cobbler had in the interval departed this life. Without[3] saying anything of his errand, he withdrew secretly, rejoicing at the opportunity thus unexpectedly afforded him of gaining[4] a pair of shoes for nothing. His conscience, however, says Seneca, would not suffer him to remain quiet under such an act of injustice ; so, taking up the money, he returned to the cobbler's shop, and, casting in the money, said, 'Go thy ways, for though he is dead to all the world besides, yet he is alive to me.'

[1] For 'a pair' use *bini*. [2] Note the Constr. of Verbs of *promising*. [3] Do not use *sine*. [4] Use *(sibi)* *parare* or *comparare*.

LI.

Socrates and the Thirty Tyrants.

While[1] Athens was governed by the thirty tyrants, Socrates, the philosopher, was summoned to the Senate House. He was there ordered by them to go with some other persons, whom they named, to seize one Leon, a man of rank and fortune, whom they determined to put out of the way, that they might enjoy his estate. This commission Socrates positively refused to execute. 'I will not willingly,' said he, 'assist in an unjust act.' Charicles sharply replied, 'Dost thou think, Socrates,

to talk in this high tone and not to suffer?' 'Far from
it [2],' replied he, 'I expect to suffer a thousand ills, but
none so great as to do unjustly.'

[1] *Dum* here takes the Present: see **Vol. I, § 143, Note.**   [2] *Immo.*

LII.

Porus and his Elephant.

King Porus, in a battle with Alexander the Great,
being severely wounded, fell from the back of his elephant. Supposing him dead, the Macedonian soldiers
pushed forward, in order to despoil him of his rich
clothing and accoutrements; but the faithful elephant,
standing over the body of his master, boldly repelled
every one who dared to approach, and while the enemy
stood at bay [1], took the bleeding Porus up on his trunk,
and placed him again on his back. By this time [2] the
troops of Porus had come to his relief, and the king was
saved; but the elephant died of the wounds which it had
received in the heroic defence of its master.

[1] 'stood at bay': use *consto* or *cunctor.*   [2] 'By this time'
is always *iam*, which (as distinguished from *nunc*) has reference
to past time, implying that 'a time *has* (or *had*) arrived when.'

LIII.

The Grasshopper and the Ants.

In the winter season a commonwealth of ants was
busily employed in the management and preservation of
their corn, which they arranged in heaps round about
their little habitation. A grasshopper, who had chanced
to outlive the summer, and was ready to starve with cold
and hunger, implored them to relieve his necessity with

one grain of wheat. One of the ants asked him how
he had disposed of his time in summer, that he had not[1]
taken pains, and laid in a stock as they had done. 'Alas!
gentlemen,' says he, 'I passed the time merrily in drinking, singing, and dancing, and never once thought of
winter.' 'If that be the case,' replied the ant, laughing,
'all I have to say is, that they who drink, sing, and dance
in the summer, must starve in winter.'

[1] 'that he had not': use *quod non* with the Indic.

LIV.

Sixtus V.

Pope Sixtus V. was so poor when he came to Rome,
that he was obliged to ask alms. Having at last saved
a small pittance, he deliberated with himself for a long
time whether he should lay it out in the purchase of
something to allay his hunger, or of a pair of shoes, of
which he was in extreme want; and his countenance
expressed the deep interest he felt in this consultation.
A merchant, seeing his embarrassment, asked him the
cause, which he ingenuously confessed to him; and did
so in a manner so agreeable, that the merchant, perceiving him to be a man of talent, took him home with him
to dinner, and thus settled the question. When Sixtus
became Pope, he did not forget his old friend the merchant, but repaid as a prince the service he had received
as a beggar.

LV.

Sabinus and his Dog.

After the execution of Sabinus, the Roman general,
who suffered death for his attachment[1] to the family of

Germanicus, his body was exposed to public view upon
the Gemonian stairs, as a warning to all who should
dare to befriend the house of Germanicus. No friend
had courage to approach the body; one only remained
true—his faithful dog. For three days the animal continued to watch the body; his pathetic howlings awakening the sympathy of every heart. Food was at last
brought him; but on taking the bread, instead of obeying
the impulse of hunger, he fondly laid it on his master's
mouth, and renewed his lamentations : days thus passed,
nor did he for a moment quit the body.

[1] Say 'to whom the attachment to (*fides in*) the family, &c.,
was for a destruction.'

LVI.

Atys and the Boar.

When a boar of huge size was destroying the cattle
on Mount Olympus, and likewise many of the country
people, persons were sent to implore the assistance of
the King. Atys, one of the King's sons, a youth of
high spirit, urged his father to let him go, and assist
in killing the boar. The King, remembering a dream,
in which he saw his son perish by a spear, refused at
first to permit him to go; reflecting, however, that the
tooth of a wild beast was not to be dreaded so much
as the pointed spear, he consented. The youth accordingly set out, and while all of them were eagerly intent
on slaying the boar, a spear thrown by one of the country
people pierced the heart of the young Atys, and thus
realised his father's dream.

LVII.

Every Man for Himself.

Two friends were travelling together on the same road, when they were met by[1] a bear. The one, in great fear, climbed up a tree, and hid himself among the branches, thinking only of himself. The other, seeing that he had no chance single-handed against the bear, threw himself on the ground, and feigned to be dead. He did this because he had heard that the bear will never touch a dead body. As he thus lay, the bear came up to his head, smelling his nose and ears, but the man held his breath, and the beast, supposing him to be dead, walked away. When the bear was out of sight, the other man came down out of the tree, and asked what it was that the bear had whispered to him ; 'for,' said he, 'I observed he put his mouth very close to your ear.' 'Well,' replied his companion, 'he only bade me never again keep company with those who, when any danger threatens, look after their own safety, and leave their friends in the lurch.'

[1] 'were met by' : turn this Act.

LVIII.

True Poverty.

One of the officers of Artaxerxes, King of Persia, of the name of Artibarzanes, solicited his majesty to confer a favour upon him, which, if granted, would be an act of injustice. The king, learning that the promise of a considerable sum of money was the only motive that induced the officer to make such an unreasonable request, ordered his treasurer to give him thirty thousand dariuses, being a present of equal value with that which he was to have received. 'Here,' says the king, giving him an order for the money, 'take this token of my friendship for you ; a gift of this nature cannot make me poor, but complying with your request would render me poor indeed, since it would make me unjust.'

LIX.

An Honest Rogue.

The Dukes of Ossuna had the privilege of visiting the galleys once a year, and releasing any slave who might appear to be the least criminal. So Ferdinando, going on board [1] for that purpose, demanded of each the nature of his crime. They all protested they were entirely innocent, and had been imprisoned from the malice and corruption of their accusers and judges, except one man, who said that, impelled by extreme distress, he had robbed a person of his money, and merited the rigour of his sentence. The Duke, striking him over the back with his cane, ordered him to quit the galley immediately, observing that ' he was too great a rogue to live among so many honest people.'

[1] 'To go on board' is *navem* or *in navem conscendere.*

LX.

The Shield of Mars.

As King Numa one morning raised his hands in prayer to Jove, from the ancient palace at the foot of the Palatine, beseeching his protection and favour for the infant state of Rome, the god let fall from heaven, as a mark of his favour, an oblong brazen shield. At the same time a voice was heard declaring that Rome should endure as long as this shield was preserved. Numa caused the sacred shield, which was believed to be that of Mars, to be carefully preserved. The better to prevent its abstraction, he ordered eleven others to be made exactly similar, and instituted for their protection the college of the Salii, twelve in number, who were selected from the noblest families in Rome.

LXI.

The Daughters of Servius.

The two daughters of Servius were married to their cousins, the two young Tarquins. The fierce Tullia was the wife of the gentle Aruns Tarquin; the gentle Tullia had married the proud Lucius Tarquin. Aruns' wife tried to persuade her husband to seize the throne that had belonged to[1] his father, and when he would not listen to her, she agreed with his brother Lucius that, while[2] he murdered her sister, she should kill his brother, and then that they should marry. The horrid deed was carried out, and old Servius, seeing what a wicked pair were likely to come after him, began to consider with the Senate whether it would not be better to have two consuls or magistrates chosen every year than a king.

[1] For ' to belong to' say ' to be of.'   [2] Note that 'while' here does not refer to time.

LXII.

Tullia and Tarquin.

This made[1] Lucius Tarquin the more furious, and, going to the Senate, where the patricians hated the king as the friend of the plebeians, he stood upon the throne, and was beginning to tell the patricians that this would be the ruin of their greatness, when[2] Servius came in and, standing on the steps of the doorway, ordered him to come down. Tarquin[3] sprang on the old man and hurled him backwards, so that the fall killed him, and his body was left in the street. The wicked Tullia, wanting to know how her husband had sped, came out in her chariot on the road. The horses started back before the corpse. She asked what was in their way; the slave who drove her told her it was the king's body. 'Drive on,' she said. The horrid deed caused the street to be known ever after as 'Scelerata,' or 'the wicked street.'

[1] 'This made Lucius': turn this Passively. In this way a change of Subject will be avoided. Note especially that Latin, unlike English, objects to a frequent change of Subject: make it a rule to change your Subject as seldom as possible.   [2] Note that 'when' here marks the real apodosis, introducing the most important Verb of the passage.   [3] Before 'Tarquin sprang' insert *Tum* or *Tum vero*. Make it a rule in Latin, wherever you can, to introduce some words or phrase at the beginning of each fresh sentence to indicate the connection with the preceding sentence. This may be a word indicating Time, or logical connection, or a Relative, or any Particle or Conjunction which serves to carry on the mind naturally from one sentence to another. Latin abhors a gap.

LXIII.

Character of the Scottish People.

I am in great hopes, through God's mercy, we shall be able this winter to give the people such an understanding of the justness of our cause, and our desires for the just liberties of the people, that the better sort of them[1] will be satisfied therewith; although I must confess, hitherto they continue obstinate. I thought I should have found in Scotland a conscientious people, and a barren country: about Edinburgh, it is as fertile for corn as any part of England; but the people generally are so given to the most impudent lying, and frequent swearing, as is incredible to be believed. I rest your Lordship's most humble servant, OLIVER CROMWELL.

[1] 'The better sort of them': say *optimus quisque.*

LXIV.

Sir Thomas More.

The greatest of men are sometimes seized with strange fancies at the very moment when one would suppose they had ceased to be occupied with the things of this world. Sir Thomas More, at his execution[1], having laid his head upon the block, and perceiving that his beard was extended in such a manner that it would be cut through by the stroke of the executioner, asked him to adjust it properly upon the block; and when the executioner told him he need not trouble himself about his beard, when his head was about to be cut off, 'It is of little consequence to me,' said ·Sir Thomas, 'but it is a matter of some importance to you, that you should understand your profession[2], and not cut through my beard, when you had orders only to cut off my head.'

[1] The proper phrase for 'to behead' is *securi ferire* or *perculere.*
[2] Say 'art.'

LXV.

A Loyal Son.

Titus Manlius was the son of a sour and imperious father, who banished him from his house as a blockhead

and a scandal[1] to the family.   This Manlius, hearing that
his father's life was in question, and a day named for his
trial, went to the tribune who had undertaken the cause,
and discoursed with him about it.   The tribune told him
the appointed time, and withal that his cruelty to his son
would be part of the charge.   Upon this, Manlius took
the tribune aside, and presenting a poniard to his breast,
'Swear,' said he, 'that you will let this cause drop, or you
shall have this dagger in your heart; it is now in your
choice which way my father shall be saved.'   The tribune
swore, and kept his word ; and made a fair report of the
whole matter to the bench.

[1] 'To be a scandal to': *dedecori* or *opprobrio esse.*

LXVI.

Oracular ambiguity.

A person who had some dangerous enemies, whom he
believed capable of attempting anything against him, consulted an oracle to know whether he should leave the
country.   The answer he obtained was, '*Domine, stes
securus* ;' a reply which led him to believe he might safely
remain at home.   Some days afterwards, his enemies set
fire to his house, and it was with great difficulty that he
escaped with his life.   On recollecting the words of the
Oracle, he perceived, when too late, that he had divided
the words wrongly, and that the oracular sentence ought
to have been read thus : *Domi ne stes securus.*

LXVII.

Pyrrhus admires his Enemies.

Pyrrhus was unwilling to fight till his allies arrived.
After a few days, the armies met on the banks of the

river, and the battle commenced. One wing of the Roman army was victorious, but the other was driven back to the camp by the elephants of Pyrrhus. The Romans fought very bravely, but were unable to withstand the second charge of the enemy. They took to flight, and on that account have been accused of cowardice. Pyrrhus gained a complete victory, and took the enemy's camp without resistance. On the following day he visited the field of battle, and, seeing the bodies of the Romans turned towards the enemy, he pronounced them brave men. Having delayed a few days, he returned to Tarentum.

LXVIII.

Battle of Lake Regillus.

Now they knew at Rome that the armies had joined battle, and as the day wore away all men longed for tidings. And the sun went down, and suddenly there were seen in the forum two horsemen, taller and fairer than the tallest and fairest of men, and they rode on white horses, and they were as men just come from the battle, and their horses were all bathed in foam. They alighted by the Temple of Vesta, where a spring of water bubbles up from the ground, and fills a small deep pool. Here they washed away the stains of the battle, and when men crowded round them, and asked for tidings, they told them how the battle had been fought, and how it was won. Then they mounted their horses, and rode from the forum, and were seen no more, and men sought for them in every place, but found them not.

LXIX.

A Cold Shoulder.

The Prince de Condé once thought himself offended by the Abbé de Voisenon : Voisenon heard this, and went to court to exculpate himself. As soon as the Prince saw him, he turned away from him. 'Thank God!' said Voisenon, 'I have been misinformed, Sir; your Highness does not treat me as if I was an enemy.' 'How do you see that, Mr. Abbé?' said his Highness, coldly, over his shoulder. 'Because, Sir,' answered the Abbé, 'your Highness never turns your back upon an enemy.' 'My dear Abbé,' exclaimed the Prince, turning round and taking him by the hand, 'it is quite impossible[1] for any man to be angry with you ;' and so ended his Highness's animosity.

[1] 'It is impossible that': *non fieri potest ut.*

LXX.

Piety.

Papirius was encamped over against the Samnites ; and perceiving that, if he fought, victory was certain, he desired the omens to be taken. The fowls refused to peck ; but the chief soothsayer, observing the eagerness of the soldiers to fight, reported to the consul that the auspices were favourable. But some among the soothsayers divulged to certain of the soldiers that the fowls had not pecked. This was told to Spurius Papirius, who reported it to the consul ; but the latter straightway bade him mind his own business, for that so far as he himself and the army were concerned, the auspices were fair. It so chanced that, as they advanced against the enemy, the chief soothsayer was killed by a spear thrown by a Roman soldier; when the consul heard this, he said, 'All goes well; for by the death of this liar the army is purged of blame.'

LXXI.

Impiety.

But an opposite course was taken by Appius Pulcher, in Sicily, in the first Carthaginian war. For desiring to join battle, he bade the soothsayers take the auspices, and on their announcing that the fowls refused to feed, he answered, 'Let us see, then, whether they will drink;' and, so saying, caused them to be thrown into the sea. After which he fought and was defeated. For this he was condemned at Rome, while Papirius was honoured; not so much because the one had gained while the other had lost a battle, as because in their treatment of the auspices the one had behaved discreetly, the other with rashness.

LXXII.

Newton and his Dog.

Sir Isaac Newton, the great philosopher, was so distinguished for his cool and even temper, that he remained calm and undisturbed under the greatest provocation. The following story is told of him. He had a favourite little dog, which he called Diamond. Being one evening called out of his study into the next room, the dog was left behind. The philosopher, on returning after a few minutes' absence, had the mortification to[1] find that Diamond had overturned a lighted candle among some papers, the nearly finished labours of many years, which were now reduced to ashes. Instead[2] of getting into a rage, however, and punishing the dog, he restrained his anger, and said in a sorrowful but quiet tone : 'O Diamond, Diamond, little do you know the mischief you have done !'

[1] 'had the mortification': say *cum magno suo dolore.*   [2] 'Instead of': say ' yet did not he . . . but.'

LXXIII.

A good old Tory.

Cato was unfortunate enough to live at a time when avarice, luxury, and ambition prevailed at Rome, when religion and the laws were disregarded, and when the whole appearance of the state was so changed and disfigured that if one of the former generation had risen from the dead he would hardly have recognised the Roman people. Cato was one of a few who supported the cause of virtue, who could neither be allured by promises nor terrified by threats, and who would not flatter the great at the expense of the truth. Though his countrymen were too depraved to be influenced by his example, they could not do otherwise than admire him in their hearts.

LXXIV.

The Caudine Forks.

Two years later the two consuls, Titus Veturius and Spurius Posthumius, were marching into Campania, when the Samnite commander, Pontius, sent forth people disguised as shepherds to entice them into a narrow mountain pass near the city of Caudium, with only one way out, which the Samnites blocked up with trunks of trees. As soon as the Romans were within this place, the other end was blocked in the same way, and thus they were all closed up at the mercy of their enemies. What was to be done with them? asked the Samnites; and they went to consult old Herennius, the wisest man in the nation. 'Either kill them all,' said he, 'or let them all go free.' Asked to explain what he meant, he said that to release them generously would be to make them friends and allies for ever; but if the war was to go on, the best thing for Samnium would be to destroy such a number of enemies at a blow.

LXXV.

The Romans pass under the Yoke.

Pontius placed two spears in the ground and laid a third across them. Under this 'yoke' the Roman army was led with its two consuls, four legates, and twelve tribunes. But when the messengers reached Rome, the whole people was moved with anger and shame. The senate declared that they, who alone had power to make treaties, had had no part in the transaction. The consuls were afraid to assume their insignia. Twice was a dictator nominated, and twice the augurs refused their assent. Nothing was done until the interrex named Cursor and Philo for the consulship. Then Postumius begged the people to reject the treaty which he himself had made: but he added that the leader who had erred must be surrendered to the Samnites. Accordingly, when he had been led by heralds into the enemy's camp, he struck one of them on the head, and exclaimed, 'I am no longer a Roman but a Samnite.'

LXXVI.

Eloquence of Cicero.

Ligarius, a Roman citizen, had attached himself to the interests and fortunes of Pompey, and after his death had retired, with Scipio, into Africa. He did everything in his power against Cæsar, who was informed of the whole by Tubero, and who, in consequence, conceived so great an aversion against Ligarius, that he thought only of revenge. Cicero undertook the defence of Ligarius; and although Cæsar at first absolutely refused to listen to him, the other, who was not to be disconcerted by the first rebuff, at last prevailed on him to listen to his justification. Cæsar, in fact, entertained no doubt that he would be able to prove his guilt by undoubted documents, and that Cicero would be unable to make any reply. But before Cicero had finished his defence of Ligarius, the letters and memorials had insensibly dropped from the hand of Cæsar; he changed his colour, his resolution, as if he had been under the influence of some charm, and not only granted a free pardon to Ligarius, but admitted him into the list of his particular friends.

LXXVII.

Cæsar approaches Britain.

From his ship Cæsar perceived the rocks covered with armed men. At this spot the sea was so close to the cliffs that a dart thrown from the heights could reach the beach. The place appeared to him in no respect convenient for landing. Cæsar cast anchor, and waited in vain till the ninth hour for the arrival of the vessels which were delayed. In the interval he called together his lieutenants and the tribunes of the soldiers, communicated to them his plan, as well as the information brought by Volusenus, and urged upon them the execution of his orders instantaneously, on a simple sign, as maritime war required, in which the manœuvres must be as rapid as they are varied. It is probable that Cæsar had till then kept secret the point of landing.

LXXVIII.

A Head of Gold.

Turgot came one day to visit Voltaire in the house of the Marquis de Villette, when he was so much tormented by the gout that he had not the free use of his limbs. ' Ah, M. Turgot,' said Voltaire, addressing him, ' how do you do?' 'I can scarcely walk for pain.' 'Gentlemen,' cried Voltaire, with enthusiasm, 'I never see M. Turgot but I think I see Nebuchadnezzar's image.' 'Yes,' answered the Minister, 'feet of clay.' 'And the head of gold, the head of gold!' replied Voltaire.

LXXIX.

A Noble Roman Matron.

This tardy gratitude consoled Cornelia, who retained in a distant retirement the memory of the greatness both of her parents and her offspring. In her dwelling on the promontory of Misenum, surrounded by the envoys of kings and the representatives of Grecian literature, she rejoiced in recounting to her admiring visitors the life and death of her noble children, without shedding a tear, but speaking calmly of them, as heroes of ancient days. Only

she would conclude her account of her father Africanus
with the words : 'The grandchildren of this great man
were my sons. They perished in the temples and groves
of the gods. They deserved to fall in those holy spots,
for they gave their lives for the noblest end, the happiness
of the people.'

LXXX.

A Multitude without a Head.

When Virginia died by her father's hand, the commons of Rome withdrew under arms to the Sacred Hill.
Whereupon the senate sent messengers to demand by
what sanction they had deserted their commanders and
assembled there in arms. And in such reverence was the
authority of the senate held, that the commons, lacking
leaders, durst make no reply. 'Not,' says Titus Livius,
' that they were at a loss what to answer, but because
they had none to answer for them ;' words which clearly
show how helpless a thing is the multitude when without
a head.

LXXXI.

Johnson on Scottish Scenery.

Mr. Ogilvie was unlucky enough to choose for the topic
of his conversation the praises of his native country. He
began with saying that there was very rich land around
Edinburgh. Goldsmith, who had studied physic there,
contradicted this, very untruly, with a sneering laugh.
Disconcerted a little by this, Mr. Ogilvie then took a new
ground, where he probably thought himself perfectly safe ;
for he observed that Scotland had a great many noble
wild prospects. ' I believe, sir,' said Johnson, ' you have

a great many; Norway, too, has noble wild prospects; and Lapland is remarkable for prodigious noble wild prospects; but, sir, let me tell you, the noblest prospect which a Scotchman ever sees is the high road that leads him to England.'

LXXXII.

Woman's Love.

Queen Elizabeth loved the Earl of Essex so dearly, that in a tender moment she gave him a ring, telling him, that if he ever should be guilty of undertaking anything against the state worthy of death, he had only to send to her that ring in order to ensure his pardon. The Earl of Essex some time afterward fell in love with another lady, engaged in treasonable practices, and was condemned to death. In the last extremity, he intrusted the ring to this lady to be conveyed to Elizabeth. As the lady knew the secret connected with the ring, she preferred keeping it and allowing her lover to be beheaded, to running the risk of seeing him unfaithful.

LXXXIII.

Why should not Plebeians be Consuls?

To such language as this the tribunes might have replied by denying that its principle was applicable to the particular point at issue; they might have urged that the admission of the commons to the consulship was not against the original and unalterable laws of the Romans, inasmuch as strangers had been admitted even to be kings at Rome; and the good king Servius, whose memory was so fondly cherished by the people, was, according to one tradition, not only a stranger by birth, but a slave. And further, they might have answered that the law of intermarriage between the patricians and commons was a breaking down of the distinction of orders, and implied that there was no such difference between them as to make it profane in either to exercise the functions of the other.

LXXXIV.

Exploit of P. Decius Mus.

In this almost hopeless danger, one of the military tribunes, Publius Decius Mus, discovered a little hill above the enemy's camp, and asked leave to lead a small body of men to seize it, since he would be likely thus to draw off the Samnites, and while they were destroying him, as he fully expected, the Romans could get out of the valley. Hidden by the wood, he gained the hill, and there the Samnites saw him, to their great amazement; and while they were considering whether to attack him, the other Romans were able to march out of the valley. Finding he was not attacked, Decius set guards, and, when night came on, marched down again as quietly as possible to join the army, who were now on the other side of the Samnite camp.

LXXXV.

A Fair Exchange.

Brebeuf, when young, had no taste for any author but Horace. One of his friends, named Gautier, on the contrary, liked nothing but Lucan. This preference was the cause of frequent disputes. To put an end to these, at last they agreed that each should read the poem which his companion preferred, examine it, and estimate its merits impartially. This was done : and the consequence was that Gautier, having read Horace, was so delighted with him that he scarcely ever left him ; while Brebeuf, enchanted with Lucan, gave himself up so wholly to the study of his manner, that he carried it to a greater extent than Lucan himself, as is evident from the translation of that poem which he has left us in French verse.

LXXXVI.

Hannibal receives a check.

Day dawned ; the main army broke up from its camp, and began to enter the defile ; while the natives, finding their positions occupied by the enemy, at first looked on quietly, and offered no disturbance to the march.   But when they saw the long narrow line of the Carthaginian army winding along the steep mountain side, and the cavalry and baggage-cattle struggling, at every step, with the difficulties of the road, the temptation to plunder was too strong to be resisted ; and from many points of the mountain, above the road, they rushed down upon the Carthaginians.   The confusion was terrible ; for the track was so narrow, that the least crowding or disorder pushed the heavily-loaded baggage-cattle down the steep below ; and the horses, wounded by the barbarians' missiles, and plunging about wildly in their pain and terror, increased the mischief.

LXXXVII.

Louis the Just.

When Louis the XII. was raised to the throne, and many were apprehensive of punishment for the outrages they had committed against him under the government of La Dame de Beaujeu, when he was Duke of Orleans, he declared, 'That the King of France did not remember the injuries of the Duke of Orleans.' This was assuredly a noble sentiment, and worthy of a king, whose virtues deservedly acquired him the surname of the Just, and the title of Father of his Country. But it has not, I think, been observed, that the Emperor Hadrian had said nearly the same thing, though not in the same words. Shortly after his elevation[1] he met with one who had been among his chief enemies while a subject, and said, ' Fellow, you are safe, for I am Emperor.'

[1] 'after his elevation': say 'after he was made emperor.'

LXXXVIII.

The Tall Poppies.

Rome was at war with the city of Gabii, and as the city was not to be subdued by force, Tarquin tried treachery. His eldest son, Sextus Tarquinus, fled to Gabii, complaining of ill-usage by his father, and showing marks of a severe scourging. The Gabians believed him, and he was soon so much trusted by them as to have the whole command of the army, and manage everything in the city. Then he sent a messenger to his father to ask what he was to do next. When the messenger arrived, it chanced that Tarquin was walking through a corn-field. He made no answer in words, but with a switch cut off the heads of all the poppies and taller stalks of corn, and bade the messenger tell Sextus what he had seen. Sextus understood, and contrived to get all the chief men of Gabii exiled or put to death, and without them the city fell an easy prey to the Romans.

LXXXIX.

Cæsar refuses a Diadem.

Cæsar was in his chair, in his consular purple, wearing a wreath of bay, wrought in gold. The honour of the wreath was the only distinction which he had accepted from the Senate with pleasure. He retained a remnant of youthful vanity, and the twisted leaves concealed his baldness. Antony, his colleague in the consulship, approached with a diadem, and placed it on Cæsar's head, saying, 'The people give you this by my hand.' He answered in a loud voice 'that the Romans had no king but God,' and ordered that the diadem should be taken to the Capitol and placed on the statue of Jupiter. The crowd burst into an enthusiastic cheer ; and an inscription on a brass tablet recorded that the Roman people had offered Cæsar the crown by the hands of the consul, and that Cæsar had refused it.

XC.

Proposal to migrate to Veii.

When Veii fell, the commons of Rome took up the notion that it would be to the advantage of their city were half their number to go and dwell there. For they argued that[1] as Veii lay in a fertile country and was a well-built city, a moiety of the Roman people might in this way be enriched ; while, by reason of its vicinity to Rome, the management of civil affairs would in no degree be affected. To the senate, however, and the wiser among the citizens, the scheme appeared so rash and mischievous that they publicly declared that they would die sooner than consent to it. The controversy continuing, the commons grew

E

so inflamed against the senate that violence and blood-
shed must have ensued, had not the senate for their
protection put forward certain old and esteemed citizens,
respect for whom restrained the populace and put a stop
to their violence.

[1] Omit 'they argued that,' and simply put the passage into
Oratio Obliqua.

XCI.

Superiority of the Roman Infantry.

By many arguments and instances it can be clearly
established that in their military enterprises the Romans
set far more store on [1] their infantry than on their cavalry,
and trusted to the former to carry out all the chief objects
which their armies were meant to effect. Among many
other examples of this, we may notice the great battle
which they fought with the Latins near the lake Regillus,
where to steady their wavering ranks they made their
horsemen dismount, and renewing the combat on foot
obtained a victory. Here we see plainly that the Romans
had more confidence in themselves when they fought
on foot than when they fought on horseback The same
expedient was resorted to by them in many of their other
battles, and always in their sorest need they found it their
surest stay.

[1] For 'set more store on' say 'estimated at a higher value.'

XCII.

A Traitor Schoolmaster.

While the Romans were besieging the city of Falerii,
a schoolmaster contrived to lead the children of the

principal men of the city into the Roman camp. The novelty of such baseness surprised the Roman commander, and he so much abhorred it, that he immediately ordered the arms of the traitor to be tied, and giving each of the scholars a whip, bade them whip their master back to the city, and then return to their parents. The boys executed their task so well in this instance, that the wretch died under their blows as they entered the city. The generosity of the Romans touched the Faliscans so sensibly, that the next day they submitted themselves to the Romans on honourable terms.

XCIII.

The Retort Pointed.

One of the most pointed and severe satires that perhaps ever was uttered, was made by Professor Porson, a short time before his death. He was in a mixed company, among which were many eminent literary characters. A certain poet, who had a very high opinion of his own talents, was one of the company, and when the conversation turned on some of his productions, he began, as usual, to extol their merits. 'I will tell you, sir,' said Mr. Porson, 'what I think of your poetical works: they will be read when Shakespeare's and Milton's are forgotten (at this every eye was instantly upon the Professor); *but not till then !*'

XCIV.

Darest thou kill Caius Marius?

Then the council decided on his death, and sent a soldier to kill him; but the fierce old man stood glaring at him and said, 'Darest thou kill Caius Marius?' The man was so frightened that he ran away, crying out, 'I cannot kill Caius Marius.' The Senate of Minturnæ took this as an omen, and remembered besides that he had been a good friend to the Italians, so they conducted him through a sacred grove to the sea, and sent him off to Africa. On landing, he sent his son to ask shelter from one of the Numidian princes, and, while waiting for an answer, received a message from a Roman officer of low rank, forbidding his presence in Africa. He made no reply till the messenger pressed to know what to say to his master. Then the old man looked up, and sternly answered, 'Say that thou hast seen Caius Marius sitting in the ruins of Carthage.'

XCV.

Idleness breeds Corruption.

It is related that the Romans, after defeating on two different occasions armies of the Samnites sent to succour the Capuans, being desirous to return to Rome, left behind two legions to defend the Capuans, that the latter might not, from being altogether deprived of protection, once more become a prey to the Samnites. But these two legions, rotting in idleness, began to take such delight therein, that, forgetful of their country and the reverence due to the senate, they resolved to seize by violence the city they were bound to guard. For to them it seemed that the citizens of Capua were unworthy to enjoy advantages which they knew not how to defend. The Romans, however, getting timely notice of this design, at once met and defeated it.

XCVI.

Women in their right place.

When the battle had come to a standstill, and Romans and Sabines were facing each other and ready to begin the battle afresh, behold, the Sabine women rushed between the combatants, praying their fathers and brothers on the one side, and their husbands on the other, to end the bloody strife or to turn their arms against themselves, the cause of the slaughter. Then the chiefs on each side came forward and consulted together and made peace; and to put an end to all disputes they decided to make one people of the Romans and Sabines, and to live peaceably together as citizens of one town. Thus the Sabines remained in Rome, and the city was doubled in size and in the number of its inhabitants, and Titus Tatius, the Sabine king, reigned jointly with Romulus.

XCVII.

A Conscientious Boy.

A certain king, while walking to the city with one of his noblemen, happened to meet a boy who was collecting some sticks from the trees which grew here and there on the road-side. The king asked him why he hesitated to go into the neighbouring forest, where he would find abundance of wood. The boy replied that it was the king's forest, and that a proclamation had been made by the king that no one was to enter the wood either to collect wood or for any other purpose. The king laughed, and said that was of little consequence: no one would know whether he entered the wood or no. At this the boy marvelled, thinking the other must be a bad man for advising him to break the law. He therefore refused to act upon the suggestion made to him ; and added, 'Be ashamed of having attempted to make a poor boy do wrong.' The good-natured monarch was so far from being angry at the boy's impertinence that he sent for him the next day, and handsomely rewarded him.

XCVIII.

A Strict Father.

The following year, Manlius, in order to restore military discipline, ordered that no one should leave his station to fight. By chance his son had approached the camp of the enemy ; and the commander of the Latin cavalry, on recognising the consul's son, said ' Will you fight with me to show how much a Latin horseman excels a Roman ?' Forgetful of the general's order, the youth rushes to the conflict, and slays the Latin. Having collected the spoils, he returns to his father. The consul at once summons the troops, and addresses his son as follows : ' Since thou, my son, hast not obeyed the order of the consul, it behoves you to restore discipline by punishment. Go, lictor, bind him to the stake.' His head was then cut off by the lictor with an axe.

XCIX.

Hannibal encourages his Men ;

When Hannibal had arrived at the foot of the Alps, and saw that the soldiers feared the exceedingly difficult and

dangerous march, he summoned an assembly and addressed it as follows (use *Oratio Recta*) : ' It has grieved
me to see that your hearts are not filled with the courage
of my own, otherwise they would not be thus paralysed
by a sudden terror ; hearts, too, ever before undaunted.
For twenty years you have served victoriously ; you did
not leave Spain until all the countries embraced by the
two seas belonged to the Carthaginians : then, in indignation at the Roman demand that all who had besieged
Saguntum should be delivered up to them, you crossed
the Ebro, in order to blot out the Roman name from the
face of the earth, and to restore freedom to the world.'

C.

and bids them not fear the Alps.

' For what are the Alps but exceedingly high mountains ? There is no spot on earth that reaches up to the
sky, or is impassable to human daring and endurance. The
Alps are inhabited ; they produce and support living
creatures ; being passable to individuals, why do you
deem them impassable for an army ? To the soldier,
who carries with him only implements of war, nothing is
insurmountable. How great the danger, how infinite the
exertions you endured for eight months, in the struggle
to take Saguntum ! If you had had no more patience
then than you show now, you would never have taken
that city. Yield then the palm of courage to the Gauls
and Romans, or else resolve that the Tiber only shall be
the goal of your march. Once across the Alps and you
are in Italy. Will you go forward, my men, or will you
not ? '

CI.

The Language of Diplomacy.

During the war between England and Spain, in the time of Queen Elizabeth, commissioners on both sides were appointed to treat for peace. The Spanish Commissioners proposed that the negotiations should be carried on in the French tongue[1], observing sarcastically that 'the gentlemen of England could not be ignorant of the language of their fellow-subjects, their Queen being Queen of France as well as England.' 'Nay, in faith, gentlemen,' replied one of the English Commissioners, 'the French is too vulgar for a business of this importance; we will therefore, if you please, rather treat in Hebrew, for since your master styles himself King of Jerusalem, you must of course be as well skilled in Hebrew as we are in French.'

[1] 'To speak Latin, Greek,' &c. is *Latine, Graece, loqui.*

CII.

From Saguntum to Cannæ.

Hannibal marched from Spain with a large army into Italy across the Alps. When he had defeated the Romans at the river Trebia, he passed into Etruria. Flaminius, having been made consul by the Romans, thought that his soldiers would be cowards if they should allow Hannibal to do injury to the allies. Therefore having followed Hannibal, Flaminius was deceived by an ambush and perished with all his soldiers at Lake Thrasymenus. But the Romans, although alarmed by the victories of the

Carthaginians, were still desirous of fighting, and having despised the advice of Fabius, they made Varro general, a man of foolish rashness, but beloved by the common people.

CIII.

Cæsar crosses the Rhine.

Having finished the German War, Cæsar resolved for many reasons that he must cross the Rhine, a very broad, deep, and rapid river, which divides Gaul from Germany. His strongest reason was that, seeing the Germans were so easily induced to make inroads into Gaul, he wished to show them that the Romans hath both the power and the courage to carry the war into their country. Accordingly, he made the necessary preparations, and, considering it neither safe, nor suitable to his own dignity and that of the Roman people, to make the passage in boats, he caused a bridge to be constructed over the river, by which to transport his troops. Having placed a strong guard at either end of the bridge, he marched the rest of his army with all possible speed into the territories of the Sygambri.

CIV.

What is an Enemy?

A Chinese emperor was told that his enemies had raised an insurrection against him in one of his distant provinces. 'Come, then, my friends,' said he, 'follow me, and I promise you that I will quickly destroy them.' He marched against his rebellious subjects, but they submitted on his approach. All now expected that he would take the most signal revenge upon them. Instead of

doing so, however, the captives were treated with mild-
ness and humanity. 'How is this?' exclaimed his chief
minister; 'you gave your royal word that your enemies
should be destroyed; and, behold, you have pardoned
them all, and even bestowed favours upon some of them.'
'I promised,' replied the emperor, 'to destroy my
enemies, and I have kept my word; for see, they are
enemies no longer: I have made friends of them.'

CV.

Stratagem of Septimuleius.

After the Romans had nearly exhausted themselves
in fruitless efforts to break through the barbarian line,
their leader Septimuleius bethought himself of a stratagem
which seemed to offer a last hope of safety. He commanded a soldier to set fire to the baggage, in order to
excite the cupidity of the Germans and distract their attention from the battle. The night was already approaching, and no sooner did the barbarians behold the rapidly
spreading blaze, than they feared that the rich booty
would be torn from their grasp. They began therefore to
be less eager for the fight; whole ranks soon abandoned
the unprofitable toil of conflict, and rushed to the burning
pile. Hermann sought first by threats and then by
prayers to restrain his men. Let them only endure, he
said, a little longer: within an hour every man of the
hated race would meet with the death which he had
deserved, while they themselves would win eternal fame;
nor was it right that at such a moment they should think
of gain, while battling for the freedom of their fatherland.

CVI.

War with Veii.

Violent dissensions breaking out in Rome between the commons and the nobles, it appeared to the Veientines and Etruscans that now was their time to deal a fatal blow to the Roman supremacy. Accordingly, they assembled an army and invaded the territories of Rome. The senate sent Caius Manlius and Marcus Fabius to meet them, whose forces encamping close by the Veientines, the latter ceased not to reproach and vilify the Roman name with every sort of taunt and abuse, and so incensed the Romans by their unmeasured insolence that from being divided they became reconciled, and giving the enemy battle, broke and defeated them. The Veientines imagined that they could conquer the Romans by attacking them while they were at feud among themselves; but this very attack reunited the Romans and brought ruin on their assailants.

CVII.

A Consul insulted at Tarentum.

Now there were two towns close to one another in that part of the country, and it happened that a quarrel broke out amongst the inhabitants of one of them, called Tarentum. This furnished the excuse which the Romans wanted to conquer the country; so Postumius, having been elected to the consulship, was at once despatched by the senate with orders to complain of any wrong done to Roman citizens. Upon his arrival, he at once proceeded to the senate-house, and would have made a speech : but the people laughed at his bad Greek, asked him who it was that had brought him there, and told him to go home again.   Having endured this patiently for a long time, he was just going away when a rude fellow threw some dirt on him ; whereat the people only laughed the more.   Then Postumius, holding up his white gown stained with dirt for all to see, cried out in rage : ' Laugh on now, Tarentines, but you will soon have to weep : I tell you that this dirt will be washed white in your blood.'

CVIII.

The Tarentines call in Pyrrhus.

The Romans were reluctant to engage in another war at this time ; but, when they heard how Postumius had been treated by the people of Tarentum, they were so enraged that they resolved to take vengeance on that unfortunate city. Accordingly, next year, one of the consuls marched against the Tarentines with a large army.   The better classes were eager .to save the city by timely submission ; but the mass of the people, hating the Romans, were ready to do or suffer anything rather than yield. After considering what was the best course to pursue in such perilous circumstances, it was finally decided by the citizens of Tarentum to summon to their assistance Pyrrhus, the celebrated King of Epirus.   This prince, who was not only an excellent general but also a bold and experienced ruler, had recently failed in his attempt to make himself master of Macedonia, and he gladly acceded to the request of the Tarentines, in the hope that, having defeated the Romans, he might conquer the whole of Italy.

CIX.

Death of Pompey.

A great part of the voyage was accomplished, when the deathlike silence which reigned in the ship began to fill Pompey with uneasiness; he attempted however to conceal his fear by talking. So turning to Septimius, he said, 'If I mistake not, my friend, your face is known to me; were we not once comrades in the field?' Septimius nodded without speaking; and the same silence as before prevailed, until they reached the shore. The moment Pompey took the hand of his freedman Philippus, in order to rise with the greater ease, Septimius ran him through the body with his sword from behind. Seeing that he could not save his life, Pompey drew his toga over his face, and endured every stab that was inflicted upon him with the greatest fortitude, until he fell lifeless on the shore.

CX.

Presence of Mind.

The orator Domitius was once in great danger from an inscription which he had put upon a statue erected by him in honour of Caligula, wherein he had declared that that prince was a second time consul at the age of twenty-seven. This he intended as an encomium; but Caligula, taking it as a sarcasm upon his youth, and his infringement of the laws, raised a process against him, and pleaded himself in person. Instead of making a defence, Domitius repeated part of the emperor's speech with the highest marks of admiration, after which he fell upon his knees, and begging pardon, declared that he dreaded more the eloquence of Caligula than his imperial power. This piece of flattery succeeded so well, that the emperor not only pardoned, but also raised him to the consulship.

CXI.

March to Mount Algidus.

Then the master of the people and the master of the horse went together into the forum, and bade every man to shut up his booth, and stopped all causes at law, and gave an order that none should look to his own affairs till the consul and his army were delivered from the enemy. They ordered also that every man who was of military age should be ready in the Field of Mars before sunset, bringing with him victuals for five days, and twelve stakes ; and the older men dressed the victuals for the soldiers, whilst the soldiers cut their stakes where they would, without any hindrance. So the army was ready at the time appointed, and they marched forth with such haste, that ere the night was half spent they came to Algidus.

CXII.

Hanno's Prudent Advice.

After routing the Romans at Cannæ, Hannibal sent messengers to Carthage to announce his victory, and to ask support. A debate arising in the Carthaginian senate as to what was to be done, Hanno, an aged and wise citizen, advised that they should prudently take advantage of their victory to make peace with the Romans, while as conquerors they might have it on favourable terms, and

not wait to make it after a defeat; they should show the
Romans that they were strong enough to fight them, but
not to peril the victory they had won in the hope of winning a greater. This advice was not followed by the
Carthaginian senate, but its wisdom was well seen later,
when the opportunity to act upon it was gone.

CXIII.

Coriolanus in Exile.

Coriolanus, having left Rome, retired to the country of
the Volsci. Here Attius Tullius, a distinguished man and
bitter enemy to the Romans, received him kindly into his
house, and formed a strong friendship with him. The
Volscians hoped that he would assist them in their wars.
Not long afterwards, war was declared between them and
the Romans, and having divided their army into two
parts, they gave one to Coriolanus, and the other to
Attius. Coriolanus got possession of many cities, some
of which belonged to the Romans, and some to the Latins.
At length he approached Rome, and pitched his camp
five miles from the city. The plebeians were unwilling
to take up arms, and the senate sent ambassadors to the
camp to sue for peace.

CXIV.

P. Decius Mus devotes himself.

Decius, having resolved to devote himself, called out to
Manlius with a loud voice, and demanded of him how to
devote himself and what form of words he should use.
By his directions, therefore, being clothed in a long robe,

his head covered, and his arms stretched forward, standing upon a javelin, he devoted himself to the gods for the safety of Rome. Then arming himself, and mounting his horse, he rode furiously into the midst of the enemy, striking terror wherever he came, till he fell covered with wounds. The Roman army considered this deed as an omen of success ; and having put the Latins to flight, they pursued them with so great slaughter that scarcely a fourth part of them escaped.

CXV.

C. Fabricius and the Elephant.

The Romans wanted to treat about the prisoners Pyrrhus had taken, so they sent Caius Fabricius to the Greek camp for the purpose. Kineas reported him to be a man of no wealth, but esteemed as a good soldier and an honest man. Pyrrhus tried to make him take large presents, but nothing would Fabricius touch ; then, in the hope of alarming him, in the middle of a conversation one side of the tent suddenly fell, and disclosed the biggest of all the elephants, who waved his trunk over Fabricius and trumpeted frightfully. The Roman quietly turned round and smiled, as he said to the king, ' I am no more moved by your great beast than by your gold.' At supper there was a conversation on Greek philosophy, of which the Romans as yet knew nothing. When the doctrine of Epicurus was mentioned, that man's life was given to be spent in the pursuit of joy, Fabricius greatly amused the company by crying out, ' O Hercules ! grant that the Greeks may be heartily of this mind so long as we have to fight with them.'

CXVI.

A Consul leads the Opposition.

Thereupon the consul declared that he, for one, would never consent to the passing of such a measure. The question was too important to be disposed of in so summary a manner. If the object of the measure was no greater than could be inferred from the speeches of its supporters, why did they not limit its operation to the particular circumstances of time and place in which the abuses complained of had occurred? If the bill were passed in its present shape, it would be impossible for any man engaged in the most ordinary mercantile transaction to secure himself from a charge of fraud.

CXVII.

Pythias and Damon.

It was during the reign of Dionysius of Syracuse, when all the noblest spirits were imprisoned or put to death, that a certain Pythagorean philosopher, called Pythias, amongst others, incurred the tyrant's resentment. Sentenced to death, and having large properties in Greece, he entreated to be allowed to return thither to arrange his affairs. Upon the tyrant's laughing his request to scorn, Pythias told him he had a friend called Damon who would stand surety for him, and who had promised he would die in his stead should he himself not return. Dionysius at last consented; time went on; no Pythias appeared; but Damon continued serene and content, his trust in his friend so perfect that he did not even grieve because he had to die for a faithless friend. At length the

F

fatal hour arrived: a few minutes more, and Damon would without doubt have been executed, had not Pythias appeared at that very moment, and embraced his friend, expressing great joy that he had arrived in time.

CXVIII.

Trajan the Just.

The emperor Trajan would never suffer any one to be condemned upon suspicion, however strong and well grounded ; saying it was better that a thousand criminals should escape unpunished, than that one innocent person be condemned.   When he appointed Subarranus Captain of his Guards, and presented him according to custom with a drawn sword, the badge of his office, he used these memorable words : 'Employ this sword for me, but if I deserve it, turn it against me.'   Nor would he allow his freedmen any share in the administration. Some persons having a suit with one of them of the name of Eurythmus, seemed to fear the influence of the imperial freedman ; but Trajan assured them that the cause should be decided according to the strictest law of justice, adding, 'For neither is he Polycletus, nor I Nero.' Polycletus, it will be recollected, was the freedman of Nero, and as infamous as his master for rapine and injustice.

CXIX.

Alexandria founded.

When Alexander the Great thought to add to his renown by founding a city, Dinocrates the architect advised him to build it on Mount Athos ; which not only offered a strong position, but could be so handled that the city built there might present the semblance of the human form, which would be a thing strange and striking, and worthy of so great a monarch. But on Alexander asking how the inhabitants were to live, Dinocrates answered that he had not thought of that. Whereupon Alexander laughed, and leaving Mount Athos as it stood, built Alexandria; where the fruitfulness of the soil, and the vicinity of the Nile and the sea, might attract many to take up their abode.

CXX.

Cæsar crushes the Veneti.

The naval battle between the forces of Cæsar and the Veneti lasted from the fourth hour till sundown, and although the barbarians showed the greatest possible valour, the superior skill of the Romans won the day. Having lost their bravest warriors and all their ships, the Veneti were so completely crushed that they were unable to resist any longer, and they surrendered themselves and their possessions to Cæsar. He was by nature of a merciful disposition, and he would have been willing to pardon the Veneti, if they had not shown themselves to be cruel and treacherous. On this occasion he deemed it advisable to use severity, in order that the barbarians might learn for the future not to injure the ambassadors of the Roman people. Accordingly the whole of the senate was put to death, and the rest of the tribe sold into slavery.

CXXI.

After Hastings.

Meanwhile Duke William went back to Hastings, leaving a garrison in the fort which he had built there. He waited there some days thinking that men would come in and bow to him, but none came. So he set out to win the land bit by bit. First he went to Romney. It seems that some of his people had been there already ; perhaps one or more of the ships had gone astray and got on shore there. At all events there had been a fight between some of his men and the men of Romney, in which many were killed on both sides, but in the end the English had driven the Frenchmen away. So Duke William now, we are told, took from the men of Romney what penalty or satisfaction he chose for the men whom they had killed, as if he had been making them pay a fine. I suppose this means that he put them all to death.

CXXII.

How to get a majority.

Clearchus, tyrant of Heraclea, being in exile, it so happened that on a feud arising between the commons and the nobles of that city, the. latter, perceiving they were weaker than their adversaries, began to look with favour on Clearchus, and conspiring with him, in opposition to the popular voice, recalled him to Heraclea and deprived the people of their freedom. Clearchus, finding himself thus placed between the arrogance of the nobles, whom he could in no way either satisfy or correct, and the fury of the people, who could not put up with the loss of their freedom, resolved to rid himself at one stroke of the harassment of the nobles, and recommend himself to the people. Wherefore, watching his opportunity, he caused all the nobles to be put to death, and thus satisfied the popular desire for vengeance.

CXXIII.

A True General.

His influence over his men was supreme. He knew just what his troops could do, and would do, and when. He led them frequently in person and they never failed to follow. Everyone remembers the occasion when he changed the whole course of a battle by his single presence. But he possessed the same power with individuals as with masses. A soldier, wounded under his eyes, stumbled, and was falling to the rear, but the General cried : ' Never mind, my man, there's no harm done ; ' and the soldier went on till he dropped dead on the field.

CXXIV.

The Dangers of Peace.

After subduing Africa and Asia, and reducing nearly the whole of Greece to submission, the Romans became perfectly assured of their freedom, and seemed to themselves no longer to have any enemy to fear. But this security and the weakness of their adversaries led them, in conferring the consulship, no longer to look to merit, but only to favour, selecting for the office those who knew best how to pay court to them, not those who knew best how to vanquish their enemies. And afterwards, instead of selecting those who were best liked, they came to select those who had most influence ; and in this way, from the imperfection of their institutions, good men came to be wholly excluded.

CXXV.

Claverhouse, Viscount Dundee.

Dundee was obliged continually to shift his quarters by prodigious marches, in order to avoid or harass his enemy's army, or to obtain provisions; the first messenger of his approach was generally his army in sight: the first intelligence of his retreat brought accounts that he was already out of the enemy's reach. If any good thing was brought him to eat, he sent it to a faint or sick soldier; if a soldier was weary, he would offer to carry his arms. It was one of his maxims, that no general should fight with an irregular army unless he was acquainted with every man he commanded. Yet, with these habits of familiarity, the severity of his discipline was dreadful; the only punishment he inflicted was death. 'All other punishments,' he said, 'disgraced a gentleman, and all who were with him were of that rank; but death was a relief from the consciousness of crimes.'

CXXVI.

Harold's rash Advance.

Harold hastened by quick marches to reach this new invader; but though he was reinforced at London and other places with fresh troops, he found himself also weakened by the desertion of his old soldiers, who from fatigue, and discontent at Harold's refusing to divide the Norwegian spoil among them, secretly withdrew from their colours. His brother Gurth, a man of bravery and conduct, began to entertain apprehensions of the event, and remonstrated with the king that it would be better policy to prolong the war; urging that, if the enemy were harassed with small skirmishes, straitened in provisions, and fatigued with the bad weather and deep roads during the winter season, which was approaching, they must fall an easy and a bloodless prey.

CXXVII.

How a Philosopher uses Victory.

When Dio had seized the town of Syracuse, and his friends exhorted him to give the persons and property of his enemies over to the fury of the soldiery, he answered as follows (*Oratio Obliqua*): 'All other generals care for nothing but the business of war and the practice of arms: I have devoted myself for many years to the study of philosophy, and think more of conquering anger, hatred, and revenge than of vanquishing an enemy. This is a victory which is won not by a courteous attitude towards friends, but by a spirit of forgiveness and gentleness towards one's enemies. I believe I shall gain more by mercy than by rigour.'

CXXVIII.

A Candid Courtier.

It is said that Dionysius, tyrant of Syracuse, was a fluent writer of verse, and that he prided himself more on his literary achievements than on his military successes. The poet Philoxenus, however, who had heard some of these verses read aloud, frankly avowed that he entertained a poor opinion of them. The result was that he was ordered off to the stone quarries, which served as a kind of public prison at Syracuse. He was subsequently pardoned, and again admitted to the king's table. The tyrant once more read a trifle which he had composed to Philoxenus, and handing him the poem asked him to give his opinion of it. 'Surely,' he thought, 'the fear of the prison will make him give me a word of praise.' Philoxenus made no answer, but calling the officers, requested them to take him straight off to the stone quarries. Nor did his wit and courage meet with punishment.

CXXIX.

Francis I. surprises Italy.

When Francis I. of France in the year 1515 resolved on invading Italy in order to recover the province of Lombardy, those hostile to his attempt looked mainly to the Swiss, who it was hoped would stop him in passing through their mountains. But this hope was disappointed by the event. For leaving on one side two or three defiles which were guarded by the Swiss, the king advanced by another unknown pass, and was in Italy and upon his enemies before they knew. Whereupon they fled terror-stricken into Milan; while the whole population of Lombardy, finding themselves deceived in their expectation that the French would be detained in the mountains, went over to their side.

CXXX.

An Infallible Storm-Gauge.

A Jesuit, who had been particularly recommended to the captain of a vessel, was sailing from France to America. The captain, who saw that a storm was approaching, said to him, 'Father, you are not accustomed to the rolling of a vessel, you had better get down as fast as possible into the hold. As long as you hear the sailors swearing and blaspheming, you may be assured that there are good hopes: but if you should hear them embracing and re-conciling themselves to each other, you may make up your accounts with heaven.' As the storm increased, the Jesuit, from time to time, dispatched his companion to the hatchway to see how matters went on deck. 'Alas! Father,' said he, returning, 'all is lost, the sailors are swearing like demoniacs ; their very blasphemies are enough to sink the vessel.'—'Oh! heaven be praised,' said the Jesuit, 'then all is well.'

CXXXI.

Leather Money.

Lycurgus, the founder of the Spartan Republic, did all he could to prevent intercourse with strangers ; with which object, besides refusing these the right to marry, the right of citizenship, and all such other social rights as induce men to become members of a community, he ordained that in this republic of his the only money current should be of leather, so that none might be tempted to repair thither to trade or to carry on any art. Under such circumstances the number of the inhabitants of that State could never much increase. For as all our actions imitate nature, and it is not possible that a puny stem should carry a great branch, so a small republic can-not assume control over cities or countries stronger than herself; or, doing so, will resemble the tree whose boughs being greater than its trunk, are supported with difficulty, and snapped by every gust of wind.

CXXXII.

Murder will out.

In the dead of night his friend appeared to him in his sleep and begged him for help against the host, who was about to murder him. He rose, but seeing nothing, lay down again. Again the vision of his friend presented itself, praying him that, since he had not come to his aid while alive, he should at any rate not suffer his death to be unavenged: he related that he had been murdered by the host and cast upon a cart, and that his body had been covered with manure. He besought him to be present next morning early at the city gate, before the cart left the town. Deeply agitated by the vision, he did as he was bidden, and on seeing a cart there asked the driver what was in it; the latter fled in terror, and beneath the heap of manure the dead body was discovered.

CXXXIII.

A Sentinel surprised.

On the night after the dreadful battle of Arcola, Buonaparte disguised himself in the dress of an inferior officer, and traversed the camp. In the course of his round he discovered a sentinel leaning on the butt end of his musket, in a profound sleep. Buonaparte, taking the musket from under him, placed his head gently on the ground and kept watch for two hours in his stead; at the end of which the regular guard came to relieve him. On awakening, the soldier was at first astonished; but when he recognised the commander-in-chief, his astonishment was converted into terror. 'The General!' he exclaimed;

'I am then undone.' Buonaparte, with the utmost gentleness, replied, 'Not so, fellow soldier; recover yourself;
after so much fatigue, a brave man like you may be
allowed for a while to sleep; but, in future, choose your
time better.'

CXXXIV.

Military Discipline.

In the course of a war against Austria, Frederick the
Great, afraid lest his place of encampment should be
discovered to the enemy, had ordered that every light
should be put out by a certain hour. Anyone disobeying
the order was to be put to death. To find out whether
commands were being obeyed, the king one night passed
all through the camp ; and on seeing a light burning in
one of the tents, he pushed aside the curtain which served
for a door, and went in. He there found an officer seated
at a table, about to seal a letter which he had just written.
The king sternly asked why he had disobeyed his order :
the officer replied that he had been writing a short letter,
in anticipation of next day's battle, to his wife. 'By
all means despatch your letter,' said the King ; 'but before
closing it, add the following words: "By the time you
receive this letter, I shall be put to death for disobeying
the king's commands."'

CXXXV.

Trajan the Just.

As Trajan was once setting out for Rome, at the head
of a numerous army, to make war in Wallachia, he was
suddenly accosted by a woman, who called out in a
pathetic but bold tone, 'To Trajan I appeal for justice !'
Although the emperor was pressed by the affairs of a most

urgent war, he instantly stopped, and alighting from his horse, heard the suppliant state the cause of her complaint.   She was a poor widow, and had been left with an only son, who had been foully murdered; she had sued for justice on his murderers, but had been unable to obtain it.   Trajan, having satisfied himself of the truth of her statements, decreed her on the spot the satisfaction which she demanded, and sent the mourner away comforted.   So much was this action admired, that it was afterwards represented on the pillar erected to Trajan's memory, as one of the most resplendent instances of his goodness.

CXXXVI.

Wealth is not always Strength.

We are told that Crœsus, king of Lydia, after showing Solon the Athenian much besides, at last displayed to him the boundless riches of his treasure-house, and asked him what he thought of his power.   Whereupon Solon answered that he thought him no whit more powerful in respect of these treasures, for as war is made with iron and not with gold, another coming with more iron might carry off his gold.   Again, we hear how, after the death of Alexander the Great, a tribe of Gauls, passing through Greece on their way into Asia, sent envoys to the King of Macedonia to treat for terms of accord ; when the king, to dismay them by a display of his resources, showed them great store of gold and silver.   But these barbarians, when they saw all this wealth, were so anxious to possess it, that though before they had looked on peace as settled, they broke off the negotiations ; and thus the king was ruined by those very treasures he had amassed for his defence.

CXXXVII.

The King hears of Becket's Death.

The king had gone to an upland town called Argenton. The night before the news arrived (so ran the story), an aged inhabitant of Argenton was startled in his sleep by a scream rising as if from the ground, and forming itself into these portentous words : 'Behold, my blood cries from the earth more loudly than the blood of righteous Abel, who was killed at the beginning of the world.' The old man, on the following day, was discussing with his friend what this could mean, when suddenly the tidings arrived that Becket had been slain at Canterbury. When the King heard it, he instantly shut himself up for three days, refused all food except milk, vented his grief in frantic lamentations, and called God to witness that he was in no way responsible for the Archbishop's death, unless that he loved him too little. He continued in this solitude for five weeks, neither riding nor transacting public business, but exclaiming again and again, 'Alas ! alas ! that it ever happened !'

CXXXVIII.

Wallenstein.

Wallenstein had no suspicion of the conspiracy which was being formed against his life. In the full confidence that his indulgence and benevolence had won over all his enemies, he had dismissed his body-guard and retired to the privacy of the Bürgermeister's house, where he spent a short time in peace and quiet. But his energetic spirit could not rest content with the eminence which his successful career had already reached ; he therefore determined, in his eagerness to have a hand in some great and important enterprise, to renew the war on his own account; and commenced making the necessary preparations. He sent sixteen thousand men into Saxony, and took all means to secure his position in Austria during his absence. His friends, convinced that he was aiming at the throne, thought that an opportunity had now come of gaining it for him.

CXXXIX.

The Child Father to the Man.

Wordsworth says that 'the child is father to the man;' and the following anecdote of Peter Gassendi, the great French astronomer, shews that in his case at least the saying came true. Even in his childhood he was fond of watching the movements of the heavenly bodies; he would often rise out of his bed by night to see the moon and stars moving across the sky. One evening, when Peter was walking with two or three companions about the same age as himself, the full moon was shining in the sky, and a great many thin clouds were drifting before the wind. The other boys argued that it was the clouds that stood still, and that it was the moon that moved. Young Peter insisted that it was not the moon that moved, but that the clouds were being driven by the wind. The dispute was kept up for a good while. At last Peter took his companions under a tree, and bade them look up at the moon through the branches. They now saw that the moon seemed to stand still between the same leaves and branches, while the clouds passed quickly over the tree and disappeared from their view. They thus saw that Peter was in the right, and that they were entirely in the wrong.

CXL.

A Navy built in Sixty Days.

The quinquereme was not merely twice as large as a trireme, but was of a different build and construction. It was necessary, therefore, to obtain either shipwrights or a model from some nation to which such moving castles had been long familiar. Here chance was on the side of the Romans. A Carthaginian quinquereme had run ashore on the coast of Bruttium two or three years before, and had fallen into the hands of the Romans. This served as a model; and it is asserted by more than one writer that within sixty days a growing wood was felled and transformed into a fleet of a hundred ships of the line and twenty triremes. The next difficulty was to find men for the fleet, and when they had been found, to train them for their duties.

CXLI.

Defeat turned into Victory.

The battle raged with great fury, and victory was already doubtful, when the Rája of Anhalwára arrived with a strong reinforcement to the Hindùs. This unexpected addition to their enemies so dispirited the Mussulmans that they began to waver, when Mahmud, who had prostrated himself to implore the divine assistance, leaped upon his horse, and cheered his troops with such energy, that, ashamed to abandon a king under whom they had so often fought and bled, they, with one accord, gave a loud shout, and rushed forwards with an impetuosity which could no longer be withstood. Five thousand

Hindùs lay dead after the charge; and so complete was the rout of their army, that the garrison gave up all hopes of further defence, and, breaking out to the number of four thousand men, made their way to their boats; and, though not without considerable loss, succeeded in escaping by sea.

CXLII.

Cross Questions.

Frederick the Great, king of Prussia, paid so much attention to his regiments of guards, that he knew personally every one of his soldiers. Whenever he saw a new face in the ranks, he invariably put the following three questions, generally in the same order: 'How old are you?' 'How long have you been in the army?' 'Have you received your pay and your arms?' It happened that a young Frenchman, who did not understand German, enlisted into the Prussian service. The comrades of the young recruit taught him the answers, in case he should be asked the questions. A few days after, Frederick discovered the novice, and proceeded to question him. Unfortunately, on this occasion, he began with the second question: 'How long have you been in the army?' 'Twenty-one years, sire!' replied the Frenchman. The king continued: 'How old are you, then?' 'Six months, sire!' was the reply. 'Upon my word,' said Frederick, 'either you or I must be a fool.' 'Both regularly, sire!' replied the soldier. The king saw the man's mistake at once; and only advised him to learn German as quickly as possible.

CXLIII.

Either Side better than no Side.

After Hieronymus, the Syracusan tyrant, was put to death, there being at that time a great war between the Romans and the Carthaginians, the citizens of Syracuse fell to disputing among themselves with which nation they should take part. And so fierce grew the controversy, that no course could be agreed on, and they took part with neither; until Apollonides, one of the foremost of the Syracusan citizens, told them in a speech replete with wisdom, that neither those who inclined to hold by the Romans, nor those who chose rather to side with the Carthaginians, were deserving of blame; but that what was utterly to be condemned was doubt and delay in taking one side or other. For from such uncertainty he clearly foresaw the ruin of their republic; whereas, by taking a decided course, whatever it might be, some good might come.

CXLIV.

Cicero's proudest Moment.

He descended into the Forum, and returned to his own house. The people thronged round him with acclaiming shouts, and it was perhaps then that Cato, as we are told by Appian, hailed him father of his country. 'A bright light,' says Plutarch, 'shone through the streets from the lamps and torches set up at the doors, and the women showed lights from the tops of the houses in honour of Cicero, and to behold him returning with a splendid train of the principal citizens.' He always looked back to this as the proudest moment of his life, and yet it was

G

the beginning of infinite sorrow and trouble to him, for, as we shall see, his exile from Rome and the ruin of his fortunes may be distinctly traced to his conduct on this day. He had put to death Roman citizens without a trial ; and this was the accusation which was henceforth to be the watchword of his enemies, and to overshadow the rest of his life.

CXLV.

The English rally after Defeat.

Night was now coming on, and, under cover of the darkness, the light-armed took to flight. Some fled on foot, some on the horses which had carried the fallen leaders to the battle. The Normans pursued, and, as in an earlier stage of the day, the fleeing English found means to take their revenge on their conquerors. On the north side of the hill the descent is steep, almost precipitous, the ground is irregular and marshy. No place could be less suited for horsemen unaccustomed to the country to pursue, even by daylight, light-armed foot, to many of whom every step of ground was familiar. In the darkness or imperfect light of the evening, their case was still more hopeless than in the similar case, earlier in the day. In the ardour of pursuit horse and man fell head foremost over the steep, where they were crushed by the fall, smothered in the morass, or slain outright by the swords and clubs of the English.

CXLVI.

Raleigh and Queen Elizabeth.

The people mourned bitterly over their beloved prince. They thought that he had been poisoned. Suspicions were entertained against different men about the court, and these were even shared by the queen. The queen seems still to have remained Raleigh's friend, but could do nothing for him. He had addressed her a letter before, asking her to exert herself to obtain his liberation, that he might assist in the plantation of his former colony of Virginia. He had heard with interest of the new attempt to plant this colony, and of the difficulties through which it had to struggle, till at last it was placed on a secure footing. He must have longed to be able to aid in carrying on the work which he had himself first begun. 'I do still humbly beseech your majesty,' he writes to the queen, ' that I may rather die in serving my queen and my country than perish here.'

CXLVII.

Scythian Diplomacy.

The Scythian princes despatched a herald to the Persian camp with presents for the king. These were a bird, a mouse, a frog, and five arrows. The Persians asked the bearer to tell them what these gifts might mean ; but he made answer that he had no orders save to deliver them and to return again with all speed. If the Persians were wise, he added, they would find out the meaning for themselves. So when they heard this, they held a council to consider the matter. Darius gave it as his opinion that the Scythians intended a surrender of themselves and all their country, both land and water, into his hands. This he conceived to be the meaning of the gifts, because the mouse is an inhabitant of the earth and eats the same food as man, while the frog passes his life in the water; the bird bears a great resemblance to the horse, and the five arrows might signify the surrender of all their power.

To the explanation of Darius, Gobryas offered another, which was as follows : 'Unless, Persians, ye can turn into birds, and fly up into the sky, or become mice and burrow underground, or make yourselves frogs and take refuge in the fens, ye will never make your escape from this land, but die pierced by our arrows.'

CXLVIII.

Death of Caracalla.

The Emperor Caracalla, being with his armies in Mesopotamia, had with him Macrinus, who was more of a statesman than a soldier, as his prefect. But because princes who are not themselves good are always afraid lest others treat them as they deserve, Caracalla wrote to his friend Maternianus in Rome to learn from the astrologers whether any man had ambitious designs upon the empire, and to send him word. Maternianus, accordingly, wrote back that such designs were entertained by Macrinus. But this letter, ere it reached the emperor, fell into the hands of Macrinus, who, seeing when he read it that he must either put Caracalla to death before further letters arrived from Rome, or else die himself, committed the business to a centurion, named Martialis, whom he trusted, and whose brother had been slain by Caracalla a few days before, who succeeded in killing the emperor.

CXLIX.

Alexander succeeds to Empire.

Alexander, the son of Philip, was just twenty years of age at the death of his father ; and those who had admired the talents of the father believed that his great projects would die with him. At Athens the news awakened the wildest delight : Demosthenes appeared in the assembly, crowned with flowers. But the friends of liberty and of Greece cherished empty hopes. There is an idle story that the temple of Diana at Ephesus was burned to the ground on the very day that Alexander was born, and although the story is clearly false, and invented to reflect glory on the hero (a man named Erostratus having kindled the fire), it shows how far the son of Philip rose above his sire. Alexander, the pupil of Aristotle, surpassed perhaps every one that ever existed in the endowments that fit a man to be a conqueror.

CL.

Thermopylæ.

Having advanced thus far without hindrance, Xerxes now heard with surprise that a handful of Greeks made a show as if they thought of intercepting his march. He waited at the opening of the mountains four days, to give them time to recover their senses. But in vain ; he then sent a message to Leonidas, commanding him to quit the post he had chosen, and deliver up his arms ; to which Leonidas with Spartan brevity replied, 'Come and take them.' Xerxes at last became convinced that nothing but force would move this heroic band. He believed, however, that a show of force would be sufficient for the purpose, and ordered the Medes to go and bring the defenders of the pass, with Leonidas their chief, alive into his presence. The Medes met with a different reception from what their sovereign expected, and were driven back with disgrace.

CLI.

Hannibal in Italy.

From farthest Spain he had come into Italy, he had wasted the whole country of the Romans and their allies with fire and sword for more than six years, had slain more of their citizens than were now alive to bear arms against him, and at last he was shutting them up within their city, and riding freely under their walls, while none dared meet him in the field. If anything of disappointment depressed his mind at that instant; if he felt that Rome's strength was not broken, nor the spirit of her people quelled, that his own fortune was wavering, and that his last effort had been made, and made in vain; yet thinking where he was, and of the shame and loss which his presence was causing to his enemies, he must have wished that his father could have lived to see that day, and must have thanked the gods of his country that they had enabled him so fully to perform his vow.

Arnold.

CLII.

Napoleon against the World.

On the Rhine had Napoleon paused, facing the waves of avenging hosts. He had lifted up his finger, like King Canute of old, and he had said: 'Thus far and no farther.' Yet the waves still roared, and the tide still rose. Would he be submerged? Would his evil genius fail him at last? These were the supreme questions of that autumn. The whole world was against him; nay, the world, and the sea, and the sky! Yet he had overcome these before; he might overcome them again. His word was still a power, his presence an inspiration. He might emerge again, and then? There was little left for the stabbed and bleeding earth but to die; for, alas! she could bear no more.

CLIII.

How Law began.

These diversities in the form of Government spring up among men by chance. For in the beginning of the world, its inhabitants, being few in number, for a time lived scattered after the fashion of beasts; but afterwards, as they increased and multiplied, gathered themselves into societies, and, the better to protect themselves, began to seek who among them was the strongest and of the highest courage, to whom, making him their head, they rendered obedience. Next arose the knowledge of such things as are honourable and good, as opposed to those which are bad and shameful. For observing that when a man wronged his benefactor, hatred was universally felt for the one and sympathy for the other, and reflecting that the wrongs they saw done to others might be done to themselves, they resorted to making laws and fixing punishments against any who should transgress them; and in this way grew the recognition of Justice. Whence it came that afterwards, in choosing their rulers, men no longer looked about for the strongest, but for him who was the most prudent and the most just.

CLIV.

How Argyle was taken.

All thought of prosecuting the war was at an end; the chiefs of the expedition took flight in different directions. Hume reached the Continent in safety. Argyle hoped to find a secure asylum under the roof of one of his old servants, who lived near Kilpatrick. But this hope was disappointed, and he was forced to cross the Clyde. Assuming the dress of a peasant, he journeyed, with a single trusted friend, as far as Inchinnan. At this point two streams, the Black and the White Cart, mingle before they join the Clyde. The ford was guarded by a party of soldiers. Some questions were asked: Argyle's companion tried to draw suspicion on himself to save his friend. But the questioners, not believing that Argyle was only a simple peasant, laid hands upon him. He broke loose, and sprang into the water. He was instantly chased. After standing at bay for a short time against five assailants, he was struck down with a broad-sword and secured.

CLV.

Argyle's Last Sleep.

So completely had religious faith composed his spirits, that on the very day on which he was to die he dined with appetite, and lay down afterwards, as was his wont, to take a few hours of peaceful slumber, in order that his mind and body might be in full vigour when the fatal moment should arrive. Just then, one of the nobles who had formerly been Argyle's friend came to the castle, and asked whether he could be allowed to see the earl. He was informed that he was asleep. Believing this to be a

subterfuge, he forced his way in : the door was opened,
and there lay Argyle on the bed, sleeping, in his irons,
the sleep of infancy. He turned away sick at heart, fled
from the castle, and rushing to his own house, flung himself on a couch. His wife thought that he was ill, and
begged him to take some wine. ' No, no,' he cried, ' that
will do me no good.' She then prayed him to tell her
what had disturbed him : ' I have seen Argyle,' he said,
' within an hour of his death sleeping as sweetly as a
child.'

CLVI.

The True Policy for Princes.

Any one, therefore, who undertakes to control a people,
either as their prince or as the head of a commonwealth,
and does not make sure work with all who are hostile to
his new institutions, founds a government which cannot
last long. Undoubtedly those princes are to be reckoned
unhappy, who, to secure their position, are forced to advance by unusual and irregular paths, and with the people
for their enemies. For while he who has to deal with a
few adversaries only, can easily and without much or
serious difficulty secure himself, he who has an entire
people against him can never feel safe ; and the greater
the severity he uses, the weaker his authority becomes ;
so that his best course is to strive to make the people his
friends.

CLVII.

' The Ides of March are come ;'

The house was full. The conspirators were in their
places with their daggers ready. Attendants came in to
remove Cæsar's chair. It was announced that he was

not coming. Delay might be fatal. They conjectured that he already suspected something. A day's respite, and all might be discovered. Decimus Brutus, whom it was impossible for him to distrust, went to entreat his attendance, giving reasons to which he knew that Cæsar would listen, unless the plot had been actually betrayed. It was now eleven in the forenoon. Cæsar shook off his uneasiness, and rose to go. As he crossed the hall, his statue fell, and shivered on the stones. As he still passed on, a stranger thrust a scroll into his hand, and begged him to read it on the spot. It contained a list of the conspirators, with a clear account of the plot. He supposed it to be a petition, and placed it carelessly among his other papers. The fate of the Empire hung upon a thread, but the thread was not yet broken.

CLVIII.

'*But they are not passed.*'

As he was carried to the senate house in a litter, a man gave him a writing and begged him to read it instantly; but he kept it rolled in his hand without looking. As he went up the steps he said to the augur Spurius, 'The Ides of March are come.' 'Yes, Cæsar,' was the answer, 'but they are not passed.' A few steps further on, one of the conspirators met him with a petition, and the others joined in it, clinging to his robe and his neck, till another caught his toga, and pulled it over his arms, and then the first blow was struck with a dagger. Cæsar struggled at first as all fifteen tried to strike at him, but when he saw the hand uplifted of his treacherous friend Decimus, he exclaimed, 'Et tu, Brute!' drew his toga over his head, and fell dead at the foot of the statue of Pompeius.

CLIX.

Consternation at the Murder of Cæsar.

Waving his dagger dripping with Cæsar's blood, Brutus shouted to Cicero by name, congratulating him that liberty was restored. The Senate rose with shrieks and confusion, and rushed into the Forum. The crowd outside caught the words that Cæsar was dead, and scattered to their houses. Antony, guessing that those who had killed Cæsar would not spare himself, hurried off into concealment. The murderers, bleeding some of them from wounds which they had given one another in their eagerness, followed, crying that the tyrant was dead, and that Rome was free ; and the body of the great Cæsar was left alone in the house where a few weeks before Cicero told him that he was so necessary to his country that every senator would die before harm could reach him !

CLX.

Pitt as a War Minister.

Pitt came in to conduct a war, and this time a necessary war ; for the perfidy and rapine of Bonaparte made peace impossible, and the struggle with him was a struggle for the independence of all nations against the disciplined hordes of a conqueror as cruel as Attila. If utter selfishness, if the reckless sacrifice of humanity to your own interest and passions be vileness, history has no viler name. We may look with pride upon the fortitude and constancy which England displayed in the contest with the universal tyrant. The position in which it left her at its close was fairly won : though she must now be content to retire from this temporary supremacy, and fall back into her place as one of the community of nations. But Pitt was still destined to fail as a war minister; and Trafalgar was soon cancelled by Austerlitz. 'How I leave my country!' Such, it seems, is the correct version of Pitt's last words. Those words are perhaps his truest epitaph. They express the anguish of a patriot who had wrecked his country.

Goldwin Smith.

CLXI.

Pitt breathes his last.

Pitt ceased to breathe on the morning of the 23rd of January, 1806. It was said that he died exclaiming, 'O my country.' This is a fable; but it is true that his last words referred to the alarming state of public affairs. He was in his 47th year. For nineteen years he had been undisputed chief of the administration. No English statesman has held supreme power so long. It was proposed that Pitt should be honoured with a public funeral and a monument. This proposal was opposed by Fox. His speech was a model of good taste and good feeling. The task was a difficult one. Fox performed it with humanity and delicacy. The motion was carried in spite of the speech, and the 22nd of February was fixed for the ceremony.

CLXII.

The three first Kings of Rome.

When we contemplate the excellent qualities of Romulus, Numa, and Tullus, the first three kings of Rome, and note the methods which they followed, we recognise the extreme good fortune of that city in having her first king fierce and warlike, her second peaceful and religious, and her third, like the first, of a high spirit and more disposed to war than to peace. For it was essential for Rome that almost at the outset of her career, a ruler should be found to lay the foundations of her civil life ; but, after that had been done, it was necessary that her rulers should return to the virtues of Romulus, since otherwise the city must have grown feeble, and become a prey to her enemies.

CLXIII.

The Dictatorship.

Those citizens who first devised a dictatorship for Rome have been blamed by certain writers, as though this had been the cause of the tyranny afterwards established there. For these authors allege that the first tyrant of Rome governed it with the title of Dictator, and that, but for the existence of that office, Cæsar could never have cloaked his usurpation under a constitutional name. He who first took up this opinion had not well considered the matter, and his conclusion has been accepted without good ground. For it was not the name or office of Dictator which brought Rome to servitude, but the influence which certain of her citizens were able to assume from the prolongation of their term of power ; so that even had the name of Dictator been wanting in Rome, some other had been found to serve their ends, since power may readily give titles, but not titles power.

CLXIV.

After Cannæ.

It was reported afterwards, that some of the young nobles at Canusium, headed by a Metellus, had formed a plan to fly from Italy, and offer their services to some foreign prince; that young P. Scipio, now about nineteen years old, had gone instantly to the house of Metellus, and standing over him with drawn sword had made him swear neither to desert the Republic himself, nor to allow others to do so ; and that to support the noble conduct of Scipio, Varro had himself moved his headquarters to Canusium, and had used all his efforts to collect the remains of the defeated army. Having given up his command to Marcellus, Varro set out for Rome. As he drew near to the city, the Senate and people went out to meet him, and publicly thanked him that he had not despaired of the Republic. History presents no nobler spectacle than this. Had he been a Carthaginian general, he would have been crucified.

CLXV.

The Power of Good Looks.

The duke was indeed a very extraordinary person : and never any man in any age, nor, I believe, in any country or nation, rose in so short a time to so much greatness of honour, fame, and fortune, upon no other advantage or recommendation, than that of the beauty and gracefulness and becomingness of his person. And I have not the least purpose of undervaluing his good parts and qualities, of which there will be occasion shortly to give some testimony, when I say that his first introduction into favour was purely from the handsomeness of his person.

CLXVI.

The Normans and the English.

The safety of his soldiers, he said, and the honour of their country, were in their own hands : defeated, they had no hope and no retreat ; conquerors, the glory of victory and the spoils of England lay before them. But of victory there could be no doubt : God would fight for those who fought for the righteous cause, and what people could ever withstand the Normans in war? They were the descendants of the men who had won Neustria from the Franks, and who had reduced Frankish kings to submit to the most humiliating of treaties. Were they to yield to the felon English, never renowned in war, whose country had been over and over again harried and subdued by the invading Dane? Let them lift up their banners and march on; let them spare no man in the hostile ranks; they were marching on to certain victory, and the fame of their exploits would resound from one end of heaven to the other.

CLXVII.

The Protector's End.

And now the Protector's foot was on the threshold of success. His glory, the excellence of his administration, his personal dignity and virtues, were founding his government in the allegiance of the people. The friends of order were beginning to perceive that their best chance of order

lay in giving stability to his throne. Some of the great
families, acting on this view, had connected themselves by
marriage with his house. His finances were embarrassed ;
but he was about again to meet a Parliament which would
probably have voted him supplies, and concurred with him
in settling the constitution. His foot was on the threshold
of success ; but on the threshold of success stood Death.
It was death in a strange form for him : for after all his
battles and storms, and all the plots of assassins against
his life, this terrible chief died of grief at the loss of his
favourite daughter, and of watching at her side.

Goldwin Smith.

CLXVIII.

Nothing New under the Sun.

Any one comparing the present with the past will soon
perceive that in all cities and in all nations there prevail
the same desires and passions as always have prevailed ;
for which reason it should be an easy matter for him who
carefully examines past events, to foresee those which are
about to happen in any republic, and to apply such
remedies as the ancients have used in like cases; or,
finding none which have been used by them, to strike
out new ones, such as they might have used in similar
circumstances. But these lessons being neglected or not
understood by readers, or, if understood by them, being
unknown to rulers, it follows that the same disorders are
common to all times.

CLXIX.

All great Calamities are foretold.

Whence it happens I know not, but it is seen, from
examples both ancient and recent, that no grave calamity

has ever befallen any city or country which has not been foretold by vision, by augury, by portent, or by some other Heaven-sent sign. And not to travel too far afield for evidence of this, every one knows that long before the invasion of Italy by Charles VIII. of France, his coming was foretold by the friar Girolamo Savonarola; and how, throughout the whole of Tuscany, the rumour ran that over Arezzo horsemen had been seen fighting in the air. And who is there who has not heard that before the death of the elder Lorenzo de' Medici, the highest pinnacle of the cathedral was rent by a thunderbolt, to the great injury of the building?

CLXX.

Medicine and Doctors.

Medicine has been defined· to be the art or science of amusing a sick man with frivolous speculations about his disorder, and of temporising ingeniously till nature either kills or cures him. A young man intending to study medicine, communicated his design to Voltaire. 'What is that you propose doing?' said he, laughing; 'you are going to put drugs, of which you know nothing, into bodies, of which you know still less.' On another day speaking warmly in praise of the famous physician Haller, in presence of a flatterer who was living in his house, 'Ah, sir,' said this person, 'if Mr. Haller would but speak of your works as you speak of his!' Voltaire answered, 'Possibly we are both mistaken.'

CLXXI.

Battle of Hastings.

Gradually, after so many brave warriors had fallen, resistance grew fainter; but still even now the fate of the battle seemed doubtful. While Harold lived, while the horse and the rider still fell beneath his axe, the heart of England failed not, the hope of England had not wholly died away. Around the two-fold ensigns the war was still fiercely raging, and to that point every eye and every arm in the Norman host was directed. The battle had raged ever since nine in the morning, and evening was now drawing in. New efforts, new devices were needed to overcome the resistance of the English, diminished as were their numbers, and wearied as they were with the livelong toil of that awful day. The Duke ordered his archers to shoot in the air, that their arrows might, as it were, fall straight from heaven. The effect was immediate and fearful. No other device of the wily Duke that day did such frightful execution.

CLXXII.

Burial of Pitt.

The corpse was borne to Westminster Abbey with great pomp. A splendid train of princes, nobles, bishops, and councillors followed. The grave of Pitt had been made near to the spot where his great father lay; it was also near to the spot where his great rival was soon to lie. The sadness of the assistants was beyond that of ordinary mourners; for Pitt had died of sorrows and anxieties in which they had a share. Wilberforce, who carried the banner, describes the ceremony with deep feeling. As the coffin descended into the earth, he says, the eagle face of Chatham from above seemed to look down with consternation into the dark house which was receiving all that remained of so much power and glory.

CLXXIII.

An Approaching Election.

But, gentlemen, though the summer is fast approaching, we shall not, I fancy, be found indulging in ease and indolence, but on the contrary entering upon a new and arduous field of activity. Our labours will no longer be confined to the walls of this house; the battle will be fought out in the heat and in the dust, in full armour and before the face of the world; we shall have to meet the enemies of the State; we shall have to meet the determined onslaught of the enemies of the Church, and to meet them with a bold heart; our weapons will be public speeches and literature. And let us not forget that it will behove us to be eloquent as Ulysses, cunning as Mercury, and deft as Vulcan.

CLXXIV.

An Exhortation before Battle.

On receiving the intelligence that their ally, the King of Sweden, was dead, the general addressed his soldiers and exhorted them not to lose heart. Heaven, he said, would smile upon them and their cause, inasmuch as they had been true to their oath; while their enemies would be found to have incurred the displeasure of the powers above, for having held their vows so cheap. Let them only remember their ancestors, who with small armies had often defeated immense forces arrayed against them; let them not show themselves unworthy of such a lineage. It was only a few days since they had won a victory against overwhelming odds, and victory, moreover, that involved the annihilation of their enemy, a victory won in a battle fought for a cause not their own.

CLXXV.

The Bench and the Bar.

In legal procedure, the duties of the judge and advocate are opposed in every point to each other. The judge labours to discover the truth, the advocate to conceal or disguise it. The judge seeks the golden mean, which is the seat of equity; the advocate the extremes. The judge must be rigid, inflexible; the advocate ought to be supple, pliant, accommodating, entering into the views of his client, and espousing his interests. The judge should be constant, uniform, invariable, walking always in the same path; the advocate should assume all shapes. The judge ought to be passionless; the advocate labours to excite the passions, and to appear impassioned even in a cause in which he feels but a slender interest. The judge should hold the balance in equilibrium; the advocate throws into it the weight which makes his own side preponderate. The judge is armed with the sword of the law; the advocate seeks to disarm him.

CLXXVI.

Man and Woman.

Now their separate characters are briefly these. The man's power is active, progressive, defensive. He is eminently the doer, the creator, the discoverer, the defender. His intellect is for speculation and invention ; his energy for adventure, for war, and for conquest, wherever war is just, wherever conquest necessary. But the woman's power is for rule, not for battle,—and her intellect is not for invention or creation, but for sweet ordering, arrangement, and decision. She sees the qualities of things, their claims, and their places. Her great function is praise : she enters into no contest, but infallibly adjudges the crown of contest.

Ruskin.

CLXXVII.

Abdication of Vitellius.

He issued from the palace, clothed in black, his family in mourning around him. His infant child was borne in a litter. The procession might have been taken for a funeral. The people applauded compassionately, but the soldiers frowned in silence. Vitellius made a short harangue in the Forum, and then, taking his dagger from his side, as the ensign of power, tendered it to the consul Cæcilius. The soldiers murmured aloud, and the consul, in pity or from fear, declined to accept it. He then turned towards the temple of Concord, meaning there to leave the symbols of imperial office, and retire to the house of his brother. But the soldiers now interposed.

They would not suffer him to hide himself in a private dwelling, but compelled him to retrace his steps to the palace, which he entered once more, hardly conscious whether he were still emperor or not.

CLXXVIII.

A Brush with Antony.

As soon as we got through the woods, we drew up the twelve cohorts in order of battle. The other two legions had not yet come up. Antony immediately brought all his troops out of the village, ranged likewise in order of battle, and without delay engaged us. At first they fought so briskly on both sides that nothing could possibly be fiercer; though the right wing, in which I was, with eight cohorts of the Martial legion, put Antony's thirty-fifth legion to flight at the first onset, and pursued it above five hundred paces from the place where the action began. Wherefore, observing the enemy's horse attempting to surround our wing, I began to retreat, and ordered the light-armed troops to make head against them, and prevent their coming upon us from behind.

CLXXIX.

The Black Hole of Calcutta.

There was an apartment which had been sometimes used as a prison. It was eighteen feet square, and fit for two or three persons in such a climate as that of Calcutta. It was above ground and had two windows. It was not like a dungeon or black hole, but it will be called the ' Black Hole' as long as language lasts. One hundred and forty-six prisoners were ordered into this apartment. When it was full they were driven in. There they were kept through the summer night. No cries for air availed : the viceroy was asleep, he must not be disturbed. While he was asleep, the prisoners were dying fast. When the door was opened in the morning, twenty-three were alive. They looked so ghastly that their own friends did not know them.

CLXXX.

Freedom of Thought at Athens.

About twenty years before a similar charge had been brought against Protagoras for having treated the same question in too speculative a manner. For in the beginning of one of his books he had said that, ' whether the Gods did or did not exist, was a question which he could not either affirm or deny : for the life of man was too short for the solution of such a problem.' But it was intolerable to the Athenians that such a question should be a subject of doubt ; so ordering all persons who had any copies of this book to bring them to the magistrates, they caused them all to be burned in the market-place : and had not Protagoras himself taken quickly to flight, he would in all probability have been put to death.

CLXXXI.

A War should be Great and Short.

Whosoever makes war, whether from policy or ambition, means to acquire and to hold what he acquires, and to carry on the war he has undertaken in such a manner that it shall enrich and not impoverish his native country

and state. It is necessary, therefore, whether for acquiring
or holding, to consider how cost may be avoided, and
everything done most advantageously for the public
welfare. But whoever would effect all this, must take the
course and follow the methods of the Romans; which
consisted, first of all, in making their wars, as the French
say, *great and short.* For, entering the field with strong
armies, they brought to a speedy conclusion whatever
wars they had with the Latins, the Samnites, or the
Etruscans.

CLXXXII.

The Valour of Rome.

But, be this as it may, certain it is that in every
country of the world, even the least considerable, the
Romans found a league of well-armed republics, most
resolute in the defence of their freedom, whom it is clear
they never could have subdued had they not been endowed
with the rarest and most astonishing valour. To cite a
single instance, I shall take the case of the Samnites, who,
strange as it may now seem, were, on the admission of
Titus Livius himself, so powerful and so steadfast in arms,
as to be able to withstand the Romans down to the consulship of Papirius Cursor, son to the first Papirius, a period
of six and forty years, in spite of numerous defeats, the loss
of many of their towns, and the great slaughter which over-
took them everywhere throughout their country. And this
is the more remarkable when we see that country, which
once contained so many noble cities, and supported so
great a population, now almost uninhabited.

CLXXXIII.

Ulysses welcomed in Phæacia.

She, admiring to hear such complimentary words proceed out of the mouth of one whose outside looked so
rough and uncompromising, made answer: 'Stranger, I
discern neither sloth nor folly in you; and yet I see that
you are poor and wretched: from which I gather that
neither wisdom nor industry can secure felicity; only
Jove bestows it upon whomsoever he pleases. He, perhaps, has reduced you to this plight. However, since your
wanderings have brought you so near to our city, it lies in
our duty to supply your wants. Clothes, and what else
a human hand should give to one so suppliant, and so
tamed with calamity, you shall not want. We will show you
our city, and tell you the name of our people. This is the
land of the Phæacians, of which my father, Alcinous, is
king.'

Charles Lamb.

CLXXXIV.

The first Battle inside Rome.

The Senate believed that now at length the moment for
action had arrived. They implored Marius the consul to
place himself at their head, and having hastily armed and
collected all the bravest of their own order, and all such
equites as were opposed to mob ascendency, they marched
into the Forum to do battle with the populace. Here a
hand-to-hand conflict took place; and Roman annalists
have recorded that this was the first battle ever fought
within the walls of the city. The battle resulted in the
defeat and flight of the insurgents: they took refuge in

the Capitol, where they were besieged, and their supplies
of water being cut off, they were compelled to surrender.
Marius hoped to be able to save some of his former associates, and with this object he shut them up in the Senate-
house.   But some of the assailants climbed up on to the
roof, uncovered it, and pelting the defenceless prisoners
with javelins from above, put every one of them to death.

CLXXXV.

Characteristics of Roman Families.

Manners and institutions, differing in different cities,
seem here to produce a harder and there a softer race ;
and a like difference may also be discerned in the character
of different families in the same city.   And while this holds
good of all cities, we have many instances of it in reading
the history of Rome.   For we find the Manlii always stern
and stubborn ; the Valerii kindly and courteous ; the Clau-
dii haughty and ambitious ; and many families besides
similarly distinguished from one another by their peculiar
qualities.   These qualities we cannot refer wholly to the
blood, for that must change as a result of repeated inter-
marriages, but must ascribe rather to the different training
and education given in different families.   For much turns
on whether a child of tender years hears a thing well or
ill spoken of, since this must needs make an impression on
him whereby his whole conduct in after-life will be influenced.

CLXXXVI.

The Brave Sir Andrew.

He was in the Highlands with a small body of followers,
when the King of England suddenly came on him.   Being

about to hear mass, he would not permit his devotions to be interrupted. That done, his people pressed him to retreat. But Murray still said there was no heed for haste. At length his horse was brought out, and all thought that the army would now retreat. Murray, however, observed that a strap in his armour had given way, and he would not move until he had with his own hand cut and fitted the strap which he wanted. Then at last he gave the word for retreat : and though at the time the delay seemed endless to his followers, they became steady and composed from beholding the confidence of their leader.

CLXXXVII.

Marcus Aurelius Antoninus.

The virtue of Marcus Aurelius Antoninus was of a severer and more laborious kind. It was the well-earned harvest of many a learned conference, of many a patient lecture, and many a midnight lucubration. At the age of twelve years, he embraced the rigid system of the Stoics, which taught him to submit his body to his mind, his passions to his reason ; to consider virtue as the only good, vice as the only evil, all things external as things indifferent. His meditations, composed in the tumult of a camp, are still extant ; and he even condescended to give lessons of philosophy in a more public manner than was perhaps consistent with the modesty of a sage, or the dignity of an emperor. But his life was the noblest commentary on the precepts of Zeno. He was severe to himself, indulgent to the imperfections of others, just and beneficent to all mankind.

Gibbon.

CLXXXVIII.

March of Nero to the Metaurus.

Nero's determination was soon taken. Legally he had no power to quit this part of Italy, but in this emergency he resolved to set all laws at defiance. He picked out 6000 foot and 1000 horse, the flower of his army, and gave out that he would march at nightfall into Lucania. As soon as it was dark, he set out, but the soldiers soon perceived that Lucania was not their destination. They were marching northwards towards Picenum, and they found that provisions and beasts of burthen were ready for them all along the road by the Consul's orders. As soon as he was well advanced upon his march, he addressed his men and told them that 'in a few days they would join their countrymen under Livius in his camp in Umbria; that combined they would intercept Hasdrubal and his army; that victory was certain; that the chief share of the glory would be theirs.' The men answered such an address as soldiers should, and everywhere as they passed, the inhabitants came out to meet them, offering them all that they could want.

Liddell.

CLXXXIX.

Philip and Velasquez.

'Some of the painters tell me,' said Philip to Velasquez one day, 'that your pictures are unequal, and that you only paint heads well.' 'They are mistaken, Sire,' replied Velasquez: '*no one* paints heads really well.' The most important painting he ever executed, and by some considered his masterpiece, was a large group known as 'The Maids of Honour.' Into this painting Velasquez introduced a picture of himself. King Philip was mightily interested in this picture, and came daily to watch its progress. At length Velasquez declared the painting finished. 'Not quite,' said the king; 'one detail is lacking.' With that he took up the brush and sketched rapidly on the breast of the painter's portrait the cross of the Order of Santiago, one of the highest honours which it was in his power to bestow.

CXC.

A Dirty Trick.

When the masses at Athens had become more and more preponderant, the Areopagus was attacked in the following manner by Ephialtes, a man reputed incorruptible in his loyalty to democracy, and who had become leader of the Commons. He first put to death many of its members by impeaching them of offences committed in their administration. He then despoiled the Council of all its recently-acquired attributes ; and distributed these amongst the Senate, the Assembly, and the Courts of Law. In this work he had the co-operation of Themistocles, who, though himself an Areopagite, was expecting to be accused of treasonable correspondence with Persia. Desiring the ruin of the Council, Themistocles warned Ephialtes that it was going to imprison him ; and at the same time told the Council that he would shew them a band of traitors in the act of conspiring against the State. Then, conducting a committee of their number to the residence of Ephialtes, he shewed them the gang assembling, and held them in conversation on the spot; Ephialtes fled panic-struck to the altar, clad in nothing but his tunic, and sat there to the amazement of all beholders. *Aristotle.*

CXCI.

A Beloved Ass.

La Fleur offered him money. The mourner said he did not want it. It was not the value of the ass but the loss of him. The ass, he said, he was assured loved him, and upon this told them a long story of a mischance upon their passage over the Pyrenean mountains which had separated them from each other three days; during which time the ass had sought him as much as he had sought the ass, and that they had scarce either eat or drank till they met. 'Thou hast one comfort, friend,' said I, 'at least, in the loss of thy poor beast; I'm sure thou hast been a merciful master to him.' 'Alas!' said the mourner, 'I thought so, when he was alive; but now that he is dead I think otherwise. I fear the weight of myself and my afflictions together have been too much for him, they have shortened the poor creature's days, and I fear I have them to answer for.' 'Shame on the world!' said I to myself; 'did we love each other as this poor soul but loved his ass, it would be something.'

Sterne.

CXCII.

Orders Happily Disobeyed.

The winter's day was not far advanced when the rearward columns of the republican army were descried in the distance. Making a selection of some six hundred picked cavalry, with a thousand infantry, Don John ordered them to hang on the rear of the enemy, and to do him all the damage possible consistent with the possibility of avoiding a general engagement. The orders were at first strictly obeyed. But at last Gonzaga, the commander, observing that a spirited cavalry officer had advanced too far, sent hastily to recall him. The order was flatly disobeyed. ' Tell Gonzaga,' said the officer, ' that I have never turned my back upon the enemy, and that I shall not begin now. And besides, retreat is impossible.' At this juncture Alexander of Parma rode up to reconnoitre. He saw that the enemy was marching unsteadily to avoid a deep ravine into which they were being forced. Seizing the opportunity, he dashed forward with these words : 'Tell Don John of Austria that Alexander of Parma has plunged into the abyss, to perish there or come forth victorious.'

CXCIII.

Pompeians defeated.

The Pompeians were too much dispirited to make any resistance ; shivered once more at the first onset, they poured in broken masses over hill and plain. But Cæsar was not yet satisfied. Allowing a part of his troops only to return to the camp, he led four legions in hot pursuit by a shorter or better road, and drew them up at a distance of six miles from the field of battle. The fugitives finding their retreat intercepted halted on an eminence overhanging a stream. Cæsar set his men immediately to throw up intrenchments and cut off their approach to the water. This last labour was accomplished before nightfall, and when the Pompeians perceived that their means of watering were intercepted, they listened to the summons of the heralds who required their surrender.

PART IV.

More difficult Passages for Translation into Latin Prose.

—•—

CXCIV.

Second Year of the Crimean War.

If the ardour, never great, of France for the war had somewhat abated, such was not the case with England. She was more than ever bent upon pursuing it to an effective close. All her energies had been devoted to strengthening herself for the task. She was determined to show that, if her system had brought suffering and disaster on her soldiers, she knew how to make atonement for the past by a future, in which their endurance and their valour should be put to no unfair trial through want of due provision for the contingencies of warfare. Our dockyards and arsenals were busily adding to the already overwhelming strength of our fleet, and the country provided with lavish hands whatever funds were necessary to enable its generals to lead their troops wherever they determined that the enemy might be assailed with the best assurance of success.

Prince Consort.

1

CXCV.

The Northern Pirates.

A letter which a Roman provincial, Sidonius Apollinaris, wrote in warning to a friend who had embarked as an officer in the fleet, gives us a glimpse of these freebooters as they appeared to the civilised world of the fifth century. 'When you see their rowers,' says he, 'you may make up your mind that every one of them is an arch-pirate, with such wonderful unanimity do all of them at once command, obey, teach, and learn their business of brigandage. This is why I have to warn you to be more than ever on your guard in this warfare. Your foe is of all foes the fiercest. He attacks unexpectedly; if you expect him, he makes his escape; he despises those who seek to block his path; he overthrows those who are off their guard; he cuts off any enemy whom he follows; while, for himself, he never fails to escape when he is forced to fly. These men know the dangers of the deep like men who are every day in contact with them; for since a storm throws those whom they wish to attack off their guard, while it hinders their own coming onset from being seen from afar, they gladly risk themselves in the midst of wrecks and sea-beaten rocks, in the hope of making profit out of the very tempest.'   *J. Green.*

CXCVI.

The Vicar in Prison.

After reading I entered upon my exhortation, which was rather calculated at first to amuse them than to reprove. I previously observed that no other motive but their welfare could induce me to this; that I was their fellow-prisoner, and now got nothing by preaching. I was sorry, I said, to hear them so very profane; because they got nothing by it, but might lose a great deal; 'for be assured, my friends,' cried I, '—for you are my friends, however the world may disclaim your friendship,—though you swore twelve thousand oaths in a day, it would not put one penny in your purse. Then what signifies calling every moment upon the devil, and courting his friendship, since you find how scurvily he uses you? He has given you nothing here, you find, but a mouthful of oaths and an empty belly; and, by the best accounts I have of him, he will give you nothing that's good hereafter.'

Goldsmith.

CXCVII.

The News of Thrasimene.

But her spirit was invincible. When the tidings of the disaster of Thrasymenus reached the city, the people crowded to the forum and called upon the magistrates to tell them the whole truth. The praetor peregrinus, M. Pomponius Matho, ascended the rostra, and said to the assembled multitude, 'We have been beaten in a great battle; our army is destroyed; and C. Flaminius, the consul, is killed.' Our colder temperaments scarcely enable us to conceive the effect of such tidings on the lively feelings of the people of the south, or to image to ourselves the cries, the tears, the hands uplifted in prayer, or clenched in rage, the confused sound of ten thousand voices giving utterance with breathless rapidity to their feelings of eager interest, of terror, of grief, or of fury. All the northern gates of the city were beset with crowds of wives and mothers, imploring every fresh fugitive from the fatal field for some tidings of those most dear to them.   *Arnold.*

CXCVIII.

Death of Leo X.

Strange and delusive destiny of man ! The pope was at his villa of Malliana when he received intelligence that his party had triumphantly entered Milan : he abandoned himself to the exultation arising naturally from the successful completion of an important enterprise, and looked cheerfully on at the festivities his people were preparing on the occasion. He paced backwards and forwards till deep in the night, between the window and a blazing hearth—it was the month of November. Somewhat exhausted, but still in high spirits, he arrived at Rome, and the rejoicings there celebrated for his triumph were not yet concluded when he was attacked by a mortal disease. ' Pray for me,' said he to his servants, 'that I may yet make you all happy.' We see that he loved life ; but his hour was come, he had not time to receive the viaticum nor extreme unction. So suddenly, so prematurely, and surrounded by hopes so bright, he died—as the poppy fadeth.   *Ranke.*

CXCIX.

Can Friends disagree?

A question was started, how far people who disagree in a capital point can live in friendship together : Johnson said they might. Goldsmith said they could not, as they had not the 'idem velle atque idem nolle,' the same likings and the same aversions. Johnson : 'Why, sir, you must shun the subject as to which you disagree. For instance, I can live very well with Burke ; I love his knowledge, his genius, his diffusion, and affluence of conversation ; but I would not talk to him of the Rockingham party.' Goldsmith : 'But, sir, when people live together who have something as to which they disagree, and which they want to shun, they will be in the situation mentioned in the story of Bluebeard. You may look into all the chambers but one. But we should have the greatest inclination to look into that chamber, to talk of that subject.' Johnson (with a loud voice) : 'Sir, I am not saying that you could live in friendship with a man from whom you differ as to some point, I am only saying that I could do it. You put me in mind of Sappho in Ovid.'

Boswell.

CC.

The Empire in its Iron Age.

The worst kind of government is that which is regarded by its subjects as divine, and at the same time is really weak. Such was the government of Constantius, of Honorius, of Valentinian III ; imbecile, and at the same time despotic, plaguing the world like an angry deity, and misgoverning it like an angry child. But these were exceptional cases. Government during this period was commonly at a higher level. It was Asiatic, but it was commonly able. Compared with Asiatic governments it was good. If the emperor was regarded as a divinity, at least he earned his deification for the most part by merit. He was not such a deity as those which Egypt worshipped, a sacred ape or cat, but rather a Hercules or Quirinus, who had risen by superhuman labours to divine honours.   But compared with the government of the Antonines, it was barbaric.   The empire has fallen into a lower class of states.   Reason and simplicity have disappeared from it.   Subjects have lost all rights, and government all responsibility.   The reign of political superstition has set in.   Abject fear paralyses the people, and those that rule are intoxicated with insolence and cruelty.   It is an Iron Age.   *Seeley.*

CCI.

Know your own place.

Our family had now made several attempts to be fine; but some unforeseen disaster demolished each as soon as projected.   I endeavoured to take the advantage of every disappointment to improve their good sense, in proportion as they were frustrated in ambition.   'You see, my children,' cried I, 'how little is to be got by attempts to impose upon the world in coping with our betters.   Such as are poor, and will associate with none but the rich, are hated by those they avoid, and despised by those they follow.   Unequal combinations are always disadvantageous to the weaker side, the rich having the pleasure, and the poor the inconveniences, that result from them.   But, come Dick, my boy, and repeat the fable you were reading to-day, for the good of the company.'

Goldsmith.

CCII.

Death of Theodoric.

After the mutual and repeated discharge of missile weapons, in which the archers of Scythia might signalize their superior dexterity, the cavalry and infantry of the two armies were furiously mingled in closer combat. The Huns, who fought under the eyes of their king, pierced through the doubtful and feeble centre of the allies, separated their wings from each other, and wheeling with a rapid effort to the left, directed their whole force against the Visigoths. As Theodoric rode along the ranks, to animate his troops, he received a mortal wound from the javelin of Andages, a noble Ostrogoth, and immediately fell from his horse. The wounded king was oppressed in .the general disorder, and trampled under the feet of his own cavalry; and this important death served to explain the ambiguous answer of the haruspices. *Gibbon.*

CCIII.

Return from the Caudine Forks.

In far different plight, and with far other feelings than those with which they had entered the pass of Caudium, did the Roman army issue out from it again upon the plain of Campania. Defeated and disarmed, they knew not what reception they might meet with from their Campanian allies; it was possible that Capua might shut her gates against them, and go over to the victorious enemy. But the Campanians behaved faithfully and generously; they sent supplies of arms, of clothing, and of provisions, to meet the Romans even before they arrived at Capua; they sent new cloaks, and the lictors and fasces of their own magistrates, to enable the consuls to resume their fitting state; and when the army approached their city, the Senate and people went out to meet them, and welcomed them both individually and publicly with the greatest kindness. No attentions, however, could soothe the wounded pride of the Romans: they could

not bear to raise their eyes from the ground, nor to speak
to anyone. Full of shame they continued their march to
Rome; when they came near to it, all those soldiers who
had a home in the country dispersed, and escaped to their
several homes singly and silently : whilst those who lived
in Rome lingered without the walls till the sun was set,
and stole to their homes under cover of the darkness.

Arnold.

CCIV.

A Speech by Scipio.

Scipio having assembled the troops together, exhorted
them not to be disheartened by the loss which they had
sustained. That their defeat was by no means to be ascribed to the superior courage of the Carthaginians; but
was occasioned only by the treachery of the Spaniards,
and the imprudent division which the generals, reposing
too great a confidence in the alliance of that people, had
made of their forces : that the Carthaginians themselves
were now in the same condition with respect to both
these circumstances; for besides that they were divided
into separate camps they had also alienated by injurious
treatment the affections of their allies, and had rendered
them their enemies; that from thence it had happened
that one part of the Spaniards had already sent deputies
to the Romans; and that the rest, as soon as the Romans
should have passed the river, would hasten with alacrity
to join them; not so much indeed from any motive of
affection, as from a desire to revenge the insults which
they had suffered from the Carthaginians. With all
these advantages in prospect, they should now, therefore,
pass the river with the greatest confidence, and leave to
himself, and to the rest of the commanders, the whole
care of what was afterwards to be done.

CCV.

Monarchy a Law of Nature.

Where was there ever such peace, such tranquillity, such justice, such honours paid to virtue, such rewards distributed to the good and punishments to the bad; when was ever the state so wisely guided, as in the time when the world had obtained one head, and that head Rome? the very time wherein God deigned to be born of a Virgin, and to dwell upon earth. To every single body there has been given a head; the whole world therefore also, which is called by the poet a great body, ought to be content with one temporal head. For every two-headed animal is monstrous; how much more horrible and hideous a portent must be a creature with a thousand different heads, biting and fighting against one another! If, however, it is necessary that there be more heads than one, it is nevertheless evident that there ought to be one to restrain all and preside over all, so that the peace of the whole body may abide unshaken. Assuredly both in heaven and in earth the sovereignty of one has always been best.

CCVI.

Unfortunate Great Men.

The vigilant Peter the Headstrong was not to be deceived. Sending privately for the commander-in-chief of all the armies, and having heard all his story with the customary pious oaths, protestations, and ejaculations, 'Harkee, comrade,' cried he, 'though by your own account you are the most brave, upright, and honourable

man in the whole province, yet do you lie under the misfortune of being traduced and immeasurably despised.
Now, though it is certainly hard to punish a man for his
misfortunes, I cannot consent to venture my armies with
a commander whom they despise, or to trust the welfare
of my people to a champion whom they distrust. Retire,
therefore, my friend, from the irksome cares and toils of
public life with this comforting reflection—that if guilty,
you are but enjoying your just reward ; and if innocent,
you are not the first great and good man who has most
wrongfully been slandered and maltreated in this wicked
world, doubtless to be better treated in another world,
where there shall be neither error nor calumny nor persecution. In the meantime, let me never see your face
again, for I have a horrible antipathy to the countenances
of unfortunate great men like yourself.'

Washington Irving.

CCVII.

How we got the Town.

The town is most pleasantly seated, having a very
good wall with round and square bulwarks, after the old
manner of fortifications. We came thither in the night,
and indeed were very much distressed by sore and tem-
pestuous wind and rain. After a long march, we knew
not well how to dispose of ourselves ; but finding an old
abbey in the suburbs, and some cabins and poor houses,
we got into them, and had opportunity to send the garrison a summons. They shot at my trumpeter, and
would not listen to him for an hour's space ; but having
some officers in our party whom they knew, I sent them
to let them know I was there with a good part of the
army. We shot not a shot at them ; but they were very

angry, and fired very earnestly upon us, telling us it was not a time of night to send a summons. But yet in the end the governor was willing to send out two commis-sioners,—I think rather to see whether there was a force sufficient to force him, than to any other end. After almost a whole night spent in treaty, the town was de-livered to me the next morning, upon terms which we usually call honourable; which I was the willinger to give, because I had little above two hundred foot, and neither ladders nor guns, nor anything else to force them.

Cromwell.

CCVIII.

Before Hastings.

On the morning the Duke called together the most considerable of his chieftains and made them a speech suitable to the occasion. He represented to them that the event which they and he had long wished for was approaching, and the whole fortune of war now depended on their sword, and would be decided in a single action. That never army had greater motives for exerting a vigorous courage, whether they considered the prize that would attend their victory, or the inevitable destruction that must ensue on their discomfiture. That if once their martial and veteran bands could break those raw soldiers who had rashly dared to approach them, they conquered a kingdom at one blow, and were justly entitled to all their possessions as the reward of their prosperous valour; that on the contrary, if they remitted in the least their wonted prowess, an enraged enemy hung upon their rear, the sea met them in their retreat, and an ignomini-ous death was the certain punishment of their cowardice. He then ordered the signal of battle to sound, and the whole army, moving at once and singing the hymn of Roland the famous peer of Charlemagne, advanced in order and with alacrity against the enemy.

Hume.

CCIX.

Life like a Sparrow's Flight.

Another of the king's chief men, approving of his words and exhortations, presently added : 'The present life of man, O king, seems to me, in comparison of that time which is unknown to us, like to the swift flight of a sparrow through the room wherein you sit at supper in winter with your commanders and ministers, and a good fire in the midst, whilst the storms of rain and snow prevail abroad ; the sparrow, I say, flying in at one door, and immediately out at another, whilst he is within, is safe from the wintry storm ; but after a short space of fair weather, he immediately vanishes out of your sight, into the dark winter from which he had emerged. So this life of man appears for a short space, but of what went before, or what is to follow, we are utterly ignorant. If, therefore, this new doctrine contains something more certain, it seems justly to deserve to be followed.' The other elders and king's counsellors, by Divine inspiration, spoke to the same effect.

J. Green.

CCX.

St. Paul approaches Rome.

In such a time as this, did the prince of the Apostles advance towards the heathen city, where, under divine guidance, he was to fix his seat. He toiled along the

stately road which led him straight onwards to the capital
of the world. He passed under the high gate, and wandered on amid high palaces and columned temples; he
met processions of heathen priests and ministers in
honour of their idols; he met the wealthy lady, borne on
her litter by her slaves; he met the stern legionaries
who had been the ' massive iron hammers' of the whole
earth; he met the busy politician and the orator returning home surrounded by his young admirers and his
grateful or hopeful clients. He saw about him a vigorous
power, formed and matured in its religion, its laws, its
civil tradition, its imperial extension through the history
of many centuries; and what was he but a poor, feeble,
aged, stranger, in nothing different from the multitude
of men, an Egyptian, or a Chaldean, or perhaps a Jew,
some Eastern or other, as passers-by would guess according to their knowledge of human kind, carelessly looking
at him, as we might turn our eyes upon a Hindu or a
gipsy, as they met us, without the shadow of a thought
that such a one was destined then to commence an age
of religious sovereignty, in which the heathen state might
live twice over, and not see its end.   *Farrar.*

CCXI.

Approach of the Crimean War.

Looking back upon the troubles which ended in the
outbreak of war, one sees the nations at first swaying
backward and forward like a throng so vast as to be
helpless, but afterwards falling slowly into warlike array.
And when one begins to search for the man or the men
whose volition was governing the crowd, the eye falls
upon the towering form of the Emperor Nicholas. He

was not single-minded, and therefore his will was un-
stable, but it had a huge force ; and, since he was armed
with the whole authority of his Empire, it seemed plain
that it was this man—and only he—who was bringing
danger from the north. And at first, too, it seemed that
within his range of action there was none who could be
his equal: but in a little while the looks of men were
turned to the Bosphorus, for thither his ancient adversary
was slowly bending his way. To fit him for the encounter, the Englishman was clothed with little authority
except what he could draw from the resources of his own
mind, and from the strength of his own wilful nature.
Yet it was presently seen that those who were near him
fell under his dominion, and did as he bid them, and that
the circle of deference to his will was always increasing
around him ; and soon it appeared that, though he moved
gently, he began to have mastery over a foe who was
consuming his strength in mere anger. When he had
conquered, he stood as it were with folded arms, and
seemed willing to desist from strife.   *Layard.*

CCXII.

A New Arcadia.

With these discourses they went on their way, until
they arrived at the very spot where they had been
trampled upon by the bulls. Don Quixote knew it again,
and said to Sancho, ' This is the meadow where we
alighted on the gay shepherdesses and gallant shepherds,
who intended to revive in it and imitate the pastoral
Arcadia ; in imitation of which, if you approve it, I could
wish, O Sancho, we might turn shepherds, at least for
the time I must live retired. I will buy sheep and all

other materials necessary for the pastoral employment; we will range the mountains, and woods, and the meadows, singing here, and complaining there, drinking the liquid crystal of the fountains, of the limpid brooks, or of the mighty rivers. The oaks with a plentiful hand shall give their sweetest fruit; the trunks of the hardest cork-trees shall afford us seats; the willows shall furnish shade, and the roses scent; the spacious meadow shall yield us carpets of a thousand colours; the air, clear and pure, shall supply breath, the moon and stars afford light; singing shall furnish pleasure, and complaining yield delight; Apollo shall provide verses and love-conceits; with which we shall make ourselves famous and immortal, not only in the present but in future ages.'

Don Quixote.

CCXIII.

William enters Exeter.

The road, all down the long descent, and through the plain to the banks of the river, was lined, mile after mile, with spectators. From the West Gate to the Cathedral Close the pressing and shouting on each side was such as reminded Londoners of the crowds on the Lord Mayor's Day. Doors, windows, balconies, and roofs were thronged with gazers. An eye accustomed to the pomp of war would have found much to criticise in the spectacle. For several toilsome marches in the rain, through roads where one who travelled on foot sank at every step up to the ancles in clay, had not improved the appearance of men or their accoutrements. But the people of Devonshire, altogether unused to the splendour of well-ordered camps, were overwhelmed with delight and awe. Descriptions of the martial pageant were circulated all over the·kingdom. They contained much that was well-fitted to gratify the vulgar appetite for the marvellous. For the Dutch army, composed of men who had been born in various climates, and had served under various standards, presented an aspect at once grotesque, gorgeous, and terrible to islanders, who had, in general, a very indistinct notion of foreign countries. *Macaulay.*

CCXIV.

A Candidate for a Greek Chair.

I set boldly forward the next morning. Every day lessened the burden of my moveables, like Æsop and his basket of bread; for I paid them for my lodgings to the Dutch, as I travelled on. When I came to Louvain I was resolved not to go to the lower professors, but openly tendered my talents to the Principal himself. I went, had admittance, and offered him my service as a master of the Greek language, which I had been told was a desideratum in his University. The Principal seemed at first to doubt of my abilities; but of these I offered to convince him, by turning a part of any Greek author into Latin. Finding me perfectly earnest in my proposal, he addressed me thus: ' You see me, young man; I never learned Greek, and I don't find that I have ever missed it. I have had a doctor's cap and gown without Greek; I eat heartily without Greek; and, in short,' continued he, ' as I don't know Greek, I do not believe there is any good in it.' *Goldsmith.*

CCXV.

Pompey returns to the Optimates.

Nature had destined Pompeius, if ever any one, to be a member of an aristocracy; and nothing but selfish

motives had carried him over as a deserter to the demo-
cratic camp. That he should now revert to his Sullan
traditions, accorded alike with his character and his
interest. Perhaps the majority, at any rate the flower
of the citizens, belonged to the constitutional party: it
wanted nothing but a leader. Marcus Cato, its present
head, did the duty as he understood it, of its leader
amidst daily peril to his life, and perhaps without hope
of success; his fidelity to duty deserves respect, but more
than this is required of a commander. If, instead of this
man, who knew not how to act either as party chief, or
as general, a man of the political and military mark of
Pompeius should raise the banner of the existing constitution, the free townsmen of Italy would necessarily
flock towards it in crowds, that under it they might help
to fight, if not for the kingship of Pompeius, at any rate
against the kingship of Cæsar.

Adapted from Mommsen.

CCXVI.

The Relief of Derry.

Meantime the tide was rising fast. The Mountjoy
began to move, and soon passed safe through the broken
stakes and floating spars. But her brave master was no
more. A shot from one of the batteries had struck him;
and he died by the most enviable of all deaths, in sight of
the city which was his birthplace, which was his home,
and which had just been saved by his courage and self-
devotion from the most frightful form of destruction.
The night had closed in before the conflict at the boom
began; but the flash of guns was seen, and the noise
heard, by the lean and ghastly multitude which covered

K

the walls of the city. When the Mountjoy grounded, and when the shout of triumph rose from the Irish on both sides of the river, the hearts of the besieged died within them. Even after the barricade had been passed, there was a terrible hour of suspense. It was ten o'clock before the ships arrived at the quay. The whole population was there to welcome them.   *Macaulay.*

CCXVII.

Reforms of Ximenes.

His success in this scheme for reducing the power of the nobility encouraged him to attempt a diminution of their possessions, which were no less exorbitant. During the contest and disorder inseparable from the feudal government, the nobles, ever attentive to their own interests, and taking advantage of the weakness and distress of their monarchs, had seized some parts of the royal demesne, obtained grants of others, and having gradually wrested almost the whole out of the hands of the princes, had annexed them to their own estates. The titles by which most of the grandees held their lands were extremely defective: it was from some successful usurpation, which the crown had been too feeble to dispute, that many derived their only claim to possession. An inquiry carried back to the origin of these encroachments, which were almost coeval with the feudal system, was impracticable ; as it would have stripped every nobleman in Spain of great part of his lands, it must have excited a general revolt.   *Robertson.*

CCXVIII.

Reforms of Ximenes (continued).

Such a step was too bold even for the enterprising spirit of Ximenes. He confined himself to the reign of Ferdinand : and beginning with the pensions granted during that time, refused to make any further payment, because all right to them expired with his life. He then called to account such as had acquired crown-lands under the administration of that monarch, and at once resumed whatever he had alienated : the effects of this revocation extended to many persons of high rank, for, though Ferdinand was a prince of little generosity, yet he and Isabella having been raised to the throne of Castile by a powerful faction of the nobles, they were obliged to reward the zeal of their adherents with great liberality, and the royal demesnes were their only fund for that purpose. *Robertson.*

CCXIX.

Execution of Hippolytus.

Hippolytus issued from the prison, looking more like a young martyr than a criminal. He was now perfectly quiet, and a sort of unnatural glow had risen into his cheeks, the result of the enthusiasm and conscious self-sacrifice into which he had worked himself during the night. He had only prayed, as a last favour, that he might be taken through the street in which the house of the Metelli stood ; for he had lived, he said, as everybody knew, in great hostility with that family, and he now felt none any longer, and wished to bless their house as he passed it. The magistrates, for more reasons than one, had no objection; the old priest, with tears in his eyes, said that the dear boy would still be an honour to his family, as surely as he would be a saint in heaven; and the procession moved on. The main feeling of the crowd, as usual, was one of curiosity; but there were few indeed in whom it was not mixed with pity, and many women found the sight so intolerable that they were seen moving away down the streets, weeping bitterly, and unable to answer the questions of those they met.

CCXX.

The Virginian Colony.

After his departure everything tended to the wildest anarchy. Faction and discontent had often risen so high among the old settlers that they could hardly be kept within bounds. The spirit of the new-comers was too ungovernable to bear any restraint. Several among them of better rank were such dissipated, hopeless young men as their friends were glad to send out in quest of whatever fortune might betide them in a foreign land. Of the lower order, many were so profligate or desperate, that their country was happy to throw them out as nuisances to society. Such persons were little capable of the regular subordination, the strict economy, and persevering industry, which their situation required. The Indians, observing their misconduct, and that every precaution for sustenance or safety was neglected, not only withheld the supplies of provisions which they were accustomed to furnish, but also harassed them with continual hostilities. All their subsistence was derived from the stores which they had brought from England: these were soon con-

sumed ; then the domestic animals sent out to breed in
the country were devoured ; and by this inconsiderate
waste they were reduced to such extremity of famine, as
not only to eat the most nauseous and unwholesome roots
and berries, but to feed on the bodies of the Indians
whom they slew, and even on those of their companions
who sank under the oppression of such complicated distresses. In less than six months, of five hundred persons
whom Smith left in Virginia, only sixty remained : and
they so feeble and dejected that they could not have
survived for ten days if succour had not arrived from a
quarter whence they did not expect it.   *Robertson.*

CCXXI.

The Roman Exercises.

It is not the purpose of this work to enter into any
minute descriptions of the Roman exercises. We shall
only remark that they comprehended whatever could add
strength to the body, activity to the limbs, or grace to the
motions. The soldiers were diligently instructed to march,
to run, to leap, to swim, to carry heavy burdens, to handle
every species of arms that was used either for offence or
for defence, either in distant engagement or in a closer
onset : to form a variety of evolutions ; and to move to
the sound of flutes, in the Pyrrhic or martial dance. In
the midst of peace, the Roman troops familiarised themselves with the practice of war ; and it is prettily remarked
by an ancient historian who had fought against them. that
the effusion of blood was the only circumstance which
distinguished a field of battle from a field of exercise.

Gibbon.

CCXXII.

Cupid.

But, before we acquaint you with the purport of her speech, we must premise, that in the land of Lycia, which was at that time pagan, above all their other gods the inhabitants did in an especial manner adore the deity who was supposed to have influence in the disposing of people's affections in love. This god, by the name of Cupid, they feigned to be a beautiful boy, and winged; as indeed, between young persons, these frantic passions are usually least under constraint; while the wings might signify the haste with which these ill-judged attachments are commonly dissolved; and they painted him blindfolded, because these silly affections of lovers make them blind to the defects of the beloved object, which every one is quick-sighted enough to discover but themselves; or because love is for the most part led blindly, rather than directed by the open eye of the judgment, in the hasty choice of a mate.   *C. Lamb.*

CCXXIII.

Periods of Prolonged Misery.

But the prospect at home was not over-clouded merely; it was the very deepest darkness of misery. It has been well said that long periods of general suffering make far less impression on our minds, than the short sharp struggle in which a few distinguished individuals perish; not that we over-estimate the horror and the guilt of times of open blood-shedding, but we are much too patient of the greater misery and greater sin of periods of quiet legalised oppression; of that most deadly of all evils, when law, and even religion herself, are false to their

divine origin and purpose, and their voice is no longer
the voice of God, but of his enemy. In such cases the
evil derives advantage, in a manner, from the very amount
of its own enormity. No pen can record, no volume can
contain, the details of the daily and hourly sufferings of
a whole people, endured without intermission, through
the whole life of man, from the cradle to the grave. The
mind itself can scarcely comprehend the wide range of
the mischief. *Arnold.*

CCXXIV.

Need for Monarchy.

At such times, society, distracted by the conflict of individual wills, and unable to attain by their free concurrence to a general will, which might unite and hold them
in subjection, feels an ardent desire for a sovereign
power, to which all individuals must submit; and as soon
as any institution presents itself which bears any of the
characteristics of legitimate sovereignty, society rallies
round it with eagerness; as people under proscription
take refuge in the sanctuary of a church. This is what
has taken place in the wild and disorderly youth of
nations, such as those we have just described. Monarchy
is wonderfully suited to those times of strong and fruitful
anarchy, if I may so speak, in which society is striving to
form and regulate itself, but is unable to do so by the free
concurrence of individual wills. There are other times
when monarchy, though from a contrary cause, has the
same merit. Why did the Roman world, so near dissolution at the end of the republic, still subsist for more
than fifteen centuries under the name of an empire,
which, after all, was nothing but a lingering decay, a protracted death-struggle? Monarchy only could produce
such an effect.

CCXXV.

Difficulties of Velasquez.

In this embarrassing situation he formed the chimerical scheme, not only of achieving great exploits by a deputy, but of securing to himself the glory of conquests which were to be made by another. In the execution of this plan, he fondly aimed at reconciling contradictions. He was solicitous to choose a commander of intrepid resolution, and of superior abilities, because he knew these to be requisite in order to secure success; but, at the same time, from the jealousy natural to little minds, he wished this person to be of a spirit so tame and obsequious, as to be entirely dependent on his will. But when he came to apply those ideas in forming an opinion concerning the several officers who occurred to his thoughts as worthy of being intrusted with the command, he soon perceived that it was impossible to find such incompatible qualities united in one character. Such as were distinguished for courage and talents were too high-spirited to be passive instruments in his hands. Those who appeared more gentle and tractable were destitute of capacity, and unequal to the charge. This augmented his perplexity and his fears.   *Robertson.*

CCXXVI.

Public Liberty.

Many politicians of our time are in the habit of laying it down as a self-evident proposition that no people ought to be free till they are fit to use their freedom. The maxim is worthy of the fool in the old story, who resolved not to go into the water until he had learned to swim. If men are to wait for liberty till they become wise and good in slavery, they may indeed wait for ever. Therefore it is that we decidedly approve of the conduct of Milton and the other wise and good men, who, in spite of much that was ridiculous and hateful in the conduct of their associates, stood firmly by the cause of public liberty. We are not aware that the poet has been charged with personal participation in any of the blameable excesses of his time.   *Macaulay.*

CCXXVII.

William's Perplexities.

He felt that it would be madness in him to imitate the example of Monmouth, to cross the sea with a few British adventurers, and to trust to a general rising of the population. It was necessary, and it was pronounced necessary by all those who invited him over, that he should carry an army with him. Yet who could answer for the effect which the appearance of such an army might produce? The government was indeed justly odious. But would the English people, altogether unaccustomed to the interference of continental powers in English disputes, be inclined to look with favour on a deliverer who was surrounded by foreign soldiers? If any part of the royal forces resolutely withstood the invaders, would not that part soon have on its side the patriotic sympathy of millions? A defeat would be fatal to the whole undertaking. A bloody victory gained in the heart of the island by the mercenaries of the States General over the Coldstream Guards and the Buffs would be almost as great a calamity as a defeat. Such a victory would be the most

cruel wound ever inflicted on the national pride of one of
the proudest of nations. The crown so won would never
be worn in peace or security. Many, who had hitherto
contemplated the power of France with dread and loath-
ing, would say that, if a foreign yoke must be borne, there
was less ignominy in submitting to France than in submitting to Holland.   *Macaulay.*

CCXXVIII.

The Blues and the Greens.

Their first complaints were respectful and modest;
they accused the subordinate ministers of oppression, and
proclaimed their wishes for the long life and victory of the
emperor. 'Be patient and attentive, ye insolent railers!'
exclaimed Justinian; 'be mute, ye Jews, Samaritans, and
Manichæans!' The greens still attempted to awaken his
compassion. 'We are poor, we are innocent, we are
injured, we dare not pass through the streets : a general
persecution is exercised against our name and colour.
Let us die, O emperor! but let us die by your command,
and for your service!' But the repetition of partial and
passionate invectives degraded, in their eyes, the majesty
of the purple; they renounced allegiance to the prince
who refused justice to his people; lamented that the
father of Justinian had been born ; and branded his son
with the opprobrious names of an homicide, an ass, and a
perjured tyrant. 'Do you despise your lives?' cried the
indignant monarch : the blues rose with fury from their
seats ; their hostile clamours thundered in the hippo-
drome ; and their adversaries, deserting the unequal
contest, spread terror and despair through the streets of
Constantinople.   *Gibbon.*

CCXXIX.

Weighty Magistrates.

The burgomasters were generally chosen by weight. It is a maxim observed in all honest plain-thinking cities that an alderman should be fat, and the wisdom of this can be proved to a certainty. A lean, spare, diminutive body is generally accompanied by a petulant, restless, meddling mind, whereas your round sleek unwieldy periphery is ever accompanied by a mind like itself, tranquil, torpid, and at ease. Who ever hears of fat men leading a riot, or herding together in turbulent mobs?

Washington Irving.

CCXXX.

Siege of Harlem.

The tidings of despair created a terrible commotion in the starving city. There was no hope either in submission or resistance. Massacre or starvation were the only alternative. But if there was no hope within the walls, without there was still a soldier's death. For a moment the garrison and the able-bodied citizens resolved to advance from the gates in a solid column, to cut their way through the enemy's camp, or to perish on the field. It was thought that the helpless and the infirm, who would alone be left in the city, might be treated with indulgence after the fighting men had all been slain. At any rate, by remaining, the strong could neither protect nor comfort them. As soon, however, as this resolve was known, there was such wailing and outcry of women and children as pierced the hearts of the soldiers and burghers, and caused them to forego the project. They felt that it was

cowardly not to die in their presence.   It was then determined to form all the females, the sick, the aged, and the
children, into a square, to surround them with all the
able-bodied men who still remained, and thus arrayed to
fight their way forth from the gates, and to conquer by
the strength of despair, or at least to perish all together.

Motley.

CCXXXI.

From Morte d'Arthur.

Then they lightly avoided their horses, and put their
shields afore them and drew their swords and ran together
like two fierce lions, and either gave other such buffets
upon their helms that they reeled both backwards two
strides, and then they recovered both and hewed great
pieces from their harness and their shields that a great
part fell in the fields.   And thus they fought till it was
past noon and would not stint till at last they both lacked
wind, and then they stood wagging, staggering, panting,
blowing and bleeding, so that all those that beheld them
for the most part wept for pity.   And when they had
rested them a while they went to battle again trasing,
rasing, and foyning, as two boars, and sometime they ran
the one against the other as it had been two wild rams, and
hurtled so together that they fell to the ground grovelling :
and sometime they were so amazed that either took other's
swords in stead of their own.   Thus they endured till
even-song time, that there was none that there beheld
them might know whether was likliest to win the battle,
and their armour was so sore hewn that men might see
their naked sides, and in other places they were naked
but ever the naked places they defended.   And thus by
assent of them both they granted each other to rest a

while, and so they set them down upon two mole hills there beside the fighting place, and each of them unlaced his helm and took the cold wind, for either of their pages were fast by them to come when they called for them to unlace their harness.   *Malory.*

CCXXXII.

Waterloo.

When the remnant of the Old Guard gave way, and Bulow's Prussians marched up from the valley to the chaussée, they found the main body of the French flying in utter disorder along the road and across the fields. The great high road was choked up by the fugitives ; the very efforts of the pursuers were obstructed by the chaos into which they plunged.   Arms were thrown down, packs cast off, guns abandoned.   The British and the Prussians, converging upon the Charleroi road between La Belle Alliance and Rossomme, forced all they did not take or slay into the fields or the main road.   Darkness had settled over the field ; the masses, moving through the obscurity, hurtled against each other, and more than once friends were mistaken for foes.   But in the gloom of that summer evening, lighted only by a rising moon, there was such exultation as men can feel only when, by fortitude and skill, they have snatched a brilliant victory from the very jaws of destruction.   As the Prussians came up from the bloodstained village of Plancheroit, their bands played ' God save the King,' and the heroic British infantry in the van answered with true British cheers.   *Hooper.*

CCXXXIII.

Revolt and Blockade of Mytilene.

The beginning of the following year saw the revolt of Mytilene. The news was received at first with incredulity by the Athenians who were all but crushed by the recent plague and harassed by the repeated invasions of the Spartans. But when confirmation of the tidings left no room for doubt that the state was threatened by a new and unexpected danger, a blaze of indignation ensued. Athens had never subjected Mytilene to harsh or overbearing rule: when almost every other state in the confederacy had been reduced to a position of dependence, Mytilene had enjoyed equal rights and had been treated with marked distinction, paying no tribute and retaining its fortifications and its navy. Now on the flimsy pretext that they had no assurance of safety in the future, and were unwilling to go hand in hand with the Athenians in their schemes for the subjugation of the whole of Greece, their allies had seized the moment when they fancied Athens was tottering to its fall to revolt to the enemy. If this example were followed, if Athens were stripped one by one of the supports on which it leant, what hope of success remained? How could the state continue the struggle against overwhelming odds when it was already plunged in such difficulties? Exasperated as much by the insolence as by the treachery of their ally, the Athenians determined to prove that their power was not at so low an ebb as was imagined, and accordingly equipped a powerful fleet and despatched it to blockade Mytilene.

CCXXXIV.

Mytilene sues for Pardon.

Disappointed at length in their hopes of assistance from the Spartans, and reduced to utter despair by the growing pressure of famine, the Mytilenæan authorities determined on arming the populace and making a sortie against the blockading force. But the result of this step was different from their expectations. The starving citizens who had never been in sympathy with the revolt no sooner found themselves possessed of weapons than they declined to face so perilous an enterprise. Secret complaint and discontent changed to open menace and abuse of their masters. The cry was raised, invariable at such a moment, that the authorities had stored up great quantities of food which they shared with the rich, while the poor were dying of starvation. Unless they brought the contents of their granaries into the light of day and distributed them at large, immediate surrender was threatened. Well aware that this meant their own certain destruction, the magistrates preferred themselves to take the initiative in this movement, and opened negotiations with the Athenian general, the result being that the town was conditionally made over to him, while an embassy was despatched to Athens to sue for pardon.

CCXXXV.

Cruel Decree of the Athenians.

The exultation at Athens was unbounded. At last the opportunity had come for wreaking vengeance on the Mitylenæans. In the blind resentment of the moment all prayers for mercy were rejected, and it was resolved to put to death the whole male population of military age, and to sell the women and children as slaves. This frightful decision was taken mainly on the advice of Cleon, a man of low extraction, who at that time commanded most influence with the populace. But hardly had the assembly broken up before the citizens began to repent of their headlong haste. Reflexion showed them that it was a piece of monstrous cruelty to cut off a whole population at a blow: their anger would fall on innocent and guilty alike, and the honour of Athens would be seriously compromised. In this state of public feeling, Diodotus and others who were advocates of milder measures succeeded with little difficulty in getting the magistrates to call a second meeting on the morrow for the purpose of giving the whole question fresh consideration.

CCXXXVI.

Second meeting: the Decree reversed.

Next day in the assembly Cleon violently attacked the populace for the inconstancy they had displayed, warning them at the same time that it was the height of madness for a people with such imperial responsibilities as theirs to give way to unwise tenderness of heart. The Mytilenæans had inflicted on them grievous injury without provocation, and unless stern justice were meted out, there would be fresh outbreaks of these troubles in the not distant future. They ought to adhere to their former decision and turn a deaf ear to politicians whose prime aim was not the commonwealth but self. On the other hand Diodotus argued the folly of deciding a matter of such moment under the influence of strong passion.

Even if considerations of expediency weighed more with them than those of honour, some mitigation of their harsh sentences was called for. It would not prevent any other of the allied states from revolting if a fair chance of success appeared : and beyond all question a revolted ally would resort to the most desperate measures rather than fall into the hands of so pitiless a foe. Happily for Mitylene the party of mercy carried the day, and messengers were at once dispatched with orders for the Athenian general to spare the vanquished city.

Adapted from Grote.

CCXXXVII.

An Incident in the Mutiny.

Meantime a flag of truce arrived from the enemy inviting us to a conference outside the fort, and professing that they had a communication to make which they hoped would put an end to hostilities. On one of our officers being ordered out, the Rajah assured him that in attacking our cantonments he had not acted on his own will or judgment, but under compulsion from his people; that, though nominally commander, his authority over his soldiers was hardly equal to that which they exercised over himself. He was not, he added, so ignorant as to believe that his forces could defy the power of England : but he had found it impossible to resist the general rising of his nation. Now that he had discharged the duties of a patriot, he earnestly warned the general to save himself and his soldiers. He offered his solemn oath to guide them in safety through his own territory to the next cantonments. In doing this he should, he said, both serve his own countrymen, and show substantial gratitude for

L

past favours to his English friends. Only let there be no delay or hesitation. Before three days were over the insurgents would be largely reinforced, and all hope of safety would have disappeared.

After Orme.

CCXXXVIII.

A Veritable Ghost.

A late very pious but very credulous bishop was relating a strange story of a demon, that haunted a girl in Lothbury, to a company of gentlemen in the City, when one of them told his lordship the following adventure :—

'As I was one night reading in bed, as my custom is, and all my family were at rest, I heard a foot deliberately ascending the stairs, and as it came nearer I heard something breathe. While I was musing what it should be, three hollow knocks at my door made me ask who was there, and instantly the door blew open.' 'Ah! sir, and pray what did you see?' 'My lord, I'll tell you. A tall thin figure stood before me, with withered hair, and an earthly aspect; he was covered with a long sooty garment, that descended to his ankles, and his waist was clasped close within a broad leathern girdle. In one hand he held a black staff taller than himself, and in the other a round body of pale light, which shone feebly every way.' 'That's remarkable! pray, sir, go on.' 'It beckoned to me, and I followed it downstairs, and there it left me, and made a hideous noise in the street.' 'This is really odd and surprising; but, pray now, did it give you no notice what it might particularly seek or aim at?' 'Yes, my lord, it was the watchman, who came to show me that my servants had left all my doors open.'

Researches of a Psychical Society.

CCXXXIX.

The Giant Tree-Creeper.

The Blacks ascend the trees by the aid of a ring formed of a stout piece of the stem of a creeper, which is excessively strong and supple; one end is tied into a loop, and the other thrown round the tree is passed through the loop and bent back: the end being secured forms a ready and perfectly safe ring, which the operator passes over his waist. The stumps of the fallen leaves form projections which very much assist him in getting up the tree. This is done by taking hold of the ring with each hand, and by a succession of jerks the climber is soon up at the top, with his empty gourds hung round his neck. With a pointed instrument he taps the tree at the crown, and attaches the mouth of a gourd to the aperture, or he takes advantage of the grooved stem of a leaf cut off short to use as a channel for the sap to flow into the gourd suspended below. *Monteiro.*

CCXL.

The Giant Tree-Creeper (continued).

Its stem is sometimes as thick as a man's thigh, and in the dense woods at Quiballa I have seen a considerable extent of forest festooned down to the ground, from tree to tree, in all directions with its thick stems, like great hawsers; above, the trees were nearly hidden by its large, bright, dark-green leaves, and studded with beautiful branches of pure white star-like flowers, most sweetly scented. Its fruit is the size of a large orange, of a yellow colour when ripe, and perfectly round, with a hard brittle shell; inside it is full of a soft reddish pulp in which the

L 2

seeds are contained. This pulp is of a very agreeable acid flavour, and is much liked by the natives. The ripe fruit, when cleaned out, is employed by them to contain small quantities of oil, &c. It is not always easy to obtain ripe seeds, as this creeper is the favourite resort of a villainous, semi-transparent, long-legged red ant—with a stinging bite, like a red-hot needle—which is very fond of the pulp and seeds.   *Monteiro.*

CCXLI.

Kosciusko.

In the invasion of France, many years after, some Polish regiments in the service of Russia, passed through the village where this exiled patriot then lived. Some pillaging of the inhabitants brought Kosciusko from his cottage. 'When I was a Polish soldier,' said he, addressing the plunderers, 'the property of the peaceful citizen was respected.' 'And who art thou?' said an officer, 'who addresses us with a tone of authority?' 'I am Kosciusko.' There was magic in the word. It ran from corps to corps. The march was suspended. They gathered round him, and gazed with astonishment and awe upon the mighty ruin he presented. 'Could it indeed be their hero, whose fame was identified with that of their country?' A thousand interesting reflections burst upon their minds; they remembered his patriotism, his devotion to liberty, his triumphs, and his glorious fall. Their iron hearts were softened; the tears trickled down their faces as they grieved in idle indignation over their country's shameful doom, nor is it difficult to conceive what would be the feelings of the hero himself in such a scene.   *Percy Anecdotes.*

CCXLII.

Columbus and the Eclipse.

By his skill in astronomy he knew that there was shortly to be an eclipse of the moon. He assembled all the principal persons of the district around him on the day before it happened, and, after reproaching them for their fickleness in withdrawing their affection and assistance from men whom they had lately revered, he told them that the Spaniards were servants of the Great Spirit who dwells in heaven, who made and governs the world; that he, offended at their refusing to support men who were the objects of his peculiar favour, was preparing to punish this crime with signal severity, and that very night the moon should withhold her light, and appear of a bloody hue, as a sign of the divine wrath and of the vengeance ready to fall upon them. To this marvellous prediction some of them listened with the careless indifference peculiar to the people of America; others, with the credulity natural to barbarians. But when the moon began gradually to be darkened, and at length appeared of a red colour, all were struck with terror. They ran with consternation to their houses, and returning instantly to Columbus loaded with provisions, threw them at his feet, conjuring him to intercede with the Great Spirit to avert the destruction with which they were threatened.   *Robertson.*

CCXLIII.

James I. repents his Rashness.

No sooner was the king alone, than his temper, more cautious than sanguine, suggested very different views of the matter, and represented every difficulty and danger which could occur.   He reflected that, however the world might pardon this folly of youth in the prince, they would never forgive himself, who, at his years, and after his experience, could entrust his only son, the heir of his crown, the prop of his age, to the discretion of foreigners, without so much as providing the frail security of a safe conduct in his favour; that if the Spanish monarch were sincere in his professions, a few months must finish the treaty of marriage, and bring the Infanta into England; if he were not sincere, the folly was still more egregious of committing the prince into his hands; that Philip, when possessed of so invaluable a pledge, might well rise in his demands, and impose harder conditions of treaty; and that the temerity of the enterprize was so apparent, that the event, how prosperous soever, could not justify it; and if disastrous, it would render himself infamous to his people, and ridiculous to all posterity.   *Hume.*

CCXLIV.

Aeolus wrecks an Armada.

It was now broad day; the hurricane had abated nothing of its violence, and the sea appeared agitated with all the rage of which that destructive element is capable; all the ships on which alone the whole army knew that their safety and subsistence depended were driven from their anchors, some dashing against each other, some beat to pieces on the rocks, many forced ashore, and not a few sinking in the waves.   In less than an hour, fifteen ships of war, and one hundred and forty transports with eight thousand men perished: and such of the unhappy crews as escaped the fury of the sea, were murdered without mercy by the Arabs, as soon as they

reached land.   The Emperor stood in silent anguish and
astonishment, beholding the fatal event which at once
blasted all his hopes of success, and buried in the depths
the vast stores which he had provided as well for annoy-
ing the enemy as for subsisting his own troops ... At
last the wind began to fall and to give some hopes that
as many ships might escape as would be sufficient to save
the army from perishing by famine and transport them
back to Europe.   But these were only hopes : the approach of evening covered the sea with darkness ; and it
being impossible for the officers aboard the ships which
had outlived the storm, to send any intelligence to their
companions who were ashore, they remained during the
night in all the anguish of suspense and uncertainty.

Robertson.

CCXLV.

Cicero's Tusculan Villa.

From the hill on which this villa stood the spectator
surveyed a wide and various prospect, rich at once in
natural beauty and historic associations. The plain at his
feet was the battle-field of the Roman kings and of the
infant commonwealth ; it was strewn with the marble
sepulchres of patricians and consulars : across it stretched
the long straight lines of the military ways which trans-
ported the ensigns of conquest to Parthia and Arabia.
On the right over meadow and woodland, lucid with rivulets, he beheld the white turrets of Tibur, Æsula, Præ-
neste, strung like a row of pearls on the bosom of the
Sabine mountains ; on the left, the glistening waves of
Alba sunk in their green crater, the towering cone of the
Latin Jupiter, the oaks of Aricia and the pines of Lauren-
tum, and the sea bearing sails of every nation to the strand
of Ostia.

Merivale.

CCXLVI.

The Campagna.

Perhaps there is no more impressive scene on earth than the solitary extent of the Campagna of Rome under evening light. Let the reader imagine himself for a moment withdrawn from the sounds and motions of the living world, and sent forth alone into this wild and wasted plain. The earth yields and crumbles beneath his foot, tread he never so lightly, for its substance is white, hollow and carious, like the dusty wreck of the bones of men. The long knotted grass waves and tosses feebly in the evening wind, and the shadows of its motion shake feverishly along the banks of rivers that lift themselves to the sunlight. Hillocks of mouldering earth heave around him, as if the dead beneath were struggling in their sleep ; scattered blocks of black stone, foursquare, remnants of mighty edifices, not one left upon another, lie upon them to keep them down. A dull purple poisonous haze stretches level along the desert, veiling its spectral wrecks of mossy ruins, on whose rents the red light rests like dying fire on defiled altars. The blue ridge of the Alban Mount lifts itself against a solemn space of green clear quiet sky. Watch-towers of dark clouds stand steadfastly along the promontories of the Apennines. From the plain to the mountains, the shattered aqueducts, pier beyond pier, melt into the darkness, like shadowy and countless troops of funeral mourners, passing from a nation's grave. *Ruskin.*

CCXLVII.

Young St. Giles.

Some time after, the people discovered their sentiments in such a manner as was sufficient to prognosticate to the priests the fate which was awaiting them. It was usual on the festival of St. Giles, the tutelar saint of Edinburgh, to carry in procession the image of that saint; but the Protestants, in order to prevent the ceremony, found means, on the eve of the festival, to purloin the statue from the church; and they pleased themselves with imagining the surprise and disappointment of his votaries. The clergy, however, framed hastily a new image, which, in derision, was called by the people young St. Giles; and they carried it through the streets, attended by all the ecclesiastics in the town and neighbourhood. The multitude abstained from violence so long as the queen-regent continued a spectator, but the moment she retired, they invaded the idol, threw it in the mire, and broke it in pieces. The flight and terror of the priests and friars, who, it was remarked, deserted, in his greatest distress, the object of their worship, was the source of universal mockery and laughter.   *Hume.*

CCXLVIII.

The Hardy North.

These northern people were distinguished by tall stature, blue eyes, red hair and beards. They were indefatigable in war, but indolent in sedentary labours. They endured hunger more patiently than thirst, and cold than the heat of the meridian sun. They disdained towns as the refuge of a timorous, and the hiding-places of a thievish populace. They burnt them in the countries which they conquered, or suffered them to fall into decay; and centuries elapsed before they surrounded their villages with walls. Their huts, dispersed like those of the Alpine people, were placed on the banks of rivulets, or near fountains, or in woods, or in the midst of fields. Every farm constituted a distinct centre round which the herds of the owner wandered, or where, among agricultural tribes, the women and slaves tilled the land. The Germans used very little clothing, for the habit of enduring cold served them in its stead. The hides of beasts, the spoils of the chase, hung from the shoulders of the warriors; and the women wore woollen coats ornamented with feathers, or with patches of skins which they selected for their splendid and various tints. The use of clothes which, fitting accurately the different parts of the body, covered the whole of it, was introduced many ages afterwards, and was looked upon even then as a signal corruption of manners.   *Burke.*

CCXLIX.

Julian and his Army.

As soon as the approach of the troops was announced, the Cæsar went out to meet them, and ascended his tribunal, which had been erected in a plain before the gates of the city. After distinguishing the officers and soldiers who by their rank or merit deserved a peculiar attention, Julian addressed himself in a studied oration to the surrounding multitude: he celebrated their exploits with grateful applause; encouraged them to accept, with alacrity, the honour of serving under the eyes of a powerful and liberal monarch; and admonished them that the commands of Augustus required an instant and cheerful obedience. The soldiers, who were apprehensive of offending their general by an indecent clamour, or of belying their sentiments by false and venal acclamations, maintained an obstinate silence; and after a short pause were dismissed to their quarters. The principal officers were entertained by the Cæsar, who professed, in the warmest language of friendship, his desire and inability to reward, according to their deserts, the brave companions of his victories. They retired from the feast full of grief and perplexity; and lamented the hardship of their fate, which tore them from their beloved general and their native country. The only expedient which could prevent their separation was boldly agitated and approved; the popular resentment was insensibly moulded into a regular conspiracy; their just reasons of complaint were heightened by passion, and their passions were inflamed by wine, as on the eve of their departure the troops were indulged in licentious festivity.

Gibbon.

CCL.

The House of Cornelia.

On the promontory of Misenus is yet standing the mansion of Cornelia, mother of the Gracchi; and, whether from the reverence of her virtues and exalted name, or that the gods preserve it as a monument of womanhood, its exterior is yet unchanged. Here she resided many years, and never would be induced to revisit Rome after the murder of her younger son. She cultivated a variety of flowers, and naturalised several plants, and brought together trees from vale and mountain, trees unproductive of fruit but affording her in their superintendence and management a tranquil and expectant pleasure.   We read that the Babylonians and Persians were formerly much addicted to similar places of recreation.   I have no knowledge in these matters; and the first time I went thither I asked many questions of the gardener's boy, a child about nine years old.   He thought me still more ignorant than I was, and said among other such remarks, 'I do not know what they call this plant at Rome, or whether they have it there; but it is among the commonest here, beautiful as it is, and we call it cytisus.' 'Thank you, child,' said I smiling; and pointing towards two cypresses, 'pray what do you call these high and gloomy trees, at the extremity of the avenue, just above the precipice?' 'Others like them,' replied he, 'are called cypresses; but these, I know not why, have always been called Tiberius and Caius.'

Landor.

CCLI.

The Cilician Pirates.

The pirates called themselves Cilicians; in fact their vessels were the rendezvous of desperadoes and adventurers from all countries—discharged mercenaries from the recruiting-grounds of Crete, burgesses from the destroyed townships of Italy, Spain, and Asia, soldiers and officers from the armies of Fimbria and Sertorius, in a word the ruined men of all nations, the hunted refugees of all vanquished parties, every one that was wretched and daring—and where was there not misery and violence in this unhappy age? It was no longer a gang of robbers who had flocked together, but a compact soldier-state, in which the freemasonry of exile and crime took the place of nationality, and within which crime redeemed itself, as it so often does in its own eyes, by displaying the most generous public spirit. If the banner of this state was inscribed with vengeance against the civil society which, rightly or wrongly, had ejected its members, it might be a question whether this device was much worse than those of the Italian oligarchy and the Oriental sultanship which seemed in the course of dividing the world between them.

Mommsen.

CCLII.

Hyder Ali bursts upon the Carnatic.

He resolved in the gloomy recesses of a mind capacious of such things to leave the whole Carnatic an everlasting monument of vengeance, and to put perpetual desolation as a barrier between him and those against whom the faith which holds the moral elements of the world together was no protection. He became at length so confident of his force, so collected in his might that he made no secret whatever of his dreadful resolution. Having terminated his dispute with every enemy and every rival, who buried their mutual animosities in their common detestation against the creditors of the Nabob of Arcot, he drew from every quarter whatever a savage ferocity could add to his new rudiments in the arts of destruction ; and, compounding all the materials of fury, havoc, and desolation into one black cloud he hung for a while on the declivities of the mountains ; whilst the authors of all these evils were idly and stupidly gazing on the menacing meteor which blackened all their horizon, it suddenly burst and poured down the whole of its contents upon the plains of the Carnatic. Then ensued a scene of woe, the like of which no eye had seen, no heart conceived, and which no tongue can adequately tell.   All the horrors of war before known or heard of were mercy to that new havoc.   A storm of universal fire blasted every field, consumed every house, destroyed every temple.   The miserable inhabitants flying from the flaming villages in part were slaughtered; others, without regard to sex, to age, to the respect of rank or the sacredness of function—fathers torn from children, husbands from wives, enveloped in a whirlwind of cavalry, and amidst the goading spears of drivers and the trampling of pursuing horses—were swept into a captivity in an unknown and hostile land.   Those who were able to avoid this tempest fled to the walled cities; but escaping from fire, sword, and exile, they fell into the jaws of famine.   *Burke.*

CCLIII.

Tropical Africa.

Into the heart of this mysterious Africa I wish to take you with me now.   And let me magnify my subject by saying at once that it is a wonderful thing to see.   It is a wonderful thing to start from the civilization of Europe, pass up these mighty rivers and work your way into that unknown land,—work your way alone and on feet, mile after mile, month after month, among strange birds and beasts and plants and insects, meeting tribes which have no name, speaking tongues which no man can interpret, till you have reached its secret heart and stood where white man has never trod before.   It is a wonderful thing to look at this weird world of human beings—half animal, half children, wholly savage and wholly heathen; and to turn and come back again to civilization before the impressions have had time to faint and while the myriad problems of so strange a spectacle are still seething in the mind. It is an education to see this sight, an education in the meaning and history of man. To have been here is to have lived before Menes. It is to have watched the dawn of evolution. It is to have the great moral and social problems of life, of anthropology, of ethnology and even of theology, brought home to the imagination in the new and startling light. *Drummond.*

CCLIV.

Augustus and Charles IV.

If we annihilate the interval of time and space between Augustus and Charles, strong and striking will be the contrast between the two Cæsars; the Bohemian, who concealed his weakness under the mask of ostentation, and the Roman, who disguised his strength under the semblance of modesty. At the head of his victorious legions, in his reign over the sea and land, from the Nile and Euphrates to the Atlantic ocean, Augustus professed himself the servant of the senate and the equal of his fellow citizens. The conqueror of Rome and her provinces assumed the popular and legal form of the censor, a consul, and a tribune. His will was the law of mankind, but in the declaration of his laws he borrowed the voice of the senate and people; and, from their decrees, their master accepted and received his temporary commission, to administer to the republic. In his dress, his domestics, his titles, in all the offices of social life, Augustus maintained the character of a private Roman; and his most artful flatterers respected the secret of absolute and perpetual monarchy. *Gibbon.*

CCLV.

Two Armies of Martyrs.

Here, therefore, we are to enter upon one of the grand scenes of history; a solemn battle fought out to the death, yet fought without ferocity, by the champions of rival principles. Heroic men had fallen, and were still fast falling, for what was called heresy; and now those who had inflicted death on others were called upon to bear the same witness to their own sincerity. England became the theatre of a war between two armies of martyrs, to be waged, not upon the open field, in open action, but on the stake and on the scaffold, with the nobler weapons of passive endurance. Each party were ready to give their own blood; each party were ready to shed the blood of their antagonists; and the sword was to single out its victims in the rival ranks, not, as in peace, among those whose crimes made them dangerous to society, but as on the field of battle, where the most conspicuous courage most challenges the aim of the enemy. It was war though under the form of peace; and if we would understand the true spirit of the time, we must regard Catholics and Protestants as gallant soldiers, whose deaths, when they fall, are not painful, but glorious; and whose devotion we are equally able to admire, even where we cannot equally approve their cause.   *Froude.*

CCLVI.

The Libertine Destroyed.

This calls to my mind a thing that really happened not many years ago. A young fellow of some rank and fortune, just let loose from the university, resolved, in order to make a figure in the world, to assume the shining character of what he called a rake. By way of learning the rudiments of his intended profession, he frequented the theatres, where he was often drunk and always noisy. Being one night at the representation of that most absurd play, *The Libertine Destroyed,* he was so charmed with the profligacy of the hero of the piece, that, to the edification of the audience, he swore many oaths that he would be the libertine destroyed. A discreet friend of his, who sat by him, kindly represented to him that to be the libertine was a laudable design which he greatly approved of; but that to be the libertine destroyed seemed to him an unnecessary part of his plan, and rather rash. He persisted, however, in his first resolution, and insisted upon being the libertine and destroyed. Probably he was so ; at least the presumption is in his favour. There are, I am persuaded, so many cases of this nature, that for my own part I would desire no greater step towards the reformation of manners for the next twenty years, than that our people should have no vices but their own. *Chesterfield.*

CCLVII.

Rome under Valentinian.

As early as the time of Cicero and Varro it was the opinion of the Roman augurs that the twelve vultures which Romulus had seen represented the twelve centuries assigned for the fatal period of his city. This prophecy, disregarded perhaps in the season of health and prosperity, inspired the people with gloomy apprehensions when the twelfth century, clouded with disgrace and misfortune, was almost elapsed ; and even posterity must acknowledge with some surprise that the arbitrary

interpretation of an accidental or fabulous circumstance
has been seriously verified in the downfall of the Western
Empire. But its fall was announced by a clearer omen
than the flight of vultures : the Roman Government
appeared every day less formidable to its enemies, more
odious and oppressive to its subjects. The taxes were
multiplied with the public distress ; economy was neglected in proportion as it became necessary ; and the
injustice of the rich shifted the unequal burden from
themselves to the people, whom they defrauded of the
indulgences that might sometimes have alleviated their
misery. The severe inquisition, which confiscated their
goods and tortured their persons, compelled the subjects
of Valentinian to prefer the more simple tyranny of the
barbarians, to fly to the woods and mountains, or to
embrace the vile and abject condition of mercenary servants. They abjured and abhorred the name of Roman
citizen, which had formerly excited the ambition of mankind. . . . If all the barbarian conquerors had been annihilated in the same hour, their total destruction would
not have restored the empire of the West ; and if Rome
still survived, she survived the loss of freedom, of virtue,
and of honour.   *Gibbon.*

CCLVIII.

Second Invasion of Attica, B.C. 430.

Over and above the raging epidemic, they had just gone
over Attica and ascertained the devastations committed
throughout all the territory (except the Marathonian
Tetrapolis and Dekeleia districts spared, as we are told,
through indulgence founded on an ancient legendary
sympathy) during their long stay of forty days. The rich
had found their comfortable mansions and farms, the poor
their modest cottages, in the various demes, torn and

ruined. Death, sickness, loss of property, and despair of the future, now rendered the Athenians angry and intractable to the last degree ; and they vented their feelings against Pericles, as the cause, not merely of the war, but also of all that they were now enduring. Either with or without his consent, they sent envoys to Sparta to open negotiations for peace, but the Spartans turned a deaf ear to the proposition. This new disappointment rendered them still more furious against Pericles, whose longstanding political enemies now doubtless found strong sympathy in their denunciations of his character and policy. That unshaken and majestic firmness which ranked first among his many eminent qualities, was never more imperiously required and never more effectively manifested. *Grote.*

CCLIX.

Slow Decay of Rome.

It was scarcely possible that the eyes of contemporaries should discover in the public felicity the latent causes of decay. This long peace and the uniform government of the Romans introduced a slow and secret poison into the vitals of the empire. The minds of men were gradually reduced to the same level, the fire of genius was extinguished, and even the military spirit evaporated. The natives of Europe were brave and robust; Spain, Gaul, Britain, and Illyricum supplied the legions with excellent soldiers, and constituted the real strength of the monarchy. Their personal valour remained, but they no longer possessed that public courage which is nourished by the love of independence, the presence of danger, and the habit of command. They received laws and governors from the will of their sovereign, and trusted for their defence to a mercenary army.

The posterity of their boldest leaders was contented with the rank of citizens and subjects. The most aspiring spirits resorted to the court or standard of the emperors; and the deserted provinces, deprived of political strength or union, insensibly sunk into the languid indifference of private life. *Gibbon.*

CCLX.

Assassination of President Lincoln.

I mourn for Mr. Lincoln, as man should mourn the fate of man, when it is sudden and supreme. I hate regicide as I do populicide—deeply, if frenzied; more deeply, if deliberate. But my wonder is in remembering the tone of the English people and press respecting this man during his life, and in comparing it with their sayings of him in his death. They caricatured him and reviled him when his cause was poised in deadly balance; when their praise would have been grateful to him and their help priceless. They now declare his cause to have been just, when it needs no aid; and his purposes to have been noble, when all human thoughts of them have become vanity; and will never so much as mix their murmurs in his ears with the sentence of the Tribunal which has summoned him to receive a juster praise and tenderer blame than ours. *Ruskin.*

CCLXI.

Pitt's Devotion to Parliament.

The details of the childhood of great men are apt to be petty and cloying. But, in the case of Pitt, those details are doubly important. They alone explain that political precocity and that long parliamentary ascendancy, which still puzzle posterity. For he went into the House of Commons as an heir enters his home; he breathed in it his native atmosphere—he had indeed breathed no other; in the nursery, in the schoolroom, at the University, he lived in its temperature; it had been, so to speak, made over to him as a bequest by its unquestioned master. Throughout his life, from the cradle to the grave, he may be said to have known no wider existence. The objects and amusements, that other men seek in a thousand ways, were for him, all concentrated there. It was his mistress, his stud, his dice-box, his game preserve; it was his ambition, his library, his creed. For it, and for it alone, had the consummate Chatham trained him from his birth. No young Hannibal was ever more solemnly devoted to his country than Pitt to Parliament. And the austerity of his political consecration lends additional interest to the records of his childhood; for they furnish almost the only gleams of ease and nature that play on his life. He was destined, at one bound, to attain that supreme but isolated position, the first necessity of which is self-control; and, behind the imperious mask of power, he all but concealed the softer emotions of his earlier years. From the time that he went to Cambridge, as a boy of fourteen with his tutor and his nurse, he seems, with one short interval, to have left youth and gaiety behind.

Lord Rosebery.

CCLXII.

A Patriot King.

What spectacle can be presented to the eye of the mind so rare, so nearly divine, as a king possessed of absolute power, neither usurped by fraud, nor maintained by force, but the genuine effect of esteem, of confidence, and affection; the free gift of liberty, who finds her greatest security in this power, and would desire no other, if the prince on the throne could be, what his people wish him to be, immortal?   Civil fury will have no place in this draught : or, if the monster is seen, he must be seen subdued, bound, chained, and deprived entirely of power to do hurt.   In his place concord will appear, brooding peace and prosperity on the happy land : joy sitting in every face, content in every heart ; a people unoppressed, undisturbed, unalarmed ; busy to improve their private property and the public stock ; fleets covering the ocean, bringing home wealth by the returns of industry, carrying assistance or terror abroad by the direction of wisdom, and asserting triumphantly the right and the honour of Great Britain, as far as waters roll, and as winds can waft them.   *Bolinbroke.*

CCLXIII.

Pitt on the Slave Trade.

It was in 1792 that Pitt set an imperishable seal on his advocacy of the question, by the delivery of a speech which all authorities concur in placing before any other effort of his genius ; and certainly no recorded utterance of his touches the imaginative flight of the peroration. He rose exhausted, and immediately before rising was obliged to take medicine to enable him to speak.   But his prolonged and powerful oration showed no signs of disability ; indeed, for the last twenty minutes he seemed, said shrewd critics, to be nothing less than inspired.   He burst, as it were, into a prophetic vision of the civilization that shall dawn upon Africa, and recalled the not less than African barbarism of heathen Britain ; exclaiming, as the first beams of the morning sun pierced the windows of Parliament, and appeared to suggest the quotation—

Nos ubi primus equis Oriens afflavit anhelis,
Illic sera rubens accendit lumina Vesper.

Fox was loud in his generous admiration.   Windham,
an even more hostile critic, avowed that, for the first
time, he understood the possible compass of human
eloquence.   Sheridan, most hostile of all, was even passionate in his praise.   Grey, who ceded to none in the
bitterness and expression of his enmity, ceded also to
none in his enthusiasm of eulogy.   To those who consider
Pitt a sublime parliamentary hack, greedy of power and
careful only of what might conduce to power, his course
on the Slave Trade, where he had no interest to gain,
and could only offend powerful supporters, may well be
commended.   *Lord Rosebery.*

CCLXIV.

Mary declares War against France.

That he might work on these with greater facility and
more certain success, he set out for England.   The Queen
who during her husband's absence had languished in perpetual dejection, resumed fresh spirits on his arrival: and
without paying the least attention either to the interests
or the inclinations of her people, entered warmly into all
his schemes.   In vain did the Privy Council remonstrate
against the imprudence as well as the danger of involving
the nation in unnecessary war ; in vain did they put her
in mind of the solemn treaties subsisting between England and France, which the conduct of that nation had
afforded her no pretext to violate.   Mary, soothed by
Philip's caresses, or intimidated by the threats which his
ascendancy over her emboldened him at some times to
throw out, was deaf to everything that could be urged in
opposition to his sentiments, and insisted with the greatest

vehemence on an immediate declaration of war against France. The Council, though all Philip's address and Mary's authority were employed to gain or overthrow them, after struggling long, yielded at last, not from conviction, but merely from deference to the will of their sovereign. War was declared against France, the only one perhaps against that kingdom into which the English ever entered with reluctance.   *Robertson.*

CCLXV.

Roman Noses.

Among the ancient Romans the great offices of state were all elective, which obliged them to be very observant of the shape of the noses of those persons to whom they were to apply for votes. Horace tells us that a sharp nose was an indication of satirical wit and humour; for when speaking of his friend Virgil, though he says, 'At est bonus, ut melior non alius quisquam,' yet he allows he was no joker, and not a fit match at the sneer for those of his companions who had sharper noses than his own. They also looked upon short noses, with a little inflection at the end tending upwards, as a mark of the owner's being addicted to jibing; for the same author, talking of Mæcenas, says that though he was born of an ancient family, yet was he not apt to turn persons of low birth into ridicule, which he expresses by saying that 'he had not a turn-up nose.' Martial, in one of his epigrams, calls this kind of nose the rhinocerotic nose, and says that everyone in his time affected this kind of snout, as an indication of his being *master of the talent of humour.*   *James Ridley.*

CCLXVI.

Genius not Hereditary.

Cicero, in order to accomplish his son in that sort of learning which he designed him for, sent him to the most celebrated academy of that time in the world, where a vast concourse out of the most polite nations could not but furnish the young gentleman with a multitude of great examples and accidents which might insensibly have instructed him in his designed studies. He placed him under the care of Cratippus who was one of the greatest philosophers of the age, and, as if all the books which were then written were not sufficient for his use, he composed others on purpose for him. Notwithstanding all this, history informs us that Marcus proved a mere blockhead and that Nature, who it seems was even with the son for her prodigality to the father, rendered him incapable of improving by all the rules of eloquence, precepts of philosophy, his own endeavours, and the most refined conversation of Athens.

CCLXVII.

A King on Politicians.

Neither do I say this with the least intention to detract from the many virtues of that excellent king, whose character, I am sensible, will, on this account, be very much lessened in the opinion of an English reader; but, I take this defect among them to have arisen from their ignorance, by not having hitherto reduced politics into a science, as the more acute wits of Europe have done. For, I remember very well, in a discourse one day with

the king, when I happened to say, 'there were several
thousand books among us written upon the art of government,' it gave him (directly contrary to my intention) a
very mean opinion of our understandings. He professed
both to abominate and despise all mystery, refinement,
and intrigue, either in a prince or in a minister. He
could not tell what I meant by secrets of state, where an
enemy, or some rival nation, were not in the case. He
confined the knowledge of governing within very narrow
bounds, to common sense and reason, to justice and
lenity, to the speedy determination of civil and criminal
causes ; with some other obvious topics, which are not
worth considering. And he gave it for his opinion :
'That whoever could make two ears of corn, or two
blades of grass, to grow upon a spot of ground where
only one grew before, would deserve better of mankind,
and do more essential service to his country, than the
whole race of politicians put together.'   *Swift.*

CCLXVIII.

Political Causation.

In most cases where a permanent change has been
effected in the government and in the modes of political
thinking of a country, this has been mainly because the
nation has become ripe for it through the action of general
causes. A doctrine which had long been fervently held,
and which was interwoven with the social fabric, is sapped
by intellectual scepticism, loses its hold on the affections
of the people, and becomes unrealised, obsolete and incredible. An institution which was once useful and
honoured has become unsuited to the altered conditions
of society. The functions it once discharged are no

longer needed, or are discharged more efficiently in other ways, and as modes of thought and life grow up that are not in harmony with it, the reverence that consecrates it slowly ebbs away. Social and economical causes change the relative importance of classes and professions till the old political arrangements no longer reflect with any fidelity the real disposition of power. Causes of this kind undermine institutions and prepare great changes, and it is only when they have finally done their work that the men arise who strike the final blow and whose names are associated with the catastrophe. So eminently is this the case that some distinguished writers have maintained that the action of special circumstances and of individual genius, efforts, and peculiarities counts for nothing in the great march of human affairs, and that every successful revolution must be attributed solely to the long train of intellectual influences that prepared and necessitated its triumph. *Lecky.*

CCLXIX.

Union or Separation.

The soundest and healthiest bonds which can unite people are old traditions and a common history, provided always that the connection is voluntary. Pedants or fanatics who would disturb it, reviving antipathies that slumber or creating them where they had never existed, unsettling the minds of the young with their crude theories and furnishing pretexts to scheming politicians, are the pests of modern civilization. Where incurable antipathy does exist, however it has been brought about, whether by real wrongs inflicted and endured or by the evil activity of literary vermin, disruption had better take place. Anything for peace. Anything rather than this prolonged military hubbub which throws back civilization and postpones the dawn of the new era in which the working men of Europe shall come by their own. But to my mind it is a nobler spectacle when men of different blood and various speech can consent to live together under one polity subordinating the barbarous prejudices of race to the common ends of civil association.

CCLXX.

The Cæsars.

Such, amidst the superhuman grandeur and hallowed privileges of the Roman emperor's office, were the extra-ordinary perils which menaced the individual officer. The office rose by its grandeur to a region above the clouds and vapours of earth : the officer might find his personal security as unsubstantial as those wandering vapours. Nor is it possible that these circumstances of violent opposition can be better illustrated than in this tale of Herodian. Whilst the emperor's mighty arms were stretched out to arrest some potentate in the heart of Asia, a poor slave is silently and stealthily creeping round the base of the Alps, with the purpose of winning his way as a murderer to the imperial bed-chamber ; Cæsar is watching some potent rebel of the Orient, at a distance of two thousand leagues, and he overlooks the dagger which is within three stealthy steps, and one tiger's leap, of his own heart. All the heights and depths which belong to man's frailty, all the contrasts of glory and meanness, the extremities of what is highest and lowest in human casualties, meeting in the station of the Roman Cæsar Semper Augustus—have combined to call him into high marble relief, and to make him the

most interesting study of all whom history has em-
blazoned with colours of fire and blood, or has crowned
most lavishly with diadems of cypress and laurel.

De Quincey.

CCLXXI.

Ancient Republics.

The austere frugality of the ancient republicans, their
carelessness about the possession and the pleasures of
wealth, the strict regard for law among the people, its
universal steadfast loyalty during the happy centuries
when the constitution, after the pretensions of the aristocracy had been curbed, was flourishing in its full per-
fections,—the sound feeling which never amid internal
discord allowed of an appeal to foreign interference,—the
absolute empire of the laws and customs and the steadiness with which nevertheless whatever in them was no
longer expedient was amended, the wisdom of the constitution and of the laws,—the ideal perfection of fortitude
realised in the citizens and in the state,—all these qualities unquestionably excite a feeling of reverence, which
cannot be awakened equally by the contemplation of any
other people. Yet after all, if we bring those ages vividly
before our minds, something of horror will mingle with
our admiration. For those virtues from the earliest times
were leagued and compromised with the most fearful
vices ; insatiable ambition, unprincipled contempt for the
rights of foreigners, unfeeling indifference for their sufferings, avarice, even while rapine was yet a stranger, and,
as a consequence of the severance of ranks, inhuman
hard-heartedness, not only toward slaves or foreigners,
but even toward fellow-citizens. Those very virtues prepared the way for all these vices to get the mastery, and
so were themselves swallowed up.

CCLXXII.

The Gods of Rome.

What the religion of Greece was to philosophy and art, that the Roman religion may be said to have been to political and social life. It was the religion of the family: the religion also of the empire of the world. Beginning in rustic simplicity, the traces of which it ever afterwards retained, it grew with the power of the Roman state, and became one with its laws. No fancy or poetry moulded the forms of the Roman gods: they are wanting in character, and hardly distinguishable from one another. Not what they were, but their worship is the point of interest about them. Those inanimate beings occasionally said a patriotic word at some critical juncture of the Roman affairs, but they had no attributes or qualities : they are the mere impersonation of the needs of the state.

CCLXXIII.

Large States and Small.

On the whole comparison there can be little doubt that the balance of advantage lies in favour of the modern system of large states. The small republic indeed develops its individual citizens to a pitch which in the large kingdom is utterly impossible. But it so develops them at the cost of bitter political strife within, and of almost constant warfare without. It may even be doubted whether the highest form of the city-commonwealth does not require slavery as a condition of its most perfect development. The days of glory of such a commonwealth are indeed glorious beyond comparison ; but it is a glory

which is too brilliant to last, and in proportion to the
short splendour of its prime is too often the unutterable
wretchedness of its long old age.   The republics of Greece
seem to have been shown to the world for a moment, like
some model of glorified humanity, from which all may
draw the highest of lessons, but which none may hope to
reproduce in its perfection.   As the literature of Greece is
the groundwork of all later literature, as the art of Greece
is the groundwork of all later art, so in the great democracy
of Athens we recognise the parent state of law and justice
and freedom, the wonder and the example of every later
age.   But it is an example which we can no more reproduce than we can call back again the inspiration of the
Homeric singer, the more than human skill of Pheidias,
or the untaught and inborn wisdom of Thucydides.   We
can never be like them, if only because they have gone
before.

CCLXXIV.

Political Gamblers.

Such will be the impotent condition of those men of
great hereditary estates who indeed dislike the designs
that are carried on, but whose dislike is rather that of
spectators than of parties that may be concerned in the
catastrophe of the piece.   But riches do not in all cases
secure an inert and passive resistance.   There are always
in that description men whose fortunes, when their minds
are once vibrated by passion or evil principle, are by no
means a security from their actually taking their part
against the public tranquillity.   We see to what low and
despicable passions of all kinds many men in that class
are ready to sacrifice the patrimonial estates, which might
be perpetuated in their families, with splendour and with

the fame of hereditary benefactors of mankind, from generation to generation. Do we not see how lightly people treat their fortunes, when under the influence of the passion of gaming? The game of ambition or resentment will be played by many of the rich and great as desperately and with as much blindness to the consequences as any other game.

CCLXXV.

The British Monarchy.

We all feel that our old, limited, hereditary monarchy is a blessing to the country, if it be only on account of the quiet and good order which its principle of succession ensures, compared with the mischief which would follow, if the post of chief magistrate among us were to be intrigued for by the ringleaders of clubs, or fought for by ambitious soldiers. It is, of course, impossible to secure a succession of good and wise princes; nor can human foresight calculate when a Marcus Aurelius will be followed by a Commodus. Hence, our constitution is rightly cautious and restrictive. It is framed not for a single generation, or with reference to the personal qualities of a particular ruler; but it is the fruit of the experience of many ages, and is designed for duration and permanence. It therefore provides checks and securities against the ambition, and passions, and weaknesses of human nature; it fixes limitations sufficient to secure a large amount of good government, and to protect liberty, even under a bad prince. But it leaves open a wide field for the exercise of the virtues of a good one. The constitutional sovereigns of England who understand and act up to their true political duties; who also employ the high

influence of their station and example for the encourage-
ment of social and domestic virtue, for the advancement
of learning, and the well-judged patronage of art, earn
nobly the gratitude of the people : and that debt would
be paid honestly, if requisite, in act as well as in feeling.

CCLXXVI.

Punishment for Political Crime.

In the great lottery of civil war the prizes are enormous,
and when such prizes may be obtained by a course of
action which is profoundly injurious to the State, the
deterrent influence of severe penalties is especially necessary. In the great majority of cases, the broad distinction
which it is now the fashion to draw between political and
other crimes, is both pernicious and untrue. There is no
sphere in which the worst passions of human nature may
operate more easily or more dangerously than in the
sphere of politics. There is no criminal of a deeper dye
than the adventurer who is gambling for power with the
lives of men. There are no crimes which produce vaster
and more enduring sufferings than those which sap the
great pillars of order in the State, and destroy that respect
for life, for property, and for law, on which all true progress depends. So far the rebellion had been not only
severely but mercilessly suppressed. Scores of wretched
peasants, who were much more deserving of pity than of
blame, had been shot down. Over great tracts of country
every rebel's cottage had been burnt to cinders. Men
had been hanged who, although they had been compelled
or induced to take a leading part in the rebellion, had so
comported themselves as to establish the strongest claims
to the clemency of the Government. But what inconsist-

N

ency, what injustice, it was asked, could be more flagrant, than at this time to select as special objects of that clemency, the very men who were the authors and the organizers of the rebellion—the very men who, if it had succeeded, would have reaped its greatest rewards ?

Lecky.

CCLXXVII.

Cæsar.

Far as the greatness of his genius raised Cæsar above the level of ordinary men, he was nevertheless prone to certain weaknesses, to which those are often found to suc- cumb, who are attended in life by unvarying success and good fortune. Cæsar's luck in all the chances and changes of his life, the flattering encomiums with which he was everywhere received, and the distinguished offices which the Roman people conferred upon him, gradually filled him with such a degree of pride, that he took little pains to disguise the contempt with which he regarded the mass of his fellow citizens. It is true that after winning a complete victory over his opponents, he took steps to win over and enlist on his side the favour and affection of Rome. But, none the less, he was so far from hiding his arrogant pride, that he was considered a tyrant rather than a merciful victor, and many patriotic Romans lamented the overthrow and decay of freedom, and sought to avenge it.   *Froude.*

CCLXXVIII.

Cicero and Cæsar.

Literature was a neutral ground on which he could approach his political enemy without too open discredit, and he courted eagerly the approval of a critic whose literary genius he esteemed as highly as his own. Men of genuine ability are rarely vain of what they can do really well. Cicero admired himself as a statesman with the most unbounded enthusiasm. He was proud of his verses, which were hopelessly commonplace. In the art in which he was without a rival he was modest and diffident. He sent his various writings for Cæsar's judgment. ' Like the traveller who has overslept himself,' he said, 'yet by extraordinary exertions reaches his goal sooner than if he had been earlier on the road, I will follow your advice and court this man. I have been asleep too long. I will correct my slowness with my speed ; and as you say he approves my verses, I shall travel not with a common carriage, but with a four-in-hand of poetry.' *Froude.*

CCLXXIX.

Cæsar as a General.

He was rash, but with a calculated rashness, which the event never failed to justify. His greatest successes were due to the rapidity of his movements, which brought him on the enemy before they heard of his approach. He travelled sometimes a hundred miles a day, reading or writing in his carriage, through countries without roads, and crossing rivers without bridges. In battle he sometimes rode ; but he was more often on foot, bareheaded, and in a conspicuous dress, that he might be seen and recognised. Again and again by his own efforts he recovered a day that was half-lost. He once seized a panic-stricken standard-bearer, turned him round, and told him that he had mistaken the direction of the enemy. He never misled his army as to an enemy's strength, or, if he misstated their numbers, it was only to exaggerate. *Froude.*

CCLXXX.

Cromwell.

Of his genius there is little question.   Clarendon himself could not be blind to the fact that such a presence as that of this Puritan soldier had seldom been felt upon the scene of history.   Necessity, who will have the man and not the shadow, had chosen him from among his fellows and placed her crown upon his brow.   I say again let us never glorify revolution ; let us not love the earthquake and the storm more than the regular and beneficent course of nature.   Yet revolutions send capacity to the front with volcanic force across all the obstacles of envy and of class.   It was long before law-loving England could forgive one who seemed to have set his foot on law ; but there never perhaps was a time when she was not at heart proud of his glory, when she did not feel safer beneath the ægis of his victorious name.   As often as danger threatens us, the thought returns that the race which produced Cromwell, may, at its need, produce his peer, and that the spirit of the Great Usurper may once more stand forth in arms.   *Goldwin Smith.*

CCLXXXI.

Cromwell the Offspring of his Age.

To whatever age they may belong, the greatest, the most god-like of men, are men, not gods.   They are the offspring, though the highest offspring, of their age.   They would be nothing without their fellow-men.   Did Cromwell escape the intoxication of power which has turned the brains of other favourites of fortune, and bear himself always as one who held the government as a trust from

God? It was because he was one of a religious people. Did he, amidst the temptations of arbitrary rule, preserve his reverence for law, and his desire to reign under it? It was because he was one of a law-loving people. Did he, in spite of fearful provocation, show on the whole remarkable humanity? It was because he was one of a brave and humane people. A somewhat larger share of the common qualities—this, and this alone it was which, circumstances calling him to a great trust, had raised him above his fellows.   *Goldwin Smith.*

CCLXXXII.

Augustus.

Yet the secret of his power escaped perhaps the eyes of Augustus himself, blinded as they doubtless were by the fumes of national incense. Cool, shrewd, and subtle, the youth of nineteen had suffered neither interest nor vanity to warp the correctness of his judgments. The accomplishment of his designs was marred by no wandering imaginations. His struggle for power was supported by no belief in a great destiny, but simply by observation of circumstances, and a close calculation of his means. As he was a man of no absorbing tastes or fervid impulses, so he was also free from all illusions. The young Octavius commenced his career as a narrow-minded aspirant for material power. But his intellect expanded with his fortunes, and his soul grew with his intellect. The emperor was not less magnanimous than he was magnificent. With the world at his feet, he began to conceive the real grandeur of his position. He became the greatest of Stoic philosophers, inspired with the strongest enthusiasm, impressed the most deeply

with a consciousness of divinity within him. He acknow-
ledged, not less than a Cato or a Brutus, that the man-God
must suffer as well as act divinely; and though his human
weakness still allowed some meannesses and trivialities
to creep to light, his self-possession both in triumphs and
reverses was consistently dignified and imposing.

Merivale.

CCLXXXIII.

The Prince Consort.

His countenance never had a nobler aspect than in the
last years of his life. The character is written in the face:
here were none of those fatal lines which indicate craft or
insincerity, greed or sensuality. All was clear, open,
pure-minded, honest. He was patient in bearing criticism
and contradiction. He delighted in wit and humour.
Few men had a greater love of freedom in its deepest,
and in its widest sense, than the prince. As all know,
he was a man of many pursuits and various accomplishments, with an ardent admiration for the beautiful, both
in nature and in art. There was one very rare quality to
be noticed in him: he had the greatest delight in anybody
else saying a fine thing, or doing a great deed. He delighted in humanity doing well. We meet with people
who can say fine sayings, and do noble actions, but who
do not like to speak of the great sayings and noble deeds
of other persons. It is said there might be some great
and peculiar moral derived from the life of any man, if
we knew it intimately. I think I can see the moral to be
derived from a study of the prince's life. It is one which
applies to a few amongst the highest natures: he cared
too much about too many things. And everything in

which he was concerned must be done supremely well to please and satisfy him. The great German poet, Goethe, had the same defect, or rather the same super-abundance. He took great pains in writing a short note, that it should be admirably written. He did not under-stand the merit of second best. Everything that was done must be done perfectly. It was thus with the prince.

Theodore Martin.

CCLXXXIV.

Henry VIII.

Instead of a monarch, jealous, severe, and avaricious, who, in proportion as he advanced in years, was sinking still deeper in these unpopular vices, a young prince of eighteen had succeeded to the throne, who even in the eyes of men of sense gave promising hopes of his future conduct, much more in those of the people, always en-chanted with novelty, youth, and royal dignity. The beauty and vigour of his person, accompanied with dex-terity in every manly exercise, were further adorned with a blooming and ruddy countenance, with a lively air, with the appearance of spirit and activity in all his demeanour. His father, in order to remove him from the knowledge of public business, had hitherto occupied him entirely in the pursuits of literature, and the proficiency which he made gave no bad prognostic of his parts and capacity. Even the vices of vehemence, ardour, and impatience. to which he was subject, and which afterwards degenerated into tyranny, were considered only as faults incident to unguarded youth, which would be corrected when time had brought him to greater moderation and maturity.

Hume.

CCLXXXV.

Shakespeare.

Shakespeare was the man, who, of all modern, and perhaps ancient poets, had the largest and most comprehensive soul. All the images of nature were present to him; and he drew them not laboriously but luckily. When he describes anything, you more than see it, you feel it. Those who accuse him to have wanted learning, give him the greater commendation. He was naturally learned; he needed not books to read nature; he looked inwards and he found her there. I cannot say he is everywhere alike; but he is always great when some great occasion is presented to him. No man can say he ever had a fit subject for his wit, and did not then raise himself high above the rest of poets.   *Dryden.*

CCLXXXVI.

Louis XVI.

The unhappy Louis XVI was a man of the best intentions that probably ever reigned. He was by no means deficient in talents. He had a most laudable desire to supply, by general reading, and even by the acquisition of elemental knowledge, an education in all points originally defective; but nobody told him (and it was no wonder he should not himself divine it) that the world of which he read, and the world in which he lived, were no longer the same. Desirous of doing everything for the best, fearful of cabal, distrusting his own judgment, he sought his ministers of all kinds upon public testimony. But as courts are the field for caballers, the public is the theatre for mountebanks and imposters. The cure for both these evils is in the discernment of the prince. But an accurate and penetrating discernment is what in a young prince could not be expected.

CCLXXXVII.

Hannibal.

If the character of men be estimated according to the steadiness with which they have followed the true principle of action, we cannot assign a high place to Hannibal. But if patriotism were indeed the greatest of virtues, and a resolute devotion to the interests of his country were all the duty that a public man can be expected to fulfil, he would then deserve the most lavish praise. Nothing can be more unjust than the ridicule with which Juvenal has treated his motives, as if he had been actuated merely by a romantic desire of glory. On the contrary, his whole conduct displays the loftiest genius, and the boldest spirit of enterprise, happily subdued and directed by a cool judgment, to the furtherance of the honour and interests of his country; and his sacrifice of selfish pride and passion, when after the battle of Zama, he urged the acceptance of peace, and lived to support the disgrace of Carthage, with the patient hope of one day repairing it, affords a strong contrast to the cowardly despair with which some of the best of the Romans deprived their country of their services by suicide. Of the extent of his abilities, the history of his life is the best evidence; as a general, his conduct remains uncharged by a single error; for the idle censure which Livy presumes to pass on him for not marching to Rome after the battle of Cannæ, is founded on such mere ignorance, that it does not deserve any serious notice.   *Arnold.*

CCLXXXVIII.

Dryden.

Dryden began to write about the time of the Restoration, and continued long in his literary career. He brought to the study of his native tongue a vigorous mind fraught with various knowledge. There is a richness in his diction, a copiousness, ease, and variety in his expression, which have never been surpassed by any of those who have succeeded him. His clauses are never balanced, nor his periods modelled; every word seems to drop by chance, though it falls into its proper place; nothing is cold or languid; the whole is airy, animated, and vigorous; what is little is gay; what is great is splendid. Though all is easy, nothing is feeble: though all seems careless, there is nothing harsh; and though, since the publication of his works, more than a century has elapsed, yet they have nothing uncouth or obsolete.

Johnson.

CCLXXXIX.

Cato of Utica.

There was one contemporary figure, the most famous Stoic of the age, the younger Cato, who shows us in a striking form the strength and weakness of the standard by which he ruled his life. No one had more than he the courage to avow his principles and act up to his convictions; in an age of political corruption there was no stain upon his honour; and his moral influence, when once exerted to check the bribery of candidates for office,

did more, we are told, than all the laws and penal sanc-
tions which enforced them. In the worst crisis of the
revolution, when the spirits of other men were soured,
and the party cries grew fiercer, his temper seemed to
become gentler, and to forebode the miseries of civil war.
Inflexible before, he pleaded for concessions to avert the
storm ; and when they were refused, he raised his voice
still for moderate counsels, and spoke to unwilling ears of
the claims of humanity and mercy.

CCXC.

Pitt.

The memory of Pitt has been assailed times innumerable, often justly, often unjustly; but it has suffered much
less from his assailants than from his eulogists. For,
during many years, his name was the rallying cry of a
class of men with whom at one of those terrible conjunc-
tures which confound all ordinary distinctions, he was
accidentally and temporarily connected, but to whom, on
almost all great questions of principle, he was diametrically opposed. . . . . History will vindicate the real man
from calumny under the semblance of adulation, and will
exhibit him as what he was, a minister of great talents
and honest intentions, pre-eminently qualified intellec-
tually and morally for the part of a parliamentary leader,
and capable of administering with prudence and moderation the government of a prosperous and tranquil country,
but unequal to surprising and terrible emergencies, and
liable, in such emergencies, to err grievously both on the
side of weakness and on the side of violence.

Macaulay.

CCXCI.

Voltaire.

Voltaire's wits came to their maturity twenty years sooner than the wits of other men, and remained in full vigour thirty years longer. The charm which our style in general gets from our ideas, his ideas got from his style. Voltaire is sometimes afflicted, sometimes strongly moved; but serious he never is. His very graces have an effrontery about them. He had correctness of judgment, liveliness of imagination, nimble wits, quick taste, and a moral sense in ruins. He is the most debauched of spirits, and the worst of him is that one gets debauched along with him. If he had been a wise man, and had had the self-discipline of wisdom, beyond a doubt half his wit would have been gone; it needed an atmosphere of license in order to play freely. Those people who read him every day, create for themselves, by an invincible law, the necessity for liking him. But those people who, having given up reading him, gaze steadily down upon the influences which his spirit has shed abroad, find themselves in simple justice and duty compelled to detest him. It is impossible to be satisfied with him, and impossible not to be fascinated by him. *M. Arnold.*

CCXCII.

Lord Rockingham.

He is gone, my friend, my munificent patron, and not less the benefactor of my intellect! He who, beyond all other men known to me, added a fine and ever-wakeful sense of beauty to the most patient accuracy in experimental philosophy and the profounder researches of meta-physical science; he who united all the play and spring of fancy with the subtlest discrimination and an inexorable judgment; and who controlled an almost painful ex-quisiteness of taste by a warmth of heart which, in the practical relations of life, made allowance for faults as quickly as the moral taste detected them: a warmth of heart which was indeed noble and pre-eminent, for alas! the genial feelings of health contributed no spark towards it. Were it but for the remembrance of him alone, and of his lot here below, the disbelief of a future state would sadden the earth around me, and blight the very grass in the field.   *Burke.*

CCXCIII.

Darnley.

Darnley's external accomplishments had excited that sudden and violent passion which raised him to the throne. But the qualities of his mind corresponded ill with the beauty of his person. Of a weak understanding, and without experience, conceited at the same time of his own abilities, he ascribed his extraordinary success entirely to his distinguished merit. All the queen's favours made no impression on such a temper. All her gentleness could not bridle his imperious and ungovernable spirit. All her attention to place about him persons capable of directing his conduct, could not preserve him from rash and imprudent actions. Fond of all amusements, and ever prone to all the vices of youth, he became by degrees careless of her person and a stranger to her company. To a woman, and a queen, such behaviour was intolerable. The lower she had stooped in order to raise him, his behaviour appeared the more ungenerous and criminal;

and in proportion to the strength of her first affection, was the violence with which her disappointed passion operated.   *Robertson.*

CCXCIV.

The Earl of Peterborough.

He was pronounced guilty of the act of which he had in the most solemn manner protested he was innocent; he was sent to the Tower: he was turned out of all his places, and his name was struck out of the Council Book. It might well have been thought that the ruin of his fame and of his fortunes was irreparable. But there was about his nature an elasticity which nothing could subdue. In his prison, indeed, he was as violent as a falcon just caged, and would, if he had been long detained, have died of mere impatience. His only solace was to contrive wild and romantic schemes for extricating himself from his difficulties and avenging himself on his enemies. When he regained his liberty, he stood alone in the world, a dishonoured man, more hated by the Whigs than any Tory, and by the Tories than any Whig, and reduced to such poverty that he talked of retiring to the country, living like a farmer and putting his Countess into the dairy to churn and to make cheeses. Yet, even after this fall, that mounting spirit rose again, and rose higher than ever. When he next appeared before the world, he had inherited the earldom of the head of his family: he had ceased to be called by the tarnished name of Monmouth; and he soon added new lustre to the name of Peterborough. He was still all air and fire. His ready wit and his dauntless courage made him formidable: some amiable qualities which contrasted strangely with his vices, and some great exploits of which the effect was heightened by the careless levity with which they were performed, made him popular ; and his countrymen were willing to forget that a hero of whose achievements they were proud, and who was not more distinguished by parts and valour than by courtesy and generosity, had stooped to tricks worthy of the pillory.   *Macaulay.*

CCXCV.

Marcus Aurelius.

Of the outward life and circumstances of Marcus Aurelius, beyond these notices which he has himself supplied, there are few of much interest and importance. There is the fine anecdote of his speech when he heard of the assassination of the revolted Avidius Cassius, against whom he was marching : he was sorry, he said, to be deprived of the pleasure of pardoning him. And there are one or two more anecdotes of him which show the same spirit. But the great record for the outward life of a man who has left such a record of his lofty inward aspirations as that which Marcus Aurelius has left, is the clear consenting voice of all his contemporaries,—high and low, friend and enemy, pagan and Christian,—in praise of his sincerity, justice, and goodness. The world's charity does not err on the side of excess, yet the world was obliged to declare that he walked worthily of his profession. Long after his death, his bust was to be seen in the houses of private men through the wide Roman empire ; these busts of Marcus Aurelius, in the homes of Gaul, Britain, and Italy, bore witness, not to the inmates' frivolous curiosity about princes and palaces, but to their reverential memory of the passage of a great man upon the earth.   *M. Arnold.*

CCXCVI.

The Emperor Frederick II.

Through the mist of calumny and fable it is but dimly that the truth of the man can be discerned, and the outlines that appear serve to quicken rather than appease the curiosity with which we regard one of the most extraordinary personages in history. A sensualist, yet also a warrior and a politician; a profound lawgiver and an impassioned poet; in his youth, fired by crusading fervour, in later life, persecuting heretics, while himself accused of blasphemy and unbelief; of winning manners, and ardently beloved by his followers, but with the stain of more than one cruel deed upon his name, he was the marvel of his own generation, and succeeding ages looked back with awe, not unmingled with pity, upon the inscrutable figure of the last Emperor who had braved all the terrors of the Church, and died beneath her ban, the last who had ruled from the sands of the ocean to the shores of the Sicilian sea. But while they pitied they condemned. The undying hatred of the Papacy threw round his memory a lurid light; him and him alone of all the imperial line, Dante, the worshipper of the Empire, must perforce deliver to the flames of hell. *Bryce.*

CCXCVII.

A Model Advocate.

He was a man of personage proper, inclined to tallness, in his youth valiant and active, towards his latter age full and corpulent, of a full face and clear complexion, with an erected forehead, and a large grey eye bright and quick. Sound and sure he was of his words, true and faithful to

his friends, somewhat choleric, yet apt to forgive, cheerful in his journeys or at his meals, of a sound and deep
judgment, with a strong memory, both which were much
beautified with his well-composed language and graceful
delivery. He was somewhat prodigally inclined in his
youth, and generously thrifty in his age, giving good
example to his greatest neighbours by his constant
hospitality. Earnest he was and sincere in the rightful
cause of his client, pitiful in the relief of the distressed,
and merciful to the poor. *James Howel.*

CCXCVIII.

A Trimmer.

Our Trimmer, therefore, inspired by this divine virtue,
thinks fit to conclude with these assertions, that our
climate is a Trimmer, between that part of the world
where men are roasted, and the other where they are
frozen: That our church is a Trimmer, between the frenzy
of platonic visions, and the lethargic ignorance of popish
dreams: That our laws are Trimmers, between the excess of unbounded power, and the extravagance of liberty
not enough restrained: That true virtue hath ever been
thought a Trimmer, and to have its dwelling in the middle
between the two extremes: That even God Almighty
himself is divided between His two great attributes, His
Mercy and His Justice. *Halifax*

CCXCIX.

Falkland.

He had a courage of the most clear and keen temper,
and so far from fear, that he seemed not without some
appetite of danger; and therefore, upon any occasion of

action, he always engaged his person in those troops, which he thought, by the forwardness of the commanders, to be the most like to be farthest engaged; and in all such encounters he had about him an extraordinary cheerfulness, without at all affecting the execution that usually attended them, in which he took no delight, but took pains to prevent it, when it was not, by resistance, made necessary; insomuch that at Edgehill, when the enemy was routed, he was like to have incurred great peril, by interposing to save those who had thrown away their arms, and against whom, it may be, others were more fierce for their having thrown them away: so that a man might think he came into the field chiefly out of curiosity to see the face of danger, and charity to prevent the shedding of blood.   *Clarendon.*

CCC.

Facility of Charles II.

It is creditable to Charles's temper that, ill as he thought of his species, he never became a misanthrope. He saw little in man but what was hateful. Yet he did not hate them. Nay, he was so far humane that it was highly disagreeable to him to see their sufferings, or to hear their complaints. This, however, is a sort of humanity which, though amiable and laudable in a private man, whose power to help or hurt is bounded by a narrow circle, has in princes often been rather a vice than a virtue. More than one well-disposed ruler has given up whole provinces to rapine and oppression, merely from a wish to see none but happy faces round his own board and his own walks. No man is fit to govern great societies who hesitates about disobliging the few who have access to him for the sake of the many whom he will never see. The facility of Charles was such as perhaps has never been found in any man of equal sense.

Macaulay.

CCCI.

Antony and Cleopatra.

Though her own security had been the first object, and her ambition the second, the inspirer of so many licentious passions was at last enslaved herself. She might disdain the fear of a rival potentate, and defy the indignation of Octavius, but her anxiety about his sister was the instinct of the woman, rather than of the queen. She could not forget that a wife's legitimate influence had once detained her lover from her side for more than two whole years : she might still apprehend the awakening of his reason, and his renunciation of an alliance which at times he felt, she well knew, to be bitterly degrading. To retain her grasp of her admirer, as well as her seat upon the throne of the Ptolemies, she must drown his scruples in voluptuous oblivion, and invent new charms to revive and amuse his jaded passion.   *Merivale.*

CCCII.

Modesty without Diffidence.

The modesty which made him so slow to advance and easy to be repulsed, was certainly no suspicion of deficient merit, or unconsciousness of his own value : he appears to have known in its whole extent the dignity of his own character, and to have set a very high value on his own powers and performances. He probably did

O 2

not offer his conversation because he expected it to be solicited; and he retired from a cold reception not submissive but indignant, with such deference of his own greatness as made him unwilling to expose it to neglect or violation. His modesty was by no means inconsistent with ostentatiousness; he is diligent enough to remind the world of his merit, and expresses with very little scruple his high opinion of his own powers; but his self-commendations are read without scorn or indignation; we allow his claims and love his frankness. He has been described as magisterially presiding over the younger writers, and assuming the distribution of poetic fame; but he who excels has a right to teach, and he whose judgment is incontestable may without usurpation examine and decide.

CCCIII.

Queen Elizabeth.

A warm concern for the interest and honour of the nation, a tenderness for her people, and a confidence in their affections were appearances that ran through her whole public conduct, and gave life and colour to it. She did great things, and she knew how to set them off according to their full value, by her manner of doing them. In her private behaviour she showed great affability, she descended even to familiarity; but her familiarity was such as could not be imputed to her weakness, and was, therefore, most justly ascribed to her goodness. Though a woman, she hid all that was womanish about her: and if a few equivocal marks of coquetry appeared on some occasions, they passed like flashes of lightning, vanished as soon as they were discerned, and imprinted no blot on her character. She had private friendships, she had favourites: but she never suffered her friends to forget she was their queen; and when her favourites did, she made them feel that she was so.　　　　*Bolinbroke.*

CCCIV.

Character of a Divine.

He had that general curiosity to which no kind of knowledge is indifferent or superfluous; and that general benevolence by which no order of men is hated or despised. His principles both of thought and action were great and comprehensive. By a solicitous examination of objections and judicious comparison of opposite arguments, he attained what inquiry never gives but to industry and perspicuity, a firm and unshaken settlement of conviction. But his firmness was without asperity; for knowing with how much difficulty truth is sometimes found, he did not wonder that many missed it. His delivery, though unconstrained, was not negligent, and, though forcible, was not turbulent; disdaining anxious nicety of emphasis, and laboured artifice of action, it captivated the hearer by its natural dignity; it roused the sluggish and fixed the volatile, and detained the mind upon the subject without directing it to the speaker.

S. Johnson.

CCCV.

Savonarola.

Perhaps, while no preacher ever had a more massive influence than Savonarola, no preacher ever had more heterogeneous materials to work upon. And one secret of the massive influence lay in the highly mixed character of his preaching. Baldassarre, wrought into an ecstasy of self-mastering revenge, was only an extreme case among the partial and narrow sympathies of that audience. In Savonarola's preaching there were strains that appealed to the very finest susceptibilities of men's natures, and there were elements that gratified low egoism, tickled gossiping curiosity, and fascinated timorous superstition. His need of personal predominance, his labyrinthine allegorical interpretations of the Scriptures, his enigmatic visions, and his false certitude about the Divine intentions, never ceased, in his own large soul, to be ennobled by that fervid piety, that passionate sense of the infinite, that active sympathy, that clear-sighted demand for the subjection of selfish interests to the general good, which he had in common with the greatest of mankind. But for the mass of his audience all the pregnancy of his preaching lay in his strong assertion of supernatural claims, in his denunciatory visions, in the false certitude which gave his sermons the interest of a political bulletin ; and having once held that audience in his mastery, it was necessary to his nature—it was necessary for their welfare—that he should *keep* the mastery.

George Elliot.

CCCVI.

Alexander Severus. .

Alexander rose early; the first moments of the day were consecrated to private devotion, and his domestic chapel was filled with the images of those heroes, who, by improving or reforming human life, had deserved the grateful reverence of posterity. But, as he deemed the service of mankind the most acceptable worship of the gods, the greatest part of his morning hours was employed in his council, where he discussed public affairs, and determined private causes, with a patience and discretion above his years. The dryness of business was relieved by the charms of literature; and a portion of time was always set apart for his favourite studies of poetry, history, and philosophy. The works of Virgil and Horace, the Republics of Plato and Cicero, formed his taste, enlarged his understanding, and gave him the noblest ideas of man and government. The exercises of the body succeeded to those of the mind; and Alexander, who was tall, active, and robust, surpassed most of his equals in the gymnastic arts. His table was served with the most frugal simplicity; and whenever he was at liberty to consult his own inclination, the company consisted of a few select friends, men of learning and virtue, amongst whom Ulpian was constantly invited.

Gibbon.

CCCVII.

Goethe and the Court.

As we familiarise ourselves with the details of this episode, there appears less and less plausibility in the often iterated declamation against Goethe on the charge of his having 'sacrificed his genius to the Court.' It becomes indeed a singularly foolish display of rhetoric. Let us for a moment consider the charge. He had to choose a career. That of poet was then, as it is still, terribly delusive; verses could create fame, but no money; *fama* and *fames* were then, as now, in terrible contiguity. No sooner is the necessity for a career admitted than much objection falls to the ground : for those who reproach him with having wasted his time on court festivities and the duties of government, which others could have done as well, must ask whether he would have saved that time had he followed the career of jurisprudence, and jostled lawyers through the courts at Frankfort? Or would they prefer seeing him reduced to the condition of poor Schiller, wasting so much of his precious life in literary 'hackwork,' translating French books for a miserable pittance? *Time*, in any case, would have been claimed; in return for that given to Karl August, he received, as he confesses in the poem addressed to the Duke, 'what the great seldom bestow—affection, leisure, confidence, garden, and house. No one have I had to thank but him; and much have I wanted, who as a poet ill understood the arts of gain. If Europe praised me, what has Europe done for me? Nothing. Even my works have been an expense to me.'   *Lewes.*

CCCVIII.

Sir John Moore.

Thus ended the career of Sir John Moore, a man whose uncommon capacity was sustained by the purest virtue, and governed by a disinterested patriotism more in keeping with the primitive than the luxurious age of a great nation. His tall graceful person, his dark searching eyes, strongly defined forehead, a singularly expressive mouth, indicated a noble disposition and a refined understanding. The lofty sentiments of honour habitual to his mind, adorned by a subtle playful wit, gave him in conversation an ascendancy that he could well preserve by the decisive vigour of his actions. He maintained the right with a vehemence bordering upon fierceness, and every important transaction in which he was engaged increased his reputation for talent, and confirmed his character as a stern enemy to vice, a stedfast friend to merit, a just and faithful servant of his country. The honest loved him, the dishonest feared him; for while he lived, he did not shun, but scorned and spurned the base, and, with characteristic propriety, they spurned at him when he was dead.

Napier.

CCCIX.

My own Life.

I am, or rather was,—for that is the style I must now use in speaking of myself, which emboldens me the more to speak my sentiments ;—I was, I say, a man of mild dispositions, of command of temper, of an open, social, and cheerful humour, capable of attachment, but little susceptible of enmity, and of great moderation in all my passions. Even my love of literary fame, my ruling passion, never soured my temper, notwithstanding my frequent disappointments. My company was not unacceptable to the young and careless as well as to the studious and literary ; and as I took a particular pleasure in the company of modest women, I had no reason to be displeased with the reception I met with from them. In a word, though most men anywise eminent have found reason to complain of calumny, I never was touched, or even attacked by her baleful tooth : and though I wantonly exposed myself to the rage of both civil and religious factions, they seemed to be disarmed in my behalf of their wonted fury. My friends never had occasion to vindicate any one circumstance of my character and conduct : not but that the zealots, we may well suppose, would have been glad to invent and propagate any story to my disadvantage, but they could never find any which they thought would wear the face of probability. I cannot say there is no vanity in making this funeral oration of myself, but I hope it is not a misplaced one ; and this is a matter of fact which is easily cleared and ascertained.

Hume.

CCCX.

Richard, Earl of Scarborough.

He joined to the noblest and strictest principles of honour and generosity the tenderest sentiments of benevolence and compassion; and as he was naturally warm, he could not even hear of an injustice or a baseness without a sudden indignation, nor of the misfortunes or miseries of a fellow-creature without melting into softness, and endeavouring to relieve them. This part of his character was so universally known, that our best and most satirical English poet says;

> *'When I confess, there's one who feels for fame,*
> *And melts to goodness, Scarb'rough need I name?'*

He had not the least pride of birth and rank, that common narrow notion of little minds, that wretched mistaken succedaneum of merit; but he was jealous to anxiety of his character, as all men are who deserve a good one. And such was his diffidence upon that subject, that he never could be persuaded that mankind really thought of him as they did. For surely never man had a higher reputation, and never man enjoyed a more universal esteem. Even knaves respected him; and fools thought they loved him. If he had any enemies, for I protest I never knew one, they could only be such as were weary of always hearing of Aristides the Just.   *Chesterfield.*

CCCXI.

Tiberius.

At the same time with all his frugality Tiberius obtained the rare praise of personal indifference to money, and forbearance in claiming even his legitimate dues. In many cases in which the law enriched the emperor with the property of a condemned criminal, he waived his right and allowed it to descend to the heir. He frequently refused to accept inheritances bequeathed him by persons who were not actually related to him, and checked the base subservience of a death-bed flattery. With all these generous merits towards the common-wealth he was not blind to the advantage he might derive from pretending to another virtue which ranked high in the estimation of the Romans, but to which he had no real claim. From the commencement of his principate he affected the most obsequious deference to the State as represented by the Senate, the presumed exponent of its will. His first care was to make it appear to the world that his own pre-eminence was thrust upon him by that body alone which could lawfully invest him with it. We have seen under what disguises, and by what circuitous processes, he had gradually drawn into his own hands the powers by which he seemed only seeking to enrich the Senate at the expense of every other order in the commonwealth.   *Merivale.*

CCCXII.

William III.

Such situations bewilder and unnerve the weak, but call forth all the strength of the strong. Surrounded by snares in which an ordinary youth would have perished, William learned to tread at once warily and firmly. Long before he reached manhood he knew how to keep secrets, how to baffle curiosity by dry and guarded answers, how to conceal all passions under the same show of grave tranquillity. Meanwhile he made but little proficiency in fashionable and literary accomplishments. The manners of the Dutch nobility of that age wanted the grace which was found in the highest perfection among the gentlemen of France, and which, in an inferior degree, embellished the court of England; and his manners were altogether Dutch. Even his countrymen thought him blunt. To foreigners he often seemed churlish. In his intercourse with the world in general he appeared ignorant or negligent of those arts which double the value of a favour, and take away the sting of a refusal.   *Macaulay.*

CCCXIII.

Essex.

Nothing in the political conduct of Essex entitles him to esteem; and the pity with which we regard his early and terrible end is diminished by the consideration, that he put to hazard the lives and fortunes of his most attached friends, and endeavoured to throw the whole country into confusion, · for objects purely personal. Still it is impossible not to be deeply interested for a man so brave, high spirited, and generous; for a man who, while he conducted himself towards his Sovereign with a boldness such as was then found in no other subject, conducted himself towards his dependents with a delicacy such as has been rarely found in any other patron. Unlike the vulgar herd of benefactors, he desired to inspire not gratitude, but affection. He tried to make those whom he befriended feel towards him as an equal. His mind—ardent, susceptible, naturally disposed to admiration of all that is great and beautiful— was fascinated by the genius and accomplishments of

Bacon. A close friendship was soon formed between them, a friendship destined to have a dark, a mournful, a shameful end. *Macaulay.*

CCCXIV.

The Regent Murray.

There is no person in that age about whom historians have been more divided, or whose character has been drawn in such opposite colours. Personal intrepidity, military skill, sagacity, and vigour in the administration of civil affairs, are virtues which even his enemies allow him to have possessed in an eminent degree. His moral qualities are more dubious, and ought neither to be praised nor censured without great reserve, and many distinctions. In a fierce age he was capable of using victory with humanity, and of treating the vanquished with moderation; a patron of learning, which, among martial nobles, was either unknown or despised; zealous for religion, to a degree which distinguished him, even at a time when professions of that kind were not uncommon. His confidence in his friends was extreme, and inferior only to his liberality towards them, which knew no bounds. A distinguished passion for the liberty of his country prompted him to oppose the pernicious system which the Princes of Lorraine had obliged the Queen-mother to pursue. On Mary's return into Scotland, he served her with a zeal and affection to which he sacrificed the friendship of those who were most attached to his person. But, on the other hand, his ambition was immoderate; and events happened that opened to him vast projects which allured his enterprising genius, and led him to actions inconsistent with the duty of a subject. His treatment of the Queen, to whose bounty he was so much indebted, was unbrotherly and ungrateful. The dependence on Elizabeth, under which he brought Scotland, was disgraceful to the nation. He deceived and betrayed Norfolk with a baseness unworthy of a man of honour.   *Robertson.*

CCCXV.

The Hardships of the Scholar.

I say, then, that the hardships of the scholar are these : In the first place, poverty : not that they are all poor, but I would put the case in the strongest' manner possible ; and when I have said that he endures poverty, methinks no more need be said to show his misery; for he who is poor is destitute of everything. But notwithstanding all this, it is not so great but that he still eats, though somewhat later than usual, either of the rich man's scraps or leavings, or, which is the scholar's greatest misery, by going a-begging. Neither do they always want a fire-side or chimney-corner of some other person, which, if it does not quite warm them, at least abates their extreme cold ; and lastly, at night they sleep somewhere under cover. By this painful way they arrive to the degree they desire; which being attained, we have seen many who, from a chair, command and govern the world ; their hunger converted into fulness, their pinching cold into refreshing coolness, their nakedness into embroidery, and their sleeping on a mat to reposing in fine linen and damask.

Don Quixote.

CCCXVI.

The Hardships of the Warrior.

But their hardships fall far short of those of the warrior, as I shall presently show. Since in speaking of the scholar, we began with his poverty, let us see whether the soldier be richer; and we shall find that poverty itself is not poorer: for he depends on his wretched pay, which comes late, or perhaps never; or else on what he can pilfer, with great peril of his life and conscience. And sometimes his nakedness is such, that his laced-jacket serves him both for finery and shirt; and, in the midst of winter, being in the open field, he has nothing to warm him but the breath of his mouth, which, issuing from an empty place, must needs come out cold. But let us wait until night, and see whether his bed will make amends for these inconveniences; and that, if it be not his own fault, will never offend in point of narrowness; for he may measure out as many feet of earth as he pleases, and roll himself thereon at pleasure, without fear of rumpling the sheets.

Don Quixote.

CCCXVII.

The Warrior's Reward.

Suppose, now, the day and hour come of taking the degree of his profession,—I say, suppose the day of battle come, and then his academical cap will be of lint, to cure some wound made by a musket-shot which, perhaps, has gone through his temples, or lamed him a leg or an arm. And though this should not happen, but he should escape unhurt, he shall remain, perhaps, in the same poverty as before: and there must happen a second and a third engagement, and battle after battle, and he must come off victor from them all, to get anything considerable by it. But these miracles are seldom seen. And tell me, gentlemen, how much fewer are they who are rewarded for their services in war, than those who have perished in it? The dead cannot be reckoned up, whereas those who live, and are rewarded, may be numbered right easily. All this is quite otherwise with scholars, who are all handsomely provided for. Thus, though the hardships of the soldier are greater, his reward is less.   *Don Quixote.*

CCCXVIII.

Evil Communications.

The old proverb holds true : 'Tell me the company you keep, and I will tell you what you are.' The first company to which a young man really attaches himself often fixes his career. This, however, he often falls into at random, or more frequently has not decision of character to cast off when detected. Among many things which render bad company poisonous, one of the saddest is the extreme difficulty of getting rid of a deceitful friend. In the position which I occupy I am constantly observing that this or that youth is held down by the weight of evil comrades. To shake them off is a Herculean task ; the ill attachment sticks like the coat of Nessus. Indeed, solitary amendment is, often easier than disentangling oneself from corrupting alliance.

CCCXIX.

The Contemplation of Death.

There is a sort of delight which is alternately mixed with terror and sorrow, in the contemplation of death. The soul has its curiosity more than ordinarily awakened when it turns its thoughts upon the subject of such as have behaved themselves with an equal, a resigned, a cheerful, a generous, or heroic temper in that extremity. We are affected with these respective manners of behaviour, as we secretly believe the part of the dying person imitable by ourselves, or such as we imagine ourselves more particularly capable of. Men with exalted minds march before us like princes, and are, to the ordinary race of mankind, rather subjects for their admiration than example.

Steele.

CCCXX.

What we get from Literature.

Why should we ever treat of any dead authors but the famous ones? Mainly for this reason : because, from these famous personages, home or foreign, whom we all know so well, and of whom so much has been said, the amount of stimulus which they contain for us has been in a great measure disengaged ; people have formed their opinion about them, and do not readily change it. One may write of them afresh, combat received opinions about them, even interest one's readers in so doing ; but the interest one's readers receive has to do, in general, rather with the treatment than with the subject ; they are susceptible of a lively impression rather of the course of the discussion itself,—its turns, vivacity, and novelty, —than of the genius of the author who is the occasion of it. And yet what is really precious and inspiring, in all that we get from literature, except this sense of an immediate contact with genius itself, and the stimulus towards what is true and excellent which we derive from it?

M. Arnold.

CCCXXI.

Use what quality you have.

'Thou sayest, "Men cannot admire the sharpness of thy wits." Be it so ; but there are many other things of

P

which thou canst not say, "I am not formed for them by nature." Show those qualities, then, which are altogether in thy power,—sincerity, gravity, endurance of labour, aversion to pleasure, contentment with thy portion and with few things, benevolence, frankness, no love of superfluity, freedom from trifling, magnanimity. Dost thou not see how many qualities thou art at once able to exhibit, as to which there is no excuse of natural incapacity and unfitness, and yet thou still remainest voluntarily below the mark ? Or art thou compelled, through being defectively furnished by nature, to murmur, and to be mean, and to flatter, and to find fault with thy poor body, and to try to please men, and to make great display, and to be so restless in thy mind? No, indeed ; but thou mightest have been delivered from these things long ago.'   *M. Arnold.*

CCCXXII.

The Perfect Character.

The mere philosopher is a character which is commonly but little acceptable in the world, as being supposed to contribute little either to the advantage or pleasure of society ; while he lives remote from communication with mankind, and is wrapped up in principles and notions equally remote from their comprehension. On the other hand, the mere ignorant is still more despised; nor is anything deemed a surer sign of an illiberal genius in an age and nation where the sciences flourish, than to be entirely destitute of all relish for those noble entertainments. The most perfect character is supposed to be between those extremes : retaining an equal ability and taste for books, company, and business ; preserving in conversation that discernment and delicacy which arise from polite letters ; and in business that probity and accuracy which are the natural result of a just philosophy. In order to diffuse and cultivate so accomplished a character, nothing can be more useful than compositions of easy style and manner which draw not too much from life, require no deep application or retreat to be comprehended, and send back a student among mankind full of noble sentiments and wise precepts, applicable to every exigence of human life. By means of such compositions virtue becomes amiable, science agreeable, company instructive, and retirement entertaining. *Hume.*

CCCXXIII.

Why we commend the Past.

Men do always, but not always with reason, commend the past and condemn the present, and are so much the partisans of what has been, as not merely to cry up those times which are known to them only from the records left by historians, but also, when they grow old, to extol the days in which they remember their youth to have been spent. And although this preference of theirs be in most instances a mistaken one, I can see that there are many causes to account for it ; chief of which I take to be that in respect of things long gone by we perceive not the whole truth, those circumstances that would detract from the credit of the past being for the most part hidden from us, while all that gives it lustre is magnified and embellished. For the generality of writers render this tribute to the good fortune of conquerors, that they not merely exaggerate the great things they have done, but also lend such a colour to the actions of their enemies, that any one born afterwards has cause to marvel at these men and these times, and is constrained to praise and love them beyond all others.

CCCXXIV.

The Epicureans.

The Epicurean school professes, in the first instance, to be founded on the senses and the feeling, to be based on reality, as popularly understood. It appeals to our immediate perception and feeling, and declares that these must never be recklessly set aside. What we immediately feel and perceive, that is true ; what we directly find ourselves to be, that is what we ought to do. Act what thou art is its motto, and sense and feeling tell thee with sufficient distinctness what thou art. But the promise thus held out is certainly not kept to the letter. What we supposed to be our feelings and sensations turn out to be less trustworthy than we had been, up to this point, led to suppose. The greater number of our beliefs and opinions are due to hasty and erroneous inferences. What seemed to be perception was really reasoning. We must, therefore, get back to our original perceptions. We were told originally that we must believe nothing for which we have not the evidence of the senses and the feeling. It becomes apparent that that evidence does not go so far as we had supposed. Our senses and our feelings seem to mislead, and yet, if we reject all sense and feeling, knowledge is made impracticable.

CCCXXV.

The Stoics.

The wise man alone is free, the Stoics said, for he can make himself independent of the whims of fortune, can rise superior to so-called troubles, guard himself alike from care and fear and passionate desire, and enjoy the bliss of an unruffled calm.   It is true that in another sense he is not free, has indeed less sense of freedom than the careless crowd, for he can recognise the general law of destiny within which all things revolve.   His will, he knows, is mysteriously linked to the long chain of natural causes, but he seems free in that he can willingly obey the dictates of his nature without being helplessly determined by things external to himself. He decides on that which reason points to, and he acts under no sense of constraint or irksome pressure, for his will and universal intellect are one.

CCCXXVI.

Knowledge of Languages.

It is scarcely possible that the translation of a book of the highest class can be equal to the original.   But though much may be lost in the copy, the great outline must remain.   So the genius of Homer is seen in the poorest version of the Iliad.   Let it not be supposed that I wish to dissuade any person from studying either the ancient languages or those of modern Europe.   Far from it !   I prize most highly those keys of knowledge.   I always much admired a saying of the Emperor Charles V. 'When I learn a new language,' he said, 'I feel as if I had got a new soul.'   But I would console those who have not time to make themselves linguists by assuring them that by means of their own mother-tongue they may obtain access to vast intellectual treasures, treasures such as might have been envied in the age of Charles the Fifth, surpassing those which were possessed by Aldus, by Erasmus, by Melanchthon.   *Brougham.*

CCCXXVII.

Wisdom and Virtue.

If it be true that the understanding and the will are the two eminent faculties of the reasonable soul, it follows necessarily that wisdom and virtue, which are the best improvement of those two faculties, must be the perfection also of our reasonable being, and, therefore, the undeniable foundation of a happy life. There is not any duty to which Providence has not annexed a blessing; not any institution of Heaven, which even in this life we may not be the better for; nor any temptation, either of fortune or of appetite, that is not subject to our reason; not any passion or affliction, for which virtue has not provided a remedy. So that it is our own fault, if we either fear or hope for anything terrestrial ; and these two affections are at the root of all our miseries.

CCCXXVIII.

Passion for Money-getting.

One very common and at the same time the most absurd ambition that ever showed itself in human nature is that which comes upon man with experience and old age, the season when it might be expected he should be the wisest, and therefore cannot receive any of those lessening circumstances which do in some measure excuse the disorderly ferments of youthful blood ; I mean the passion for getting money, exclusive of the character of the provident father, the affectionate husband, or the generous friend. It may be remarked for the comfort of honest poverty that this desire reigns most in those who have but few qualities to recommend them. This is a weed that will grow in a barren soil. Humanity, good nature, and the advantage of a liberal education are incompatible with avarice. 'Tis strange to see how suddenly this abject passion kills all the noble sentiments and generous ambitions that adorn human nature; it renders the man who is overrun with it a peevish and cruel master, a severe parent, an unsociable husband, a distant and mistrustful friend. But it is more to the present purpose to consider it as an absurd passion of the heart rather than as a vicious affection of the mind. As there are frequent instances to be met with of a proud humility, so this passion, contrary to most others, affects applause by avoiding all show and appearance; for this it will not sometimes endure even the decencies of apparel.

Spectator.

CCCXXIX.

Natural Religion.

But the hopes and fears of man are not limited to this short life, and to this visible world. He finds himself surrounded by the signs of a power and wisdom higher than his own; and, in all ages and nations, men of all orders of intellect, from Bacon and Newton, down to the rudest tribes of cannibals, have believed in the existence of some superior mind. Thus far the voice of mankind is almost unanimous. But whether there be one God, or many, what may be his natural and what his moral attributes, in what relation his creatures stand to him, whether he have ever disclosed himself to us by any other revelation than that which is written in all the parts of the glorious and well-ordered world which he has made, whether his revelation be contained in any permanent record, how that record should be interpreted, and whether it have pleased him to appoint any unerring interpreter on earth, these are questions respecting which there exists the widest diversity of opinion, and respecting which a large part of our race has, ever since the dawn of regular history, been deplorably in error.

CCCXXX.

Common Indifference to Truth.

Though it is scarcely possible to avoid judging, in some way or other, of almost everything which offers itself to one's thoughts; yet it is certain, that many persons, from different causes, never exercise their judgment upon what comes before them, in the way of determining whether it be conclusive, and holds. They are perhaps entertained with some things, not so with others; they like, and they dislike; but whether that which is proposed to be made out be really made out or not; whether a matter be stated according to the real truth of the case, seems to the generality of people merely a circumstance of no consideration at all. Arguments are often wanted for some accidental purpose; but proof, as such, is what they never want for themselves, for their own satisfaction of mind, or conduct in life. Not to mention the multitude who read merely for the sake of talking, or to qualify themselves for the world, or some such kind of reasons; there are, even of the few who read for their own entertainment, and have a real curiosity to see what is said, several, which is prodigious, who have no sort of curiosity to see what is true.   *Butler.*

CCCXXXI.

Socrates on Immortality.

I have often observed a passage in Socrates' behaviour at his death, in a light wherein none of the critics have considered it. That excellent man, entertaining his friends a little before he drank the bowl of poison, with a discourse on the immortality of the soul, at his entering upon it, says, that he does not believe any of the most comic genius can censure him for talking upon such a subject at such a time. This passage, I think, evidently glances upon Aristophanes, who writ a comedy on purpose to ridicule the discourses of that divine philosopher. It has been observed by many writers, that Socrates was so little moved at this piece of buffoonery, that he was several times present at its being acted on the stage, and never expressed the least resentment of it. But with submission, I think the remark I have here made shows us that this unworthy treatment made an impression upon his mind, though he had been too wise to discover it.

Spectator.

CCCXXXII.

The Soul after Death.

The soul after death takes its way to the regions below, and there stands unveiled before the bar of judgment, and nothing can possibly hinder the judges from searching all its secrets. Men's souls contract sores and ulcers from the vices they have committed in this life. The judges again mark closely the nature of the sores, and judge whether the sores are curable or not. If so, they are chastised and corrected by punishment and healed.

When incurable, they are tortured for ever and ever with the direst agony, from which they themselves derive no benefit, but are held out as examples for others. Those who have remained their whole life through free from great sins pass into the islands of the blessed, and there live an enjoying life of bliss. I believe then this tale, dear Callicles, and have ever deemed it my supreme duty to present myself before my judge with the healthiest of souls: and I entreat you to keep yourself chaste and pure, and to dismiss all vain pursuits. Otherwise when you come to the judgment seat below, you will be wracked with pain, may be, and will hesitate, and be at your wits' end for excuses, and be visited with the utmost contumely.

Plato.

CCCXXXIII.

Insincerity in Conversation.

Amongst too many instances of the great corruption and degeneracy of the age in which we live, the great and general want of sincerity in conversation is not the least. The world is grown so full of dissimulation and compliment, that men's words are hardly any signification of their thoughts: and if any man measure his words by his heart, and speak as he thinks, and do not express more kindness to every man, than men usually have for any man, he can hardly escape the censure of breeding. The old English plainness and sincerity, that generous integrity of nature, and honesty of disposition, which always argue true greatness of mind, and are usually accompanied with undaunted courage and resolution, are in a great measure lost amongst us; there has been a long endeavour to transform us into foreign manners and fashions, and to bring us to a servile imitation of some of

the best of our neighbours in some of the worst of their qualities. The dialect of conversation is now-a-days so swelled with vanity and compliment, and so surfeited, as I may say, of expressions of kindness and respect, that if a man that lived an age or two ago should return into the world again, he would really want a dictionary to help him to understand his own language, and to know the true intrinsic value of the phrase in fashion, and would hardly at first believe at what a low rate the highest strains and expressions of kindness imaginable do commonly pass in common payment; and when he should come to understand, it would be a great while before he could bring himself with a good countenance and a good conscience to converse with men upon equal terms and in their own way. *Spectator.*

CCCXXXIV.

Epicurus and Pleasure.

Were it possible for you to have spent an hour with Epicurus, you would have been delighted with him, for his nature was like the better part of yours. He who shows us how fear may be reasoned with and purified, how death may be disarmed of terrors, how pleasure may be united with innocence and constancy; he who persuades us that vice is painful and vindictive, and that ambition, deemed the most manly of our desires, is the most childish and illusory, deserves our gratitude. If you must quarrel with Epicurus on the principal good, take my idea. The happy man is he who distinguishes the boundary between desire and delight, and stands firmly on the higher ground; he who knows that pleasure not only is not possession, but is often to be lost and always

to be endangered by it. In life, as in those prospects
which if the sun were above the horizon we would see
from hence, the objects covered with the softest light,
and offering the most beautiful forms in the distance, are
wearisome to attain and barren.

CCCXXXV.

Work and Play.

With every power that we have we can do two things:
we can work, and we can play. Every power that we
have is at the same time useful to us and delightful to us.
Even when we are applying them to the furtherance
of our personal objects, the activity of them gives us
pleasure; and when we have no useful end to which to
apply them, it is still pleasant to us to use them; the
activity of them gives us pleasure for its own sake. There
is no motion of our body or mind which we use in work,
which we do not also use in play or amusement. If we
walk in order to arrive at the place where our interest
requires us to be, we also walk about the fields for enjoyment. If we apply our combining and analysing powers
to solve the problems of mathematics, we use them sometimes also in solving double acrostics.   *M. Arnold.*

CCCXXXVI.

Tardy Resolves.

The ambassador being present in the council when
these matters were being discussed, told them 'that he
thought it of far greater moment for them to consider
what they were to do than what they were to say; for

when their resolves were formed, it would be easy to clothe them in fit words.' Now this was sound advice, and such as every prince and people should lay to heart. But not less mischievous than doubtful resolves are those which are late and tardy, especially when they have to be made on behalf of a friend. For from their lateness they help none, and hurt ourselves. Tardy resolves are due to want of spirit or want of strength, or to the perversity of those who have to determine, who being moved by a secret desire to overthrow the government, or to carry out some selfish purpose of their own, suffer no decision to be come to, but only thwart and hinder. Whereas, good citizens, even when they see the popular mind to be bent on dangerous courses, will never oppose the adoption of a fixed plan, more particularly in matters which do not brook delay.

CCCXXXVII.

The Limits of Time.

Men are apt enough of themselves to fall into the most astonishing delusions about the opportunities which time affords, but they are even more deluded by the talk of the people about them. When children hear that a new carriage has been ordered of the builder, they expect to see it driven up to the door in a fortnight, with the paint quite dry on the panels. All people are children in this respect, except the workman, who knows the endless details of production; and the workman himself, notwithstanding the lessons of experience, makes light of the future task. What gigantic plans we scheme, and how little we advance in the labour of a day! If there is one lesson which experience teaches, surely it is this, to make plans that are strictly limited, and to arrange our work in a practicable way within the limits that we must accept.   *Hamerton.*

CCCXXXVIII.

True Affection.

There are wonders in true affection; it is a body of enigmas, mysteries, and riddles, wherein two so become one as they both become two; I love my friend before myself, and yet methinks, I do not love him enough. Some few months hence, my multiplied affection will make me believe I have not loved him at all. When I am from him, I am dead till I am with him. United souls are not satisfied with embraces, but desire to be truly each other, which being impossible, these desires are infinite, and must proceed without a possibility of satisfaction. Another misery there is in affection, that whom we truly love like our own selves, we forget their looks, nor can our memory retain the idea of their faces; and it is no wonder, for they are ourselves, and our affections make their looks our own. This noble affection falls not on vulgar and common constitutions, but on such as are marked for virtue. He that can love his friend with this noble ardour will, in a competent degree, affect all.

Sir Thomas Browne.

CCCXXXIX.

The Duty of Silence.

Silence is a privilege of the grave, a right of the departed: let him, therefore, who infringes that right by speaking publicly of, for, or against, those who cannot speak for themselves, take heed that he opens not his mouth without a sufficient sanction. Only to philosophy enlightened by the affections does it belong justly to esti- mate the claims of the deceased on the one hand, and of the present age and future generations on the other, and to strike a balance between them. Such philosophy runs a risk of becoming extinct among us, if the coarse in- trusions into the recesses, the gross breaches into the sanctities, of domestic life, to which we have lately been more and more accustomed, are to be regarded as indica- tions of a vigorous state of public feeling. The wise and good respect, as one of the noblest characteristics of Englishmen, that jealousy of familiar approach, which, while it contributes to the maintenance of private dignity, is one of the most efficacious guardians of rational public freedom.

CCCXL.

Plato, thou reasonest well.

It might very well be thought serious trifling to tell my readers that the greatest men had ever a high esteem for Plato ; whose writings are the touchstone of a hasty and shallow mind ; whose philosophy has been the admiration of ages ; which supplied patriots, magistrates, and law- givers to the most flourishing States, as well as Fathers to the Church, and doctors to the schools. Albeit in these days the depths of that old learning are rarely fathomed ; and yet it were happy for these lands if our young nobility and gentry, instead of modern maxims, would imbibe the notions of the great men of antiquity. It may be modestly presumed there are not many among us, even of those who are called the better sort, who have more sense, virtue, and love of their country than Cicero, who, in a letter to Atticus, could not forbear exclaiming, 'O Socrates,

et Socratici viri! nunquam vobis gratiam referam.' Would
to God many of our countrymen had the same obligations
to those Socratic writers! Certainly, where the people are
well educated, the art of piloting a State is best learned
from the writings of Plato. But among bad men, void of
discipline and education, Plato, Pythagoras, and Aristotle
themselves, were they living, could do but little good.

CCCXLI.

The Popular Verdict.

When I travelled I took a particular delight in hearing
the songs and fables that are come from father to son,
and are most in vogue among the common people of the
countries through which I passed; for it is impossible
that anything should be universally tasted and approved
by a multitude, though they are only the rabble of a
nation, which hath not in it some peculiar aptness to
please and gratify the mind of man. Human nature is
the same in all reasonable creatures; and whatever falls
in with it will meet with admirers amongst readers of all
qualities and conditions. Molière, as we are told by M.
Boileau, used to read all his comedies to an old woman
who was his housekeeper, as she sate with him at her
work by the chimney corner; and foretell the success of
his play at the theatre from the reception it met at his
fireside, for he tells us the audience always followed the
old woman, and never failed to laugh in the same place.

CCCXLII.

The Passion for Glory.

One of the strongest incitements to excel in such arts
and accomplishments as are in the highest esteem among

men, is the natural passion for glory which the mind of man has : which, though it may be faulty in the excess of it, ought by no means to be discouraged. Perhaps some moralists are too severe in beating down this principle, which seems to be a spring implanted by nature to give motion to all the latent powers of the soul, and is always observed to exert itself with the greatest force in the most generous dispositions. The men whose characters have shone brightest among the ancient Romans appear to have been strongly animated by this passion. Cicero, whose learning and services to his country are so well known, was inflamed by it to an extravagant degree, and warmly presses Lucceius, who was composing a history of those times, to be very particular and zealous in relating the story of his consulship ; and to execute it speedily, that he might have the pleasure of enjoying in his lifetime some part of the honour which he foresaw would be paid to his memory. This was the ambition of a great mind, but he is faulty in the degree of it, and cannot refrain from soliciting the historian, upon this occasion, to neglect the strict laws of history, and in praising him, even to exceed the strict bounds of truth. The younger Pliny appears to have had the same passion for fame, but accompanied with greater chasteness and modesty.   *Spectator.*

CCCXLIII.

The Supreme Rank of Poetry.

But among all the arts it is only poetry that can confer this supreme kind of fame, because speech is the only mirror in which the whole universe can be reflected. With colours or in marble we can express only what we see, but there is nothing that the mind can think which cannot be uttered in speech. And therefore, in the poetry of all ages we possess, as it were, a shifting view of the universe as it has appeared to successive generations of men. According to the predominant inclination of the human mind in each age is the poetry of that age. At one time it is busy with the brave deeds of the hero, the contest and the laurel wreath : at another time with mere enjoyment, with wine and love. Then it describes the struggle of man against destiny, heroic fortitude and endurance in the midst of little hope ; at another time it pictures man as in probation, purified in adversity, and having a hope beyond the grave. At one time it becomes idyllic, delights in country life, simple pleasures, simple loves, a wholesome and peaceful existence ; at another time it loves cities, and deals in refinements, courtesies, gallantries, gaieties. And sometimes it takes a philosophical tone, delights in the grandeur of eternal laws, aspires to communion with the soul of the world, or endeavours to discover, in the construction of things, the traces of a beneficent plan.   *Seeley.*

CCCXLIV.

Ancient Hatred of Foreigners.

That system of morality, even in the times when it was powerful and in many respects beneficial, had made it almost as much a duty to hate foreigners as to love fellow-citizens. Plato congratulates the Athenians on having shown in their relations to Persia, beyond all the other Greeks, 'a pure and heartfelt hatred of the foreign nature.' Instead of opposing, it had sanctioned and consecrated the savage instinct which leads us to hate whatever is strange or unintelligible ; to distrust those who live on the farther side of a river; to suppose that those whom we hear talking together in a foreign tongue must be plotting some mischief against ourselves. The lapse of time and the fusion of races doubtless diminished this antipathy considerably, but at the utmost it could but be transformed into an icy indifference, for no cause was in operation to convert it into kindness. On the other hand, the closeness of the bond which united fellow-citizens was considerably relaxed. Common interests and common dangers had drawn it close; these in the wide security of the Roman Empire had no longer a place. It had depended upon an imagined blood-relationship; fellow-citizens could now no longer feel themselves to be united by the tie of blood. Every town was full of resident aliens and emancipated slaves, persons between whom and the citizens nature had established no connection, and whose presence in the city had originally been barely tolerated from motives of expediency. The selfishness of modern times exists in defiance of morality; in ancient times it was approved, sheltered, and even in part enjoined by morality.

CCCXLV.

Plutocracy.

It is the curse of our species that the great and wealthy seldom or never pursue this straight and righteous path to dominion. They insist upon governing mankind without taking the trouble to acquire those qualities which make mankind willing to be governed by them. They choose to rule by mere dint of naked wealth and station, unallied with those beneficent ingredients which bestow upon rulers an empire over human hearts as well as over human persons. Then come the strain and tug to make the influence of wealth alone in worthless and ungifted hands equal to that of wealth and mental excellence united. Wealth in itself, apart from all personal merit, insures the power of conferring favours and inflicting injuries. It enables a man to deal out bribes, open or disguised, with one hand, and blows with the other. It will not indeed obtain for him the heartfelt esteem of a willing public, but it serves as a two-edged sword to compel delusive indications of it. It will steal away simulated demonstrations of esteem, and extort those votes which he has not virtue enough to earn.

CCCXLVI.

Brahmin Cosmogony.

The Brahmins assert that the world arose from an infinite spider, who spun this whole complicated mass from his bowels, and annihilates afterwards the whole, or any part of it, by absorbing it again, and resolving it into his own essence. Here is a theory which appears to us ridiculous; because a spider is a little contemptible animal, whose operations we are never likely to take for a model of the whole universe. But still it is in keeping with what goes on in our globe. And were there a world wholly inhabited by spiders (which is very possible) this theory would there appear as natural and irrefragable as that which in our planet ascribes the origin of all things to design and intelligence, as explained by Cleanthes. Why an orderly system may not be spun from the belly, as well as from the brain, it will be difficult for him to give a satisfactory reason.

CCCXLVII.

Human Nature Narrow rather than Heartless.

It is constantly said that human nature is heartless.
Do not believe it. Human nature is kind and generous;
but it is narrow and blind, and can only with difficulty
conceive anything but what it immediately sees and feels.
People would instantly care for others as well as themselves if only they could *imagine* others as well as themselves. Let a child fall into the river before the roughest
man's eyes;—he will usually do what he can to get it out,
even at some risk to himself; and all the town will triumph
in the saving of one little life. Let the same man be
shown that hundreds of children are dying of fever for
want of some sanitary measure which it will cost him
trouble to urge, and he will make no effort; and probably
all the town would resist him if he did. So also the lives
of many deserving women are passed in a succession of
petty anxieties about themselves, and gleaning of minute
interests and mean pleasures in their immediate circle,
because they are never taught to make any effort to look
beyond it, or to know anything about the mighty world
in which their lives are fading, like blades of bitter grass
in fruitless fields.   *Ruskin.*

CCCXLVIII.

The True Aristocracy.

Will you go and gossip with your housemaid, or your
stable boy, when you may talk with queens and kings; or
flatter yourselves that it is with any worthy consciousness
of your own claims to respect, that you jostle with the
hungry and common crowd for *entrée* here, and audience

there, when all the while this eternal court is open to you, with its society, wide as the world, multitudinous as its days, the chosen and the mighty of every place and time? Into that you may enter always; in that you may take fellowship and rank according to your wish; from that, once entered into it, you can never be an outcast but by your own fault; by your aristocracy of companionship there, your own inherent aristocracy will be assuredly tested, and the motives with which you strive to take high place in the society of the living, measured, as to all the truth and sincerity that are in them, by the place you desire to take in this company of the Dead.   *Ruskin.*

CCCXLIX.

Rarity of True Friendship.

When Socrates was building himself a house at Athens, being asked by one that observed the littleness of the design, why a man so eminent would not have an abode more suitable to his dignity? he replied, that he should think himself sufficiently accommodated, if he could see that narrow habitation filled with real friends. Such was the opinion of this great master of human life concerning the infrequency of such an union of minds as might deserve the name of friendship, that among the multitudes whom vanity or curiosity, civility or veneration, crowded about him, he did not expect that very spacious apartments would be necessary to contain all that should regard him with sincere kindness, or adhere to him with steady fidelity. So many qualities are indeed requisite to the possibility of friendship, and so many accidents must concur to its rise and its continuance, that the greatest part of mankind content themselves without it, and supply its place as they can, with interest and dependence. Multitudes are unqualified for a constant and warm reciprocation of benevolence, as they are incapacitated for any other elevated excellence, by perpetual attention to their interest, and unresisting subjection to their passions. Long habits may superinduce inability to deny any desire, or repress, by superior motives, the importunities of any immediate gratification, and an inveterate selfishness will imagine all advantages diminished in proportion as they are communicated.

CCCL.

Truth Overdone.

It is difficult to think too highly of the merits and delights of truth ; but there is often in men's minds an exaggerated notion of some bit of truth, which proves a great assistance to falsehood. For instance, the shame of finding that he has in some special case been led into falsehood becomes a bugbear which scares a man into a career of false dealing. He has begun making a furrow a little out of the line, and he ploughs on in it, to try and give some consistency and meaning to it. He wants almost to persuade himself that it was not wrong, and entirely to hide the wrongness from others. This is a tribute to the majesty of truth : also to the world's opinion about truth. It proceeds, too, upon the notion that all falsehoods are equal, which is not the case, or on some fond craving for a show of perfection, which is sometimes very inimical to the reality. The practical, as well as the high-minded, view in such cases, is for a man to think how he can be true now. To attain that, it may, even for this world, be worth while for a man to admit that he has been inconsistent, and even that he has been untrue. His hearers, did they know anything of themselves, would be fully aware that he was not singular, except in the courage of owning his insincerity.   *Spectator.*

CCCLI.

The Fear of Death.

I have often thought upon death, and I find it the least of evils. All that which is past is as a dream; and he that hopes or depends upon time coming dreams waking. So much of our life as we have discovered is already dead, and all those hours which we share, even from the breast of our mother, until we return to our grandmother the earth, are part of our dying day; whereof even this is one, and those that succeed are of the same nature; for we die daily, and as others have given place to us, so we must in the end give way to others. Physicians in the name of death include all sorrow, anguish, disease, calamity, or whatsoever can fall in the life of man, either grievous or unwelcome: but these things are familiar unto us, and we suffer them every hour; therefore we die daily, and I am older since I affirmed it. I know many wise men that fear to die; for the change is bitter, and flesh would refuse to prove it: besides the expectation brings terror, and that exceeds in evil. But I do not believe that any man fears to be dead, but only the stroke of death: and such are my hopes that if Heaven be pleased, and nature renew but my lease for twenty-one years more, without asking longer days, I shall be strong enough to acknowledge without mourning that I was begotten mortal.

CCCLII.

Two Theories on Land.

There are two theories on the subject of land now abroad, and in contention; both false. The first is that, by Heavenly law, there have always existed, and must continue to exist, a certain number of hereditarily sacred persons, to whom the earth, air, and water of the world belong, as personal property; of which, earth, air, and water, these persons may, at their pleasure, permit, or forbid, the rest of the human race to eat, to breathe, or to drink. This theory is not for many years longer tenable. The adverse theory is that a division of the land of the world among the mob of the world would immediately elevate the said mob into sacred personages; that houses would then build themselves, and corn grow of itself; and that everybody would be able to live, without doing any work for his living. This theory would also be found highly untenable in practice. *Ruskin.*

CCCLIII.

Satire without Sting.

I often apply this rule to myself; and when I hear of a satirical speech or writing that is aimed at me, I examine my own heart, whether I deserve it or not. If I bring in a verdict against myself, I endeavour to rectify my conduct for the future in those particulars which have drawn the censure upon me; but if the whole invective be grounded upon a falsehood, I trouble myself no further about it, and look upon my name at the head of it to signify no more than one of those

fictitious names made use of by an author to introduce
an imaginary character. Why should a man be sensible
of the sting of a reproach, who is a stranger to the guilt
that is implied in it? or subject himself to the penalty,
when he knows he has never committed the crime?
This is a piece of fortitude, which every one owes to
his own innocence, and without which it is impossible
for a man of any merit or figure to live at peace with
himself in a country that abounds with wit and liberty.

CCCLIV.

Self-Sacrifice.

It is noble to be capable of resigning entirely one's
own portion of happiness, or chances of it : but after all
this self-sacrifice must be for some end ; it is not its own
end ; and if we are told that its end is not happiness, but
virtue which is better than happiness, I ask, Would the
sacrifice be made if the hero or martyr did not believe
that it would earn for others immunity from similar
sacrifices? Would it be made if he thought that his
renunciation of happiness for himself would produce no
fruit for any of his fellow-creatures, but to make their
lot like his, and place them also in the condition of
persons who have renounced happiness? All honour
to those who can abnegate for themselves the personal
enjoyment of life, when by such renunciation they contribute worthily to increase the amount of happiness in
the world ; but he who does it, or professes to do it,
for any other purpose, is no more deserving of admiration than the ascetic mounted on his pillar. He may
be an inspiring proof of what men can do, but assuredly
is not an example of what they should.   *J. S. Mill.*

CCCLV.

Men have their Exits.

The end of a man's life is often compared to the winding-up of a well-written play, where the principal persons still act in character, whatever the fate is they undergo. There is scarce a great person in the Grecian or Roman history, whose death has not been remarked upon by some writer or other, and censured or applauded according to the genius or principles of the person who has descanted upon it. Monsieur de St. Evremont is very particular in setting forth the constancy and courage of Petronius Arbiter during his last moments, and thinks he discovers in them a greater firmness of mind and resolution than in the death of Seneca, Cato, or Socrates. There is no question but this polite author's affectation of appearing singular in his remarks, and making discoveries which had escaped the observation of others, threw him into this course of reflexion. It was Petronius' merit that he died in the same gaiety of temper in which he lived ; but as his life was altogether loose and dissolute, the indifference which he showed at the close of it is to be looked upon as a piece of natural carelessness and levity, rather than fortitude. The resolution of Socrates proceeded from very different motives, the consciousness of a well-spent life, and a prospect of a happy eternity. If the ingenious author above-mentioned was so pleased with gaiety of humour in a dying man, he might have found a much nobler instance of it in our countryman Sir Thomas More.

Addison.

CCCLVI.

The Errors of the Illustrious Dead.

Undoubtedly we ought to look at ancient transactions by the light of modern knowledge. Undoubtedly it is among the first duties of a historian to point out the faults of the eminent men of former generations. There are no errors which are so likely to be drawn into precedent, and therefore none which it is so necessary to expose, as the errors of persons who have a just title to the gratitude and admiration of posterity. In politics, as in religion, there are devotees who show their reverence for a departed saint by converting his tomb into a sanctuary for crime. Receptacles for wickedness are suffered to remain undisturbed in the neighbourhood of the church which glories in the relics of some martyred apostle. Because he was merciful, his bones give security to assassins. Because he was chaste, the precinct of his temple is filled with licensed stews. Privileges of an equally absurd kind have been set up against the jurisdiction of political philosophy. Vile abuses cluster thick round every glorious event, round every venerable name; and this evil assuredly calls for vigorous measures of literary police. But the proper course is to abate the nuisance without defacing the shrine, to drive out the gangs of thieves and prostitutes without doing foul and cowardly wrong to the ashes of the illustrious dead.

Macaulay.

CCCLVII.

All is Vanity.

The highest gratification we receive here below is mirth, which at the best is but a fluttering unquiet motion that beats about the breast for a few moments, and after leaves it void and empty. So little is there in the thing we so much talk of, and so much magnify — keeping good company. Even the best is but a less shameful act of losing time. What we call science here, and study, is little better. The greater number of arts to which we apply ourselves are mere groping in the dark ; and even the search of our most important concerns in a future being, is but a needless, anxious, and uncertain haste to be knowing sooner than we can, what without all this solicitude, we shall know a little after. We are but curious impertinents in the case of futurity. It is not our business to be guessing what the state of souls is, but to be doing what may make our own happy. We cannot be knowing, but we can be virtuous. *Pope.*

CCCLVIII.

How to deal with Passion.

When passion, whether in the political body or in the individual, is once roused, it is vain, during the paroxysm, to combat it with the weapons of reason. A man in love is proverbially inaccessible to argument, and a nation heated in the pursuit of political power is as incapable of listening either to the deductions of the understanding, or the lessons of experience. The only way in such times of averting the evil is by presenting some new object of pursuit which is attractive not only to the thinking few, but to the unthinking many ; by counteracting one passion by the growth of another, and summoning to the support of truth not only the armour of reason but the fire of imagination. *A. Alison.*

CCCLIX.

The Legal Profession.

'I see,' cries my friend, 'that you are for a speedy administration of justice; but all the world will grant, that the more time there is taken up in considering any subject, the better will it be understood. Besides, it is the boast of an Englishman, that his property is secure, and all the world will grant that a deliberate administration of justice is the best way to secure his property. Why have we so many lawyers, but to secure our property? Why so many formalities, but to secure our property? Not less than one hundred thousand families live in opulence merely by securing our property.' . . . 'But, bless me,' returned I, 'what numbers do I see here—all in black—how is it possible that half this multitude find employment?' 'Nothing so easily conceived,' returned my companion, 'they live by watching each other. For instance, the catch-pole watches the man in debt, the attorney watches the catch-pole, the counsellor watches the attorney, the solicitor the counsellor, and all find sufficient employment.' 'I conceive you,' interrupted I, 'they watch each other: but it is the client that pays them all for watching.'   *Citizen of the World.*

CCCLX.

Of Causes in Politics.

Not to lose ourselves in the infinite void of the conjectural world, our business is with what is likely to be affected for the better or the worse, by the wisdom or weakness of our plans. In all speculations upon men and human affairs, it is of no small moment to distinguish things of accident from permanent causes, and from effects that cannot be altered. It is not every irregularity in our movement that is a total deviation from our course. I am not quite of the mind of those speculators, who seem assured, that necessarily, and by the constitution of things, all states have the same periods of infancy, manhood, and decrepitude, that are found in the individuals who compose them. Parallels of this sort rather furnish similitudes to illustrate or to adorn, than supply analogies from whence to reason. The objects which are attempted to be forced into an analogy are not found in the same classes of existence. Individuals are physical beings, subject to laws universal and invariable. The immediate cause acting in these laws may be obscure : the general results are subjects of certain calculation. But commonwealths are not physical but moral essences. They are artificial combinations ; and in their proximate efficient cause, the arbitrary productions of the human mind. We are not yet acquainted with the laws which necessarily influence the stability of that kind of work made by that kind of agent. There is not in the physical order (with which they do not appear to hold any assignable connexion) a distinct cause by which any of those fabrics must necessarily grow, flourish, or decay ; nor, in my opinion, does the moral world produce anything more determinate on that subject, than what may serve as an amusement (liberal indeed, and ingenious, but still only an amusement) for speculative men. I doubt whether the history of mankind is yet complete enough, if ever it can be so, to furnish grounds for a sure theory on the internal causes which necessarily affect the fortune of a State. I am far from denying the operation of such causes : but they are infinitely uncertain, and much more obscure, and much more difficult to trace, than the foreign causes that tend to raise, to depress, and sometimes to over-whelm a community.   *Addison.*

CCCLXI.

Political Necessities.

Let us take for granted that what has been desired, what has been held good and useful by all the enlightened men of a country, without variation, during a succession of years of various governments, is a necessity of the time.   Such, gentlemen, is the liberty of the Press. . . . I do not say that governments ought to hasten to recog-nise these new necessities.   But when they have been recognised, to take back what was given, or—which comes to the same thing—to suspend it indefinitely, that is a rashness which, more than any one, I hope may not bring a sad repentance to those who have conceived the convenient but pitiful thought.   You must never com-promise the good faith of a government.   In our days it is not easy to deceive for a long time.   There is some one who has more sense than Voltaire, more sense than Bonaparte, more than any Director, more than any Minister, past, present, or to come.   That is, everybody. To undertake, or even to persist in a controversy where all the world is interested against you is a fault; and to-day all political faults are dangerous.   *Talleyrand.*

CCCLXII.

A Frenchman on the Discovery of America.

Frenchmen, brought to the colónies on military expedi-tions, came home with glowing descriptions of the wealth contained in the New World. America was on every lip. 'What should we be were it not for America?' everybody wanted to know. 'She gives us a navy,' stated M. Malouet, 'she extends our trade,' the Abbé Raynal proclaimed; 'she gives work to our overcrowded populations,' repeated the administrators of the day; 'she welcomes all restless spirits,' said the ministers; 'she is the refuge of all dissenters,' remarked the philosophers. Nothing more useful, nothing more pacific, in appearance. There was no topic of conversation but the glory attached to the discovery of America. And yet, let us sift matters to the bottom. What has been the result of all our communications with the New World? Do we see less misery around us? Have all our disorganisers disappeared? Have not the longing looks we have cast abroad lessened our love for fatherland? These newly discovered parts of the world having given England and France additional points of irritation, are not wars more frequent, longer, of greater extent, and more costly? The history of mankind supplies this sad conclusion : that the spirit of strife rushes to every spot on earth to which communication is opened. *Talleyrand.*

CCCLXIII.

O Mighty Opium.

The town of L. represented the earth, with its sorrows and its graves left behind, yet not out of sight, nor wholly forgotten. The ocean in everlasting but gentle agitation, and brooded over by a dove-like calm, might not unfitly typify the mind and the mood which then swayed it. For it seemed to me as if then first I stood at a distance and aloof from the uproar of life ; as if the tumult, the

R

fever and the strife were suspended ; or respite granted
from the secret burthens of the heart ; a sabbath of
repose, a resting from human labours.   Here were the
hopes which blossom in the paths of life reconciled with
the peace which is in the grave ; motions of the intellect as unwearied as the heavens, yet for all anxieties
a halcyon calm, a tranquility that seemed no product
of inertia, but as if resulting from mighty and equal
antagonisms ; infinite activities, infinite repose.   Oh,
just, subtle, and mighty opium ! that to the hearts of
poor and rich alike for the wounds that will never heal,
and for 'the pangs that tempt the spirit to rebel,' bringest
an assuaging balm ; eloquent opium ! that with thy potent
rhetoric stealest away the purposes of wrath ; and to the
guilty man for one night givest back the hopes of his
youth and hands washed pure from blood ; . . . . that
summonest to the chancery of dreams, for the triumphs
of suffering innocence, false witnesses ; and confoundest
perjury, and dost reverse the sentences of unrighteous
judges.   *De Quincey.*

CCCLXIV.

The Landed and Moneyed Men.

The landed men are the true owners of our political
vessel : the moneyed men, as such, are no more than
passengers in it.   To the first, therefore, all exhortations
to assume this spirit of disinterestedness should be addressed.   It is their part to set the example : and when
they do so, they have a right to expect that the passengers should contribute their proportion to save the vessel.
If they should prove refractory, they must be told that
there is a law in behalf of the public, more sacred and
more ancient too, for it is as ancient as political society,

than all those under the terms of which they would exempt themselves from any reduction of interest and consequently from any reimbursement of their principal; though this reduction and this reimbursement be absolutely necessary to restore the prosperity of the nation and to provide for her security in the meantime. The law I mean, is that which nature and reason dictate and which declares the preservation of the commonwealth to be superior to all other laws. *Bolinbroke.*

CCCLXV.

By Him were all things made.

All we see, hear, and touch, the remote sidereal firmament, as well as our own sea and land, and the elements which compose them and the ordinances they obey, are His. The primary atoms of matter, their properties, their mutual action, their disposition and collocation, electricity, magnetism, gravitation, light, and whatever other subtle principles or operations the wit of man is detecting or shall detect, are the work of his hands. From Him has been every movement which has convulsed and refashioned the surface of the earth. The most insignificant or unsightly insect is from Him, and good in its kind ; the ever-teeming, inexhaustible swarms of animalculae, the myriads of living motes invisible to the naked eye, the restless ever-spreading vegetation which creeps like a garment over the whole earth, the lofty cedar, the umbrageous banana are His. His are the tribes and families of birds and beasts, their graceful forms, their wild gestures, and their passionate cries.

J. H. Newman.

R 2

CCCLXVI.

What has Philosophy done?

In a word, from the time that Athens was the University of the world, what has Philosophy taught men, but to promise without practising, and to aspire without attaining? What has the deep and lofty thought of its disciples ended in but eloquent words? Nay, what has its teaching ever meditated, when it was boldest in its remedies for human ill, beyond charming us to sleep by its lessons, that we might feel nothing at all? like some melodious air, or rather like those strong perfumes, which at first spread their sweetness over everything they touch, but in a little while do but offend in proportion as they once pleased us. Did Philosophy support Cicero under the disfavour of the fickle populace, or nerve Seneca to oppose an imperial tyrant? It abandoned Brutus, as he sorrowfully confessed, in his greatest need, and it forced Cato, as his panegyrist strangely boasts, into the false position of defying heaven.

J. H. Newman.

CCCLXVII.

The Virtue of Restraint.

And this necessity of restraint, remember, is just as honourable to man as the necessity of labour. You hear every day greater numbers of foolish people speaking about liberty, as if it were such an honourable thing : so far from being that, it is, on the whole, and in the broadest sense, dishonourable, and an attribute of the lower creatures. No human being, however great or powerful, was ever so free as a fish. There is always something that he must or must not do ; while the fish may do whatever he likes. All the kingdoms of the world put together are not half so large as the sea ; and all the railroads and wheels that ever were, or will be, invented are not so easy as fins. You will find, on fairly thinking of it, that it is his restraint which is honourable to man, not his liberty; and, what is more, it is restraint which is honourable even in the lower animals. A butterfly is much more free than a bee ; but you honour the bee more, just because it is subject to certain laws which fit it for orderly function in bee society. And throughout the world, of the two abstract things, liberty and restraint, restraint is always the more honourable. It is true, indeed, that in these and all other matters you never can reason finally from the abstraction, for both liberty and restraint are good when they are nobly chosen, and both are bad when they are basely chosen ; but of the two, I repeat, it is restraint which characterises the higher creature and betters the lower creature ; and, from the ministering of the archangel to the labour of the insect,—from the poising of the planets to the gravitation of a grain of dust,— the power and glory of all creatures and all matter consist in their obedience, not in their freedom. The sun has no liberty—a dead leaf has much. The dust of which you are formed has no liberty. Its liberty will come—with its corruption.   *Ruskin.*

CCCLXVIII.

Broken Friendships.

But further questions arise in consequence of the changes of feeling to which human nature is liable : first, whether it is our duty to resist such changes as much as we can ; and secondly, whether if this effort fails, and love diminishes or departs, we ought still to maintain a disposition to render services corresponding to our past affection. And on these points there does not seem to be agreement among moral and refined persons. For, on the one hand, it is natural to us to admire fidelity in friendship and stability of affections, and we commonly regard these as most important excellences of character : and so it seems strange if we are not to aim at these as at all other excellences, as none more naturally stir us to imitation. And hence many would be prepared to lay down that we ought not to withdraw affection once given, unless the friend behaves ill : while some would say that even in this case we ought not to break the friendship unless the crime is very great. Yet, on the other hand, we feel that such affection as is produced by deliberate effort of will is but a poor substitute for that which springs spontaneously, and most refined persons would reject such a boon : while, again, to conceal the change of feeling seems insincere and hypocritical. I have noticed that some extend this latter view so far, that they would have us follow the spontaneous course of feeling even in the domestic relationships : and if common sense rejects this, and it seems a duty so far to force our feelings to flow in legal and customary channels, we should perhaps all the more avoid constraint as regards other affections, and let them flow in old or new courses as nature inclines. Still, all would recognise some limit to this : for it seems too inhuman to treat as a stranger one who has been a friend, unless he has deserved severe punishment.

CCCLXIX.

The Stoics.

They knew nothing of God or the gods, but they had something in themselves which made sensuality nauseating instead of pleasant to them. They had an austere sense of the meaning of the word 'duty.' They could distinguish and reverence the nobler possibilities of their nature. They disdained what was base and effeminate, and, though religion failed them, they constructed out of philosophy a rule which would serve to live by. Stoicism is a not unnatural refuge of thoughtful men in confused and sceptical ages. It adheres rigidly to morality. It offers no easy Epicurean explanation of the origin of man, which resolves him into an organization of particles, and dismisses him again into nothingness. It recognises only that men who are the slaves of their passions are miserable and impotent, and insists that personal inclinations shall be subordinated to conscience. It prescribes plainness of life, that the number of our necessities may be as few as possible; and in placing the business of life in intellectual and moral action it destroys the temptation to sensual gratifications. It teaches a contempt of death so complete that it can be encountered without a flutter of the pulse; and while it raises men above the suffering which makes others miserable, generates a proud submissiveness to sorrow which noblest natures feel most keenly, by representing this huge scene and the shows which it presents as the work of some unknown but irresistible force, against which it is vain to struggle and childish to repine. *Froude.*

CCCLXX.

Human Inconsistency.

I often consider mankind as wholly inconsistent with itself. Though we seem grieved at the shortness of life in general, we are wishing every period of it at an end. The minor longs to be at age, then to be a man of business,

then to make up an estate, then to arrive at honours, then
to retire. Thus, although the whole of life is allowed by
every one to be short, the several divisions of it appear
long and tedious. We are for lengthening our span in
general, but would fain contract the parts of which it
is composed. The usurer would be very well satisfied
to have all the time annihilated that lies between the
present moment and next quarter-day. The lover would
be glad to strike out of his existence all the moments
that are to pass away before the happy meeting. Thus,
as fast as our time runs, we should be very glad in most
parts of our lives that it ran much faster than it does.
Several hours of the day hang upon our hands, nay, we
wish away whole years ; and travel through time as through
a country filled with many wild and empty wastes, which
we would fain hurry over, that we may arrive at those
several little settlements or imaginary points of rest which
are dispersed up and down in it.   *Spectator.*

CCCLXXI.

Plainness of Speech.

A second property of the ability of speech, conferred
by Christ upon his apostles, was its unaffected plainness
and simplicity : it was to be easy, obvious, and familiar ;
with nothing in it strained or far-fetched : no affected
scheme, or airy fancies, above the reach or relish of an
ordinary apprehension ; no, nothing of all this ; but their
grand subject was truth, and consequently above all these
petit arts and poor additions, as not being capable of any
greater lustre or advantage than to appear just as it is.
For there is a certain majesty in plainness, as the proclamation of a prince never frisks it in tropes or fine

conceits, in numerous and well turned periods, but commands in sober, natural expressions. A substantial beauty, as it comes out of the hands of nature, needs neither paint nor patch ; things never made to adorn, but to cover something that would be hid. It is with expression, and the clothing of a man's conceptions, as with the clothing of a man's body. Gaudery is a pitiful and mean thing, not extending farther than the surface of the body; but indeed there may be great need of an outside, when there is little or nothing within.   *South.*

CCCLXXII.

Progressive Civilisation.

History, again, tells us of successive civilisations which have been born, have for a space thriven exceedingly, and have then miserably perished. And as it shows us samples of death and decay so it shows us samples of growth arrested, and, as far as we can tell, permanently arrested, at a particular stage of development. What is there in all this to indicate that a nation or group of nations which happens to be under observation during its period of energetic growth is either itself to be an exception to this common law, or is of necessity to find in some other race an heir charged with the task of carrying on its work ? Progressive civilisation is no form of indestructible energy which if repressed here must needs break out there, if refused embodiment in one shape must needs show itself in another. It is a plant of tender growth, difficult to propagate, not difficult to destroy, that refuses to flourish except in a soil which is not to be found everywhere, nor at all times, nor even, so far as we can see, necessarily to be found at all.

A. J. Balfour.

CCCLXXIII.

Progress.

In one generation an institution is unassailable, in the next bold men may assail it, and in the third only bold men defend it. At one time the most conclusive arguments are advanced against it in vain, if indeed they are allowed utterance at all; at another time the most childish sophistry is enough to secure its condemnation. In the first case the institution, though probably indefensible by pure reason, was congruous with the unconscious habits and modes of thought of the community. In the second these had changed from causes which the acutest analysis would probably fail to explain, and a breath sufficed to topple over the sapped structure. Progress is a misnomer for secular change. All that we can really say is that change is going on, but whether the nation is on the ascending or descending limb of the curve, which all nations seem to trace, can hardly be positively decided by contemporaries. Happily, such considerations as these, while they may chasten pride and sober temerity, cast no doubt upon the plain duties that lie before us. We can build our houses without knowing the nature of gravitation or the construction of the universe, and we need no complete scheme of statecraft to enable us to do our duty as good citizens.   *The Times.*

CCCLXXIV.

Conversation on Amusements.

Society talks, by preference, about amusements; it does so because when people meet for recreation they wish to relieve their minds from serious cares, and also for the practical reason that society must talk about what its members have in common, and their amusements are more in common than their work. As M. Thiers recommended the republican form of government in France on the ground that it was the form which divided his countrymen least, so a polite and highly civilised society chooses for the subject of general conversation the topic which is least likely to separate the different people who are present. It almost always happens that the best topic having this recommendation is some species of amusement; since amusements are easily learnt outside the business of life, and we are all initiated into them in youth.

CCCLXXV.

True Courage.

There be those who confound the foresight of death with a fearfulness of death, and talk of meeting death like brave men; and there be institutions in human society which seem made on purpose to hinder the thougnts of death from coming timeously before the deliberation of the mind. And they who die in war, be they ever so dissipated, abandoned, and wretched, have oft a halo of everlasting glory arrayed by poetry and music around their heads; and the forlorn hope of any enterprise goeth to their terrible post amidst the applauding shouts of all their comrades. And 'to die game' is a brutal form of speech which they are now proud to apply to men. And our prize-fights, where they go plunging upon the edge of eternity, and often plunge through, are applauded by tens of thousands, just in proportion as the bull-dog quality of the human creature carries it over every other.

And to run hair-breadth escapes, to graze the grass that skirts the grave, and escape the yawning pit, the impious, the daring wretches call cheating the devil; and the watchword of your dissolute, debauched people is, 'a short life, and a merry one.' All which tribes of reckless, godless people lift loud the laugh against the saints, as a sickly, timorous crew, who have no upright gait in life, but are always cringing under apprehensions of death and the devil.   *Edward Irving.*

CCCLXXVI.

The Death of the Righteous.

How much soever men differ in the course of life they prefer, and in their ways of palliating and excusing their vices to themselves; yet all agree in the one thing, desiring to 'die the death of the righteous.' This is surely remarkable. The observation may be extended further, and put thus: Even without determining what that is which we call guilt or innocence, there is no man but would choose, after having had the pleasure or advantage of a vicious action, to be free of the guilt of it, to be in the state of an innocent man. This shows at least the disturbance and implicit dissatisfaction in vice. If we inquire into the grounds of it, we shall find it proceeds partly from an immediate sense of having done evil; and partly from an apprehension that this inward sense shall, one time or other, be seconded by a higher judgment, upon which our whole being depends. Now, to suspend and drown this sense, and these apprehensions, be it by the hurry of business or of pleasure, or by superstition, or moral equivocations, this is in a manner one and the same, and makes no alteration at all in the nature of our case. Things and actions are what they are, and the consequences of them will be what they will be : why then should we desire to be deceived?　　　*J. Butler.*

CCCLXXVII.

Nullius Addictus.

It is a good rule to examine well before we addict ourselves to any sect ; but I think it is a better rule to addict ourselves to none. Let us hear them all, with a perfect indifferency on which side the truth lies; and, when we come to determine, let nothing appear so venerable to us as our own understandings. Let us gratefully accept the help of every one who has endeavoured to correct the vices, and strengthen the minds of men; but let us choose for ourselves, and yield universal assent to none. Thus, that I may instance the sect already mentioned, when we have laid aside the wonderful and surprising sentences, and all the paradoxes of the Portique, we shall find in that school such doctrines as our unprejudiced reason submits to with pleasure, as nature dictates, and as experience confirms. Without this precaution, we run the risk of becoming imaginary kings and real slaves. With it, we may learn to assert our native freedom, and live independent on fortune.　　　*Bolinbroke.*

CCCLXXVIII.

The Power of Death.

It was death, which, opening the conscience of Charles the Fifth, made him enjoin his son Philip to restore Navarre ; and King Francis the First of France to command that justice should be done upon the murderers of the Protestants in Merindol and Cabrières, which till then he neglected. It is therefore death alone that can suddenly make man to know himself. He tells the proud and insolent that they are but objects, and humbles them at the instant; makes them cry, complain, and repent; yea, even to hate their fore-passed happiness. He takes the account of the rich, and proves him a beggar; a naked beggar, which hath interest in nothing but in the gravel that fills his mouth. He holds a glass before the eyes of the most beautiful, and makes them see therein their deformity and rottenness, and they acknowledge it.

O eloquent, just and mighty death! whom none could advise, thou hast persuaded; what none hath dared, thou hast done; and whom all the world hath flattered, thou only hast cast out of the world and despised: thou hast drawn together all the far stretched greatness, all the pride, cruelty, and ambition of men, and covered it all over with these two narrow words, *Hic jacet.*

Sir Walter Raleigh.

CCCLXXIX.

The Screech-owls of Mankind.

These screech-owls seem to be settled in an opinion that the great business of life is to complain, and that they were born for no other purpose than to disturb the happiness of others, to lessen the little comforts and shorten the short pleasures of our condition by painful remembrances of the past, or melancholy prognostics of the future; their only care is to crush the rising hope, to damp the kindling transport, and alloy the golden hours of gaiety with the hateful dross of grief and suspicion.

I have known Suspirius, the screech-owl, fifty-eight years and four months, and have never passed an hour with him in which he has not made some attack on my quiet. When we were first acquainted, his great topic was the misery of youth without riches; and whenever we walked out together, he solaced me with a long enumeration of pleasures, which, as they were beyond the reach of my fortune, were without the verge of my desires, and which I should never have considered as the objects of a wish, had not his unreasonable representations placed them in my sight.

Whenever my evil star brings us together he never fails to represent to me the folly of my pursuits, and informs me we are much older than when we began our acquaintance; that the infirmities of decrepitude are coming fast upon me; that whatever I now get I shall enjoy but a little time: that fame is to a man tottering on the edge of the grave of very little importance; and that the time is at hand when I ought to look for no other pleasures than a good dinner and an easy chair.

Dr. Johnson.

CCCLXXX.

One's own Master.

To be absolute master of one's own time and actions is an instance of liberty which is not found but in solitude. A man that lives in a crowd is a slave, even though all that are about him fawn upon him and give him the upper-hand. They call him master, or lord, and treat him as such; but as they hinder him from doing what he otherwise would, the title and homage which they pay him is flattery and contradiction.

I ever loved retirement, and detested crowds; I would

rather pass an afternoon amongst a herd of deer, than half an hour at a coronation; and sooner eat a piece of apple-pie in a cottage, than dine with a judge on circuit. To lodge a night by myself in a cave would not grieve me so much as living half a day in a fair. It will look a little odd when I own that I have missed many a good sermon for no other reason but that many others were to hear it as well as myself. I have neither disliked the man, nor his principles, nor his congregation, singly; but altogether I could not abide them.

I am, therefore, exceedingly happy in the solitude which I am now enjoying. I frequently stand under a tree, and with great humanity pity one half of the world and with equal contempt laugh at the other half. I shun the company of men, and seek that of oxen, and sheep, and deer, and bushes; and when I can hide myself for the moiety of a day from the sight of every creature but those that are dumb, I consider myself as monarch of all that I see or tread upon, and fancy that Nature smiles and the sun shines for my sake only.   *Humourist.*

CCCLXXXI.

Words and Gold.

The same weakness, or defect in the mind, from whence pedantry takes its rise, does likewise give birth to avarice. Words and money are both to be regarded as only marks of things; and as the knowledge of the one, so the possession of the other, is of no use, unless directed to a farther end. A mutual commerce could not be carried on among men, if some common standard had not been agreed upon, to which the value of all the various productions of art and nature were reducible, and which might be of the same use in the conveyance of property as words are in that of ideas. Gold, by its beauty, scarceness, and durable nature, seems designed by Providence to a purpose so excellent and advantageous to mankind. Upon these considerations, that metal came first into esteem. But such who cannot see beyond what is nearest in the pursuit, beholding mankind touched with an affection for gold, and, being ignorant of the true reason that introduced this odd passion into human nature, imagine some intrinsic worth in the metal to be the cause of it. Hence the same men who, had they been turned towards learning, would have employed themselves in laying up words in their memory, are by a different application employed to as much purpose in treasuring up gold in their coffers. They differ only in the object; the principle on which they act, and the inward frame of mind, is the same in the critic and the miser.

Dr. G. Berkeley.

CCCLXXXII.

Virtue not Happiness.

It was true then, it is infinitely more true now, that what is called virtue in the common sense of the word, still more, that nobleness, godliness, or heroism of character in any form whatsoever, have nothing to do with this or that man's prosperity or even happiness. The thoroughly vicious man is no doubt wretched enough; but the worldly, prudent, self-restraining man, with his five senses, which he understands how to gratify with tempered indulgence, with a conscience satisfied with the hack routine of what is called respectability— such a man feels no wretchedness; no inward uneasiness disturbs him, no desires which he cannot gratify; and

S

this though he be the basest and most contemptible slave of his own selfishness. Providence will not interfere to punish him. Let him obey the laws under which pros-perity is obtainable, and he will obtain it, let him never fear. He will obtain it, be he base or noble. . . . And again it is not true, as optimists would persuade us, that such prosperity brings no real pleasure. A man with no high aspirations, who thrives and makes money, and envelopes himself in comforts, is as happy as such a nature can be. If unbroken satisfaction be the most blessed state for a man (and this certainly is the practical notion of happiness) he is the happiest of men. Nor are those idle phrases any truer, that the good man's good-ness is a never ceasing sunshine; that virtue is its own reward, &c., &c. If men truly virtuous care to be re-warded for it, their virtue is but a poor investment of their moral capital.   *Froude.*

CCCLXXXIII.

The Goddess Fortune.

In order to which great end, it is necessary that we stand watchful, as sentinels, to discover the secret wiles and open attacks of this capricious goddess before they reach us. Where she falls upon us unexpected, it is hard to resist; but those who wait for her will repel her with ease. The sudden invasion of an enemy overthrows such as are not on their guard; but they who foresee the war, and prepare themselves for it before it breaks out, stand, without difficulty, the first and the fiercest onset. I learned this important lesson long ago, and never trusted to fortune even while she seemed at peace with me. The riches, the honours, the reputation, and all the advantages which her treacherous indulgence poured upon me, I placed so that she might snatch them away without giving me any disturbance. I kept a great interval between me and them. She took them, but she could not tear them from me. *Bolinbroke.*

CCCLXXXIV.

The Sea.

The sea deserved to be hated by the old aristocracies as it has been the mightiest instrument in the civilisation of mankind. In the depth of winter, when the sky is covered with clouds, and the land presents one cold and blank and lifeless surface of snows, how refreshing it is to the spirits to walk upon the shore, and to enjoy the eternal freshness and liveliness of ocean. Even so, in the deepest winter of the human race, when the earth was but one chilling expanse of inactivity, life was stirring in the waters. There began that spirit whose genial influence has now reached the land, has broken the chains of winter, and covered the face of the earth with beauty. *Arnold.*

CCCLXXXV.

Taxation.

I heard a very warm debate between two professors, about the most commodious and effectual ways and means of raising money, without grieving the subject. The first affirmed, 'the justest method would be to lay a certain tax upon vices and folly; and the sum fixed upon every man to be rated, after the fairest manner, by a jury of his neighbours.' The second was of an opinion directly contrary; 'To tax those qualities of mind and body, for which chiefly men value themselves; the rate to be more or less, according to the degrees of excelling ; the decision whereof should be left entirely to their own breast.'... Wit, valour, and politeness, were likewise proposed to be largely taxed, and collected in the same manner, by every person's giving his own word for the quantum of what he possessed.   But as to honour, justice, wisdom, and learning, they should not be taxed at all; because they are qualifications of so singular a kind, that no man will either allow them in his neighbour or value them in himself.

Swift.

CCCLXXXVI.

Ill-natured Wit.

There is nothing that more betrays a base ungenerous spirit than the giving of secret stabs to a man's reputation.   Lampoons and satires, that are written with wit and spirit, are like poisoned darts, which not only inflict a wound, but make it incurable.   For this reason I am very much troubled when I see the talents of humour and ridicule in the possession of an ill-natured man. There cannot be a greater gratification to a barbarous and inhuman wit than to stir up sorrow in the heart of a private person, to raise uneasiness among near relations, and to expose whole families to derision, at the same time that he remains unseen and undiscovered.   If, besides the accomplishments of being witty and ill-natured, a man is vicious into the bargain, he is one of the most mischievous creatures that can enter into a civil society. His satire will then chiefly fall upon those who ought to be the most exempt from it.   Virtue, merit, and everything that is praiseworthy, will be made the subject of ridicule and buffoonery.

Addison.

CCCLXXXVII.

Obedience the Law of Nature.

Now if Nature should intermit her course and leave altogether, though it were only for a while, the observation of her own laws; if those principal and mother elements of the world, whereof all things in this lower world are made, should lose the qualities which now they have ; if the frame of that heavenly arch erected over our heads should loosen and dissolve itself; if celestial spheres should forget their wonted motion, and by irregular volubility turn themselves any way as it might happen ; if the prince of the lights of heaven, which now as a giant doth run his unwearied course, should as it were through a languishing faintness begin to stand and to rest himself; if the moon should wander from her beaten way ; the times and seasons of the year blend themselves by disordered and confused mixture ; the winds breathe out their last gasp, the clouds yield no rain, and the earth be defeated by heavenly influence ; the fruits of the earth pine away as children at the withered breasts of their mother, no longer able to give them relief. What would become of man himself, whom these things now do all serve ? See we not plainly that the obedience of creatures to the law of nature is the stay of the whole world ?

Hooker.

CCCLXXXVIII.

Man helpless in his own Nature.

This writer went through all the usual topics of moralists, showing how diminutive, contemptible, and helpless an animal was man in his own nature; how unable to defend himself from the inclemencies of the air or the fury of wild beasts; how much he was excelled by one creature in strength, by another in speed, by a third in foresight, by a fourth in industry. He added that Nature was degenerated in these latter declining ages of the world, and would now produce only small abortive births in comparison of those in ancient times. He said it was very reasonable to think not only that the species of men were originally much larger, but also that there must have been giants in former ages; which as it is asserted by history and tradition, so it hath been confirmed by huge bones and skulls, casually dug up in several parts of the kingdom, far exceeding the common dwindled race of man in our days. He argued that the very laws of nature absolutely required we should have been made in the beginning of a size more large and robust, not so liable to destruction from every little accident of a tile falling from a house, or a stone cast from the hand of a boy, or being drowned in a little brook. From this way of reasoning the author drew several moral applications useful in the conduct of.life, but needless here to repeat.

CCCLXXXIX.

The Honourable Profession of the Law.

There is a society of men among us, bred up from their youth in the art of proving, by words multiplied for the purpose, that white is black, and black is white, according as they are paid. To this society all the rest of the people are slaves. For example, if my neighbour has a mind to my cow, he has a lawyer to prove that he ought to have my cow from me. I must then hire another to defend my right, it being against all rules of law that any man should be allowed to speak for himself. Now, in this case, I, who am the right owner, lie under two great disadvantages : first, my lawyer, being practised almost from his cradle in defending falsehood, is quite out of his element when he would be an advocate for justice, which is an unnatural office he always attempts with great awkwardness, if not with ill will. The second disadvantage is, that my lawyer must proceed with great caution, or else he will be reprimanded by the judges, and abhorred by his brethren, as one that would lessen the practice of the law. And therefore I have but two methods to preserve my cow. The first is, to gain over my adversary's lawyer with a double fee, who will then betray his client, by insinuating that he has justice on his side. The second way is, for my lawyer to make my cause appear as unjust as he can, by allowing the cow to belong to my adversary, and this, if it be skilfully done will certainly bespeak the favour of the bench.

Swift.

CCCXC.

A Cultivated Woman.

Thus a cultivated woman is like a good old-fashioned Scotch garden. Inside, somewhat screened from view, are all the products of what our English friends call the kitchen-garden : the homely vegetables which feed the family kail-pot ; the native fruits of which the winter preserves are made : but there is thyme and lavender in it, as well as carrots, turnips, and potatoes ; roses are not wanting ; and it is set all round with bright sweet-scented perennial flowers, which grow sweeter and richer

as they grow older. Yet even a garden may be over-
cultivated ; and a too ambitious sowing may but betray
the poverty of the soil.   *G. G. R.*

CCCXCI.

The Power of Common Words.

It is by means of familiar words that style takes hold of
the reader and gets possession of him. It is by means
of these that great thoughts get currency and pass for
true metal, like gold and silver which have had a recognised stamp put upon them. They beget confidence in
the man who, in order to make his thoughts more clearly
perceived, uses them ; for people feel that such an employment of the language of common human life betokens
a man who knows that life and its concerns, and who
keeps himself in contact with them. Besides, these words
make a style frank and easy. They show that an author
has long made the thought or the feeling expressed his
mental food ; that he has so assimilated them and familiarised them, that the most common expressions suffice
him in order to express ideas which have become every-
day ideas to him by the length of time they have been in
his mind. And lastly, what one says in such words looks
more true ; for, of all the words in use, none are so clear
as those which we call common words ; and clearness is
so eminently one of the characteristics of truth, that often
it even passes for truth itself.   *M. Arnold.*

CCCXCII.

Spots on the Sun.

We must take men as we find them. No man can live
up to the best which is in him. To expect a human crea-

ture to be all genius, all intellect, all virtue, all dignity, would be as absurd as to expect that midnight should be all stars. Curiosity in the lives of great men is to a certain degree legitimate, and even profitable; but there is perhaps a danger of it being carried too far. To find the great on a level with ourselves may gratify our vanity, but it may sometimes lead to very erroneous results. Mr. Hookham Frere once related the following anecdote about Canning: 'I remember one day going to consult Canning on a matter of great importance to me, when he was staying at Enfield. We walked into the woods. As we passed some ponds I was surprised to find that it was new to him that tadpoles turn into frogs. "Now, don't you," he added, "go and tell that story to the next fool you meet." Canning could rule, and did rule, a great nation; but people are apt to think that a man who does not know the natural history of frogs must be an imbecile in the treatment of men.'

CCCXCIII.

Fiction more true than History.

What do we look for in studying the history of a past age? Is it to learn the political transactions and characters of the leading public men? Is it to make ourselves acquainted with the life and being of the time? If we set out with the former grave purpose, where is the truth, and who believes that he has it entire? As we read in these delightful volumes of the Spectator, the past age returns, the England of our ancestors is revivified. The Maypole rises in the Strand again in London, the churches are thronged with daily worshippers, the beaux are gathering in the coffee-houses, the gentry are going to the drawing-room, the ladies are thronging to the toy-shops, the chairmen are jostling in the streets, the footmen are running with links before the chariots or fighting round the theatre. I say the fiction carries a greater amount of truth in solution than the volume which purports to be all true. Out of the fictitious book I get the expression of the life of the time ; of the manners, of the movement, the dress, the pleasures, the laughter, the ridicule of society— the old times live again, and I travel in the old country of England.   *Thackeray.*

CCCXCIV.

Machines.

Take of deities, male and female, as many as you can use. Separate them into two equal parts, and keep Jupiter in the middle. Let Juno put him in a ferment, and Venus mollify him. Remember on all occasions to make use of volatile Mercury. If you have need of devils, draw them out of Milton's Paradise, and extract your spirits from Tasso. The use of these machines is evident ; for since no epic poem can possibly subsist without them, the wisest way is to reserve them for your greatest necessities. When you·cannot extricate your hero by any human means, or yourself by your own wit, seek relief from heaven, and the gods will do your business very readily. This is according to the direct prescription of Horace in his Art of Poetry :

Nec Deus intersit, nisi dignus vindice nodus
Inciderit.—
Never presume to make a God appear
But for a business worthy of a God.—Roscommon.

That is to say, a poet should never call upon the gods for their assistance, but when he is in great perplexity.

A. Pope.

CCCXCV.

Poetry and Music.

I know very well that many, who pretend to be wise by the forms of being grave, are apt to despise both poetry and music as toys and trifles too light for the use or entertainment of serious men : but whoever find themselves wholly insensible to these charms, would, I think, do well to keep their own counsel, for fear of reproaching their own temper, and bringing the goodness of their natures, if not of their understandings, into question : it may be thought at least an ill sign, if not an ill constitution, since some of the fathers went so far as to esteem the love of music a sign of predestination, as a thing divine and reserved for the felicities of heaven itself. While this world lasts, I doubt not but the pleasure and requests of these two entertainments will do so too : and happy those that content themselves with these, or any other so easy and so innocent, and do not trouble the world, or other men, because they cannot be quiet themselves though nobody hurts them !

When all is done, human life is, at the greatest and the best, but like a froward child, that must be played with and humoured a little to keep it quiet till it falls asleep, and then the care is over. *Sir William Temple.*

CCCXCVI.

Preface to Hammond's Elegies.

The author compósed them ten years ago, before he was twenty-two years old, an age when fancy and imagination commonly riot at the expense of judgment and correctness, neither of which seem wanting here ; but sincere in his love as in his friendship, he wrote to his mistresses as he spoke to his friends, nothing but the true genuine sentiments of his heart. He sat down to write what he thought, not to think what he should write ; it was nature and sentiment only that dictated to a real mistress, not youthful and poetic fancy to an imaginary one. Elegy, therefore, speaks here her own proper native language, the unaffected plaintive language of the tender passions. The true elegiac dignity and simplicity are preserved and united, the one without pride, the other without meanness. Tibullus seems to have been the model our author judiciously preferred to Ovid, the former writing directly from the heart to the heart, the latter too often yielding and addressing himself to the imagination.   *Lord Chesterfield.*

CCCXCVII.

Time mellows all.

Time mellows ideas as it mellows wine. Things in themselves indifferent acquire a certain tenderness in recollection ; and the scenes of our youth, though re-markable neither for elegance nor feeling, rise up to our memory dignified at the same time and endeared. As countrymen in a distant land acknowledge one another as friends, so objects, to which when present we give but little attention, are nourished in distant remembrance with a cordial regard. If in their own nature of a tender kind, the ties which they had on the heart are drawn still closer, and we recall them with an enthusiasm of feeling which the same objects of the immediate time are unable to excite. The ghosts of our departed affections are seen through that softening medium, which, though it dims their brightness, does not impair their attraction; like the shade of Dido, appearing to Aeneas,

Demisit lacrimas, dulcique affatus amore est.

The hum of a little tune, to which in our infancy we have often listened, the course of a brook which in our child-hood we have frequently raced, the ruins of an ancient building which we remember almost entire : these re-membrances sweep over the mind with an enchanting power of tenderness and melancholy, at whose bidding the pleasures, the business, the ambition of the present moment fade and disappear.

CCCXCVIII.

Preface to Endymion.

Knowing within myself the manner in which this poem has been produced, it is not without a feeling of regret that I make it public. What manner I mean will be quite clear to the reader, who must soon perceive great inexperience, immaturity, and every error denoting a feverish attempt, rather than a deed accomplished. The two first books, and indeed the two last, I feel sen-sible are not of such completion as to warrant their passing the press ; nor should they, if I thought a year's castigation would do them any good ;—it will not : the foundations are too sandy. It is just that the youngster should die away : a sad thought for me, if I had not some hope that while it is dwindling I may be plotting and fitting myself for verses fit to live. This may be speak-ing too presumptuously and may deserve a punishment : but no feeling man would be forward to inflict it : he will leave me alone with the conviction that there is no fiercer torment than the failure in a great object.

This is not written with the least atom of purpose to fore-
stall criticisms, but from the desire I have to conciliate
men who are competent to look, and who do look, with a
jealous eye to the honour of English literature. The
imagination of a boy is healthy, and the mature imagination of a man is healthy, but there is a space of life
between, in which the soul is in a ferment, the character
undecided, the way of life uncertain, the ambition thick-
sighted : thence proceeds mawkishness, and all the
thousand bitters which · those men I speak of must
necessarily taste in going over the following pages. I
hope I have not in too late a day touched the beautiful
mythology of Greece and dulled its brightness, for I wish
to **try** once more before I bid it farewell.   *Keats.*

CCCXCIX.

Statuary, Painting and Description.

Among the different kinds of representation, statuary
is the most natural, and shows us something likest the
object that is represented. To make use of a common
instance, let one who is born blind take an image in his
hands, and trace out with his fingers the different furrows
and impressions of the chisel, and he will easily conceive
how the shape of a man or beast may be represented by
it ; but should he draw his hand over a picture where all
is smooth and uniform, he would never be able to imagine
how the several prominences and depressions of a human
body could be shown on a plain piece of canvas, that has
in it no unevenness or irregularity. Description runs
yet further from the thing it represents than painting ; for
a picture bears a real resemblance to its original, which

letters and syllables are wholly void of. Colours speak all languages, but words are understood only by such a people or nation. We are told that in America, when the Spaniards first arrived there, expresses were sent to the Emperor of Mexico in paint, and the news of his country delineated by the strokes of a pencil, which was a more natural way than that of writing, though at the same time much more imperfect, because it is impossible to draw the little connexions of speech, or to give the picture of a conjunction or an adverb.

CCCC.

Ovid.

I have now gone through the whole of Ovid's works, and heartily tired I am of him and them. Yet he is a wonderfully clever man. But he has two insupportable faults. The one is that he will always be clever; the other that he never knows when to have done. He is rather a rhetorician than a poet. There is little feeling in his poems; even in those which were written during his exile. The pathetic effect of his supplications and lamentations is injured by the ingenious turns of expression, and by the learned allusions, with which he sets off his sorrow. He seems to have been a very good fellow : rather too fond of women ; a flatterer and a coward ; but kind and generous, and free from envy, though a man of letters, and though sufficiently vain of his literary performances. The *Art of Love,* which ruined poor Ovid, is, in my opinion, decidedly his best work.

Macaulay.

CCCCI.

Thucydides' Set Speeches.

'Set speeches,' says Voltaire, 'are a sort of oratorical lie, which the historian used to allow himself in old times. He used to make his heroes say what they might have said. . . . At the present day these fictions are no longer tolerated. If one put into the mouth of a prince a speech which he had never made, the historian would be regarded as a rhetorician.' How did it happen that Thucydides allowed himself this 'oratorical lie,'—Thucydides, whose strongest characteristic is devotion to the truth, impatience of every inroad which fiction makes into the province of history, laborious persistence in the task of separating fact from fable; Thucydides, who was not constrained, like later writers of the old world, by an established literary tradition; who had no Greek predecessors in the field of history, except those chroniclers whom he despised precisely because they sacrificed truth to effect? Thucydides might rather have been expected to express himself on this wise: 'The chroniclers have sometimes pleased their hearers by reporting the very words spoken. But, as I could not give the words, I have been content to give the substance, when I could learn it.'   *R. C. Jebb.*

CCCCII.

The Classical Languages.

But in the great typical qualities which are the basis of all language: in logical symmetry and simplicity; in obedience to great cardinal principles, of which the letter may sometimes apparently be violated, but the spirit

never; in that inexorable demand for accuracy which
inflection produces, and which makes it impossible for an
error or a confusion of thought to pass undetected: in
these points the Classical languages are incomparable.
In addition, they exhibit all the qualities that make up
style: simplicity, directness, truth, force, point, terse-
ness, euphony—all the points in which modern language,
modern English especially, is so deficient. The same
great typical qualities distinguish the literature, the
history, the philosophy, the art of antiquity. All is
monumental, great, original; displaying the fundamental
faculties of man as developed in two marvellously
gifted races; man first risen to his strength, and exer-
cising it on a fresh world, in which the ever-recurring
problems of humanity presented themselves in clear and
simple forms, unclouded by centuries of confused tradition, unencumbered by the chaos of details, the maze of
interlocking causes, which make modern life so complex,
modern books so innumerable, the formulating of great
principles about modern affairs so difficult, originality of
thought and language in dealing with them well-nigh
impossible. *G. G. R.*

CCCCIII.

Danger of reading Latin and Greek Books.

And as to Rebellion in particular against Monarchy, one
of the most frequent causes of it, is the Reading of the
books of Policy, and Histories of the antient Greeks, and
Romans; from which, young men, and all others that are
unprovided of the antidotes of solid Reason, receiving a
strong, and delightful impression, of the great exploits
of warre, atchieved by the Conductors of their Armies,
receive withall a pleasing Idea of all they have done

T

besides; and imagine their great prosperity, not to have proceeded from the æmulation of particular men, but from the vertue of their popular forme of government : Not considering the frequent Seditions, and Civill Warres, produced by the imperfection of their Policy.   From the reading, I say, of such books, men have undertaken to kill their Kings, because the Greek and Latine writers, in their books, and discourses of Policy, make it lawfull, and laudable, for any man so to do ; provided, before he do it, he call him a tyrant.   *Hobbes.*

CCCCIV.

Protestant and Jesuit Learning in the Seventeenth Century.

It may often happen that Scaliger is wrong, and Petavius right.   But single-eyed devotion to truth is an intellectual quality, the absence of which is fatal to the value of any investigation.   Jesuit learning is a sham learning, got up with great ingenuity in imitation of the genuine, in the service of the church.   It is related of the Chinese that when they first, in the war of 1841, saw the effect of our steam vessels, they set up a funnel and made a smoke with straw on the deck of one of their junks in imitation, while the paddles were turned by men below.   Such a mimicry of the philology of Scaliger and Casaubon was the philology of the Jesuit.   It was vitiated by his *arrière-pensée*.   The search of truth was falsified by its interested motive, the interest not of an individual but of a party.   It was that caricature of the good and great and true, which the good and great and true invariably calls into being ; a phantom which sidles up against the reality, mouths its favourite words as a third-rate actor does a great part, undermimics its wisdom, overacts its folly, is by half the world taken for it, goes some way to suppress it in its own time, and lives for it in history.   *M. Pattison.*

CCCCV.

The use of French Terms.

I have often wished that, as in our constitution there are several persons whose business it is to watch over our laws, our liberties and commerce, certain men might be set apart as superintendents of our language, to hinder any words of a foreign coin from passing among us, and in particular to prohibit any French phrases from being current in this kingdom, when those of our own stamp are altogether as valuable. The present war has so adulterated our tongue with strange words, that it would be impossible for one of our great grandfathers to know what his posterity have been doing, were he to read their exploits in a modern newspaper. Our warriors are very industrious in propagating the French language, at the same time that they are so gloriously successful in beating down their power. Our soldiers are men of strong heads for action, and perform such feats as they are not able to express. They want words in their own tongue to tell us what it is they achieve, and therefore send us over accounts of their performances in a jargon of phrases, which they learn among their conquered enemies. They ought, however, to be provided with secretaries, and assisted by our foreign ministers, to tell their stories for them in plain English, and to let us know in our mother-tongue what it is our brave countrymen are about.   *Addison.*

T 2

Character and Culture.

It is common to hear remarks on the frequent divorce between culture and character, and to infer from this that culture is a mere varnish, and that character only deserves any serious attention. No error can be more fatal. Culture without character is, no doubt, something frivolous, vain, and weak; but character without culture is, on the other hand, something raw, blind, and dangerous. The most interesting, the most truly glorious peoples, are those in which the alliance of the two has been effected most successfully, and its result spread most widely. This is why the spectacle of ancient Athens has such profound interest for a rational man, that it is the spectacle of the culture of a people. It is not an aristocracy, leavening with its own high spirit the multitude which it wields, but leaving it the unformed multitude still; it is not a democracy, acute and energetic, but tasteless, narrow-minded, and ignoble; it is the middle and lower classes in the highest development of their humanity that these classes have yet reached. It was the many who relished those arts, who were not satisfied with less than those monuments. In the conversations recorded by Plato, or even by the matter-of-fact Xenophon, which for the free yet refined discussion of ideas have set the tone for the whole cultivated world, shopkeepers and tradesmen of Athens mingle. For any one but a pedant, this is why a handful of Athenians of two thousand years ago are more interesting than the millions of most nations our contemporaries.

M. Arnold.

CCCCVII.

Books without Reading.

The whole course of things being thus entirely changed between us and the ancients, and the moderns wisely sensible of it, we of this age have discovered a shorter and more prudent method to become scholars and wits, without the fatigue of reading or of thinking. The most accomplished way of using books at present is two-fold : either, first, to serve them as some men do lords, learn their titles exactly, and then brag of their acquaintance ; or, secondly, which is indeed the choicer, the profounder, and politer method, to get a thorough insight into the index, by which the whole book is governed and turned, like fishes by the tail. For to enter the palace of learning at the great gate requires an expense of time and forms ; therefore men of much haste and little ceremony are content to get in by the back-door. Thus are the sciences found, like Hercules's oxen, by tracing them backwards. Thus are old sciences unravelled, like old stockings, by beginning at the foot. Besides all this, the army of the sciences has been of late, with a world of martial discipline, drawn into its close order, so that a view or muster may be taken of it with abundance of expedition. For this great blessing we are wholly indebted to systems and abstracts, in which the modern fathers of learning, like prudent usurers, spent their labour for the ease of us their children. For labour is the seed of idleness, and it is the peculiar happiness of our noble age to gather the fruit. *Swift.*

CCCCVIII.

Favourite Writers.

A great writer is the friend and benefactor of his readers; and they cannot but judge of him under the deluding influence of friendship and gratitude. We all know how unwilling we are to admit the truth of any disgraceful story about a person whose society we like, and from whom we have received favours; how long we struggle against evidence; how fondly, when the facts cannot be disputed, we cling to the hope that there may be some explanation or extenuating circumstance with which we are unacquainted. Just such is the feeling which a man of liberal education naturally entertains towards the great minds of former ages. The debt which he owes to them is incalculable. They have guided him to truth. They have filled his mind with noble and graceful images. They have stood by him in all vicissitudes, comforters in sorrow, nurses in sickness, companions in solitude. These friendships are exposed to no danger from the occurrences by which other attachments are weakened or dissolved. Time glides on; fortune is inconstant; tempers are soured; bonds which seemed indissoluble are daily sundered by interest, by emulation, or by caprice. But no such cause can affect the silent converse which we hold with the highest of human intellects. That placid intercourse is disturbed by no jealousies or resentments. These are the old friends who are never seen with new faces, who are the same in wealth and in poverty, in glory and in obscurity.

Macaulay.

CCCCIX.

The Temper for Right Taste.

The temper, therefore, by which right taste is formed, is characteristically patient. It dwells upon what is submitted to it. It does not trample upon it, lest it should be pearls, even though it look like husks. It is a good ground, soft, penetrable, retentive; it does not send up thorns of unkind thoughts, to choke the weak seed; it is hungry and thirsty too, and drinks all the dew that falls on it. It is an honest and good heart, that shows no too ready springing before the sun be up, but fails not afterwards; it is distrustful of itself, so as to be ready to believe and to try all things, and yet so trustful of itself that it will neither quit what it has tried, nor take anything without trying. And the pleasure which it has in things that it finds true and good is so great, that it cannot possibly be led aside by any tricks of fashion, or diseases of vanity; it cannot be cramped in its conclusions by partialities and hypocrisies; its visions and its delights are too penetrating, too living, for any whitewashed object or shallow fountain long to endure or supply. .... The conclusions of this disposition are sure to be eventually right; more and more right according to the general maturity of all the powers; but it is sure to come right at last, because its operation is in analogy to, and in harmony with, the whole spirit of the Christian moral system, and must ultimately love and rest in the great sources of happiness common to all the human race, and based on the relations they hold to their Creator.

Ruskin.

CCCCX.

Beatrice and Benedick.

D. Pedro. The lady Beatrice hath a quarrel to you; the gentleman that danced with her told her she is much wronged by you.

Benedick. O, she misused me past the endurance of a block! an oak but with one green leaf on it would have answered her; my very visor began to assume life and scold with her: she told me, not thinking I had been myself, that I was the prince's jester: that I was duller than a great thaw; huddling jest upon jest with such impossible conveyance upon me, that I stood like a man at a mark, with a whole army shooting at me; she speaks poniards, and every word stabs; if her breath were as terrible as her terminations there were no living near her, she would infect to the north star. I would not marry her, though she were endowed with all Adam had left him before he transgressed; she would have made Hercules have turned spit; yea, and have cleft his club to make the fire too. Come, talk not of her; you shall find her the infernal Ate in good apparel. I would to God some scholar would conjure her; for certainly while she is here a man may live as quiet in hell as in a sanctuary; and people sin upon purpose, because they would go thither: so indeed all disquiet, horror, and perturbation follow her.   *Shakespeare.*

CCCCXI.

The False Ideal.

Of this final baseness of the false ideal, its miserable waste of the time, strength, and available intellect of man,

by turning, as I have said above, innocence of pastime
into seriousness of occupation, it is of course hardly
possible to sketch out even so much as the leading mani-
festations. The vain and haughty projects of youth for
future life; the giddy reveries of insatiable self-exaltation;
the discontented dreams of what might have been or
should be, instead of the thankful understanding of what
is; the casting about for sources of interest in senseless
fiction, instead of the real human histories of the people
round us; the prolongation from age to age of romantic
historical deception instead of sifted truth ; the pleasures
taken in fanciful portraits of rural or romantic life in
poetry and on the stage, without the smallest effort to
rescue the living rural population of the world from its
ignorance or misery ; the excitement of the feelings by
laboured imagination of spirits, fairies, monsters, and
demons, issuing in total blindness of heart and sight to
the true presences of beneficent or destructive spiritual
powers around us ; in fine, the constant abandonment
of all the straightforward paths of sense and duty, for
fear of losing some of the enticement of ghostly joys, or
trampling somewhat ' *sopra lor vanità, che par persona*';
all these forms of false idealism have so entangled the
modern mind, often called, I suppose ironically, practical,
that I truly believe there never yet was idolatry of stock
or staff so utterly unholy as this our idolatry of shadows.

Ruskin.

CCCCXII.

The Drama.

By what has been said of the manners, it will be easy
for a reasonable man to judge, whether the characters be
truly or falsely drawn in a tragedy : for if there be no

manners appearing in the characters, no concernment for the persons can be raised, no pity or honor can be moved but by vice or virtue; therefore without them, no person can have any business in the play. If the inclinations be obscure, it is a sign the poet is in the dark, and knows not what manner of man he presents to you; and consequently you can have no idea, or very imperfect, of that man, nor can judge what resolutions he ought to take. or what words or actions are proper for him. Most comedies, made up of accidents or adventures, are liable to fall into this error, and tragedies with many turns are subject to it; for the manners can never be evident where the surprises of fortune take up all the business of the stage, and where the poet is more in pain to tell you what happened to such a man than what he was. It is one of the excellencies of Shakespeare that the manners of his persons are generally apparent, and you see their bent and inclination.   *Dryden.*

CCCCXIII.

Supereminence of the Athenians.

As a nation, Athens is the school of Greece; and her individual citizens are the most accomplished specimens of the human race. Nor is this idle boasting; for experience and reality are its warrants. The powers and protection of Athens are felt in every land; and the fears or gratitude of mankind are the noblest evidence of her greatness. And such a country well deserves that her children should die for her. They have died for her, and her praise is theirs. My task is then mostly completed: yet it may be added that their glorious and beautiful lives have been crowned by a most glorious death. Enjoying and enjoyed as has been their life, it never tempted them to seek by unworthy fear to lengthen it. To repel their country's enemies was dearer to them than the fairest prospect that added years could offer them ; having gained this they were content to die ; and their last field witnessed their brightest glory, undimmed by a single thought of weakness.

Pericles.

CCCCXIV.

Ministers the true Innovators.

These are maxims so old and so trite, that no man cares to dwell on them, for fear of being told that he is repeating what he learned of his nurse. But they are not the less true for being trite ; and when men suffer themselves to be hurried away by a set of new-fangled notions diametrically opposite, they cannot be repeated too often. If we persist in the other course, we must go on increasing our debt till the burden of our taxes becomes intolerable. That boasted constitution, which we are daily impairing, the people will estimate not by what it once has been, or is still asserted to be in the declamations against anarchy, but by its practical effects ; and we shall hardly escape the very extreme we are so anxiously desirous of shunning. The old government of France was surely provided with sufficient checks against the licentiousness of the people ; but of what avail were those checks when the ambition and prodigality of the Government had exhausted every resource by which established governments can be supported ? Ministers attempt to fix upon others the charge of innovation, while they themselves are, every session, making greater innovations than that which they now call the most dreadful of all, namely, a reform in the representa-

tion in parliament. But it is the infatuation of the day
that, while fixing all our attention upon France, we
almost consider the very name of liberty as odious :
nothing of the opposite tendency gives us the least
alarm.

CCCCXV.
I die Content.

Detesting the corrupt and destructive maxims of despotism, I have considered the happiness of the people as
the end of government. Submitting my actions to the
laws of prudence, of justice, and of moderation, I have
trusted the event to the care of Providence. Peace was
the object of my counsels as long as peace was consistent
with the public welfare ; but when the imperious voice
of my country summoned me to arms, I exposed my
person to the dangers of war, with the clear foreknow-
ledge (which I had acquired from the art of divination)
that I was destined to fall by the sword. I now offer
my tribute of gratitude to the Eternal Being, who has
not suffered me to perish by the cruelty of a tyrant, by
the secret dagger of conspiracy, or by the slow tortures
of lingering disease.

CCCCXVI.
Improvement in Surgery.

The highest orders in England will always be able to
procure the best medical assistance. Who suffers by
the bad state of the Russian school of surgery? The
Emperor Nicholas? By no means ! The whole evil
falls on the peasantry. If the education of a surgeon
should become very expensive, if his fees should consequently rise, if the supply of regular surgeons should

diminish, the sufferers would be, not the rich, but the poor in our villages, who would again be left to barbers and old women. The honourable gentleman speaks of sacrificing the interests of humanity to those of science. This is not a mere question of science ; it is a question between health and sickness, between ease and torment, between life and death. Does the honourable gentleman know from what cruel sufferings the improvement of surgery has rescued our species ? I will tell him a story, the first that comes into my head. He may have heard of Leopold, Duke of Austria, the same who imprisoned our Richard Cœur de Lion. Leopold's horse fell under him, and crushed his leg. The doctors said the limb must be amputated, but none of them knew how to do it. Leopold—in his agony—laid a hatchet on his thigh, and ordered his servant to strike with a mallet. The leg was cut off, and the Duke died of the loss of blood. Such was the end of that powerful prince ! There is now no labouring man who falls from a ladder in England who cannot obtain better assistance than the sovereign of Austria in the thirteenth century.

Macaulay.

CCCCXVII.

Return from the Crimea.

'Officers, non-commissioned officers, and soldiers ! I wish personally to convey through you, to the regiments assembled here this day, my hearty welcome on their return to England in health and full efficiency. Say to them, that I have watched anxiously over the difficulties and hardships which they have so nobly borne, that I have mourned with deep sorrow for the brave men who have fallen in their country's cause, and that I have felt proud of that valour, which, with their gallant allies, they have displayed on every field. I thank God that your dangers are over, while the glory of your deeds remains; but I know, that should your services be again required, you will be animated with the same devotion, which in the Crimea has rendered you invincible.'

The Prince Consort.

CCCCXVIII.

Liberty or Death.

I have but one lamp by which my feet are guided, and that is the lamp of experience. I know of no way of judging the future but by the past. And, judging by the past, I wish to know what there has been in the conduct of the British Ministry to justify those hopes with which gentlemen have been pleased to solace themselves? Is it that insidious smile with which our petition has been lately received? Trust it not, sir; it will prove a snare to your feet. Suffer not yourselves to be betrayed with a kiss. Ask yourselves how this gracious reception comports with those warlike preparations which cover our waters and darken our land. Are fleets and armies necessary to a work of love and reconciliation? These are the implements of war and subjugation, the last arguments to which kings resort. Our chains are forged. Their clanking may be heard on the plains of Boston. The war is inevitable, and let it come. Gentlemen may cry, peace, peace—but there is no peace. The next gale that sweeps from the north will bring to our ears the clash of resounding arms. Is life so dear, or peace so sweet, as to be purchased at the cost of chains and slavery? Forbid it, Almighty God! I know not what course others may take, but as for me, give me liberty or give me death.

Patrick Henry.

CCCCXIX.

True Freedom.

I call that mind free which protects itself against the usurpations of society, which does not cower to human opinion, which feels itself accountable to a higher tribunal than man's, which respects a higher law than fashion, which respects itself too much to be the slave or tool of the many or the few. I call that mind free which, through confidence in God and in the power of virtue, has cast off all fear but that of wrong-doing, which no menace or peril can enthral, which is calm in the midst of tumults, and possesses itself though all else be lost. I call that mind free which resists the bondage of habit, which does not mechanically repeat itself and copy the past, which does not live on its old virtues, which does not enslave itself to precise rules, but which forgets what is behind, listens for new and higher monitions of conscience, and rejoices to pour itself forth in fresh and higher exertions. I call that mind free which is jealous of its own freedom, which guards itself from being merged in others, which guards its empire over itself as nobler than the empire of the world. *Channing.*

CCCCXX.

Safety a Benefit.

It is a truth, Mr. Speaker, and a familiar truth, that safety and preservation are to be preferred before benefit or increase, inasmuch as those counsels which tend to preservation seem to be attended with necessity; whereas, those deliberations which tend to benefit, seem only accompanied with persuasion. And it is ever gain and no loss, when at the foot of the account there remains the purchase of safety. The prints of this are everywhere to be found : the patient will ever part with some of his blood to save and clear the rest; the sea-faring man will, in a storm, cast over some of his goods to save and assure the rest: the husbandman will afford some foot of ground for his hedge and ditch, to fortify and defend the rest. Why, Mr. Speaker, the disputer will, if he be wise and cunning, grant somewhat that seemeth to make against him, because he will keep himself within the strength of his opinion, and the better maintain the rest.

CCCCXXI.

Safety in Distance.

'No, sir,' replied I, 'I am for liberty! that attribute of God's! Glorious liberty! that theme of modern declamation! I would have all men kings : I would be a king myself. We have all naturally an equal right to the throne : we are all originally equal. This is my opinion, and was once the opinion of a set of honest men who were called Levellers. . They tried to erect themselves into a community, where all should be equally free. But, alas! It would never answer; for there were some among them stronger and some more cunning than others, and these became masters of the rest; for, as sure as your groom rides your horses, because he is a cunninger animal than they, so surely will the animal that is cunninger or stronger than he, sit upon his shoulders in turn. Since, then, some are born to command and others to obey, the question is, as there must be tyrants, whether it is better to have them in the same house with us, or in the same village, or, still further off in the metropolis.' *Goldsmith.*

CCCCXXII.

Liberty of Speech.

This government holds a man responsible for every thought that an indiscreet or an incautious friend, or a concealed enemy, or a tool of power, reveals. If it succeeds in this attempt, it will not rest satisfied with this victory over the remnant of our freedom. It is not in the nature of things that it should. A government that will not tolerate censure must forbid discussion. You are now asked to put down writing. When that has been done conversation will be attacked. Paris will resemble Rome under the successors of Augustus: already the suppression of the press has produced a malaise which I never felt or observed before. What will be the feelings of the nation when all that is around it is concealed, when every avenue by which light could penetrate is stopped, when we are exposed to all the undefined terrors and exaggerated dangers that accompany utter darkness?

Guizot.

CCCCXXIII.

Πολεμοῦμεν ἵν' εἰρήνην ἄγωμεν.

It is true, my lords, that I have, perhaps more than any other man in this country, struggled to maintain a state of peace. I have done so, because I thought it a duty to the people of this country, a duty to God and man, first to exhaust every possible measure to obtain peace before we engaged in war. I may own, though I trust my conscience acquits me of not having done the utmost, that I only regret not having done enough, or

U

lest I may have lost some possible means of averting what
I consider the greatest calamity that can befall a country.
It has been said that my desire for peace unfits me to
make war; but how and why do I wish to make war? I
wish to make war in order to obtain peace, and no
weapon that can be used in war can make the attainment
of peace so sure and speedy, as to make that war with
the utmost vigour and determination.

CCCCXXIV.

A Tribune of the Plebs.

I am not unaware how vast are the resources at the
command of that nobility whom I, single-handed, powerless, with nothing but the empty semblance of office, am
undertaking to dislodge from their supremacy; I know
full well with how much more safety a guilty faction can
act, than innocence when unsupported. But over and
above the good hope which I have of your assistance—a
hope which has conquered fear—I have come to the
settled conviction that it is better for a brave man to fight
and fail for freedom's sake, than not to fight at all. Yet
so it is that all others, who have been elected to maintain
your rights, have turned against you all the weight and
influence of their high positions, and count it better to
sin for gain, than to do right for nothing. And, accordingly, all have now given way to the tyranny of a few
who have seized upon the treasury, upon armies, kingdoms, and provinces : while you, the commonalty, yield
yourselves up, like cattle, to individuals for their possession and profit, stripped of all that heritage which your
ancestors bequeathed to you.

CCCCXXV.

Speech in the American Senate.

Sir, does he suppose it in his power to exhibit a Carolina name so bright as to produce envy in my bosom? No, sir, increased gratification and delight rather. I thank God that if I am gifted with little of the spirit which is able to raise mortals to the skies, I have yet none, as I trust, of that other spirit which would drag angels down. When I shall be found, sir, in my place here in the Senate, or elsewhere, to sneer at public merit, because it happens to spring up beyond the little limits of my own State or neighbourhood; when I refuse for any such cause, or for any cause, the homage due to American talent or elevated patriotism, to sincere devotion to liberty and the country; or if I see an uncommon endowment of Heaven, if I see extraordinary capacity and virtue in any son of the south, and if, moved by local prejudice or gangrened by State jealousy, I get up here to abate the tithe of a hair from his just character and just fame, may my tongue cleave to the roof of my mouth !   *Calhoun.*

CCCCXXVI.

Death a Gain.

I have great hopes, O my judges, that it is infinitely to my advantage that I am sent to death ; for it must of necessity be that one of these two things must be the consequence : death must take away all these senses, or convey me to another life. If all sense is to be taken away, and death is no more than that profound sleep without dreams in which we are sometimes buried, O

heavens, how desirable is it to die! How many days do
we know in this life preferable to such a state ? But if
it be true that death is but a passage to places which
they who lived before us do now inhabit, how much still
happier is it to go from those who call themselves judges
to appear before those who are really such, and to meet
men who have lived with justice and truth? Do you
think it nothing to speak with Orpheus, Musæus, Homer,
and Hesiod? I would indeed suffer many deaths to enjoy
these things.   *Plato.*

CCCCXXVII.

Appeal to the French Assembly.

I am grieved, gentlemen, if I offend you; though many
of you are older in years than I am, not one probably is
so old in public life. I may be addressing you for the
last time, and I feel that my last words ought to contain
all the warnings that I think may be useful to you. This
Assembly will soon end as all its predecessors have
ended ; its acts, its legislation, may perish with it, but
its reputation, its fame 'for good or for evil, will survive.
Within a few minutes you will do an act by which that
reputation will be seriously affected, by which it may be
raised, by which it may be deeply, perhaps irrecoverably,
sunk. Your vote to-night will show whether you possess
freedom, and whether you deserve it. As for myself, I
care but little, a few months or even years of imprison-
ment are among the risks which every public man who
does his duty in revolutionary times must encounter, and
which the most important men of the country have
incurred, either at the outset of their career or at its
close.

CCCCXXVIII.

Our Great Men.

And, sir, if he who now addresses you finds some work to do in life, it is because he belongs to a land which men like these have raised to fame, to power, to greatness ; not least of all because he practises, to the utmost limits of his strength, qualities in which they stood pre-eminent—fair dealing, industry, self-control, the protection of the distressed, the detestation of the bad—an affinity of habits scarcely, I imagine, less close than that of which noble lords can boast, community of blood and identity of name.

CCCCXXIX.

Loyalty without Flattery.

I am sensible that our happiness depends on the security of his Majesty's title, and the preservation of the present government upon those principles which established them at the late glorious revolution ; and which, I hope, will continue to actuate the conduct of Britons to the latest generations. These have always been my principles ; and whoever will give himself the trouble of looking over the course of these papers, will be convinced that they have been my guide ; but I am a blunt plain-dealing old man, who am not afraid to speak the truth ; and as I have no relish for flattery myself, I scorn to bestow it on others. I have not, however, been sparing of just praise, nor slipped any reasonable opportunity to distinguish the royal virtues of their present Majesties. More than this I cannot do ; and more than this will not, I hope, be expected. Some of my expres-

sions, perhaps, may have been thought too rough and
unpolished for the climate of a court ; but they flowed
purely from the sincerity of my heart ; and the freedom
of my writings has proceeded from my zeal for the
interest of my king and country.

CCCCXXX.

Conscience before Popularity.

I defy the noble lord to point out a single action of my
life in which the popularity of the times ever had the
smallest influence on my determinations. I thank God,
I have a more permanent and steady rule for my conduct,—the dictates of my own breast. Those who have
forgone that pleasing adviser, and given up their mind to
be the slave of every popular impulse, I sincerely pity ; I
pity them still more, if their vanity leads them to mistake
the shouts of a mob for the trumpet of fame. Experience
might inform them that many who have been saluted
with the huzzas of a crowd one day, have received their
execrations the next ; and many, who by the popularity
of their times have been held up as spotless patriots, have
nevertheless appeared upon the historian's page, when
truth has triumphed over delusion, the assassins of liberty.
Why then the noble lord can think I am ambitious of
present popularity, that echo of folly and shadow of renown, I am at a loss to determine.

CCCCXXXI.

A Horrible Crime.

Gentlemen, it is a most extraordinary case. This
bloody drama excited no suddenly-exerted, ungovernable

rage. The actors in it were not surprised by a lion-like temptation springing upon their virtue, and overcoming it before resistance could begin. Nor did they do the deed to glut savage vengeance or satiate long-settled or deadly hate. It was a cool, calculating, money-making murder. It was all hire and salary, not revenge. It was the weighing of money against life; the counting out of so many pieces of silver against so many ounces of blood. The circumstance now clearly in evidence spread out the whole scene before us. A healthful old man, to whom sleep was sweet, the first sound slumbers of the night held him in their soft but strong embrace. The assassin enters through the window already prepared, with noise-less foot he paces the lonely hall, winds up the stairs to the door of the chamber, moves the lock till it turns on its hinges without noise : the beams of the moon resting on the gray locks show him where to strike. The victim passes without a struggle to the repose of death. His assassin retraces his steps to the window and escapes. No eye has seen him, no ear has heard him. The secret is his own, and it is safe! Ah! gentlemen, that was a dreadful mistake, such secrets of guilt are never safe from detection even by men.   *Webster.*

CCCCXXXII.

A Traitor to the Union.

Even then and there men condemned such deeds, although they were not wholly without excuse. But now, when tens of thousands of brave souls have gone up to God under the shadow of the flag. when thousands more, maimed and shattered in the contest, are sadly awaiting the deliverance of death, now when three years of terrific warfare have raged over us, when our armies have pushed the rebellion back over mountains and rivers, and crowded it into narrow limits, until a wall of fire girds it : now, when the uplifted hand of a majestic people is about to hurl the bolts of its conquering power upon the rebellion ; now, in the quiet of this Hall, hatched in the lowest depths of a similar dark treason, there rises a Benedict Arnold, and proposes to surrender all, body and spirit, the nation and the flag, its genius and its honour, once and for ever, to the accursed traitors of our country. And that proposition comes—God forgive and pity my beloved State—it comes from a citizen of the time-honoured and loyal commonwealth of Ohio! I implore you, brethren in this House, to believe that not many births ever gave pangs to my mother-state such as she suffered when that traitor was born. I beg you not to believe that on the soil of that State another such growth deforms the face of nature and darkens the light of God's day.

CCCCXXXIII.

Is there no Danger?

Does a design against the constitution of this country exist? If it does, and if it is carried on with increasing vigour and activity by a restless faction, and if it receives countenance by the most ardent and enthusiastic applauses of its object, in the great council of this kingdom, by men of the first parts, which this kingdom produces, perhaps by the first it has ever produced, can I think that there is no danger? If there be danger, must there be no precaution at all against it? If you ask whether I think the danger urgent and immediate, I answer, thank God, I do not. The body of the people is yet sound, the

constitution is still in their heart, while wicked men are
endeavouring to put another into their heads. But if I see
the very same beginnings, which have commonly ended
in great calamities, I ought to act as if they might produce
the very same effects. Early and provident fear is the
mother of safety; because in that state of things the mind
is firm and collected, and the judgment unembarrassed.
But when the fear, and the evil feared, come on together,
press at once upon us, deliberation itself is ruinous, which
saves upon all other occasions; because when perils are
instant, it delays decision, the man is in a flutter, and in
a hurry, and his judgment is gone.

CCCCXXXIV.

An Appeal to the King.

You ascended the throne with a declared, and, I doubt
not, a sincere resolution of giving universal satisfaction to
your subjects. You found them pleased with the novelty
of a prince whose countenance promised even more than
his words, and loyal to you not only from principle but
passion. It was not a cold profession of allegiance to the
first magistrate, but a partial, animated attachment to a
favourite prince, the native of their country. They did not
wait to examine your conduct, nor to be determined by
experience, but gave you a generous credit for the future
blessings of your reign, and paid you in advance the
dearest tribute of their affections. Such, sir, was once the
disposition of a people who now surround your throne
with reproaches and complaints. Do justice to yourself.
Banish from your mind those unworthy opinions with
which some interested persons have laboured to possess
you. Distrust the men who tell you that the English are

naturally light and inconstant, that they complain without a cause. Withdraw your confidence equally from all parties—from ministers, favourites, and relations; and let there be one moment in your life in which you have consulted your own understanding.   *Junius.*

CCCCXXXV.

No Liberty without Law.

Laws must not only be made, they must be enforced. Peisistratus enforced Solon's laws. He insisted on peace and order in the city. He stopped by main force the perpetual political agitation which is the ruin of any commonwealth. Let the reader remember that without sound intellectual culture all political training is and must be simply mischievous. A free constitution is perfectly absurd, if the opinion of the majority is incompetent. I fear it is almost hopeless to persuade English minds that a despotism may in some cases be better for a nation than a more advanced constitution. And yet no students of history can fail to observe that even yet very few nations in the world are fit for diffused political privileges. The nations that are fit are so manifestly the greatest and best, and consequently the most prosperous, that inferior races keep imitating their institutions, instead of feeling that these institutions are the result and not the cause of true national greatness. In the case of the Irish the English nation has in vain given them its laws, and even done something to enforce them. I believe the harshest despotism would be more successful, and perhaps in the end more humane.

CCCCXXXVI.

Pride in our Indian Empire.

If I thought that our power in India had originated in crime and was maintained by brute force, it would have no interest for me. In that case I should turn my attention to other matters and leave a hopeless system to reach its natural end by its own road. I feel, however, that such a view is utterly false, and that we, the English nation, can hardly degrade ourselves more deeply than by repudiating the achievements of our ancestors, apologising for acts of which we ought to feel as proud as the inheritors of great names and splendid titles must feel of the deeds by which they were won, and evading like cowards and sluggards the arduous responsibilities which have devolved upon us. I say, let us acknowledge them with pride. Let us grapple with them like men. That will enable our sons to praise us for something more manly than reviling our fathers. Let them praise us, not for atoning for the misdeeds, but for following the examples of Clive and Hastings, and the two Wellesleys, and Dalhousie, and Canning, and Henry Lawrence, and Havelock, and others, whom I do not mention because they still live, and because I have the honour to call some of them my friends. I deny that ambition and conquest are crimes; I say that ambition is the greatest incentive to every manly virtue, and that conquest is the process by which every state in the world has been built up.

CCCCXXXVII.

Parliamentary Reform.

Two centuries ago the people of this country were engaged in a fearful conflict with the Crown. A despotic and treacherous monarch assumed to himself the right to levy taxes without the consent of Parliament and the people. That assumption was resisted. This fair island became a battlefield, the kingdom was convulsed, and an ancient throne overturned. And if our forefathers two hundred years ago resisted that attempt, if they refused to be the bondmen of a king, shall we be the born thralls of an aristocracy like ours? Shall we, who struck the lion down, pay homage to the wolf? Or shall we not by a manly and united expression of public opinion at once and for ever put an end to this giant wrong? Our cause is at least as good as theirs. We stand on higher vantage-ground; we have larger numbers at our back; we have men of wealth, intelligence, and union, and we understand better the rights and true interests of the country; and, what is more than all this, we have a constitutional weapon which we intend to wield, and by means of which we are sure to conquer, our laurels being gained, not in bloody fields, but upon the election hustings, and in courts of law.   *J. Bright.*

CCCCXXXVIII.

Robespierre's Murderers.

But who gave Robespierre the power of being a tyrant? And who were the instruments of his tyranny? The present virtuous constitution-mongers. He was a tyrant, they were his satellites and his hangmen. Their sole merit is in the murder of their colleagues. They have expiated their other murders by a new murder. It has always been the case among this banditti : they have always had the knife at each other's throats, after they had almost blunted it at the throat of every honest man. These people thought that in the commerce of murder, he was like to have the better of the bargain if any time was lost; they therefore took one of their short revolutionary methods, and massacred him in a manner so perfidious and cruel as would shock all humanity if the stroke was not struck by the present rulers on one of their associates. But this last act of infidelity and murder is to expiate all the rest, and to qualify them for the amity of a humane and virtuous sovereign and civilised people.

Burke.

CCCCXXXIX.

Should we Tax America.

Sir, I think you must perceive that I am resolved this day to have nothing at all to do with the question of the right of taxation. Some gentlemen startle,—but it is true; I put it totally out of the question. It is less than nothing in my consideration. The question with me is, not whether you have a right to render your people miserable, but whether it is not your interest to make them happy. It is not what a lawyer tells me I may do, but what humanity, reason, and justice tell me I ought to do. Is a politic act the worse for being a generous one I Is no concession proper, but that which is made from your want of right to keep what you grant? Or does it lessen the grace or dignity of relaxing in the exercise of an odious claim, because you have your evidence-room full of titles, and your magazines stuffed with arms to enforce them? What signify all those titles and all those arms? Of what avail are they, when the reason of the thing tells me that the assertion of my title is the loss of my suit; and that I could do nothing but wound myself by the use of my own weapons?

Burke.

CCCCXL.

Speech of Sir John Eliot.

The Rhodians had a story of their island, he said, that when Jupiter, who ruled them, was delivered of Pallas, it rained there gold in abundance; and this, after their fashion, they moralised. Pallas, so born, they held to signify both prowess and policy, martial worth and wisdom : wisdom too, both human and divine, implying not only instruction for the affairs of men but in the service and worship of the gods. The fable, Eliot thought, might have just application to members of that house, and some instruction for their purpose. Aforetime might their island have been taken for a Rhodes, the proper seat of gods, wherein, when action had been added unto counsel, and counsel joined to action, when religion and resolution had come together, there wanted nothing of the felicity or blessing that wealth and honour could impart. Wisdom and valour singly had availed not ; Apollo had not satisfied, Mars had been too weak; but both their virtues meeting with religion, and concurring in that centre—as in the person of their Pallas, their Minerva, their last great queen !—never had those failed in their chronicles and stories to give both riches and reputation, the true showers of gold mentioned in the fable.   *J. Foster.*

CCCCXLI.

The Goddess Criticism.

Momus, having thus delivered himself, staid not for an answer, but left the goddess to her own resentment. Up she rose in a rage, and, as it is the form upon such occasions, began a soliloquy. ' It is I,' said she, ' who gave wisdom to infants and idiots ; by me children grew wiser than their parents, by me beaux became politicians, and schoolboys judges of philosophy ; by me sophisters debate, and conclude upon the depths of knowledge ; and coffee-house wits, instinct by me, can correct an author's style, and display his minutest errors without understanding a syllable of his matter or his language ; by me striplings spend their judgement, as they do their estate, before it comes into their hands. It is I who have deposed wit and knowledge from their empire over poetry, and advanced myself in their stead. And shall a few upstart ancients dare to oppose me ? '

Swift.

CCCCXLII.

A United Empire.

Hence that unexampled unanimity which distinguishes the present season. In other wars we have been a divided people ; the effect of our external operations has been in some measure weakened by intestine dissension. When peace has returned, the breach has widened, while parties have been formed on the merits of particular men, or of particular measures. These have all disappeared : we have buried our mutual animosities in a regard to the common safety. The sentiment of self-preservation, the first law which nature has impressed, has absorbed every other feeling ; and the fire of liberty has melted down the discordant sentiments and minds of the British Empire into one mass, and propelled them in one direction. Partial interests and feelings are suspended, the spirits of the body are collected at the heart, and we are awaiting with anxiety, but without dismay, the discharge of that mighty tempest which hangs upon the skirts of the horizon, and to which the eyes of Europe and of the world are turned in silent and awful expectation. While we feel solicitude, let us not betray dejection, nor be alarmed at the past successes of our enemy, since they have raised him from obscurity to an elevation which has made him giddy, and tempted him to suppose everything within his power. The intoxication of his success is the omen of his fall. *Robert Hall.*

CCCCXLIII.

To the Bristol Electors, 1780.

And now, gentlemen, on this serious day, when I come, as it were, to make up my account with you, let me take to myself some degree of honest pride on the nature of the charges that are against me. I do not here stand before you accused of venality or of neglect of duty. It is not said that, in the long period of my service, I have in a single instance sacrificed the slightest of your interests to my ambition or to my fortune. It is not alleged that to gratify any anger or revenge of my own, or of my party, I have had a share in wronging or oppressing any description of men, or any one man in any description. No! the charges against me are all of one kind—that I have pushed the principles of general justice and benevolence too far; further than a cautious policy would warrant; and further than the opinions of many would go along with me. In every accident which may happen through life, in pain, in sorrow, in depression and distress, I will call to mind this accusation, and be comforted. *Burke.*

British Responsibility for India.

But again let me ask what are your hearts doing? These millions, 180 millions—for I cannot too often remind you that we have here to answer for about a fifth portion of the earth's inhabitants, men like yourselves, where are your hearts when your eyes fall on them, and see them at the foot of your armies and governed by your own sons, brothers, countrymen? Soldiers flow into the country and give up their lives in war to duty when it calls them, and even in peace to the more terrible demands of a climate which wears them out, and to disease, which occasionally breaks out in fierceness and cuts them off by tens and hundreds in a day. Civilians flow in also, eager for employment, until now the stream is checked because it is superabounding. Merchants and men of business add themselves to the gathering waters, peopling the Presidential towns and directing the whole course of trade, which in remote corners of the land feels everywhere their presiding influence. Barristers and solicitors succeed and reap from a litigious people harvests of gold, which after a few years of strenuous work, they carry back with them to their native soil, there in comfort and in rest to end their days. Engineers and artisans follow, making locomotion easy and distributing with swiftness and precision the produce which the land yields and the intelligence which interests all nations. We rule the land ; upon the whole unselfishly and wisely. We restrain such evil as an honest love of right and truth can put down, by instruments far from perfect, but the best which the land furnishes. *Bishop Douglas of Bombay.*

X

CCCCXLV.

Political Responsibility.

In this crisis I must hold my tongue, or I must speak with freedom. Falsehood and delusion are allowed in no case whatever; but, as in the exercise of all the virtues, there is an economy of truth. It is a sort of temperance by which a man speaks truth with measure that he may speak it the longer. But as the same rules do not hold in all cases, what would be right for you, who may presume on a series of years before you, would have no sense for me, who cannot, without absurdity, count on six months of life. What I say, I must say at once. Whatever I write is in its nature testamentary. It may have the weakness, but it has the sincerity of a dying declaration. For the few days I have to linger here, I am removed completely from the busy scene of the world; but I hold myself to be still responsible for everything that I have done whilst I continued in the place of action. If the rawest tyro in politics has been influenced by the authority of my grey hairs, and led by anything in my speeches or my writings to approve this war, he has a right to call upon me to know why I have changed my opinions, or why, when those I voted with have adopted better notions, I persevere in exploded error.

CCCCXLVI.

Conciliation with America.

The last cause of this disobedient spirit in the colonies is hardly less powerful than the rest, as it is not merely moral, but laid deep in the natural constitution of things.

Three thousand miles of ocean lie between you and them. No contrivance can prevent the effect of this distance in weakening government. Seas roll, and months pass, between the order and the execution; and the want of a speedy explanation of a single point is enough to defeat a whole system. You have, indeed, winged ministers of vengeance, who carry your bolts in their pounces to the remotest verge of the sea. But there a power steps in that limits the arrogance of raging passions and furious elements, and says 'So far shalt thou go and no farther.' Who are you that should fret and rage, and bite the chains of nature? Nothing worse happens to you than does to all nations who have extensive empire; and it happens in all the forms into which empire can be thrown. In large bodies, the circulation of power must be less vigorous at the extremities. Nature has said it. The Turk cannot govern Egypt and Arabia and Kurdistan as he governs Thrace; nor has he the same dominion in Crimea and Algiers which he has at Brusa and Smyrna. Despotism itself is obliged to truck and huckster. The Sultan gets such obedience as he can. He governs with a loose rein, that he may govern at all, and the whole of the force and vigour of his authority in the centre is derived from a prudent relaxation in his borders. Spain in her provinces is perhaps not so well obeyed as you are in yours. She complies too, she submits, she watches times. This is the immutable condition, the eternal law of extensive and detached empires.   *Burke, 1775.*

CCCCXLVII.

Burke on the Hustings.

But if I profess all this impolitic stubbornness, I may chance never to be elected into Parliament. It is certainly

not pleasing to be put out of the public service. But I
wish to be a member of Parliament to have my share of
doing good and resisting evil. It would therefore be
absurd to renounce my objects in order to obtain my
seat. I deceive myself indeed most grossly if I had not
much rather pass the remainder of my life hidden in the
recesses of the deepest obscurity, feeding my mind even
with the visions and imaginations of such things, than to
be placed on the most splendid throne in the universe,
tantalised with a denial of the practice of all which can
make the greatest situation any other than the greatest
curse. Gentlemen, I have had my day. I can never
sufficiently express my gratitude to you for having set
me in a place wherein I could lend the slightest help to
great and laudable designs. If by my vote I have aided
in securing to families the best possession, peace; if I
have joined in reconciling kings to their subjects and subjects to their prince; if I have thus taken part with the
best of men in the best of their actions, I can shut the
book. I might wish to read a page or two more; but this
is enough for my measure,—I have not lived in vain.

Burke.

CCCCXLVIII.

Defence of Thomas Hardy.

Driven from the accusation upon the subject of pikes,
and even from the very colour of accusation, and knowing
that nothing was to be done without the proof of arms, we
have got this miserable, solitary knife, held up to us as
the engine which was to destroy the constitution of this
country; and Mr. Groves, an Old Bailey solicitor, employed as a spy upon the occasion, has been selected to
give probability to this monstrous absurdity by his re-

spectable evidence. I understand that this same gentleman has carried his system of spying to such a pitch as to
practice it since this unfortunate man has been standing a
prisoner before you, professing himself as a friend to the
committee preparing his defence, that he might discover
to the Crown the materials by which he meant to defend
his life. I state this only from report, and I hope in God
I am mistaken; for human nature starts back appalled
from such atrocity, and shrinks and trembles at the very
statement of it. But as to the perjury of this miscreant, it
will appear palpable beyond all question, and he shall
answer for it in due season. He tells you he attended at
Chalk Farm; and that there, forsooth, amongst about
seven or eight thousand people he saw two or three
persons with knives. He might, I should think, have
seen many more, as hardly any man goes without a knife
of some sort in his pocket. He asked, however, it seems,
where they got these knives, and was directed to Green,
a hairdresser, who deals besides in cutlery; and accordingly this notable Mr. Groves went (as he told us) to
Green's, and asked to purchase a knife, when Green, in
answer to him, said, ' Speak low, for my wife is a damned
aristocrat.' This answer was sworn to by this wretch, to
give you the idea that Green, who had his knives to sell,
was conscious that he kept them for an illegal and wicked
purpose, and that they were not to be sold in public.

Lord Erskine, 1794.

CCCCXLIX.

Irish Emigration.

No one has deplored in more emphatic terms than
myself the circumstances which compel so many noble-

hearted Irishmen to leave the land of their birth. But to lament an emigration you are unable to arrest, and which is composed of those you cannot employ, is a useless waste of feeling. There are few human passions with which I have greater sympathy, or which I can better understand, than the love of home. But in this life no one can arrange his destiny altogether to his taste; and to sally forth and battle with the world is one of the most universal conditions of existence. It is all very well to talk pathetically of the hardship endured by the Irish peasant in quitting the home of his childhood, but to dwell for ·ever in the home of one's childhood is almost the rarest earthly luxury which can be mentioned ; not one man in ten thousand expects to enjoy it; no woman desires it. Law in France, custom in America, discourage such permanent arrangements, while in England they are only within the reach of a comparatively small minority.

CCCCL.

Bribery and Corruption.

Our shame stalks abroad in the open face of day; it is become too common even to excite surprise. We treat it as a matter of small importance that some of the electors of Great Britain have added treason to their corruption, and have traitorously sold their votes to foreign Powers ; that some of the members of our Senate are at the command of a distant tyrant ; that our Senators are no longer the representatives of British virtue, but the vices and pollutions of the East.   *W. Pitt.*

CCCCLI.

American Address to Trinity College, Dublin, July 7, 1892.

To the plaudits of British and Continental scholars the Americans add their tributes of grateful reverence. We bring you salutations from the New World, a barren wilderness when Trinity College was founded, now a vigorous forest where acorns of British oaks have taken root and grown. We have come to greet living friends, in whose companionship our scholars walk through the fields of ancient and modern literature, survey the heavens, enter the abstract realms of mathematics and philosophy, and dwell in the earthly paradise of science and art. At the stately portal of Trinity College we have been met by your Goldsmith, and ours, and we have heard him say, in the phrases of the immortal Vicar ; here is a college to be preferred, 'as I chose my wife, as she chose her wedding gown, not for a fine glossy surface, but for such qualities as would wear well'; and when we turned to salute the other guardian of the threshold, we heard the clarion voice of Edmund Burke, our Burke as well as yours, defending the cause of American freedom, and were set to musing whether, if his warnings had been heeded, we should now be present as freemen of the United Kingdom, and not as citizens of the United States. Therefore to-day, before these scholars assembled from every land of Christendom, the Americans do homage to the University of Dublin, for its present, and for its past.

D. C. Gilman.

CCCCLII.

Rhetorical Blandishments.

My Lords, I should be ashamed if at this moment I attempted to use any sort of rhetorical blandishments whatever. Such artifices would neither be suitable to the body that I represent, to the cause which I sustain, or to my own individual disposition upon such an occasion. My Lords, we know very well what these fallacious blandishments too frequently are. We know that they are used to captivate the benevolence of the court, and to conciliate the affections of the tribunal rather to the person than to the cause. We know that they are used to stifle the remonstrances of conscience in the judge and to reconcile it to the violation of his duty, and that thus all parties are induced to separate in a kind of good humour as if they had nothing more than a verbal dispute to settle, or a slight quarrel over a table to compromise : while nations, whole suffering nations, are left to beat the empty air with cries of suffering and anguish, and to cast forth to an offended heaven the imprecations of disappointment and despair.

Burke.

CCCCLIII.

Protection in America.

Ours is not a destructive party. We are not at enmity with the rights of any of our fellow-citizens. We are not recklessly heedless of any American interests, nor will we abandon our regard for them, but, invoking the love, fairness, and justice which belong to true Americanism, and upon which the Constitution rests, we insist that no plan of tariff legislation shall be tolerated which has for its object and purpose a forced contribution from the earnings and income of the masses of our citizens to swell directly the accumulations of a favoured few, nor will we permit pretended solicitude for American labour or any other specious pretext of benevolent care for others to blind the eyes of the people to the selfish schemes of those who seek, through the aid of unequal tariff laws, to gain unearned and unreasonable advantages at the expense of their fellows. *Mr. Cleveland.*

CCCCLIV.

Self-Depreciation.

But that which makes me wonder most of all is, how it could occur to you that you can no longer be of any use to your country or your friends, and therefore that you have no motive for desiring to live. I will say no more, nor will I attempt to express what I think on this subject, further than this, which I declare and will maintain as long as I live, that I have derived more advantage from my acquaintance with you, than from all the time I have spent on my travels. This is enough for the present. But, my dear Hubert, do not think it is either arrogance, which I hope is not one of my faults, nor mere loquacity, which, however, Xenophon thought no fault in young Cyrus, but an inclination, or rather impulse of my mind that has moved me to write thus much to you: I was desirous to do what I could to relieve you from that distress, which I perceived was somewhat disturbing you; and yet I readily allow that all this comes under the proverb, *Sus Minervam.*

Humbled, but not humiliated.

Had it pleased God to continue to me the hopes of succession, I should have been according to my mediocrity, and the mediocrity of the age I live in, a sort of founder of a family: I should have left a son, who, in all the points in which personal merit can be viewed, would not have shown himself inferior to the Duke, or to any of those whom he traces in his line. But a Disposer whose power we are little able to resist, and whose wisdom it behoves us not at all to dispute, has ordained it in another manner, and, whatever my querulous weakness might suggest, a far better. The storm has gone over me. I am stripped of all my honours, I am torn up by the roots, and lie prostrate on the earth! There, and prostrate there, I most unfeignedly recognise the divine justice, and in some degree submit to it. But whilst I humble myself before God, I do not know that it is forbidden to repel the attacks of unjust and inconsiderate men. The patience of Job is proverbial. After some of the convulsive struggles of our irritable nature, he submitted himself, and repented in dust and ashes. But even so, I do not find him blamed for reprehending, and with a considerable degree of verbal asperity, those ill-natured neighbours of his, who visited his dunghill to read moral, political, and economical lectures on his misery. I am alone. I have none to meet my enemies in the gate. Indeed, my lord, I greatly deceive myself if, in this hard season, I would give a peck of refuse wheat for all that is called fame and honour in the world. *Burke.*

CCCCLVI.

A Letter of Condolence.

My dear friend,—I received a letter from Mrs. Damer a few days ago, informing me of the melancholy event that has taken place with you; and I have seen her since and learnt the particulars concerning it. I sympathise with you and your sister most truly: for I know well that the advanced age of a parent, which makes such a loss expected, and for which we ought to be prepared, does not, therefore, make it less afflicting. That he has lived to a great age, in health and comfort far beyond what most old people enjoy, and that your society and affection have so greatly contributed to it, is pleasing to remember; but long habits broken up, and the removal of the object of those habits, who bore to you affection of a nature which no other can bear, makes for a time a sad blank in the heart, which will not be comforted by reason. I am glad for your sakes that your father had recovered from all the fatigue of travelling before he was taken ill, and I am glad both for your sake and his own, that his illness was so short and his end without suffering.

H. Walpole.

CCCCLVII.

Intellectual Companionship.

We have shared together many hours of study, and you have been willing, at the cost of much patient labour, to cheer the difficult paths of intellectual toil by the unfailing sweetness of your beloved companionship. It seems to me that all those things which we have learned together are doubly my own; whilst those other studies which I have pursued in solitude have never yielded me more than a maimed and imperfect satisfaction. The dream of my life would be to associate you with all I do if that were possible; but since the ideal can never be wholly realised, let me at least rejoice that we have been so little separated, and that the subtle influence of your finer taste and more delicate perception is ever, like some penetrating perfume, in the whole atmosphere around me.   *Hamerton.*

CCCCLVIII.

Incorrupta fides nudaque Veritas.

Even your expostulations are pleasing to me; for though they show you angry, yet they are not without many expressions of your kindness; and therefore I am proud to be so chidden. Yet I cannot so far abandon my own defence, as to confess any idleness or forgetfulness on my part. What has hindered me from writing to you was neither ill-health nor a worse thing, ingratitude, but a flood of little businesses, which yet are necessary to my subsistence, and of which I hoped to have given you a good account before this time: but the court rather speaks kindly of me than does anything for me, though they promise largely; and perhaps they think I will advance as they go backward, in which they will be much deceived; for I can never go an inch beyond my conscience and my honour. If they will consider me as a man who has done my best to improve the language and especially the poetry of my country, and will be content with my acquiescence under the present government, and forbearing satire on it, that I can promise, because I can perform it; but I can neither take the oaths nor forsake my religion. . . . Truth is but one ; and they who have once heard of it can plead no excuse if they do not embrace it.   But these are things too serious for a trifling letter.

CCCCLIX.

A Shiftless Brother.

Dear Brother,—I should have answered your letter sooner, but in truth I am not fond of thinking of the necessity of those I love, when it is so very little in my power to help them.   I am sorry to find you are still every way unprovided for ; and what adds to my uneasiness is, that I have received a letter from my sister Johnson, by which I learn that she is pretty much in the same circumstances.   As to myself, I believe I could get both you and my poor brother-in-law something like that which you desire, but I am determined never to ask for little things, nor exhaust any little interest I may have, until I can serve you, him, and myself more effectually. As yet no opportunity has offered, but I believe you are pretty well convinced that I will not be remiss when it arrives.   The king has lately been pleased to make me Professor of Ancient History in a Royal Academy of Painting, which he has just established, but there is no salary annexed ; and I took it rather as a compliment to the institution, than any benefit to myself.   Honours to one in my situation are something like ruffles to a man that wants a shirt.   *Goldsmith.*

CCCCLX.

Reform or Revolution.

LONDON, *Sept.* 13, 1831.

My dear Sister,—I am in high spirits at the thought of soon seeing you all in London, and being again one of

a family which I love so much. It is well that one has
something to love in private life ; for the aspect of public
affairs is very menacing ; fearful, I think, beyond what
people in general imagine. Three weeks, however, will
probably settle the whole, and bring to an issue the
question, Reform or Revolution. One or the other I am
certain that we must and shall have. I assure you that
the violence of the people, the bigotry of the Lords, and
the stupidity and weakness of the Ministers alarm me so
much, that even my rest is disturbed by vexation and
uneasy forebodings ; not for myself, for I may gain and
cannot lose, but for this noble country, which seems
likely to be ruined without the miserable consolation of
being ruined by great men.   *Macaulay.*

CCCCLXI.

Pleasing the People.

No man carries further than I do the policy of making
government pleasing to the people. But the widest
range of this politic complaisance is confined within the
limits of justice. I would not only consult the interests of
the people, but I would cheerfully gratify their humours.
We are all a sort of children that must be soothed and
managed. I think I am not austere or formal in my
nature. I would bear, I would even myself play my
part in any innocent buffooneries, to divert them. But
I never will act the tyrant for their amusement. If they
will mix malice in their sports, I shall never consent to
throw them any living, sentient creature whatsoever, no,
not so much as a kitling, to torment.

CCCCLXII.

Self-Knowledge.

In the various objects of knowledge, which I have had
the pleasure of seeing you study under my care, as well
as those which you have acquired under the various
teachers who have hitherto instructed you, the most
material branch of information which it imports a human
being to know, has been entirely overlooked; I mean,
the knowledge of yourself. There are indeed very few
persons who possess at once the capability and the disposition to give you this instruction. Your parents, who
alone are perhaps sufficiently acquainted with you for
the purpose, are usually disqualified for the task, by the
very affection and partiality which would prompt them
to undertake it. Your masters, who probably labour
under no such prejudices, have seldom either sufficient
opportunities of knowing your character, or are so much
interested in your welfare, as to undertake an employment so unpleasant and laborious.   *Goldsmith.*

CCCCLXIII.

Self-Knowledge (continued).

You are as yet too young and inexperienced to perform
this important office for yourself, or indeed to be sensible
of its very great consequence to your happiness. The
ardent hopes and the extreme vanity natural to early
youth blind you at once to everything within and everything without, and make you see both yourself and the
world in false colours. This illusion, it is true, will
gradually wear away as your reason matures and your

experience increases; but the question is, What is to be done in the meantime? Evidently there is no plan for you to adopt but to make use of the reason and experience of those who are qualified to direct you. Of this, however, I can assure you, both from my own experience and from the opinions of all those whose opinions deserve to be valued, that if you aim at any sort of eminence or respectability in the eyes of the world, or in those of your friends; if you have any ambition to be distinguished in your future career for your virtues, or talents, or accomplishments, this self-knowledge of which I am speaking is above all things requisite. It is therefore my intention, in this letter, to offer you a few hints on this most important subject.   *Goldsmith.*

CCCCLXIV.

The King's Party.

The mention of this man has moved me from my natural moderation. Let me return to your Grace. You are the pillow upon which I am determined to rest all my resentments. What idea can the best of sovereigns form to himself of his own government? In what repute can he conceive that he stands with his people, when he sees beyond the possibility of a doubt that, whatever be the office, the suspicion of his favour is fatal to the candidate, and that, when the party he wishes well to has the fairest prospect of success, if his royal inclination should unfortunately be discovered, it drops like an acid, and turns the election. This event, among others, may perhaps contribute to open his Majesty's eyes to his real honour and interest. In spite of all your Grace's ingenuity, he may at last perceive the inconvenience of selecting, with such a curious felicity, every villain in the nation to fill the various departments of his government. Yet I should be sorry to confine him in the choice either of his footmen or his friends.   *Junius.*

CCCCLXV.

Family Life.

It is quite high time that I should write to you, for weeks and months go by, and it is quite startling to think how little communication I hold with many of those whom I love most dearly. And yet these are times when I am least of all disposed to loosen the links which bind me to my oldest and dearest friends, for I imagine we shall all want the union of all the good men we can get together ; and the want of sympathy which I cannot but feel towards so many of those whom I meet with, makes me think how delightful it would be to have daily intercourse with those with whom I ever feel it thoroughly. What men do in middle life without a wife and children to turn to I cannot imagine ; for I think the affections must be sadly checked and chilled, even in the best men, by their intercourse with people, such as one usually finds them in the world. I do not mean that one does not meet with good and sensible people ; but then their minds are set, and our minds are set, and they will not, in mature age, grow into each other. But with a home filled with those whom we entirely love and sympathize with, and with some old friends, to whom one can open one's heart fully from time to time, the world's society has rather a bracing influence to make one shake off mere dreams of delight.

Y

CCCCLXVI.

Work without power to work.

I covet rest neither for my friends nor yet for myself, so long as we are able to work; but, when age or weakness comes on, and hard labour becomes an unendurable burthen, then the necessity of work is deeply painful, and it seems to me to imply an evil state of society wherever such a necessity generally exists. One's age should be tranquil as one's childhood should be playful: hard work at either extremity of human existence seems to me out of place; the morning and the evening should be alike cool and peaceful; at mid-day the sun may burn, and men may labour under it.

CCCCLXVII.

Damnum reparabile.

I am heartily sensible of your loss, which yet admits of alleviation, not only from the common motives which have been repeated every day for upwards of five thousand years, but also from your own peculiar knowledge of the world and the variety of distresses which occur in all ranks from the highest to the lowest: I may add too from the peculiar times in which we live, which seem to threaten still more wretched and unhappy times to come. Nor is it a small advantage that you have a peculiar resource against distress from the gaiety of your own temper. Such is the hypochondriac melancholy complexion of us Islanders, that we seem made of butter, every accident makes such a deep impression upon us; but those elastic spirits, which are your birthright, cause the strokes of fortune to rebound without leaving a trace behind them ; though, for a time, there is and will be a gloom, which, I agree with your friends, is best dispelled at the court and metropolis, amidst a variety of faces and amusements.

CCCCLXVIII.

Ne sutor ultra crepidam.

Sir,—I think I have been more congratulated on my Egyptian appointment than on any other of the offices which I have ever held ; the reason of this is that people have supposed that I could terminate the long protracted troubles in Egypt in a manner not inconsistent with the dignity of the British nation. I hope that Heaven has approved the appointment, and will continue to stand by me when the time for action comes. One thing I have no hesitation in saying, that I will try my best to give the nation no cause to be disappointed in me. Do you, on your part, believe only what I write to the Government or yourself, and refuse to give countenance to unauthorised rumours by believing in them. It is a common experience, but I have verified it in the present war, that no one is so entirely superior to common report as not to be influenced by it in his action. In every social gathering, and—Heaven save the mark—at every dinner party, there are gentlemen to be found, who, in their own opinion, are capable of conducting an Egyptian campaign, who know where the camp should be pitched, at what time and by what route the country should be entered, where the magazines should be located, what is the right moment to commence action, and when to desist from action. Nor do they merely lay down the law as to the right course of action ; but if anything is done in a manner which does not accord with their fiat, they accuse the general as if he were on his trial. All this is a great source of difficulty to practical men. It is not given to every one to be as unflinching and resolute in the face of hostile criticism as Wellington, who deliberately preferred to have his power curtailed by the lightheadedness of the people, to discharging his duties less well for gaining a reputation. I am not one of those who think that generals should not receive advice : on the contrary, I think that the man who relies entirely upon his own unaided judgment is a coxcomb rather than a wise man. What then is my drift? Advice should be tendered in the first instance by practical men, who have had special experience in military affairs ; in the second place, by such as are present on the spot, who know the ground and the enemy, and are watching for the right moment, who row in the same boat and share the same perils. If, then, there is any one who is sure that he can advise me to the public advantage in the war on which I am about to enter, let him not refuse to help, but let him come out with me to Egypt : I will place a steamer, a camel, and a tent at his disposal, and will pay his expenses. If he is afraid to do this, and prefers an armchair at his club to service in the field, then, say I, let him not try to steer the ship from the shore. There is enough gossip in town ; let him confine his powers of talk to this area, and rest assured that I shall be satisfied with the counsel of military men.

CCCCLXIX.

Rest well earned.

I know not when I have been more delighted by any letter, than by that which I lately received from you. It contains a picture of your present state which is truly a cause for thankfulness, and, speaking after the manner of men, it is an intense gratification to my sense of justice, as well as to my personal regard for you, to see a life of hard and insufficiently paid labour well performed, now, before its decline, rewarded with comparative rest and with comfort. I rejoiced in the picture which you gave of your house and fields and neighbourhood ; there was a freshness and a quietness about it which always goes very much to my heart, and which at times, if I indulged the feeling, could half make me discontented with the perpetual turmoil of my own life. I sometimes look at the mountains which bound our valley, and think how content I could be never to wander beyond them any more, and to take rest in a place which I love so dearly. But whilst my health is so entire, and I feel my spirits still so youthful, I feel ashamed of the wish, and I trust that I can sincerely rejoice in being engaged in so active a life, and in having such constant intercourse with others.

CCCCLXX.

Putting out to sea.

We are going to leave this place, if all be well, on Monday; and I confess that it makes me rather sad to see the preparations for our departure, for it is like going out of a very quiet cove into a very rough sea ; and I am every year approaching nearer to that time of life when rest is more welcome than exertion. Yet, when I think of what is at stake on that rough sea, I feel that I have no right to lie in harbour idly ; and indeed I do yearn more than I can say to be able to render some service where service is so greatly needed. It is when I indulge such wishes most keenly, and only then, that strong political differences between my friends and myself are really painful; because I feel that not only could we not act together, but there would be no sympathy the moment I were to express anything beyond a general sense of anxiety and apprehension, in which I suppose all good men must share.

CCCCLXXI.

Party Enthusiasm.

You are now embracing the cause full of enthusiasm and zeal, and this is very well; how else could we run out the race, unless we began with some little fire? But this will not last, and unless you are warned, you may be offended and fall away. When you have lived longer in this world and outlived the enthusiastic and pleasing illusions of youth, you will find your love and pity for the race increase tenfold, your admiration and attachment to any particular party fall away altogether. You will not find the royal cause perfect any more than any other, nor those embarked in it free from mean and sordid motives, though you think now that all of them act from the noblest. This is the most important lesson that a man can learn—that all men are really alike ; that all creeds and opinions are nothing but the mere result of chance and temperament; that no party is on the whole better than another ; that no creed does more than shadow imperfectly forth some one side of truth ; and it is only when you begin to see this that you can feel that pity for mankind, that sympathy with its disappointments and follies, and its natural human hopes, which have such a little time of growth, and such a sure season of decay.   *Shorthouse.*

CCCCLXXII. ·

An Apology.

My dear Walter,—I know that you are too reasonable a man to expect anything like punctuality of correspondence from a translator of Homer, especially from one who is a doer also of many other things at the same time; for I labour hard not only to acquire a little fame for myself, but to win it also for others, men of whom I know nothing, not even their names, who send me their poetry, that, by translating it out of prose into verse, I may make it more like poetry than it was. Having heard all this, you will feel yourself not only inclined to pardon my long silence, but to pity me also for the cause of it. You may, if you please, believe likewise, for it is true, that I have a faculty of remembering my friends even when I do not write to them, and of loving them not one jot the less, though I leave them to starve for want of a letter from me. And now, I think, you have an apology both as to style, matter, and manner, altogether unexceptionable.   *W Cowper.*

CCCCLXXIII.

A Letter of Sympathy.

I cannot let this night close without offering a few lines of reply to your kind, sad letter just received. It truly grieves me that you write in so desponding a style of your health, but I trust that very great deduction must be made on the score of morbid feeling. I have known you at other times less apprehensive of the same complaint. Any thoughts of your being a traveller at this season I had, I may say, given up before; and in truth, when I found your complaint so obstinate, my wish was that you should consult your feelings and nurse yourself. I am unwilling, however, to give up the hope so long cherished of seeing you here at some time. And in spring, so far as it is right and lawful, I trust we shall meet.

CCCCLXXIV.

John Wilkes to H. C.

PARIS, *January* 20.

But I am to await the event of these two trials; and Philips can never persuade me that some risk is not run. I have in my own case experienced the fickleness of the people. I was almost adored one week; the next, neglected, abused, and despised. With all the fine things said and wrote of me, have not the public, till this moment, left me in the lurch, as to the expenses of so great a variety of law-suits? Can I trust, likewise, a rascally Court, who bribe my own servants to steal out of my house? Which of the Opposition, likewise, can call on me and expect my services? I hold no obligation to any of them, but to Lord Temple; who is really a superior being. It appears, then, that there is no call of honour. I will now go on to the public cause, that of every man—liberty. Is there then any one point behind to be tried? I think not. The two important decisions have secured for ever an Englishman's liberty and property. They have grown out of my firmness,

and the affair of the *North Briton :* but in this case neither
are we nor our posterity concerned whether John Wilkes,
or some one else, wrote and published the *North Briton.*

CCCCLXXV.

Literature or Politics?

But that a man before whom the two paths of literature
and politics lie open, and who might hope for eminence
in either, should choose politics, and quit literature, seems
to me madness.   On the one side is health, leisure, peace
of mind, the search after truth, and all the enjoyments of
friendship and conversation.   On the other side is almost
certain ruin to the constitution, constant labour, constant
anxiety.   Every friendship which a man may have, becomes precarious as soon as he engages in politics.   As
to abuse, men soon become callous to it, but the discipline
which makes them callous is very severe.   And for what
is it that a man who might, if he chose, rise and lie down
at his own hour, engage in any study, enjoy any amusement, and visit any place, consents to make himself as
much a prisoner as if he were within the rules of the
Fleet; to be tethered during eleven months of the year
within the circle of half a mile round Charing Cross; to
sit or stand night after night for ten or twelve hours, in-
haling a noisome atmosphere, and listening to harangues
of which nine-tenths are far below the level of a leading
article in a newspaper?   Is it for fame?   Who would
compare the fame of Charles Townshend to that of
Hume?   Who can look back on the life of Burke, and
not regret that the years which he passed in ruining
his health and temper by political exertions were not
passed in the composition of some great and durable
work?   But these, as I have said, are meditations in a

quiet garden, situated far beyond the contagious influence of English faction.   What I might feel if I again
saw Downing Street and Palace Yard, is another question.
I tell you sincerely my present feelings.

CCCCLXXVI.

From Columbus.

'I could have supported this evil fortune with less grief,'
Columbus wrote, 'had my person alone been in jeopardy,
since I am a debtor for my life to the Supreme Power,
and have at other times been within a step of death.   But
it was a cause of infinite sorrow and trouble to think that,
after having been illuminated with faith and certainty
to undertake this enterprise, after having victoriously
achieved it, and when on the point of convincing my
opponents, and securing to your highnesses a vast increase
of dominion, the divine majesty should be pleased to
defeat all by my death.   It would have been more sup-
portable, also, had I not been accompanied by others who
had been drawn on by my persuasions, and who in their
distress cursed not only the hour of their coming, but the
fear inspired by my words, which prevented their turning
back, as they had repeatedly determined.   My grief was
doubled when I thought of my two sons, whom I had left
at school in Spain, destitute, in a strange land, without
any testimony of services rendered by their father, which
might have induced your highnesses to befriend them.   And
although I was comforted by faith that the Deity would
not permit a work of such exaltation, wrought through so
many troubles and contradictions, to remain imperfect,
yet I reflected on my own faults and failures, which
might with perfect justice deprive me of the glory that
was almost resting on my brow.'

CCCCLXXVII.

John Shallow to Mr. Spectator.

Mr. Spectator,

The night before I left London I went to see a play called the Humorous Lieutenant. Upon the rising of the curtain I was very much surprised with the great concert of cat-calls which was exhibited that evening, and began to think with myself that I had made a mistake, and gone to a music meeting instead of the playhouse. It appeared indeed a little odd to me, to see so many persons of quality, of both sexes, assembled together at a kind of caterwauling ; for I cannot look upon that performance to have been anything better, whatever the musicians themselves might think of it. As I had no acquaintance in the house to ask questions of, and was forced to go out of town early the next morning, I could not learn the secret of this matter. What I would therefore desire of you, is, to give me some account of this strange instrument, which I found the company called a cat-call ; and particularly to let me know whether it be a piece of music lately come from Italy. For my own part, to be free with you, I would rather hear an English fiddle : though I durst not shew my dislike whilst I was in the playhouse, it being my chance to sit the very next man to one of the performers.

I am, Sir,

Your most affectionate friend and servant,

John Shallow, Esq.

Addison.

CCCCLXXVIII.

To a Friend.

WESTON, *April* 8.

Your entertaining and pleasant letter, resembling in that respect all that I receive from you, deserved a more expeditious answer; and should have had what it so well deserved, had it not reached me at a time when, deeply in debt to all my correspondents, I had letters to write without number. Like 'autumnal leaves that strew the brooks in Vallombrosa,' the unanswered farrago lay before me. If I quote at all, you must expect me henceforth to quote none but Milton, since for a long time to come I shall be occupied with him only.

I was much pleased with the extract you gave me from your sister Eliza's letter; she writes very elegantly, and (if I might say it without seeming to flatter you) I should say much in the manner of her brother. I rejoice that you are so well with the learned Bishop of Sarum, and well remember how he ferreted the vermin Lauder out of all his hidings, when I was a boy at Westminster.

What letter of the 10th of December is that which you say you have not yet answered? Consider, it is April now, and I never remember anything that I write half so long. But perhaps it relates to Calchas, for I do remember that you have not yet furnished me with the secret history of him and his family, which I demanded from you.

Adieu, Yours most sincerely,

W. COWPER.

CCCCLXXIX.

Raleigh's Last Letter.

Most sorry I am (as God knows) that being thus surprised by death, I can leave you no better estate. God is my witness, I meant you all my office of wines, or that I could have purchased by selling it; half my stuff, and all my jewels, but some one for the boy; but God hath prevented all my resolutions, even that great God that worketh all in all; but if you live free from want, care for no more, for the rest is but vanity; love God, and begin betimes to repose your trust in Him; therein shall you find true and lasting riches, and endless comfort. For the rest, when you have travailed and wearied your thoughts over all sorts of worldly cogitation, you shall but sit down by sorrow in the end. . . . Remember your poor child for his father's sake, who chose you and loved you in his happiest time. Get those letters (if it be possible), which I writ to the lords, wherein I sued for my life. God is my witness, it was for you and your's that I desired life; but it is true that I disdain myself for begging it, for know (dear wife) that your son is the son of a true man, and one who in his own respect despiseth death, and all his misshapen and ugly forms. I cannot write much, God He knoweth how hardly I steal this time while others sleep; and it is also high time that I should separate my thoughts from the world. Beg my dead body, which living was denied thee, and either lay it at Sherborne (if the land continue) or in Exeter church by my father and mother; I can say no more, time and death call me away.   *Sir W. Raleigh.*

CCCCLXXX.

Paris under the First Consul.

Nothing else (but ill health) should have detained me so long at Paris, a place which in cold weather I think excessively disagreeable and peculiarly unwholesome. In fine weather, when a stranger can visit the various works of art which the tempest has assembled here from every quarter of the globe, it is highly interesting; and it is encircled by so many delightful gardens, that one may pass the summer here without feeling one's absence from the country. Yet I have never seen a spot where I should more grieve at fixing my residence, nor a nation with which I should find it so difficult to coalesce. A revolution does not seem to be favourable to the morals of a people. In the upper classes I have seen nothing but the most ardent pursuit after sensual or frivolous pleasures, and the most unqualified egotism, with a devotion to the shrines of luxury and vanity unknown at any former period. The lower ranks are chiefly marked by a total want of probity, and an earnestness for the gain of to-day, though purchased by the sacrifice of that character which might ensure them ten-fold advantage on the morrow. You must not think me infected with national prejudice. I speak from the narrow circle of my own observation and that of my friends, and I do not include the suffering parts of the nation, who have little intercourse with strangers, and who form a society apart. I have been presented to Bonaparte and his wife, who receive with great state, ceremony, and magnificence. His manner is very good, but the expression of his countenance is not attractive. *Mrs. R. Trench.*

CCCCLXXXI.

Polished Plums.

I know that the ears of modern verse-writers are delicate to an excess, and their readers are troubled with the same squeamishness as themselves. So that if a line do not run as smooth as quicksilver they are offended. A critic of the present day serves a poem as a cook does a dead turkey, when she fastens the legs of it to a post and draws out all the sinews. For this we may thank Pope; but unless we could imitate him in the closeness and compactness of his expression, as well as in the smoothness of his numbers, we had better drop the imitation, which serves no other purpose than to emasculate and weaken all we write. Give me a manly rough line, with a deal of meaning in it, rather than a whole poem full of musical periods, that have nothing but their oily smoothness to recommend them.

I have said thus much, as I hinted in the beginning, because I have just finished a much longer poem than the last; which our common friend will receive by the same messenger that has the charge of this letter. In that poem there are many lines which an ear so nice as the gentleman's who made the above-mentioned alteration would undoubtedly condemn; and yet (if I may be permitted to say it) they cannot be made smoother without being the worse for it.

There is a roughness on a plum, which nobody that understands fruit would rub off, though the plum would be much more polished without it.　　　　　*Cowper.*

CCCCLXXXII.

A coat of many colours.

MY DEAR RANDOLPH,

I must confess it's rather hard on you that after your wholesale slaughter of wild lions (*sic*) in S. Africa, you should have made so little impression on your return upon the tame cats. I mean, of course, y^r constituents at Paddington. On the other hand (pardon a little brag) it's wonderful how popular I've lately become with the Tories. I wish you had heard my speech on the Local Government Bill for Ireland the other night in the House. 'Queen and Constitution,' 'the Emerald Isle,' 'the Union of hearts,' &c. &c. Rounds of applause followed my loyal sentiments. We're on the eve of a dissolution. The G. O. M. is, alas, as fresh as ever. Still I really felt a bit of the old love for him when he harangued the other night on 'Disestablishment of the Welsh and Scotch Churches,' 'One man one vote,' and 'Reconstruction of the House of Lords.' These were once *my* principles, you know.

Are they still? you will ask. Well, to tell you the truth I hardly know myself.

Yours ever,

JOSEPH.

The Granta.

CCCCLXXXIII.

A Letter.

MY DEAR HUNT,　　　　FLORENCE, *Nov.* 23, 1819.

Why don't you write to us? I was preparing to send you something for your 'Indicator,' but I have been a drone instead of a bee in this business, thinking that, perhaps, as you did not acknowledge any of my late enclosures, it would not be welcome to you, whatever I might send.

What a state England is in ! But you will never write politics. I don't wonder; but I wish, then, that you would write a paper in the 'Examiner' on the actual state of the country, and what, under all circumstances of the conflicting passions and interests of men, we are to expect. Not what we ought to expect, nor what, if so and so were to happen, we might expect ;—but what, as things are, there is reason to believe will come ;—and send it to me for my information. Every word a man has to say is valuable to the public now; and thus you will at once gratify your friend, nay instruct, and either exhilarate him or force him to be resigned, and awaken the minds of the people.

I have no spirits to write what I do not know whether you will care much about; I know well that if I were in great misery, poverty, &c., you would think of nothing else but how to amuse and relieve me. You omit me if I am prosperous.

I could laugh, if I found a joke, in order to put you in good-humour with me after my scolding; in good-humour enough to write to us. . . . Affectionate love to and from all. This ought not only to be the *Vale* of a letter, but a superscription over the gate of life.

Your sincere friend,
P. B. SHELLEY.

CCCCLXXXIV.

To the Master of Pembroke College.

SIR, *October* 3, 1773.

Apprehensions of gout, about this season, forbid my undertaking a journey to Cambridge with my son. I regret this more particularly, as it deprives me of an occasion of being introduced to your personal accquaintance, and that of the gentlemen of your society; a loss, I shall much wish to repair, at some other time. Mr. Wilson, whose admirable instruction and affectionate care have brought my son, early, to receive such further advantages, as he cannot fail to find, under your eye, will present him to you. He is of a tender age, and of a health not yet firm enough to be indulged, to the full, in the strong desire he has to accquire useful knowledge. An ingenuous mind and docility of temper will, I know, render him conformable to your discipline, in all points. Too young for the irregularities of a man, I trust, he will not, on the other hand, prove troublesome by the puerile sallies of a boy. Such as he is, I am happy to place him at Pembroke; and I need not say, how much of his parents' hearts goes along with him. I am, with great esteem and regard, Sir, your most faithful and most obedient humble servant,

CHATHAM.

CCCCLXXXV.

A Reformed Character.

Aug. 15, 1758.

I have already given my landlady orders for an entire reform in the state of my finances. I declaim against hot suppers, drink less sugar in my tea, and check my grate with brickbats. Instead of hanging my room with pictures I intend to adorn it with maxims of frugality. These will make pretty furniture enough, and wont be a bit too expensive; for I shall draw them all out with my own hands, and my landlady's daughter shall frame them with the parings of my black waistcoat. Each maxim is to be inscribed on a sheet of clear paper, and wrote with my best pen; of which the following will serve as a specimen. 'Look sharp'; 'Mind the main chance'; 'Money is money now'; 'If you have a thousand pound, you can put your hands by your sides and say you are worth a thousand pounds every day of the year'; 'Take a farthing from an hundred pound, and it will be an hundred pound no longer.' Thus, whichever way I turn my eyes, they are sure to meet one of those friendly monitors; and as we are told of an actor who hung his room round with looking-glasses to correct the defects of his person, my apartment shall be furnished in a peculiar manner to correct the errors of my mind.

Goldsmith.

CCCCLXXXVI.

Who wrote Ossian?

MR. JAMES MACPHERSON,

I received your foolish and impudent letter. Any violence offered me I shall do my best to repel; and what I cannot do for myself, the law shall do for me. I hope I shall never be deterred from detecting what I think a cheat, by the menaces of a ruffian.

What would you have me retract? I thought your book an imposture; I think it an imposture still. In this opinion I have given my reasons to the publick, which I here dare you to refute. Your rage I defy. Your abilities, since your Homer, are not so formidable; and what I hear of your morals inclines me to pay regard not to what you shall say, but to what you shall prove. You may print this if you will.

SAM. JOHNSON.

CCCCLXXXVII.

A New Householder.

I shall exult and triumph to you a little that I have now at last, being turned of forty, to my own honour, to that of learning, and to that of the present age, arrived at the dignity of being a householder! .About seven months ago I got a house of my own and completed a regular family; consisting of a head, viz. myself, and two inferior members, a maid and a cat. My sister has since joined me, and keeps me company. With frugality I can reach, I find, cleanliness, warmth, light, plenty, and contentment. What would you have more? Independence? I have it in a supreme degree. Honour? That is not altogether wanting. Grace? That will come in time. A wife? That is none of the indispensable requisites of life. Books? That *is* one of them, and I have more than I can use. In short I cannot find any blessing of consequence which I am not possessed of in a greater or less degree: and without any great effort of philosophy I may be easy and satisfied.   *Hume.*

CCCCLXXXVIII.

To a Noble Lord.

I have, through life, been willing to give everything to others; and to reserve nothing for myself, but the inward conscience, that I had omitted no pains to discover, to animate, to discipline, to direct the abilities of the country for its service, and to place them in the best light to improve their age, or to adorn it. This conscience I have. I have never suppressed any man; never checked him for a moment in his course, by any jealousy, or by any policy. I was always ready, to the height of my means, and they were always infinitely below my desires, to forward those abilities which overpowered my own. In that period of difficulty and danger, more especially, I consulted, and sincerely co-operated with, men of all parties, who seemed disposed to the same ends, or to any main part of them. Nothing to prevent disorder was omitted : when it appeared, nothing to subdue it was left uncounselled, nor unexecuted, as far as I could prevail. At the time I speak of, and having a momentary lead, so aided and so encouraged, and as a feeble instrument in a mighty hand—I do not say I saved my country; I am sure I did my country important service.   *Burke.*

CCCCLXXXIX.

Letter to Bonstetten.

I must not close my letter without giving you one principal event of my history; which was that, in the course of my late tour, I set out one morning before five o'clock, the moon shining through a dark and misty autumnal air, and got to the sea-coast time enough to be at the sun's levee. I saw the clouds and dark vapours open gradually to right and left, rolling over one another in great smoky wreaths, and the tide, as it flowed gently in upon the sands, first whitening, then slightly tinged with gold and blue ; and all at once a little line of insufferable brightness that, before I can write these five words, was grown to half an orb, and now to a whole one, too glorious to be distinctly seen. It is very odd it makes no figure on paper; yet I shall remember it as long as the sun, or at least as I endure. I wonder whether anybody ever saw it before ; I hardly believe it.

T. Gray.

CCCCXC.

To Mr. Spectator.

MR. SPECTATOR,

Now, Sir, the thing is this; Mr. Shapely is the prettiest gentleman about town. He is very tall, but not too tall neither. He dances like an angel. His mouth is made I do not know how, but it is the prettiest that I ever saw in my life. He is always laughing, for he has an infinite deal of wit. If you did but see how he rolls his stockings! He has a thousand pretty fancies, and I am sure, if you saw him, you would like him. He is a very good scholar, and can talk Latin as fast as English. I wish you could but see him dance. Now you must understand poor Mr. Shapely has no estate; but how can he help that, you know? and yet my friends are so unreasonable as to be always teasing me about him, because he has no estate; but I am sure he has that that is better than an estate; for he is a good-natured, ingenious, modest, civil, tall, well-bred, handsome, man; and I am obliged to him for his civilities ever since I saw him. I forgot to tell you that he has black eyes, and looks upon me now and then as if he had tears in them. And yet my friends are so unreasonable, that they would have me be uncivil to him. I have a good position which they cannot hinder me of, and I shall be fourteen on the 29th day of August next, and am therefore willing to settle in the world as soon as I can, and so is Mr. Shapely. But everybody I advise with here is poor Mr. Shapely's enemy. I desire, therefore, you will give me your advice, for I know you are a wise man; and if you advise me well, I am resolved to follow it. I heartily wish you could see him dance, and am,

Sir,

Your most humble servant,

B.D.

P.S.—He loves your Spectators mightily.

Spectator.

CCCCXCI.

A Family Letter.

Your two letters, my dear John, were very acceptable, and it gives me great pleasure to find your situation so agreeable, with a prospect also of its being so advantageous with respect to your improvement. I miss you exceedingly, but the reflection and the hope that you will profit by it reconciles me to the separation : and you may be assured I am much more happy with such prospects in view, than I should be if you were with me and without them. But, my dear John, mental advantages are not all that are to be considered : you should also have regard to your health, for without health there can be no enjoyment. Do not neglect to pay proper attention to that, and spare nothing that will continue to preserve it ; and if anything should at any time ail you, do not neglect to attend to it in time. It certainly would be my wish to have me with you, if your improvement would be promoted by it ; but when that cannot be, I must and do endeavour to reconcile myself to the separation with cheerfulness, and I am the better enabled to do this when I remember that you have, in addition to the other advantages of your situation, the (I may say) maternal care and kindness of the worthy Mrs. Knox. Indeed, I feel great regard for her on account of her attention to you, and wish with you that her situation was more suited to her merits.

CCCCXCII.

A Remarkable Woman.

On the 24th of this month passed away a woman remarkable both for herself and her associations . . . She was a woman of really rare gifts, though, as with her husband, these did not carry her into the light of public fame. Her memory was exact; her knowledge of Scottish literature well-nigh inexhaustible. She had a bright, keen humóur of her own, and could turn out epigrams and quatrains with as much facility as smartness. In her youth she sang Scottish songs with great sweetness and spirit, in her maturer age she was an inimitable story-teller, and her fund of anecdote and quotation was as a cruse of oil that never failed. No one enjoyed a good story more than she, and no one passed it on with more gusto. In her private life she was famous for her friendships and her generosities. Staunch, hospitable, sincere, she gathered round her a circle of admirers to whom she never proved either false or cold. She was the trusted confidant of both young and old, and no one who went to her for sympathy was disappointed, nor was her counsel ever other than that of the highest morality and truest practical wisdom. After an illness of over ten months . . . she peacefully slept unto death, and her friends, who are legion, mourn her as a unique figure gone from their world—one impossible to replace for wit, humour, sympathy and good judgment, combined with boundless hospitality and strong personal affection. *E. L. Lushington.*

INDEX TO SELECTED PASSAGES.

—•—

10/4/99

Clarendon Press Series.

Latin Educational Works.

GRAMMARS, LEXICONS, &c.

Allen. *Rudimenta Latina.* Comprising Accidence, and Exercises of a very Elementary Character, for the use of Beginners. By J. BARROW ALLEN, M.A. . . . . [Extra fcap. 8vo, 2s.

—— *An Elementary Latin Grammar.* By the same Author. *New Edition, Revised and Enlarged.* . . . . [Extra fcap. 8vo, 2s. 6d.

—— *A First Latin Exercise Book.* By the same Author. *Eighth Edition.* . . . . [Extra fcap. 8vo, 2s. 6d

—— *A Second Latin Exercise Book.* By the same Author. *Second Edition.* . . . . [Extra fcap. 8vo, 3s. 6d.

[*A Key to First & Second Latin Exercise Books : for Teachers only, price 5s. net.*]

Fox and **Bromley.** *Models and Exercises in Unseen Translation.* By H. F. Fox, M.A., and T. M. BROMLEY, M.A. [Extra fcap. 8vo, 5s. 6d.
[*A Key to Passages quoted in the above: for Teachers only, price 6d. net.*]

Gibson. *An Introduction to Latin Syntax.* By W. S. GIBSON, M.A. [Extra fcap. 8vo, 2s.

Jerram. *Reddenda Minora.* By C. S. JERRAM, M.A. [Extra fcap. 8vo, 1s. 6d.

—— *Anglice Reddenda.* FIRST SERIES. [Extra fcap. 8vo, 2s. 6d.

—— *Anglice Reddenda.* SECOND SERIES. [Extra fcap. 8vo, 3s.

—— *Anglice Reddenda.* THIRD SERIES. [Extra fcap. 8vo, 3s.

Lee-Warner. *Hints and Helps for Latin Elegiacs.* By H. LEE-WARNER, M.A. . . . . . . [Extra fcap. 8vo, 3s. 6d.
[*A Key is provided : for Teachers only, price 4s. 6d.*]

Lewis. *An Elementary Latin Dictionary.* By CHARLTON T. LEWIS, Ph.D.. . . . . [Square 8vo, 7s. 6d.

—— *A Latin Dictionary for Schools.* By the same Author. [Small 4to, 18s.

Lindsay. *A Short Historical Latin Grammar.* By W. M. LINDSAY, M.A.. . . . . [Crown 8vo, 5s. 6d.

Nunns. *First Latin Reader.* By T. J. NUNNS, M.A. *Third Edition.* [Extra fcap. 8vo, 2s.

Owen and **Phillimore.** *Mvsa Clavda.* Translations into Latin Elegiac Verse. By S. G. OWEN and J. S. PHILLIMORE. [Crown 8vo, paper boards, 3s. 6d.

Ramsay. *Latin Prose Composition.* By G. G. RAMSAY, M.A., LL.D. *Fourth Edition.* Extra fcap. 8vo.
Vol. I. *Syntax, Exercises with Notes, &c.,* 4s. 6d.
Or in two Parts, 2s. 6d. each, viz.
Part I. *The Simple Sentence.* Part II. *The Compound Sentence.*
*** *A Key to the above, price 5s. net. Supplied to Teachers only, on application to the Secretary, Clarendon Press.*
Vol. II. *Passages of Graduated Difficulty for Translation into Latin, together with an Introduction on Continuous Prose,* 4s. 6d.

Ramsay. *Latin Prose Versions.* Contributed by various Scholars.
Edited by G. G. RAMSAY, M.A., LL.D   .   .   .   [Extra fcap. 8vo, 5s.
Rouse. *Demonstrations in Latin Elegiac Verse.* By W. H. D. ROUSE,
M.A. .   .   .   .   [Crown 8vo, 4s. 6d.
Sargent. *Easy Passages for Translation into Latin.* By J. Y. SARGENT,
M.A. *Seventh Edition.* .   .   .   .   .   [Extra fcap. 8vo, 2s. 6d.
[A Key to this Edition is provided : for Teachers only, price 5s., net.]
—— *A Latin Prose Primer.* By the same Author. [Ex. fcap. 8vo, 2s. 6d.

King and Cookson. *The Principles of Sound and Inflexion,* as
illustrated in the Greek and Latin Languages. By J. E. KING, M.A., and
CHRISTOPHER COOKSON, M.A. .   .   .   .   .   .   [8vo, 18s.
—— *An Introduction to the Comparative Grammar of Greek and
Latin.* By the same Authors. .   .   .   .   .   [Crown 8vo, 5s. 6d.
Papillon. *A Manual of Comparative Philology.* By T. L. PAPILLON,
M.A. *Third Edition.* .   .   .   .   [Crown 8vo, 6s.

Caesar. *The Commentaries* (for Schools). With Notes and Maps.
By CHARLES E. MOBERLY, M.A.
    The Gallic War. *New Edition.* Extra fcap. 8vo—
        Books I and II, 2s. ; I–III, 2s. ; III–V, 2s. 6d. ; VI–VIII, 3s. 6d.
    The Civil War. *Second Edition.* .   .   [Extra fcap. 8vo, 3s. 6d.
Catulli Veronensis *Carmina Selecta,* secundum recognitionem
ROBINSON ELLIS, A.M. .   .   .   .   .   ˙ [Extra fcap. 8vo, 3s. 6d.
Cicero. *Selection of Interesting and Descriptive Passages.* With Notes.
By HENRY WALFORD, M.A. In three Parts. *Third Edition.*
                                    [Extra fcap. 8vo, 4s. 6d.
    Part I.   *Anecdotes from Grecian and Roman History.* . *[limp,* 1s. 6d.
    Part II. *Omens and Dreams ; Beauties of Nature..* . [„   1s. 6d.
    Part III. *Rome's Rule of her Provinces.* .   .   . [„   1s. 6d.
—— *De Amicitia.* With Introduction and Notes. By ST. GEORGE
STOCK, M.A. .   .   .   .   [Extra fcap. 8vo, 3s.
—— *De Senectute.* With Introduction and Notes. By LEONARD
HUXLEY, B.A. *In one or two Parts.* .   .   .   [Extra fcap. 8vo, 2s.
—— *Pro Cluentio.* With Introduction and Notes. By W. RAMSAY,
M.A. Edited by G. G. RAMSAY, M.A. *Second Edition.* [Extra fcap. 8vo, 3s. 6d.
—— *Pro Marcello, pro Ligario, pro Rege Deiotaro.* With Introduction
and Notes. By W. Y. FAUSSET, M.A. .   .   .   [Extra fcap. 8vo, 2s. 6d.
—— *Pro Milone.* With Notes, &c. By A. B. POYNTON, M.A.
                                    [Extra fcap. 8vo, 2s. 6d.
—— *Pro Roscio.* With Introduction and Notes. By ST. GEORGE
STOCK, M.A. .   .   .   .   [Extra fcap. 8vo, 3s. 6d.
—— *Select Orations* (for Schools). *In Verrem Actio Prima.* *De
Imperio Gn. Pompeii. Pro Archia. Philippica IX.* With Introduction and
Notes. By J. R. KING, M.A. *Second Edition.* . [Extra fcap. 8vo, 2s. 6d.
—— *In Q. Caecilium Divinatio* and *In C. Verrem Actio Prima.*
With Introduction and Notes. By J. R. KING, M.A. [Extra fcap. 8vo, 1s. 6d.
—— *Speeches against Catilina.* With Introduction and Notes. By
E. A. UPCOTT, M.A. *Second Edition.* .   .   .   [Extra fcap. 8vo, 2s. 6d.

Cicero. *Philippic Orations* (I–III, V, VII). With Notes, &c., by J. R. KING, M.A. . . . . [Extra fcap. 8vo, 3s. 6d.

—— *Selected Letters* (for Schools). With Notes. By C. E. PRICHARD, M.A., and E. R. BERNARD, M.A. *Second Edition.* [Extra fcap. 8vo, 3s.

—— *Select Letters.* With English Introductions, Notes, and Appendices. By ALBERT WATSON, M.A. *Fourth Edition.* . . [8vo, 18s.

—— *Select Letters.* Text. By the same Editor. *Second Edition.* [Extra fcap. 8vo, 4s.

Early Roman Poetry. *Selected Fragments.* With Introduction and Notes. By W. W. MERRY, D.D. . . . . . [Crown 8vo, 6s. 6d.

Horace. With a Commentary. Volume I. *The Odes, Carmen Seculare,* and *Epodes.* By EDWARD C. WICKHAM, D.D. *New Edition.* [Extra fcap. 8vo, 6s.

—— *Odes,* Book I. By the same Editor. . . [Extra fcap. 8vo, 2s.

—— *Selected Odes.* With Notes for the use of a Fifth Form. By the same Editor. . . . . [Extra fcap. 8vo, 2s.

—— *The Complete Works.* By the same Editor. [On writing-paper, 32mo, 3s. 6d.; on India paper, 5s.

Juvenal. *XIII Satires.* Edited, with Introduction, Notes, &c., by C. H. PEARSON, M.A., and H. A. STRONG, M.A. *Second Edition.* [Crown 8vo, 9s.

Livy. *Selections* (for Schools). With Notes and Maps. By H. LEE-WARNER, M.A. . . . . [Extra fcap. 8vo.
Part I. *The Caudine Disaster.* . . . . . . [limp, 1s. 6d.
Part II. *Hannibal's Campaign in Italy.* . . . [„ 1s. 6d.
Part III. *The Macedonian War.* . . . . . [„ 1s. 6d.

—— *Books V—VII.* With Introduction and Notes. By A. R. CLUER, B.A. *Second Edition.* Revised by P. E. MATHESON, M.A. [Extra fcap. 8vo, 5s.
Book V, 2s. 6d.; *Book VII,* 2s. By the same Editors.

—— *Books XXI—XXIII.* With Introduction, Notes, and Maps. By M. T. TATHAM, M.A. *Second Edition* . . . [Extra fcap. 8vo, 5s.

—— *Book XXI.* By the same Editor. . . [Extra fcap. 8vo, 2s. 6d.

—— *Book XXII.* By the same Editor. . . [Extra fcap. 8vo, 2s. 6d.

Nepos. With Notes. By OSCAR BROWNING, M.A. *Third Edition.* Revised by W. R. INGE, M.A. . . . [Extra fcap. 8vo, 3s.

—— *Lives from. Miltiades, Themistocles, Pausanias.* With Notes, Maps, Vocabularies, and English Exercises. By JOHN BARROW ALLEN, M.A. [Extra fcap. 8vo, 1s. 6d.

Ovid. *Selections* (for the use of Schools). With Introductions, Notes, and an Appendix on the Roman Calendar. By W. RAMSAY, M.A. Edited by G. G. RAMSAY, M.A. *Third Edition.* . [Extra fcap. 8vo, 5s. 6d.

—— *Tristia,* Book I. The Text revised, with an Introduction and Notes. By S. G. OWEN, B.A. *Second Edition.* . [Extra fcap. 8vo, 3s. 6d.

—— *Tristia,* Book III. With Introduction and Notes. By the same Editor. . . . . [Extra fcap. 8vo, 2s.

Persius. *The Satires.* With Translation and Commentary by J. CONINGTON, M.A., edited by H. NETTLESHIP, M.A. *Third Edition.* [8vo, 8s. 6d.

Plautus. *Captivi.* With Introduction and Notes. By W. M. LINDSAY, M.A. . . . . [Extra fcap. 8vo, 2*s.* 6*d.*

—— *Trinummus.* With Notes and Introductions. By C. E. FREEMAN, M.A., and A. SLOMAN, M.A. . . . . . [Extra fcap. 8vo, 3*s.*

Pliny. *Selected Letters* (for Schools). By C. E. PRICHARD, M.A., and E. R. BERNARD, M.A. *Third Edition.* . . . [Extra fcap. 8vo, 3*s.*

Quintilian. *Institutionis Oratoriae Liber X.* Edited by W. PETERSON, M.A. . . . . [Extra fcap. 8vo, 3*s.* 6*d.*

Sallust. *Bellum Catilinarium* and *Jugurthinum.* With Introduction and Notes, by W. W. CAPES, M.A. . . [Extra fcap. 8vo, 4*s.* 6*d.*

Tacitus. *The Annals.* Books I—IV. Edited, with Introduction and Notes for the use of Schools and Junior Students, by H. FURNEAUX, M.A. [Extra fcap. 8vo, 5*s.*

—— *The Annals.* Book I. By the same Editor. . . [*limp,* 2*s.*

—— *The Annals.* (Text only). . . . . . [Crown 8vo, 6*s.*

Terence. *Adelphi.* With Notes and Introductions. By A. SLOMAN, M.A. . . . . [Extra fcap. 8vo, 3*s.*

—— *Andria.* With Notes and Introductions. By C. E. FREEMAN, M.A., and A. SLOMAN, M.A. *Second Edition* . . [Extra fcap. 8vo, 3*s.*

—— *Phormio.* With Notes and Introductions. By A. SLOMAN, M.A. . . . . [Extra fcap. 8vo, 3*s.*

Tibullus and **Propertius.** *Selections.* Edited, with Introduction and Notes, by G. G. RAMSAY, M.A. *Second Edition.* . [Extra fcap. 8vo, 6*s.*

Virgil. With an Introduction and Notes. By T. L. PAPILLON, M.A., and A. E. HAIGH, M.A. [Crown 8vo, 2 vols., *cloth, price* 6*s. each, or in stiff covers,* 3*s.* 6*d. each.*

—— *The Text, including the Minor Works.* [On writing-paper, 32mo, 3*s.* 6*d.*; on India paper, 5*s.*

—— *Aeneid.* With Introduction and Notes, by the same Editors. In Four Parts. . . . . [Crown 8vo, 2*s. each.*

—— *Aeneid I.* With Introduction and Notes, by C. S. JERRAM, M.A. [Extra fcap. 8vo, *limp,* 1*s.* 6*d.*

—— *Aeneid IX.* Edited, with Introduction and Notes, by A. E. HAIGH, M.A. . . . [Extra fcap. 8vo, *limp,* 1*s.* 6*d. In two Parts,* 2*s.*

—— *Bucolics.* With Introduction and Notes, by C. S. JERRAM, M.A. [Extra fcap. 8vo, 2*s.* 6*d.*

—— *Bucolics and Georgics.* By T. L. PAPILLON, M.A., and A. E. HAIGH, M.A. . . . . [Crown 8vo, 2*s.* 6*d.*

—— *Georgics.* Books I, II. By C. S. JERRAM, M.A. [Extra fcap. 8vo, 2*s.* 6*d.*

—— *Georgics.* Books III, IV. By the same Editor. [Extra fcap. 8vo, 2*s.* 6*d.*

𝕺𝖝𝖋𝖔𝖗𝖉

AT THE CLARENDON PRESS

𝕷𝖔𝖓𝖉𝖔𝖓, 𝕰𝖉𝖎𝖓𝖇𝖚𝖗𝖌𝖍, 𝖆𝖓𝖉 𝕹𝖊𝖜 𝖄𝖔𝖗𝖐

HENRY FROWDE